Chapter One

It was only ten-thirty and it was already a craptastic day.

Megan Vandemeer stared at the airplane on the tarmac. What the hell was she doing? The Alaska Airlines flight was taking off in twenty minutes and she was actually going to be on it.

Her phone rang and she dug it out of her purse, cringing when she saw her best friend Blair's name on the caller ID. She answered anyway.

"How did she take it?" Blair asked.

"Well..." Megan glanced up at the digital sign at the gate. Five minutes to boarding.

"Wait." Blair's voice was short. "Tell me that you *told* her."

"I told her."

Her friend paused. "You're lying. That's your lying voice."

Megan shook her head. "I have a lying voice?"

"It goes up half an octave and gets tight at the end."

"Should it worry me that you know me that well?"

"We've been friends since kindergarten. I'd *hope* I know you that well." Blair groaned. "You might be trying to change the subject, but your mother's going to notice when you don't show up to your own wedding."

The overhead PA system blurted a fuzzy message about a changed gate and Megan covered the microphone on her phone.

"Megan, you have to tell her!" Blair said in frustration.

"I will." The digital sign now said four minutes to boarding.

"*When?*"

"Later this afternoon."

"Why not just call her now?" The overhead PA sounded again and Blair gasped. "Are you actually at the *airport?*"

"Blair..."

"You never canceled your flight, did you?"

Megan brushed her hair out of her face and leaned forward, lowering her voice. "Honestly, Blair. I forgot."

"Lie."

Tears stung Megan's eyes. "I need a friend right now, Blair. Not a damned lie detector."

"I'm sorry." Blair sighed. "You're right. Trust me, I understand why you've stalled. Your mother scares *me* and you know I don't scare easily. But you have to tell her, Megs. The longer you wait, the harder it's going to be."

"I know, but I want to tell her in person. At this point, I could hardly do anything else."

"So you're really coming home?"

Megan cast a glance at the gate. "I'm boarding the plane in two minutes."

"Okay." Blair was quiet for several seconds and Megan knew she was making some kind of plan. Blair was the one person you could count on in a crisis. If there was ever a zombie apocalypse, her best chance of survival was to stick by Blair's side. "You're going to need to escape tonight. Maybe you, me, and Libby can go out."

Megan swallowed the lump in her throat. "Thank you."

"What are best friends for? Call me when the deed is done, although I suspect I'll hear the yelling all the way downtown. If you need to stay at my place, I have a spare bed for you."

"What about Neil?"

"He's on a three-day business trip and won't be home until Friday. But even so, he doesn't like to spend weeknights together."

"But you're getting married in three months. Aren't you going to be living together?"

"Of course," she said, sounding defensive. "We'll work it out when we need to."

"I don't get it," Megan muttered, shaking her head.

"Says the woman boarding a plane to fly to her wedding even though she broke up with her fiancé five weeks ago."

"Six."

"Sadly, that makes it worse."

An airline employee at the gate counter picked up the microphone. "We are about to board Flight 365 to Kansas City. First class passengers will board first."

"Blair, I've got to go. They're boarding first class. Considering how much the ticket cost, I might as well board first and get something out of it."

"Don't forget the alcohol. You get free drinks."

Megan rolled her eyes, even if the gesture was lost on her friend. "It's not even eleven o'clock in the morning, Blair."

"Mimosas. Bloody Marys. Screwdrivers. There's a whole assortment of brunch drinks."

The overhead PA went off again. "Now boarding our first class passengers."

Megan grabbed her purse and stood. "They're boarding. I'll call you later."

"You can do it, Megs. What's the worst she can do?"

She shuddered. "I don't even want to consider it. I'll let you know how it goes." She hung up and stuffed her phone into her purse, eyeing the gate with apprehension.

The thought of boarding the plane made her nervous for another reason. Turbulence gave her horrible airsickness. But her coworker had suggested she take Dramamine as a preventive measure. While Megan hated taking medication, even aspirin for a headache, she had enough to worry about once she got off the plane. The last thing she wanted to do was spend every moment on board battling nausea. She pulled a bottle of water out of her bag, shook two pills from the travel-size container, and swallowed them, hoping they worked in time.

She stood behind a businessman with a bad comb-over, who looked to be a good twenty years older than her. He glanced over his shoulder and grinned as he eyed her up and down. "Have you considered your retirement needs?"

Her eyebrows rose. "Retirement?"

"What are you, thirty-two? Thirty-four?"

Megan shot him a glare. "Twenty-nine."

His grin widened as he moved forward with the line. "It's never too early to start. Maybe we can chat about it on the plane if we're sitting next to each other."

The way her life was going lately, it seemed almost inevitable.

But thankfully, he sat in the front row and she was in seat 3D. She stuffed her purse under the seat and looked out the window, remembering when she and Jay had bought the plane tickets to fly to Kansas City to their wedding. That should have been her first clue that Jay was an asshole she shouldn't marry. He'd insisted that they each pay for their own ticket.

"Can I get you something, Ms. Vandemeer?"

Megan turned to look at the pretty flight attendant who was smiling down at her. She was perfect from the top of her blond head to the tips of her fashionable yet practical shoes. To the untrained observer, her smile appeared friendly, but Megan had spent eighteen years under the tutelage of her impossibly perfect mother—long enough for her to know a fake smile when she saw one. And the reminder of her mother was nearly enough to send her over the edge. "Uh…a mimosa?"

The attendant nodded. "Coming right up."

Other passengers filed past Megan, and after a while she realized that the only open first class seat was next to hers. Maybe Jay had forgotten to cancel his ticket too. But that didn't seem likely. Jay was a penny-pinching snob. But what else had she expected from an investment banker? His idea of a wild night was moving her 401K into high-risk mutual funds. Creepy financial planner dude was a year too late.

The flight attendant brought her the drink and Megan sipped it faster than intended, trying to quell her nerves. The knots in her shoulders were just loosening up when one of the attendants started to shut the cabin door. The woman stopped mid-action, holding the door open to let one last passenger on board. He stood in the front of the aisle, his gaze taking in the empty seat next to hers.

Megan wasn't the only woman to notice him, even if her attention was less pointed than the others'. At least six feet tall, he had to stoop slightly to keep from bumping his head on the ceiling. The blond flight attendant who'd brought Megan's drink gave him a sideways glance of appreciation, even if he didn't notice. Then again, Megan was sure a guy like him, who epitomized the words tall, dark, and handsome, was used to women staring. Jay certainly had been.

The attendant rested her hand lightly on the man's arm and looked up at him through heavily mascaraed eyelashes, saying something softly so that she had to lean into him to be heard. Looking slightly irritated, he showed her his ticket and she pointed to the empty seat.

Megan had a neighbor.

He stuffed his overnight bag in the overhead bin and sat next to her, buckling his seatbelt. He was, without a doubt, a better option than the financial planner, but maybe not by much. She guessed him to be close to her age, and he didn't have the typical laid-back Seattle vibe. He bore a resemblance to Jay, though his thick, wavy dark brown hair wasn't trimmed as closely as her ex-fiancé's always was. His looks didn't concern her. What did concern her was the determined gleam in his dark brown eyes and the way his jaw was perpetually clenched, as if he were steeling himself against something unpleasant. He looked like he was determined to complete a mission, at any cost.

Momentary fear mingled with the inebriated fog in her head. "Are you a terrorist?" she asked before she could stop herself.

"*What?*" he asked, his eyes wide as he turned to her in horror.

She shook her head, the movement making her dizzy. "Sorry. You just had a crazed look…" She waved her hand in circles in front of her face to help justify her statement, then quickly dropped it to her lap. What on earth had possessed her to say that?

Moments later, the flirty attendant came back and leaned across the man to grab the empty glass on Megan's tray. Still bent over, the blond turned to face him, her face less than a foot from his. "Don't you worry, Mr. McMillan." She patted his arm again. "I'll come take care of you just as soon as I can."

His mouth parted slightly before he grunted, "Thanks."

Megan had to wonder what the attendant's definition of *taking care of him* included.

The flight crew started the safety demonstration and Megan leaned her head against the seat, her fingers digging into the armrest. When this flight landed, she would finally have to do what she'd been avoiding for over a month…but how? How was she going to face her mother?

"Afraid of flying?" the man next to her asked, sounding displeased by the prospect.

"No, just crashing and burning." Which was exactly what was going to happen to her after they landed.

Chapter Two

It was his turn to ask, "*What?*"

"Not the *plane*." The brunette's brown eyes fluttered open, glistening with tears. "My life."

Josh nearly panicked. He could deal with paranoid people worried about plane crashes, but he hoped to God this woman wasn't going to cry. He didn't think he could take it right now.

He wasn't supposed to be here—on this plane, with this woman, at this point in his life.

Josh McMillan wasn't the kind of man to take leaps. Every step he took was carefully plotted beforehand. Except for this one.

Ever since Josh was eight years old, he'd wanted to follow in his father's footsteps and become an engineer. Josh was sixteen when his father died, but the loss only cemented his resolve. His older brother, already an engineer, took over the family business, and Josh joined him when he graduated from college.

The firm had struggled since their father's death and the bad turn in the economy hadn't helped. But then Josh had created a revolutionary part that could be used on wind turbines to help produce more electricity with the same amount of wind power. The part had the potential to make millions. So they'd hired a patent attorney and spent a fortune they didn't have to get the patent process started, hinging the future of their business on it. And it had worked. They'd acquired interest from a serious investor who could help take their engineering firm to a whole new level.

Until last Friday, when their patent had been denied.

A firm in Kansas City, Missouri, had received approval for an identical plan, but how could a firm in Kansas City have so exactly duplicated the esoteric part? Josh had literally stumbled upon the design by accident.

Josh's company would have to pay thousands more to an attorney to fight the ruling. Thousands they couldn't afford to lose. Worse yet, the investor had caught wind and threatened to pull out of their agreement if the matter wasn't resolved within a week. The brothers went out for drinks to strategize about the ruling, which is when, after a couple of rounds, Noah confessed to having shown the plans to a friend of a friend at a conference three years before.

"Who was the friend of a friend?"

Noah looked slightly embarrassed. "She was a woman I picked up in the hotel bar. I took her to my room and the next morning she was gone and so was my bag. A copy of the plans was inside."

"And you didn't think to tell me?" Josh asked, his temper rising.

Noah slouched over the bar, cradling a glass tumbler in his hand. He lifted his shoulder into a half-shrug. "They were a copy, Josh. I didn't think anything of it."

"We have to fight this." Josh only realized he was shouting

when he took in the startled looks of the other bar patrons. "We didn't work so hard to file the patent then get this investor just to let it all be flushed down the drain."

Noah sat up and drained his drink. "Maybe there's nothing left to fight for."

Only Josh wasn't so willing to give up the fight. He'd spent the last seven years pouring his everything into making his father's company a success. He'd sacrificed his personal life, not to mention his checkbook. No, he couldn't come this close to making the company financially solvent just to lose it all. There had to be a way to fight this. There just had to be.

He went on to spend the weekend researching everything he could about PMV Engineering, the firm that had filed the patent two weeks before the McMillan brothers. PMV consisted of three partners. One had retired and moved to Belize, which—in and of itself—made Josh suspicious. The other two were still active. Andrew Peterman was the second principal, and his son Drew had joined the firm three years prior—suspicious timing, indeed. From the photos Josh found on the Internet, he made the highly unscientific judgment that the man was cold-blooded enough to set Noah up.

After hours of researching and brainstorming and only six days before the investor pulled out, Josh decided to go to Kansas City to confront the bastards in person. By a stroke of luck, the daughter of the third principal, Bart Vandemeer, was about to get married. Josh figured he could use the distraction to catch them off guard.

Noah thought he was crazy, but then again, he would. Despite being four years older, he'd never been as invested in the company. Still, in spite of his skepticism about the last-minute trip, Noah had driven him to the airport. Since the ticket had been purchased at the last minute, Josh had needed to spring for first class. It had cost a fortune, but at least he could have a beer or two and relax on the flight to Kansas City, take the opportunity to figure out a real plan.

Or at least that's what he'd thought.

He hadn't counted on being seated next to the anxious brunette. She was pretty with long, dark hair that hung past her shoulders and long, slender legs—definitely his type—but within a minute of sitting down, she'd accused him of being a terrorist and made her crash-and-burn comment.

It was going to be a long flight.

Maybe he could get the eager flight attendant to move him to coach.

After they reached cruising altitude, the airline attendant stood, and Josh grabbed her attention, not a hard thing to do since she'd kept her eye on him since before takeoff.

She walked straight toward him with a determined look. "Can I help you, Mr. McMillan?"

"I need a Jack and Coke," he said, forgoing his planned beer. The woman next to him was already driving him crazy. He was going to need something stronger than a beer to endure her tics.

"Of course. Anything else?" The attendant flashed him a blinding smile. The name tag pinned to her uniform read "Tiffani." Of course it did.

"I want another Mimosa," the woman next to him said.

The attendant barely acknowledged her order before spinning around to head to the galley.

When she returned, she leaned in closer than necessary to place the woman's drink on the tray next to him. Then she set a cup of ice along with a can of Coke and a minibar bottle on his tray. "Would you like me to make it for you?"

She was certainly attractive, but she looked too high-maintenance and more his brother's type. Josh might have been interested in her anyway at a different time, but today he didn't need the distraction. "Thanks, but I've got it."

Her smile faltered as she walked away, but while he felt a

little bad, there was no sense in leading her on. He was a man on a mission and his mission currently lacked an accompanying plan.

Josh was fixing his drink when, apropos of nothing, the woman next to him asked, "Do you get along with your mother?"

He turned to her. "My *mother?*"

"Yeah, you know," she waved her hand dismissively. "The woman who raised you."

He gave her his full attention, still confused. She looked more relaxed now, and he was sure it had something to do with the drink she'd downed before takeoff. "Maybe I was raised by two fathers," he said, keeping a straight face.

Her eyes widened as though she'd had an epiphany. "*Oh.* Were you?"

"No." He couldn't hide a smirk.

She watched him for a second and he studied her while he waited. Her big brown eyes weren't entirely focused. Could she have been drinking before she boarded the plane? She didn't seem the type, but who knew.

"So do you?" Her thin eyebrows lifted in an exaggerated movement.

"Do I what?" He'd forgotten her question as he watched her shift in her seat. Her light blue skirt hiked up to mid-thigh and stayed there, but she didn't seem to notice.

"Get along with your mother."

He grinned, surprising himself. "Yes. I love my mother."

She lifted her glass and the liquid sloshed around, nearly spilling over the side. "Now that's different. Loving your mother and getting along with her are two very. Different. Things." She waved her glass to emphasize her point.

"I guess you're right," he said, his mouth pursed. "My mother and I get along pretty well. Better than my brother and me."

"You're really, really lucky." She took a sip of her drink and turned to the window to stare out into the clouds. When she was silent for several minutes, he decided she was done and turned to face the seat in front of him.

Josh took a sip of his drink and closed his eyes. He hadn't slept well the night before and now that he was on this flight, he realized Noah was right. This caper *was* insane. He hadn't even reserved a car or hotel for his time in Kansas City.

What the hell was he doing? It wasn't like he could actually crash the Vandemeer wedding.

"Can I get you something else, Mr. McMillan?" Tiffani asked. Josh opened his eyes, a little irritated now. Wasn't it a cardinal rule for flight attendants to leave sleeping—or possibly sleeping—passengers alone?

"No, thank you."

"Can I have some water, please?" the woman next to him asked.

The flight attendant gave her a dirty look, then moved on to the next row. When she returned, she gave the woman her water and looked down at Josh, fluttering her lashes. "Mr. McMillan, if you change your mind, you let me know."

"Thank you," he said, and she walked away with a small sigh.

"Mr. McMillan," the woman next to him sing-songed in an undertone. "Will you have my babies?"

He laughed and turned to her. "She's that obvious?"

She snorted, then asked after a pause, "Are you married, *Mr. McMillan?*"

He waggled his bare left fingers at her. "Nope. You?"

She looked down at the simple diamond solitaire on her left ring finger. "Nope. Very single." Then she laughed and looked up at him with a wistful smile. "Guess why I'm going to Kansas City."

"I have no idea."

"Guess."

"You're joining the circus."

"Nope. Guess again." She leaned her head against the window, her eyes partially closed.

He found himself wondering again if she'd spent the morning at the airport bar. It seemed impossible that she could be so drunk off two drinks. "You're going to join a convent."

She laughed again and lifted her hand, showing him her ring. "I'm going home to my wedding."

"But you just said you're single."

"I am. *Now.*" She sat up and grabbed the cup of water. "I broke up with the lying, cheating bastard six weeks ago."

He shook his head. "I'm confused."

She set her glass down with a thud and water sloshed out. "I didn't tell my mother."

"So…you're going to tell her you're marrying an invisible man?"

Her eyes widened. "Do you think that would work?"

He chuckled. "No."

She flopped back in her seat with a humph. "You're probably right."

"So let me get this straight: You're going home to your wedding which is this…?"

"Saturday." She sat up again and leaned over, then picked up his half-full glass of Coke and Jack Daniel's and gulped it down in a couple of swigs.

He grabbed her arm and pried the now-empty glass out of her hands. "Whoa, slow down there, slugger."

"She'll bring you more, you know," she mumbled, leaning over the armrest toward him, trying to take the glass back.

He moved it out of reach. "Who?"

"The flight attendant. The *future* Mrs. McMillan." She burst into giggles and pointed to the glass in his hand, whispering loudly, "Those are free in first class."

"So I've been told."

"But even if they weren't, the future Mrs. McMillan would probably give them to you for free."

"You think so?" he teased, looking down the aisle at the woman in question. "What do you think? Should I propose before I get off the plane?"

The brunette scrunched her nose. "She reminds me of some of the sorority girls I knew in college."

"And is that a good thing or a bad one?"

She tried to look serious, but she needed to squint to see him. "Definitely bad. Those girls were bitches."

He laughed despite himself. "I think you just saved me from a nasty divorce."

She pointed her finger at him. "And don't forget the alimony."

"True enough. If you weren't as drunk as a sailor on shore leave, I'd buy you a free drink. Is your mother really that scary?"

Her eyes widened in horror. "Worse." She grabbed her water and drained it.

"So what are you going to do?"

She shrugged. "Tell her, I guess."

"You *guess?*"

"It might be a really, really short trip." She gave him a conspiratorial smile. "She's picking me up from the airport. I can tell her as soon as she picks me up. Shoot, I didn't even need to pack my suitcase."

"It might not be so bad," he volunteered. "She'll understand. I can't imagine a mother would want her daughter to marry a lying, cheating bastard."

She pursed her lips and shook her head. "Nope. She can't get her deposits back. She warned me last fall before making the bookings." She looked up at him. "She was pissed about my engagement. She said Jay should have asked Dad for my hand in marriage, as if it were some kind of business transaction. And the fact that I'd dated him for two years without ever bringing him home. Well...that pissed her off too."

"So why not catch a flight to KC to introduce them?" He could only imagine how upset his mother would be if he got engaged to a woman she'd never met.

She sighed. "Jay could never get away. And honestly, I've only been home once in four years. I didn't *want* him to meet them."

"So they were basically going to meet him on the way to the chapel? I can understand why she'd be pissed."

The woman gave him a frustrated glare. "Really, Mr. McMillan? I saved you from the single greatest mistake of your life—Future Mrs. McMillan up there—and you're turning on me just like that?" She tried to snap her fingers, but she fumbled with them several times before giving up.

He grinned. "When you put it that way...I'm still not surprised your mother was pissed."

"Well, it wasn't going to be like that. That's why we were coming today, so my family could spend an extra couple of days getting to know him."

"Wow." He lifted his hands off his lap. "A whole couple of extra days to meet their new son-in-law."

"You don't know my family. And the whole thing's moot. He's history and my mother has to cancel a twenty-five-thousand-dollar wedding without getting a single penny back." She took several shallow breaths and Josh realized she was about to cry.

"Hey! Maybe she can get a refund on *some* of it."

She sniffled, reaching to the floor for her purse, but the seatbelt across her lap kept it out of reach, while also protecting her from falling out of the seat and onto her head—a real danger.

"Here, let me get that for you," Josh said, already unlatching his belt. He leaned forward and grabbed the bag and set it in her lap.

She pulled out a package of tissues, struggling to tug one loose from the plastic.

He reached over and did it for her.

She blew her nose, a noisy sound, then looked up at him. "Do you want to know the worst part?"

Ordinarily, he wouldn't. He'd be looking for the first opportunity out of this crazy conversation. But God help him, he was genuinely curious when he asked, "What?"

"She's going to say, 'I told you so.'" Tears filled her eyes. "They're her favorite words."

"Maybe she won't. Families surprise you sometimes."

She shook her head. "You don't know my mother."

There was no doubt about it, she was in a difficult position, and he wasn't sure how to respond. But there was no need. Her alcohol-induced ADD kicked in and she started digging through her bag again. "Where is it?"

"What are you looking for? Maybe I can help."

"Tina lied. She swore that Dramamine would keep me from feeling sick, but I feel like I'm about to puke."

"Dramamine?"

"Maybe I should take more."

He grabbed her bag and pulled it from her. "*You took Dramamine? When?*"

"When I was boarding the plane. The last time I flew, the turbulence made me sick. I didn't want that to happen again."

"How many drinks have you had?"

"Only two," she said, looking indignant, then a little sheepish. "Plus the rest of yours."

"That's two and a half too many. You can't drink with Dramamine." He reached over his head and pushed the call light. The flight attendant appeared within seconds and he found himself mentally calling her the Almost-Future Mrs. McMillan. "Can I get more water for…" He looked at the nearly incapacitated woman, realizing he didn't even know her name.

"Megan," she offered.

"…for Megan. She's not feeling well."

The flight attendant looked disgusted. "Is she *drunk?*"

"No. She just needs water."

The woman released an exasperated sigh and spun on her heels.

"She's pissed at you, you know," Megan mumbled, leaning back in the seat. "She's jealous."

"Let her be," he grumbled. "Didn't you know you shouldn't drink with Dramamine?"

"No." She closed her eyes and rested her head against the window.

The flight attendant brought the water and handed it to Josh, who took it without giving her a glance.

"Megan, why don't you drink more water before you take a nap." He looked back at the attendant, who stood in the aisle watching. "Can you bring her a blanket?"

She stomped away, returning with the blanket a few moments later. By then he'd coaxed Megan to drink more water. He leaned her seat back and spread the blanket over her as she passed out. He watched the rise and fall of her chest for a moment, feeling a bit better when it appeared normal. As long as she was breathing okay, she'd be fine. He considered telling Tiffani what was going on, but he didn't expect much sympathy. Megan was right. The flight attendant was jealous.

He was about to engage in a last stand for the company that had been his life's work—and his father's and brother's—so how had taking care of this woman become his top priority? The only thing he knew was that it felt right.

Chapter Three

Josh spent the rest of the flight worried about the woman next to him, so much so he had trouble focusing on his own issues. How was he going to prove that Andrew Peterman and Bart Vandemeer's firm had stolen the plans? It wasn't like they were just going to hand over the information willingly. He hoped fate would intervene and do him a solid. Ten employees were counting on him, including Ted Murray, an engineer close to retirement age who'd been hired by Josh's father before Josh was even born, and Missy Dunston, their seven-months-pregnant receptionist. Neither one would have jobs lined up and waiting. They were counting on him to protect them, whether they knew it or not.

Megan was still snoring softly beside him as the plane made its descent and then landed with a hard thud on the tarmac. He pulled out his phone and turned it on, finding two missed calls and a text from his brother. His brother was the last person he wanted to deal with right now. After all, this whole mess was indisputably Noah's fault and his answer seemed to be to just throw in the towel. Josh shoved the phone back into his pocket. Well, he wasn't going down without a fight.

He turned to the sleeping woman in the next seat. "Megan."

She didn't stir.

"Megan," he said louder, giving her arm a little shake.

She roused, but her eyes were still squeezed shut. "Leave me alone."

"Megan." He jostled her harder this time. "We landed. You need to wake up."

"I'm tired," she murmured, burrowing under the blanket.

"You can sleep after you get off the plane." But he knew she couldn't. Her mother was picking her up, which meant she wouldn't get to sleep for quite some time. She'd be busy explaining why her fiancé was a no-show.

How was she going to face her mother in this condition?

She still hadn't roused by the time the plane pulled up to the gate. The first class passengers began to bolt from their seats, fumbling with the overhead bins with all the excitement of toddlers on Christmas morning. Josh waved Tiffani over, who shoved passengers out of the way in her hurry to reach him.

He motioned to Megan. "She's going to need help getting off the plane."

The flight attendant shot Megan a snotty look, then rolled her eyes. "Sure. We'll call security to take care of the problem."

"Security? Can't someone just help her off the plane? Her mother's out there waiting for her."

The attendant gave him a stern look, but he saw a flash of vindictiveness in her eyes. "We take public intoxication very seriously, Mr. McMillan."

"She's not drunk. She had a drug interaction with the alcohol she drank."

The attendant's eyebrows arched. "So she takes drugs too? Then she's a sloppy drunk."

"I told you she's not—"

"Not to worry." She patted Josh's arm. "You are so sweet to feel responsible, but you can go about your business. We'll take care of her."

Josh worried *how* she'd take care of her. He hardly knew the woman next to him, but for some reason he *did* feel responsible for her. "That's not necessary. I'll help her off."

The attendant shook her head, her mouth twisting into a mock sympathetic pout. "Sorry. You're not traveling together and we can't let an unconscious woman leave with a *stranger*. Imagine the liability to the airline."

"If she wakes up and tells you she wants to leave with me, will you let me help her?"

She studied Megan, who was audibly snoring again, for a moment before giving Josh a smug grin. "Of course." Then she returned to the front of the plane.

The cabin door opened and the passengers started to rush off. The sensible part of Josh told him to get up and walk away, but he just couldn't do it.

"Megan." He shook her arm more vigorously. The passengers exiting from the back watched the scene with morbid curiosity.

"What?" she finally groaned, turning toward him.

"The Almost-Future Mrs. McMillan is going to call security unless you get up and walk off this plane."

Her eyelids fluttered open. "Sorority Bitch?"

He grinned. "That's the one."

She tried to sit up and swayed in her seat. "Why's the plane swaying?"

"It's not. You're still out of it."

She leaned back in the seat. "I'm just gonna take a little nap…" Her voice trailed off.

"*Megan.*"

She jolted upright, her eyes wide. "What?"

"Sorority Bitch will let me help you off the plane, but you have to tell her that you want to leave with me."

She grinned and waggled her finger in his face, sing-songing, "She's not gonna like it…"

"I can deal with it. Will you tell her?"

Her grin widened, but her gaze was still unfocused. "Oh…yeah…"

Josh started to get out of his seat. "Do you have anything in the overhead bin?"

"What?… No."

She was fading again, so he quickly grabbed his overnight bag and darted into the aisle, blocking the path of an irritated passenger from the back of the plane. He set his rolling case on the seat in front of him and grabbed Megan's purse off the floor, slinging it over his shoulder. "Let's stand you up and get going."

She didn't answer, already asleep again.

He leaned over and pulled the blanket off her. "*Megan.*"

She startled and jumped up, the top of her head hitting the bottom of his chin.

"Oww!" He jerked upright and whacked the top of his head on the ceiling over the seat. Frustrated, he stopped and took a deep breath. How the hell had he gotten himself into this situation? He briefly considered running for the exit. Without her. But he couldn't. He couldn't leave her with Tiffani.

"Hey, buddy," the irritated man behind him grumbled. "Some of us want off this plane."

"Just a second," Josh barked as he glanced down at Megan and found her staring up at him. Or as much as she could through squinted eyes.

He reached for her arm and pulled her into a standing position. "First we walk off the plane, then we'll figure out the rest."

"Okay," she murmured, but her limbs were limp. He'd be lucky to get her down the short aisle. Somehow she found some inner reservoir of energy and managed to stand and maneuver her way around the seat and into the aisle.

He knew things were going too well, especially when the Almost-Future Mrs. McMillan stopped her. "Miss, are you leaving of your own accord?"

Megan shook her head and Josh's heart slammed into his chest. If she told them no, could he be arrested for kidnapping? "I don't have an Accord," Megan slurred as she began to wobble. "I have a Civic."

The flight attendant scowled. "Do you know the man you're leaving with? Do you want to leave with him?"

Megan's eyes widened as she tried to focus on the woman in front of her. She said in a mock serious tone, "Yes, I know this man." She winked up at him, then turned back to Tiffani. "He's Mr. McMillan and we're leaving here together." She stuck out her tongue at the flight attendant, who had a horrified look on her face. "So no little McMillan babies for you." Then she tried to tap the other woman on the nose, missing and jabbing her cheek instead.

"Okay…" Josh grunted, pulling Megan toward the door while he tried to maneuver his rolling carry-on bag with one hand. "Let's save the birds and the bees speech for later."

He hadn't waited for permission to take her, so he half-expected to be stopped as he coaxed Megan out of the plane and down the tunnel to the terminal. They were ten feet from the door when her knees buckled. He pulled her up against his chest, his arm wrapped around her back to support her. He glanced down at a wheelchair at the entrance to the plane. One of the baggage handlers was watching him with wide eyes.

"I don't suppose I can use that wheelchair?" Josh asked.

The man shook his head, grabbing the handle. "No can do,

Mister."

"Thanks for nothing."

The airline employee chuckled—actually chuckled—in response. If Josh had been the type of guy to write nasty letters…

"Megan?" Josh gently shook her. "Can you keep walking?"

Her eyes were tiny slits as she flopped her head back to look at him. "No, thank you. I don't want any peanut brittle…"

He supposed that was as good an answer to his question as any. Now he needed to figure how to get her, her purse, and his bag down to arrivals.

Squatting, he pressed his shoulder into her abdomen, then stood, carrying her in a fireman's hold. Her upper body dangled down his back, her drooping arms swinging and brushing his ass. This was going to look suspicious as hell, but it was the only way he could get her out without leaving their stuff behind.

He grabbed the handle of his suitcase and set her purse on top of the bag, hurrying for the door once he had her steady. He'd never flown to Kansas City, so he wasn't expecting the cramped waiting area and the dense crowd preparing to board the next flight. Thankfully, the exit was only twenty feet away.

Megan's upper body still dangled down his back. He knew they were a spectacle, and the outright stares confirmed it. "She's my fiancée," he muttered, breaking one of his cardinal rules—never explain yourself, especially not to strangers. But he knew that some of those stares were from people who were worried that he was kidnapping her. "She's not feeling well." He tugged on her legs. "Tell the people you're not feeling well, Megan."

One of her dangling hands waved around as she spoke. "I'm the one helping you. I saved you from that awful woman." Then she patted his backside. "You have a really nice ass. No wonder she wanted to have your babies."

To his horror, Josh's face began to burn. He couldn't remember the last time he'd blushed. "Megan, there are *children* around us."

Her hand dropped, but he wasn't sure if his admonishment had stopped her or if she'd simply passed out again.

She wasn't a large woman, but he hadn't been very faithful at the gym lately, so he was feeling the physical exertion of carrying her dead weight. He made it out of the secure area, despite a suspicious once-over from the security guard at the door. As soon as he stepped out into the hallway, he wondered what on earth to do with her next. A group of three people stood clustered in a group and they all turned their horrified gazes to the woman draped over his shoulder.

"It's okay," he assured them. "I'm her fiancé."

Only then did he realize one of the women was an older version of Megan.

Oh. Shit.

The woman in question looked at the woman hanging down his back. She squatted and tilted her head upside down. "*Megan?*"

Megan gave an exaggerated wave. "Hi, Mom. Why are you upside down?"

Her mother released a horrified gasp. "Are you *drunk?*"

Josh took a step toward her, his heart hammering in his chest. How the hell was he going to get himself out of this one? "She took some Dramamine and apparently it has a pretty strong effect on her. She's okay."

"How much did she *take?*"

He thought back to their conversation. "She said she took two as she was boarding."

"And you didn't see her take them?" she asked, her tone full of admonishment. The woman's eyes lifted to Josh's face and he knew he was being scrutinized. He could see why

Megan was scared of her mother. She was intimidating in the way that only stately women of a certain age could be.

An older man stepped forward and put a hand on her shoulder. "Oh, for God's sake, Nicole, let the man be. Is this really how you want to meet your future son-in-law?"

Josh shook his head. "See, there's been a misunderstanding." But he had to wonder why they didn't know what Megan's ex-fiancé looked like. Sure, they'd never met the guy, but hadn't they at least seen photos?

Megan's father shot his wife a weighted grimace. "The only misunderstanding is that Nicole is trying to micromanage everything. Like always." He stepped forward and held out his hand. "I'm Megan's father, Bart Vandemeer. Nice to finally meet the man who's marrying my little girl. It's Jay, isn't it?"

Josh gaped at the man, at a loss for words. For once in his life he hadn't bothered to come up with an intricate plan before jumping into a situation. He'd asked for fate to intervene and the very man he needed to talk to had been dropped right in front of him.

For once in his life, he was going to just go for it.

He shifted Megan on his shoulder and awkwardly held out his hand for a shake, still speechless. These people obviously had no idea he wasn't Megan's real fiancé. How wrong would it be if he used that to his advantage? After all, he'd be helping Megan too. She was in no condition to deal with her family at the moment. "Josh, actually."

Bart Vandemeer looked confused. "Megan told us your name was Jay."

"Oh…Jay is my nickname. You can call me Jay or Josh, but I usually go by Josh."

"What?" Nicole Vandemeer shrieked, her voice raising a full octave. "All the materials for the wedding list your name as Jay."

Josh struggled to keep from grimacing. "Jay is fine. It really doesn't matter."

"I don't know why Megan doesn't tell me these things," the woman grumbled. An elderly woman grinned like a Cheshire cat behind her, as if finding the whole exchange amusing.

Megan's father ignored his wife. "Well, Josh. Welcome to Kansas City." The older man beamed. "We look forward to getting to know you better."

Bart Vandemeer had no idea how much Josh was looking forward to getting to know him too.

Chapter Four

When Megan woke, she was pretty sure the pounding in her head was about to split it wide open. This was worse than the New Year's Eve party she'd gotten so drunk on tequila shooters she stood up on the coffee table and serenaded "My Heart Will Go On" to her then-boyfriend…only to break up with him an hour later when she found him kissing Lisa Menendez at midnight with enough tongue to contradict his protests that it was a friendly peck.

Now that she thought about it, cheating boyfriends had been a constant in her dating life. She knew the topic deserved closer inspection, but there was no way she could psychoanalyze herself until she'd taken an ibuprofen.

It took her a second to orient herself. She was lying on her stomach, her cheek pressed against something soft and wet. When she finally pried her eyes open, she was surprised to find herself in her old bedroom. Her vision was blurry until it focused on a familiar bulletin board attached to a lavender wall.

She'd hung the board up the summer before her freshman year of high school, ready to capture her high school memories with her two best friends, Blair and Libby. The three of them were together in plenty of the photos—at football games, class trips, and sleepovers. But there were also individual shots of Libby in her cheerleader uniform and Blair in her business suit, ready for a debate match. The familiar pang of regret and inferiority flooded her.

Megan had never found her place in high school. Part of the problem was her mom's unrelenting quest to make her into some kind of mini-me. Her mother never seemed to tire of coercing her to go on day-long shopping trips. When Megan reached high school, she finally announced that enough was enough. She would rather stand naked in history class reciting the United States Constitution than go on another torture session with her mother. Her mother had done exactly what she'd always done in response to Megan's protests: she ignored them. But one Saturday morning, mother and daughter were locked in a standoff over Nicole's meticulously planned day at the Country Club Plaza when Megan's father exercised one of his rare interventions. He told her mother that she'd had fourteen years to try to sway Megan to the dark side and failed. Then he advised Megan she had five minutes to get everything she needed for an overnight camping trip with him and her brother Kevin.

Camping hadn't figured into her plans for the weekend. What she really wanted was to go spend the afternoon with Libby. But an inmate on death row didn't protest when his reprieve meant moving to maximum security instead of freedom, so Megan had done as he'd suggested.

And to her surprise, she loved it.

She wasn't sure why. She'd never considered herself an outdoorsy person, but she began to cherish her monthly camping trips with her dad and brother.

This had irritated her mother to no end, and in fact, drove an even deeper wedge between the two. And that wedge became a gulf when Megan graduated from Missouri University and flew off to Seattle to work for a nonprofit that worked to prevent over-deforestation. At the time, her well-planned escape had been an act of rebellion. While she loved her job, and had quickly moved up the hierarchy to the position of grant coordinator and fundraiser, she now realized the move had cost her something precious—her close relationship with her father and brother.

But here she was, hip-deep in self-analysis again, when she still had no answer to the pressing issue of how she'd gotten from the plane into her old room.

It all came rushing back to her. Boarding the plane. Drinking two mimosas. Stealing Mr. McMillan's drink. Blabbering to him about the flight attendant and her defunct fiancé.

She squeezed her eyes shut in horror. She'd made an utter fool of herself.

She sat up and swiped at her wet cheek, realizing the wet sensation was the result of all the drool on her pillow. Great. As if she needed to feel any worse. At least she could take comfort in the fact that she'd never see the man again. What did it matter if he thought she was crazy? Besides, there were bigger things to worry about. She shook her head, trying to clear it, but spiking a fresh round of pain instead. She needed to focus so she could figure how she'd ended up on her bed. The last thing she remembered was snuggling under the blanket in her seat on the plane. But if she was in her room, her mother must have found her somehow.

Her mother was going to kill her. It was a wonder she hadn't taken advantage of Megan's supine state to do so already.

Megan glanced around the room and found her old digital

alarm clock on the worn white nightstand. 6:12. The sun was streaming through the blinds, but it was summer so that didn't necessarily give her a clue as to whether it was six o'clock a.m. or p.m. She supposed it didn't matter. One way or another, there would be hell to pay.

Sliding off the bed, Megan moved to her door and cautiously cracked it open. Voices floated up from downstairs, one of them clearly her mother's. Since her mother never got up before seven-thirty if she could help it, it had to be evening.

She made her way down the stairs with an anxious ball in the pit of her stomach. She was going to have some explaining to do, though she had no idea how much, because in her drugged state she could have said *anything* to her mother between meeting her in the airport and falling onto her bed. But the sound of other voices in the kitchen gave her a small measure of reassurance. Her mother's voice was light and airy—her company voice. This was good news for Megan. No matter how upset she was, Nicole Vandemeer would never under any circumstances murder someone in front of guests. No matter how justified.

"...Megan hardly told us anything," her mother was saying as Megan approached the kitchen.

"I wouldn't want to bore you with the details," a man's voice said. Why did he sound familiar?

"There she is!" Nicole Vandemeer exclaimed, clasping her hands together in glee. She was in full-on hostess mode, but she seemed even more enthusiastic than was warranted by a mere guest. "Megan! We were just talking about you!"

Had the Dramamine transported her to some sort of bizarre world?

Three people sat at the kitchen island, their backs to her, while her mother stood in front of the commercial gas cooktop, a martini glass in her hand. In tandem, the people on the barstools turned to face her. Her grandmother gave her a big smile and her father nodded, a twinkle in his eye. But it was the third person that made the floor turn to molasses.

Mr. McMillan, the man who sat next to her on the airplane, was sitting at her parents' kitchen counter.

Of course, it couldn't be true.

She squinted her eyes tight, trying to reboot her brain, but when she opened them he was still there, giving her a hesitant smile. Which left only one solution. She turned around and headed back to her room without another word. Maybe if she went back to bed, she could lie down and hit the restart button, waking up in reality.

"Megan!" her mother shouted after her. "Where are you going? Come officially introduce us to your fiancé!"

Oh, God. She really *was* hallucinating. Maybe this was some kind of psychotic break induced by extreme stress and pharmaceuticals.

"Megan, come back right now!" Her mother's tone borderlined on slipping out of character. If Megan pushed her over the edge, the consequences would be worse than she felt capable of handling at the moment. "You're being incredibly rude. Is that how they do things in the Pacific West?"

Megan cringed. Nope. This was real. Her mother was the only person on earth who dropped the North from Pacific Northwest. Megan turned around and walked back into the kitchen, stopping in the doorway. Mr. McMillan studied her with an expressionless face. What in the hell was he doing here? What had he told them?

As if reading her mind—or perhaps her face—he jumped out of his seat and walked over to her. "Hey, honey. How are you feeling?"

She looked up at him, dumbfounded. Why was he smiling at her like that? Scratch that, why was he calling her *honey*? "What the… How did you get here?"

"We picked him up from the airport, of course. Josh told us

what happened," her mother said, her voice light and breezy again. "He told us that you got airsick when you flew to Phoenix last year, so you took Dramamine on this trip as a preventive measure. You should have seen the way Josh took care of you when you got off the plane." She gave Josh a look of approval. Leave it to her mother to wait to give her elusive stamp of approval to a fake boyfriend.

"Wait. *Josh...?*"

Mr. McMillan put an arm around Megan's back, his hand resting on her hip, warm and surprisingly comforting. "I told your parents how you insist on calling me Jay even though my name is Josh."

She shook her head in confusion. "*What?*" Was this some weird joke, or had she just woken up in the *Twilight Zone?*

He gave her a patient smile. "Sweetheart, you must still be out of it. Your parents were filling me in on the wedding plans. I know you wanted it to be a surprise, but it's only a couple of days now. It sounds just as remarkable as I knew it would be."

She was wrong. This wasn't a hallucination. This was a nightmare. Anger blazed to life in her stomach, quickly spreading up through her chest. She clenched her hands into fists.

"Why didn't you bring this young man home sooner, pumpkin?" her father asked. "I can tell he's going to fit right in with our family."

Was that supposed to be a *good* thing?

"And he's got a cute patootie," her grandmother added. "I think you kids call it an ass."

"Gram!" Megan protested in shock.

Josh laughed, his hand pulling her closer. "Funny, Megan was saying the same thing today in the airport."

Megan's jaw dropped as she glared at him in disbelief.

Gram shook her head. "For the life of me, I don't know why you would call someone's back end an ass. Especially a cute one. Don't you kids know that an ass is a donkey?"

Megan didn't take her gaze off Josh for a moment, her temper about to blow. "I don't know what you think you're doing—"

Before she realized what was happening, he cupped her cheek, and kissed her, his lips soft but insistent. She put her balled hands on his chest with the intention of pushing him away, but her heart began to race in spite of herself and she leaned closer, inexplicably drawn to him as her anger bled out and her hands relaxed. His muscles were firm below her fingertips and her knees began to weaken, but the arm he'd looped around her back held her up. If this was a dream, she decided she wasn't ready to wake up.

Josh lifted his face, looking slightly dazed for a moment before he turned toward her family, still holding her in his arms. "Sorry," he murmured. "I just love her so much I can't stop myself sometimes."

Megan gaped at him as if she'd just had a lobotomy. The way her brain felt at the moment, it probably wasn't too far off.

"He doesn't look like a donkey," her grandmother said in a smug tone.

"Aww…" her mother cooed. "That's so precious. Your wedding is going to be the talk of the summer at the country club."

Megan was speechless again, but this time for an entirely different reason. What had just happened?

The door to the garage opened and Megan turned to see her older brother filling the opening, a duffel bag in his hand. "Get a room," he groaned with a grin.

"Kevin!" She broke free from Josh's hold and ran to her brother, throwing her arms around his shoulders.

"Hey, Squirt!" He dropped his bag and wrapped his arms around her back, lifting her several inches off the ground as he swung her in a circle.

"Kevin! Put her down!" their mother shouted. "If you break her leg, she'll never be able to walk down the aisle on Saturday!"

He put her down and playfully tugged a lock of her hair. "I'm not going to break her leg. I already did that when we were kids. No point in doing it again." Kevin picked her up again and swung her for several seconds more before setting her on her feet. He gave her a mischievous grin, then winked.

"What are you doing here?" she asked, surprised by how happy she was to see him.

"Rumor has it that my baby sister is getting married. I took leave so I could put the fear of God into your fiancé," he said. He narrowed his eyes on Josh, his voice taking on an air of authority. He had been teasing before, but not now. This was one of the reasons why Megan had never brought her boyfriends home when she was in high school and college. Kevin loved to intimidate any male who got within ten feet of her. But then, he'd always had a way of intimidating anyone. The marines seemed like a natural fit for him. "So are you finally gonna introduce me to the man you're marrying in three days?"

Her brother's words sobered her. "*Actually*…" She took a breath for strength, her stomach knotting equally with nerves and irritation. "There's something I need to tell all of you—"

"*Sweetheart*," Josh said, glancing at her brother, then giving her a strained look. "I know you're still irritated with me over our argument at the airport in Seattle, but there's no reason to drag your family into it."

She shot him a glare. Who was this guy and what in the hell was his end game? One thing was for sure—she wasn't about to find out in front of her mother.

Gritting her teeth, she marched toward him and grabbed his wrist, her nails digging deeper than necessary as she tugged him to the doorway. "He's right. I'm still pissed at him and we need to get this straightened out."

"Megan!" her mother shouted after her. "You're being incredibly rude."

But Megan ignored her as she climbed the stairs and dragged him into her room. It wasn't until she shut the door behind them that she realized she was still holding onto his wrist. She dropped it as though he were on fire.

"What the hell is going on?" she demanded. "Is this some kind of sick joke?"

He shook his head. "No! It's a giant misunderstanding."

"*Misunderstanding?* A misunderstanding is when you order French fries and get onion rings. The fact that my parents think a stranger is my fiancé is not a *misunderstanding*. It's a disaster. How could you let this happen?"

His face froze with fear. "Please tell me that you remember sitting by me on the plane."

"I remember that part." She rubbed her hand over her forehead as if to banish the lingering headache. "You sat down and I accused you of being a terrorist. Then I made fun of the flight attendant and stole your drink." She cringed in embarrassment. "Everything else is fuzzy after that."

"You don't remember getting off the plane?"

"No."

"The flight attendant was going to call security, so I helped you off. I had to carry you over my shoulder because you couldn't walk, and I got the impression that security wasn't going to help you find your mother. The flight attendant had it in for you."

Think, Megan. Think. She scrunched her eyes shut to remember how she got into this situation. "I vaguely remember telling her she couldn't have your babies. Then you dragged me away." She glanced up, putting her hands on her hips. "While I appreciate you for helping me not get arrested by a federal marshal, that doesn't explain how you ended up *here*. As *my fiancé*."

He held his hands up in surrender, his eyes pleading with hers, and damned if her breath didn't catch. Her pulse quickened just at the sight of him. Of course, it didn't help that their kiss was so fresh in her memory.

"You couldn't walk and you were talking nonsense, so like I said, the only way I knew how to get you out of the terminal without leaving our bags behind was to carry you over my shoulder. But people thought I was abducting you, so I told them that you were my fiancée." He heaved out a sigh of frustration. "Your family heard me and thought I was Jay. And then I got stuck."

Everything made perfect sense, but something about his delivery was off.

He narrowed his eyes and she could practically feel the judgment rolling off him. "Have they really never seen him before?"

"No," she said sharply, putting her hands on her hips. "Not that it's any of your business."

"Not even photos?" His brow lifted as though a new idea had occurred to him. "Wait. Does he even exist?"

Her mouth dropped in shock. "Of course he exists!"

"Then why no photos?"

Her back stiffened. "I have some photos of him. Just not very many. And I guess they're a little blurry."

"You have to admit that's pretty weird, since you were supposedly together for two years."

She gasped. "Who are you to judge me? You've been conscious and coherent all day, yet you were just sitting in a strange woman's kitchen pretending to be her fiancé!"

"Now, Megan. I wouldn't call you strange. A little eccentric maybe."

She balled her fists and groaned in frustration. "Are you

some creepy stalker? How did you know I'd been with Jay two years?"

"Your mother. She's very chatty when she's in a good mood."

She covered her face with her hands. "I still don't understand how this happened." Dropping her arms to her sides, she glared at him. "What are you *doing* here?"

"I told you. Your parents thought I was your fiancé."

"I mean, why didn't you *correct* them?"

He quirked his brow and smirked at her. "Says the woman who's getting married in three days to a made-up groom."

She stomped her foot. "I did *not* make him up!"

He began to pace at the foot of her bed, his pure masculinity a sharp contrast to the white and lavender ruffled comforter. "Look, in hindsight, it probably wasn't the smartest decision to call you my fiancée when I left the terminal—especially after you told me that your mother was picking you up—but I didn't know what else to do. I tried to explain the misunderstanding, but before I knew it, I was riding in your mother's Navigator to Blue Springs, Missouri." He spun around to stare at her. "Your mother is frightening."

"I told you!"

He grabbed her hand and sat down on the bed, guiding her to sit next to him. "Look. You need someone to stand in for your fake boyfriend—"

"He's not fake!"

"—and your parents think I'm him. We can make this work for you."

"What are you talking about?" she asked, ignoring the fact that his touch sent flutters through her stomach. She jerked her hand free.

If he was offended, he didn't let on. "We'll let them continue to think I'm here to marry you. Then I'll act like a jerk and break up with you in front of them. That way I'll take all the blame, which gets you off the hook. You have to admit that it's the perfect plan. Your mother won't kill you and you might not even have to return all those toasters."

"I didn't register for toasters. I registered for a bagel oven."

He looked taken aback. "You seriously registered for your fake wedding? How far were you going to take this anyway?"

She gritted her teeth, seething. "I *had* a fiancé. His name is Jay Connors. He's an investment banker and he lives in downtown Seattle in a condo that overlooks Puget Sound."

His head jerked back in disgust. "*An investment banker.* You can't be serious."

"What's wrong with dating an investment banker?"

"Nothing. If you were really engaged to one. But if you made the guy up, you could have at least given him a more exciting career. Like a firefighter. Or a trapeze artist."

"And what is it that *you* do, *Mr.* McMillan?"

"I'm an entrepreneur."

She rolled her eyes. "Like that's any better. Isn't that a fancy way of saying you don't know what to do with your life?"

He ignored her insult and pressed on. "What do your parents know about me?"

"They don't know anything! I just met you."

"Not me. Him. Your fake fiancé. The one you made up."

"I didn't make him up!" she shouted.

"Then show me a photo."

"I don't have to prove a damn thing to you."

He smirked in triumph.

Damn him. Why did she care what he thought? Yet she found herself digging her phone out of her purse anyway. She scrolled through her photos, then stopped. "Here's a picture of us at a Seahawks game."

Josh took the phone and stared at it for several seconds. "This? That looks like you've Photoshopped your head into a bad photo of James Van Der Beek."

"The guy from *Dawson's Creek?* I'm more than a little frightened you know who he is."

He shrugged. "Hey, my college girlfriend Trisha was obsessed with that show. I watched it with her. You could have used a photo of Brad Pitt or someone more current, you know."

"Wouldn't that be kind of obvious?"

He lifted his brow with a smirk. "So you admit it's a fake."

"I didn't fake this photo!" She took a deep breath to regain control. Pressing her lips together, she gave a slight nod before continuing in an ultra-calm voice. "So his face isn't very clear. The camera on my phone sucks."

He tossed the phone back to her. "I'm not convinced, but that's not the point," he added when she opened her mouth to protest. "We have a mission." He made sure he had her full attention. "I'll make myself look like an ass and break up with you, saving you from your mother's wrath."

She narrowed her eyes, her suspicion building. "Why would you do this?"

"Because I'm a nice guy." He grinned, his whole face lighting up, and in that moment she could see why the bitchy flight attendant had been so determined to snag him. If she hadn't been so suspicious of his motives, it would be easy to fall for that grin.

"Try again."

He shrugged with a good-natured smile. "I have my reasons." When she started to talk, he cut her off. "Look, I'm here in Kansas City for family reasons. I'd prefer not to be here at all—no offense—but this gives me a chance to procrastinate and not deal with the drama."

She of all people could understand avoiding family issues, but wasn't impersonating someone's fiancé a bit extreme? Then again, she'd flown home to her own wedding with no groom, so who was she to judge?

"How do I know you're not a thief? Or a murderer. Maybe you're waiting until the middle of the night and you plan to kill us all in our sleep."

"You have a very active imagination. It makes me wonder even more about the existence of your boyfriend. Why would I go to so much trouble?"

"I don't know," she said, annoyed. "How would I know how a serial killer thinks?"

"First I'm a terrorist and now I'm a serial killer? I think you need to make up your mind."

She gritted her teeth.

"I'm perfectly harmless." He held his hands out at his sides. "I promise."

She knew bullshit when she saw it. And she'd seen plenty of it in her dating life. Jay may not have been the most exciting man in the world, but at least she'd known what she was getting with him. Or at least she'd thought so until he pulled the rug out from under her. What were you supposed to do when even the "safe" guys, the ones you settled for, turned out to be cheats and liars?

She turned to Josh and jabbed her finger into his chest. "I don't trust you."

His smile didn't even dim. "And you don't have to. Just let me break up with you and then I'll be on my merry way."

"Fine." She sighed. "Let's go get it over with."

He held up his hands. "Whoa, whoa, whoa. We're not breaking up tonight."

"*What?* Why not?"

"We can't. How suspicious would that look if we were just super sweet to each other and then I suddenly broke up with you? Your parents might see through it and realize you made up your boyfriend."

"I did not make up my boyfriend!" she hissed, trying to keep her voice down.

"That's a moot point," he said, acting far too calm considering the situation. "We need to *focus*."

She took a deep breath, ready to vent her frustration. She couldn't think of the last time she'd been this angry. Fights with Jay had run more ice cold and passive-aggressive. "Fine," she huffed. "Since this is *your* crazy scheme, I take it you have some kind of plan."

"Tonight we act like a couple in love, then tomorrow, I'll start acting like an ass."

"You're doing a pretty good job right now," she said, eyebrows raised. "You take this bossy, condescending show on the road, and you're golden."

He heaved out a breath. "Do you want me to help you or not? If you'd prefer, I'll call a taxi and have them come pick me up now. Then you can explain everything yourself."

Her shoulders tensed. "You wouldn't."

He grinned. "Try me."

"You're an ass."

"You already said that," he laughed. "Oh, wait. No, you said you liked my ass."

"Not likely," she said in a snide tone, but she couldn't be sure it was true. Megan couldn't remember saying any such thing, but her gram was right. He had a nice one. Alcohol had a tendency to make her spew out all kinds of truths, embarrassing or not.

Focus, Megan.

She began to pace. If she were smart, she'd march downstairs and tell her family everything, but that had never been her style. Yes, avoidance had been Megan Vandemeer's philosophy long before this man had come into her life. The fact that she'd immediately broken it off with Jay after finding out he was screwing his secretary—and had been for months—was a huge step for her. She stopped and turned to face the man in her room. Could he really be the answer to her problem?

"Did my parents really buy the whole thing about me calling you Jay even though your name is Josh?"

"Never questioned it."

A knock on the door and Megan's mother's voice stopped her. "Megan? Is everything okay in there?"

The blood rushed from Megan's head. How much had her mother heard?

Josh reached forward and opened the door, then stepped back next to Megan.

Her mother stood in the threshold looking suspicious. "What are you two up to? Megan, did you say you'd had an argument?" Her disapproving tone made it clear whom she blamed for said argument.

Josh snaked his arm around Megan's waist and pulled her close. "Sorry we disappeared like that, Mrs. Vandemeer. We had a small disagreement before, but we worked everything out. I've been ignoring my little love bug lately." He tapped Megan's nose with his index finger, giving her a smug smile that dared her to contradict him, then he turned to face her mother. "I've been really busy at work for the past few weeks, trying to clear my plate so I could get away for the wedding and honeymoon, so..."

Megan's mother frowned. "But Megan said you were too busy to get away for a honeymoon. I thought you were flying straight back to Seattle after this weekend so you could head to work on Monday morning."

Josh's mouth dropped open. "What?" He turned to look at Megan with a wide smile. "What kind of husband would I be if I didn't take my bride on a honeymoon?" He gave her mother a sheepish grin. "I wanted it to be a surprise." Then he turned back to Megan. "Surprise, honey!"

Megan's mother placed her hand on her chest, beaming. "I told Megan she needed to go on a honeymoon, but she swore you couldn't get away and she didn't want one. Where are you taking her?"

"Well… Uh…"

"Yes, *honey*," Megan said, lifting an eyebrow. "Where are we going?"

"Uh…" He truly looked stymied for a moment, but then he said, "The Caribbean," acting as if it were a revelation.

"That's wonderful!" her mother gushed. "Which island?"

"Excuse me?" he asked, clearly uncomfortable.

"Which island?"

Megan decided to take pity on him. She still didn't trust him, and she was certain there was more to his motives than he was letting on, but he'd saved her twice. She owed him something. "I bet it's the Virgin Islands, isn't it? Ever since we met, I've been telling Josh how much I wanted to go there."

"That's it!" Josh exclaimed. "But now I've ruined the surprise."

"Oh, sweetheart," Megan drawled, patting his cheek harder than necessary. "You're just one surprise after another."

He reached up and grabbed her hand, pulling it down to his chest, where he held it over his heart. *Laying it on a bit thick?*

"You still didn't explain what you're doing up here," her mother said.

Megan was irritated. She was twenty-nine years old and her mother was still trying to control her.

Josh intervened. "Like I said, I've been working a lot…which means I haven't spent a lot of time with Megan lately." He dropped her hand and wrapped his other arm around her as he pulled her to his chest. "I assumed that you and Mr. Vandemeer would want us to sleep in separate rooms until the wedding, so I figured we could enjoy a little time alone together since we were already up here. If you know what I mean." He winked.

Megan couldn't believe he'd just said that to her mother.

She kicked his shin, but his smile barely wavered.

Her mother's face turned a pretty pink, which Megan didn't find surprising. Everything her mother did only enhanced her beauty and sophistication. She wasn't an ugly crier, so *of course* her blush would look like blush, not like the ugly splotches Megan got when she was embarrassed. There had never been any question as to why her father had married the Southern belle from Atlanta, who still carried her Southern accent around like a badge of honor. But she'd found it impossible to live in her shadow.

Her mother reached for the diamond pendant at the base of her neck. "Bart and I understand young love. We're not *that* old-fashioned. You're both grown adults, days away from your wedding. We know you…*do things*…in Seattle. So Josh, we put your bag in here with Megan's." She gestured to the suitcase Megan hadn't noticed until precisely that moment.

Josh's arms stiffened around Megan. "I wouldn't want to offend—"

"Don't be silly." She waved him off with one hand. "But save the hanky-panky for later and come down to the kitchen. The guests are arriving in twenty minutes."

"Guests?" Megan gasped.

Megan's mother shook her head. "Really, Megan. Don't you listen to a word I say?" She released an exaggerated sigh. "I told you about this *months* ago."

Megan *hadn't* paid attention. Her mother had gone Mother-of-the-Bridezilla with planning the details for the wedding, down to the exact size of the love birds her mother had monogrammed onto an old handkerchief—seven-eighths of an inch by five-eighths—and Megan had done her best to tune it all out. She was now regretting that decision.

"I had a feeling something like this would happen," her mother said. She pointed to the dresser along the far wall. "I made you both an itinerary for the rest of the week so you know where you need to be and when."

Josh glanced at the dresser, but Megan kept her attention on her mother. "So we need to be downstairs in twenty minutes?" Obviously, her mother wasn't interested in volunteering what was planned for the evening. She'd need to read it in whatever booklet—or, knowing her mother, tome—on the dresser.

Her mother rolled her eyes. Even that looked pretty on her. "Not quite. The guests *arrive* in twenty minutes. I need you downstairs pronto to help finish setting up." She took a step toward the door before turning back. "And Megan…you should consider putting on some fresh clothes and touching up your makeup a bit. You look like you've been on a two-day drinking binge." She made an exaggerated grimace, then walked out the door toward the stairs.

"I'm not sure whether to be horrified or amused that your mother called what we were doing *hanky-panky*," Josh said, shivering as though he'd narrowly escaped a brush with death.

But Megan ignored him, shutting the bedroom door—a little louder than normal but not as loud as she wanted—then running into the Jack and Jill bathroom off her room and flipping on the light.

"*Ohmygawd!*" she gushed in horror. Her mascara was smeared under her eyes and her hair looked like it belonged to a creative child's Barbie. Her natural waves had ratted into a huge mess on the right side of her head, where she'd been leaning against the plane window. She'd just had a conversation with Josh—and he'd kissed her—looking like…*this*.

"Your mother thinks we're going to sleep together tonight," he said from the bedroom.

"I know. I was privy to the conversation." She opened the linen closet and grabbed a washrag and stuck it under the running water.

"So what are we going to do?"

"I don't know. I have bigger issues to worry about."

"Your makeup? Honestly, you don't look that bad."

"Maybe not for a *zombie!*" she moaned.

"Why are you so worked up?"

"I looked like this—" she pointed to her reflection in the mirror "—down there." She pointed to the door.

"So?"

"*So?*" She shook her head, trying to swallow the burning lump in her throat. "You obviously wouldn't understand."

"Try me."

I will not cry. I will not cry. Why on earth did she care so much about what the man in the next room thought? Soon he'd be gone and she'd never see him again. But she couldn't ignore the way that kiss had felt… But even though she was mortified he'd seen her this way, it wasn't what was really bothering her. How could she even explain it? She'd spent most of the first eighteen years of her life trying to live up to her mother's expectations and she'd come up short each and every time. The last time she'd been home was last fall, to shop for her wedding. Trying on wedding dresses was supposed to be a magical experience, but with her mother in the room, each gown had felt like a gunnysack. Not to mention they hadn't seen eye to eye on any of the details for the reception and ceremony. Ultimately, she'd just given in and allowed Nicole Vandemeer to have what she wanted. So to come home and face the humiliation that would inevitably result when her mother found out the truth...Tears welled in her eyes.

She should shove Josh out the door and confess to her family, but she couldn't bear it. How much more embarrassing would it be if her mother assumed she'd hired this guy, some attractive stranger, to act as her fiancé? Because that's inevitably where her mother's mind would go. No, the answer was simple.

She and Josh needed to stage an epic breakup.

Chapter Five

He hadn't meant to kiss her. Despite the fact that he was posing as her fiancé, he hadn't given any thought to the probability that they'd have to have some type of physical contact if she agreed to play along. His sole strategy was to find proof that Bart Vandemeer's company had stolen his part. Once he did, he'd never have to see these people again.

But something had changed when he kissed her.

He'd figured out a plan on the way home from the airport. Nicole Vandemeer kept herself so busy reciting every last detail about the wedding that all he had to do was nod and say "uh-huh" every so often, and she was none the wiser that he was plotting his revenge on her husband.

Josh had to admit that Bart Vandemeer wasn't what he'd expected. He'd envisioned someone more ruthless, although he wasn't sure why. After all, there was no proof Megan's father was responsible for stealing Josh's design. In fact, his only piece of flimsy evidence pointed to Drew Peterman, Bart's partner's son. But even if Bart wasn't knowingly involved, he was still responsible—he should have asked the right questions when the design was so abruptly submitted.

And then there was Megan's wedding. Megan had told him it was a twenty-five-thousand-dollar affair, but based on the details her mother had given him, he suspected the total was much higher…which begged the question of where all that money was coming from.

He'd tried to quiz Bart about his business, just a future son-in-law making polite conversation, but Nicole had tried her best to steer the conversation away from business, frustrating Josh to no end.

One of the things Nicole had blathered on about had made an impression—she was hosting a massive party for him and Megan that evening. Josh hoped to take advantage of the distraction so he could search Bart's home office. He'd heard Nicole mention that it was upstairs. Josh could pretend he needed to use the bathroom and then find the home office and search it before anyone was the wiser. He also considered trying to steal the older man's keys for a visit to his actual office, but Josh didn't want to resort to such drastic measures. It was bad enough he was impersonating Megan's fiancé; he wasn't ready to jump the shark and resort to breaking and entering just yet. He'd save that for tomorrow night if need be.

His phone vibrated in his pocket and he pulled it out, not surprised to see that his own office was trying to reach him. He sent the call to voice mail. He knew it wasn't his brother, who always called from his cell. It was probably Angie, their business manager; though they hadn't told anyone they were in danger of losing their investor's support, Angie was perceptive and had somehow caught on to the fact that they were in dire straits. Although she'd tried to pry the truth out of both men, neither one had caved. Still, Josh was usually predictable. He didn't take unexplained and unplanned trips, so Angie had probably flipped her lid when he didn't show up today. All the more reason to ignore her call. He couldn't handle talking to her right now…and he definitely couldn't do it with Megan Vandemeer in the next room.

His entire company was depending on him to save them, whether they knew it or not. So why did he keep thinking about kissing his enemy's daughter?

He was still desperate to find the information, yes, but his traitorous mind kept thinking about her body pressed against his, the way she'd kissed him back, her lips warm and soft.

Damn it.

He needed to stop thinking about kissing her and focus on getting the information he needed to save his engineering firm. The real purpose of this trip.

It had seemed like a great lead a few hours ago—the perfect answer to his dilemma. Now, he was conflicted.

After Megan's parents and grandmother had accepted him as her fiancé at the airport, they'd moved to the baggage carousel to pick up Megan's bags.

He'd set Megan down in a chair, her head flopping to the side like a ragdoll's. She stirred and blinked up at him after a moment. "Hey," she mumbled, jabbing her fingertip into his chest. "I know you."

He forced his voice to stay light and amused when he answered, "I should hope so, honey."

She shook her head and his chest tightened with anxiety that the jig was likely up, but she closed her eyes, muttering, "I said I want the red ones."

"Red ones what?" Gram asked.

Nicole rolled her eyes. "She's talking nonsense, Mother. She's *drunk*." She spit the last part out as though announcing that Megan was Mussolini in disguise.

Josh was about to come Megan's defense when her father walked up.

"What's her luggage look like?" Bart had asked. "How many does she have?"

He knew the quantity answer since she'd mentioned she'd packed only one bag, but what on earth did they look like? "Uh…" He was never going to be able to pull this off. What had possessed him to try? He didn't know anything about this woman other than that her fiancé had cheated on her and she was terrified of her mother. Oh, and she thought he had a nice ass. *Think*. "We didn't drive to the airport together," he blurted out. "I met her at the gate. I know she has one bag, but I'm not sure which one she used."

"Don't you worry," Bart said, waving him to sit beside Megan. "We'll figure it out."

Within ten minutes, Bart had pulled a pink floral suitcase off the conveyer belt and was rolling it out the door. Nicole Vandemeer decreed that everyone else would wait for Bart to bring the car around, but after five minutes of doing just as she'd set out to do, Nicole grew impatient and decided to wait by the exit. Josh suspected that she was embarrassed to be seen next to her unconscious daughter.

Megan's grandmother plopped in the seat next to his and studied him. "You're not what I expected."

He swallowed, keeping his gaze on Nicole, whose posture was finishing-school straight as she stood in front of the sliding glass doors. Nicole Vandemeer hadn't been what he'd expected either. "Oh?" he asked, trying to sound nonchalant. "How so?"

"Your smile."

Josh blinked in surprise. "What does that mean?"

"Megan may not talk to her mother very often, but she talks to me. She tries to make out that everything's okay, but something in her voice tells me otherwise."

Josh stared at her, unsure of what to say.

Her grandmother patted his hand. "I'm glad you smile. Megan needs more smiles." She cast a frown toward Megan's mother, the older woman's daughter.

Bart had just pulled up, saving him from answering. Josh tried to wake Megan and managed to hoist her to her feet, albeit unsteadily, for long enough to get her strapped into a seat in the SUV. The whole time she kept mumbling something about gingerbread houses. The derisive looks Nicole kept casting at her made him want to avenge her in some way. But that wasn't his purpose for being here and it definitely wasn't his problem.

Now, several hours later, as he stood in her bathroom doorway while she prepared for whatever social function the queen had organized, he realized he still felt that way. He wanted to help Megan—and not just because of what she could do for him.

"Go look at the itinerary," she said, swiping mascara on her upper eyelashes. "We need to know what we're facing down there."

He walked over to the dresser and picked up one of two bound binders. The cover was inscribed with the words *The Wedding of Megan and Jay* in bold calligraphy. One booklet had *Megan* written in the upper right corner and the other read *Jay*.

He opened the book on top—Jay's—and flipped through the pages. The next three days were strictly regimented with a minute-to-minute schedule and detailed descriptions of all the activities. The entries were color-coded with highlighters, and there was a corresponding color key at the bottom of the first page.

Oh. My. God.

But even worse was the fact that Mrs. Vandemeer had booked most of the next three days of his life. How was he going to find the evidence he needed if he was required to be at all the places listed on those pages?

"Well?" Megan called out to him. "What is it?"

Oh, God. Friday morning he was scheduled for a men's

mani-pedi. *Who did that?*

"Josh!"

"Uh..." Terror washed through his body. What in the hell had he gotten himself into? "Uh..." He scanned the page. "Oh, your mom told me about this one. Seven p.m. Poolside cocktail party."

"*A cocktail party?*"

"Yeah..."

"Shit."

He looked over his shoulder at her, still in the binder's horrific thrall. "Is that bad?"

She stopped applying her mascara and glanced over at him. "It's not good. Do you have nice clothes? A dress shirt and a tie?"

He blinked. "Yeah."

"Really?"

He shot her a sideways glare. "Why do you sound so surprised?"

"It doesn't matter." She stormed out of the bathroom and squatted next to her suitcase before glancing up at him. "What are you waiting for?"

He tossed the binder on the dresser, then hefted his overnight bag onto the bed and unzipped it.

Megan came over, holding a pale blue dress, and started to dig through his clothes.

"Hey!"

She tugged out a shirt. "The white shirt with the blue tie."

"You're *dressing* me?"

"You want to sign up for this gig, it's part of it. She'll expect us to be color-coordinated. Did the itinerary say if there was a color scheme?"

"*A color scheme?*" He shook his head. "God, no."

"Good. Get dressed." She left him standing at the foot of her bed as she disappeared behind the bathroom door.

He could wear his jeans with the shirt and tie, but suspected Megan's mother would flip her lid. And while that would be amusing to say the least, he needed to stay on her good side, at least until he found his evidence. He dug a pair of dress pants out of his bag and set them on the bed, waiting for Megan to emerge from the bathroom so he could change. He heard Nicole's muffled voice calling from downstairs.

"Megan!"

He decided not to wait for the bathroom to be free. His goal was to charm Nicole Vandemeer and so far, he was succeeding. No need to be late for the first event on her endless schedule. He stripped off his shirt and slipped an arm into one of the sleeves of the button-down shirt as the bathroom door opened.

Megan stood in the doorway in a light blue sundress and he stopped dressing, his second arm partially in the sleeve.

The sight of her sucked his breath away. Megan Vandemeer was a stunningly beautiful woman. And Jay Connors was a fool.

They stared at each other for several seconds before she looked away.

"You can use the bathroom now," she mumbled, her cheeks flushing.

"Thanks." But he stayed in place, pulling his shirt on the rest of the way and starting to button it.

Her gaze moved to the bed and then to his face. "Keep the jeans."

"But I figured your mother would have a fit."

Megan glanced up at him through long dark eyelashes, a mischievous grin lighting up her face. "She'll hate it. That's why you should wear them."

"So you *want* me to piss your mother off? After you freaked out about upsetting her?"

"That's different," she said, picking up his tie off the bed.

"You get to make an exit from this horror show. I have to live with her for at least another thirty years."

She looped the tie around his neck and in that instant he knew he was in deep, deep shit. He forced his breathing to remain normal even though his heart raced. Did she even know how sexy she was right now, knotting his tie at the base of his throat?

She finished her task and appraised him. "I guess you'll do."

"You *guess?*"

She turned her attention to her suitcase and started digging around for something.

"We need a story," he forced out.

"What?"

"People are going to ask questions. We need to tell them the same thing. Does your family know how you met your fiancé?"

She turned her head and gave him a wry grin. "So you acknowledge his existence now?"

He almost laughed out loud. How he'd enjoyed riling her up about her fake fiancé.

"You showed me his blurry picture, right? But I still question his existence, if only based on the fact that the man has to be an idiot of epic proportions." Why did he admit that? *Focus, Josh. Focus.* There was only a week left until everything was lost. He needed to do what he'd come here to do and that was it.

She glanced down. "No. They hardly know anything."

"So how did we meet?"

"Friends set us up."

"Where was our first date?"

"At Six Seven Restaurant, overlooking the sound."

"Classy *and* romantic. And how did our first date go?"

She stood, holding a pair of sandals in her hand. She

flashed him a teasing grin. "You were smitten with me. I found you barely tolerable."

He stared into her twinkling eyes as she looked up at him. "And did any of that really happen on your first date with your fiancé?"

Her smile faded, making him regret the question. "No. We met at a bar downtown for drinks. He declared us compatible. We each paid for our own tab and agreed to try dinner the next week."

"Sounds very…calculated."

"That's Jay for you."

He wasn't sure how to respond. Based on what little he knew of her, he couldn't imagine her happy with someone like that. "When did you guys move in together?"

"We didn't." He expected her to sound bitter. She only sounded resigned.

Rather than commenting, he moved on to the next question. "What do you do?"

She sat on the bed and slipped on her shoes. "I'm a fundraiser for an environmental nonprofit." She glanced up, blowing away a strand of hair that fell in her face. "My mother finds it tacky that I'm paid to beg people for money. She says I could at least have chosen a well-respected cause. Suffice it to say, she wishes I would do something else."

"I bet."

"They know Jay's an investment banker…that he works long hours."

"What else did you tell them about Jay…ahem…I mean me?"

She smiled slightly as she stood, brushing out her skirt. "That you bought a condo in downtown Seattle overlooking the sound because it was a good investment. I was going to move in after the wedding. You're from Seattle. You have one brother and two parents… Oh, and they aren't coming to the wedding."

"Why not?" he asked, astounded.

"They booked a cruise and got the wedding date mixed up. They would have lost nearly ten thousand dollars."

He whistled. "Damn, it must be some cruise…"

"It's a private yacht in the Mediterranean. And Mom had already booked the botanical garden, so she couldn't change the date since we're getting married in June. She was lucky she got the date at all." Noticing his blank stare, she added, "That's where the wedding and reception are. The Powell Gardens."

"And my brother?"

"He's not coming either. He couldn't get away from work."

"Wow. Was anyone from this jerk's side coming to the wedding?"

She cringed. "A couple of friends. But obviously they aren't coming now."

From what Josh had heard he wasn't surprised. What an ass. "Let's try to stick together tonight. That way there's less of a chance we'll get our stories mixed up."

She lifted her eyebrows. "Don't you worry. I have no intention of leaving you alone. I have no idea what you are up to, but I'm going to keep an eye on you."

He flashed her his charming smile and held his hands out from his sides. "I already told you; I'm trying to avoid my family drama."

"By jumping into mine?" She sounded even more skeptical than before.

"Hey, anybody else's family drama is preferable to your own. Besides," he flashed her what he hoped was a beguiling grin, "I told you that this is mutually beneficial."

"Part of me wants to believe you, but nobody goes to this much trouble for someone they hardly know."

"Megan!" Her mother's muffled voice called up the stairs and through the closed door, louder than before.

"Maybe I'm just a nice guy."

She put her hands on her hips and narrowed her eyes as she studied him. "No. I don't think so."

He laughed. "You don't think I'm nice?"

"Not in this. You're up to something. But let me warn you," she wrapped her fingers around his tie and pulled him closer until their faces were no more than a foot apart, "if you screw me over down there, I will make you suffer for the rest of your natural life. Do I make myself clear?"

The sight of her—her eyes wild and wicked with the promise of retribution—had the opposite effect of what she'd intended. His heart began to race and he had to restrain himself from closing the distance and kissing her. "Megan, I'm here to help you." He placed his hands on her shoulders and gently rubbed the tense knots. "You need to relax."

She released his tie and brushed his hands away. "I'll relax after we've broken up. And we're breaking up *tonight*." And with that, she stormed out the door.

Oh, shit.

Chapter Six

Josh stopped her in the hallway. "Wait. Why are we breaking up tonight? I thought we were going to wait."

She shook her head. She didn't have time for this. Her mother was going to be plenty furious as it was. "My mother's party is the perfect place—in front of all her friends. There will be tons of witnesses to see that I'm the innocent in this and you're the jerk. There's no way she can blame me."

"Don't you think you're being hasty?"

And there it was again, the voice in her head that said something was screwy here. "You make it sound like you don't *want* to break up. What the hell kind of family drama are you facing in Kansas City, anyway? It's got to be pretty bad for you to throw your plans away and become my substitute fiancé. You don't even know me. And don't give me some bullshit answer." She knew she could demand all she wanted, but she was at his mercy. She had no leverage in this negotiation whatsoever and they both knew it.

His eyes softened. "Have you have ever been in a situation where you couldn't see a way out, so you gave up and left it to fate to work everything out?" His eyes widened in mock surprise. "Oh, wait. You *do* know what that's like. You're living it right now."

Now he was just pissing her off.

He put his hands on her shoulders. "Believe it or not, that's what's going on with me too. You said I looked determined when I sat down on the plane. I came to Kansas City because my family business is a mess and I'm making a last-ditch effort to save it."

When she didn't answer, he continued.

"Megan, I sat down on that plane and realized I didn't have a clue how to save my business. Then you waltzed into my life. I swear to you, I inadvertently told your parents I was your fiancé. But once your parents thought it was true, I figured what the hell? After all, you were in a messy situation too, and I had just given my life over to fate. I believe in karma. Maybe if I help you out, fate will help me out too."

She had to admit that he was pretty convincing, but something was off. "If your business is really failing and you're here to save it, why would you want to hang out at my parents' cocktail party tonight?" Then she gasped. "Oh! You're planning to sell your snake oil to my parents' wealthy friends!"

"What?"

She poked her finger into his chest. "If you so much as hint that you aren't an investment banker, or you try to sell insurance or vacation timeshares or crappy Tupperware to my parents' friends, I will make you suffer. Is that understood?"

He clasped her hand between both of his, giving her a sweet smile. "Perfectly. But you're not giving off a very loving vibe right now, sweetie. You don't want your mother to think I'm breaking up with you because you're a bitch."

"What? How *dare* you—"

Before she could react, he kissed her again, pulling her flush against his body. This kiss was different than the one he'd given her downstairs. The previous kiss hadn't exactly been chaste, but it had tested the line of inappropriate in front of her family. This kiss dropped all pretense. His hand tangled in her hair and his tongue parted her lips with an intensity and urgency she hadn't expected. And while some sane part of her knew she should resist, the rest of her eagerly welcomed it.

"Uh… Megan…" Her brother's voice broke through her lust-filled haze.

That's when reality set in. She was kissing this man, someone she'd only known for a matter of hours, in the upstairs hallway in her parents' house. She tried to pull away from Josh, but his arms held her tight against him as she glanced over her shoulder.

Kevin stood at the top of the stairs, his bag in hand, looking very uncomfortable while he studied the wall. "I need to change." His gaze returned to her. "And you're in the way."

Josh dropped one of his hands, but kept the other around her as he pulled her out of Kevin's way. "Sorry," he said, sounding like he'd been caught doing something he wasn't supposed to do.

Kevin moved toward them, looking into Josh's eyes. "At least I know you love her. Megan likes to paint a pretty picture of you, but Gram and I talk…and what we've pieced together has left me with some major doubts about you." His eyes grew cold. "Fair warning, buddy. If I find out that you hurt my sister in any way, I'm going to kick your ass. Is that clear?"

"Kevin!" Megan protested, even though guilt flooded through her for deceiving him. "I'm not fourteen years old, you know."

Kevin's face softened as he turned his attention to her. "Megan, you can be ninety and you'll never stop being my baby sister. I will *always* kick the ass of any guy who hurts you."

Pulling away from Josh, Megan rushed to her big brother and threw her arms around his neck, hanging onto him for dear life. "Where were you last month?" Her voice cracked with emotion.

Kevin pulled her back and glared at Josh. "What happened last month?" His voice took an ominous tone.

Oh, crap. What had possessed her to say that? But she hadn't seen Kevin for years and she'd forgotten what an intimidating presence he had. Sometimes it was nice to think someone else, like her alpha male big brother, could help her with her problems. But at the moment, she needed to dig herself out of the hole she'd just dug. The problem was that Kevin tended to be perceptive as hell. Megan gave him a reassuring smile. "Nothing." She dropped her hold on him. "I'm just all emotional with Mom and her big wedding plans."

"Did he—?"

"No." She grabbed Josh's arm with both hands and leaned into him. "He's great. A project at work had some issues, so it was a terrible month. I don't know what I would have done without him."

Josh kissed the top of her head.

Kevin studied them, looking like he was still unsure whether to believe her.

"*Megan!*" her mother shouted.

"Crap," Megan muttered. "She's up to level three. She raised her voice."

Kevin didn't look like he wanted to let the subject drop, but he waved to the stairs behind him. "You better get down there. Her split personality is in full bloom."

"Great."

Kevin grimaced. "She may have been Miss Georgia, but she would have been much more effective as a third-world dictator."

Didn't Megan know it? She started down the stairs, but

Josh snagged her hand and she looked back at him, searching his face for an explanation. What had happened back there? Her conversation with Kevin hadn't done a thing to make her forget that kiss. She had to admit to herself she'd never reacted to a kiss like that and part of her wanted to throw herself at him, even here on the steps, for a repeat performance.

Then it hit her.

She was an idiot. Josh had given her the single best kiss of her life to keep her brother from hearing their argument. That was the reason…the only one.

She tried to drop his hand, but he hung on, stopping at the bottom of the stairs and pulling her into an embrace. She tried to resist, but he leaned into her ear and whispered, "Your mother is watching."

She forced herself to relax.

"I'm sorry about what just happened," he continued, "but your brother was about to overhear us. In fact, from the look on his face and the way he wouldn't let it drop, I think he heard some of our conversation. I didn't mean to violate you like that. I was desperate."

"I know," she whispered back, fighting her disappointment at his confirmation. Had it really meant nothing to him? But of course it hadn't. It was a ruse. As gorgeous as he was, he'd probably kissed plenty of women, beautiful blonds like the flight attendant. To him, kissing was likely as routine as flossing had been for Jay.

"Megan!" her mother said.

She broke loose and walked into the kitchen, Josh on her heels, prepared for the lecture that was sure to come.

Megan's mother's nose wrinkled with a disapproving grimace. "Really, Megan. This party is for you and Jay—er, I mean Josh." She shook her head, and—if possible—looked even more perturbed. "And why didn't you bother to tell us he preferred Josh? We would have put it on all the invitations."

Josh slipped an arm around her back, his hand resting on the rise of her hip. "It's all my fault, Mrs. Vandemeer. On both counts. I insisted Megan help me figure out what to wear tonight, which made her late coming downstairs, and I told her to use Jay on everything for the wedding. My parents prefer it and I wanted to honor that even if they couldn't be here with us."

Megan couldn't believe how well the lies rolled off his tongue. She'd definitely have to keep that in mind. He might be helping her now, but he had some ulterior motive for doing so. Some instinct told her it had something to do with his mission to save his family business, but for the life of her she couldn't make the connection.

Nicole Vandemeer's face softened. "Aren't you just too precious? Defending Megan like that. And I insist you call me Nicole."

"Thank you, Nicole." His hand tugged Megan closer and he leaned his cheek on top of her head. "And I can't help but defend her. She's my damsel in distress."

Megan wanted to kick him in the shin again for the pun he'd made for her benefit, but her mother would notice.

Megan's mother got a dreamy look in her eyes. "Which makes you her white knight. This just makes the princess theme more perfect."

"More like my court jester," Megan mumbled, loud enough for only Josh to hear. But then she absorbed the second half of her mother's statement. "Wait. *What* princess theme?"

Her mother scowled, picking up a tray of white bowls shaped like flowers and white candles. "Take these outside and set them up." She handed the tray to Megan. "Be sure to light them too."

"Mom, what princess theme? You didn't say anything about a princess theme last fall."

"Now don't you worry, Megan. I've got everything under

control." Without another word of explanation, she walked into the dining room, leaving Megan with the tray in her hands.

"Megan," Josh said in a low voice. "Let's take the candles outside."

She glared up at him. "Why? So you can brown-nose her some more?"

"That's not fair. I was defending you."

She shot him a hateful look. "I don't need you to defend me."

"I wouldn't be too sure about that. After all, consider why I'm here in the first place."

"Exactly," she spat. "Why *are* you here?"

Josh's face was expressionless as he took the tray from her. "I'm here to help you and you're doing your best to make it difficult."

"I don't trust you."

"Which you've made abundantly clear. The way I see it, you have two options. One, we play this out, or two, I leave right now."

He was right, which irked her to no end. Why was she so irritated with him anyway? Unless he was a secret cultist looking for recruits, so far he was harmless enough. And he was right. He was helping her out of a situation she should have taken care of herself a month and a half ago. "You're right. I'm sorry."

An infectious grin spread across his face. "Now was that so hard? Come on." He turned and headed for the French doors, leaving her to trail behind.

When she stepped out the back door, she gasped, stopping in her tracks next to an equally stunned Josh.

"What the hell…?" he muttered.

"Oh. My. God." The house had a multilayered deck with a pool at the edge. The yard had been re-landscaped a few years ago and more features had been added since Megan's visit last fall. A pool house/cabana had been installed, and the pool deck had been extended and was lined with flowerbeds and potted flowers. Several bistro-sized tables with chairs were arranged around the pool, and a buffet table covered in pale pink organza and a gathered white organza overlay was set up on one level of the deck. But that wasn't what had so stunned them.

The entire area was tented with a soft white fabric lined with white twinkle lights, and a giant chandelier hung in the middle, directly over the pool.

"Does your mother think we're already married and this is the reception?" Josh asked.

"No, she wouldn't miss the opportunity to torture me before the wedding."

"What the..." He walked down the steps to the pool deck, checking out one of the bistro tables.

Megan followed in horror. Like the other tables, this one was decorated with a single blooming rose in a crystal vase, beneath which a few petals were artfully scattered on the white tablecloth. It was the domed glass covering the flower that had caught his attention.

"Is this from *Beauty and the Beast?*" Josh asked, turning back to gape at her.

She shook her head in dismay. "She said it was a princess theme."

"That must make me the Beast."

She released a short laugh. "If she originally planned it that way, I can assure you that she's turned the tables. She loves you. I'm the Beast."

He set the tray of candles on the table. "Oh, God. Is that bowl of red apples on the food table a *Snow White* reference? And the brass lamp must be a nod to *Aladdin*."

Megan shook her head, speechless.

"Seriously, Megan. What the hell?"

She stared up at him in dismay. "I don't know. I think I'm about twenty years too old for this party. And I don't even like Disney movies. She knows that."

"And I think I just lost my man card."

"Isn't it beautiful?" her mother asked, coming out the back door, tsking when she saw the tray of candles on one of the tables.

"It's something else, all right," Megan answered, taking in the decorations. A clear high heel sat atop the bar at the end of the pool, keeping company with the liquor bottles.

Her mother set an ornate picture frame containing words instead of a photo on the organza-strewn table. Megan moved closer to see it read *Megan and Josh, June 14.*

"I thought Josh told you that he preferred to use Jay on everything."

Her mother gave her a blank look. "Did he? I figured he meant the invitations. Besides, if people are going to call him Josh, it will be less confusing if the placard says Josh."

Her father emerged from the door next, a frame in his hand. Megan gasped when she realized what it was: A photo of her and Josh in her parents' kitchen.

"How did you get that?"

"The photos you sent me of you and Josh were just atrocious—all blurry and out of focus. And besides, Josh's hair is longer now and he's much cuter in person," her mother said. "So after Josh kissed you in the kitchen, your father took your picture with his phone so we could use it tonight."

"That's creepy," Megan muttered.

Her mother offered her a tight smile. "No. It was efficient. And while it's not the professional portrait I wanted...which I suggested to you many, *many* times—"

"I told you that Jay couldn't get away from work."

"—this will have to do in a pinch."

"Why do we need one at all?" Megan asked in dismay.

"We're both *here*. Our presence should be enough." Although she hoped Josh wouldn't be here for long, so she could be done with this disaster of a weekend.

She looked over her shoulder at him and mouthed *sorry*, although she wasn't entirely sure why. He gave her a sympathetic smile before she turned back to face her mother, and she was surprised by how comforting the gesture was. She couldn't help thinking what Jay would have done in this situation. No doubt he would have found a reason to blame it on her. He certainly wouldn't have done a thing to comfort her.

Her mother's brow furrowed, but not by much, making Megan wonder if she'd had Botox injections recently. "Barbara Decker's daughter's engagement party was gorgeous. You're not going to have anything less."

"Are you saying this is our *engagement* party? We're getting married in three days!"

"Barbara Decker gave her daughter an engagement party that was the talk of the country club for months." Her mouth turned down. "I won't be outdone by that social wannabe."

"So you did all of this?" Megan's voice rose as she gestured to the tent over their heads. "How much did it even cost?"

"Too much," her father grumbled.

"Bart!" her mother reprimanded. "Enough of that. You have one daughter and she will have the most beautiful wedding in all of Jackson County."

"Nicole," her father chided. "The wedding is going to be in *Johnson* County. And this isn't even the wedding."

"*Details!*" Her mother looked around, frantic and frustrated. "I wanted to hire *real* waitstaff, instead of taking a chance on these kids—" she waved at a teenage girl wearing a black skirt and blouse who was setting a plate of tiny cakes on the food table, "—but your father refused. And we haven't had ample time to prepare after your foolish antics at the airport, Megan

Nicole."

Shoot me now, Megan thought.

Her brother came out the back door and helped her grandmother out onto the deck. Her grandmother had changed into a flamboyant green and blue dress, paired with a headband of giant feathers. It made her hair look snow white.

"The guests are about to arrive and the candles aren't lit yet," her mother called over her shoulder as she moved toward the French doors. "Quit dilly-dallying, dear." She stopped and looked Gram up and down before shaking her head. "I'm not even…" Her voice trailed off as she entered the house.

Megan smiled to herself at her grandmother's choice of attire—probably partially chosen to irritate Nicole. Megan grabbed two candles off the tray and Josh leaned close to her ear. "Where are we supposed to set these things up, anyway? The small tables are covered with the Disney props."

"I don't care, just set them off to the side," she grumbled, her smile fading. This was going to be a total disaster.

"How about you set them out and I'll light them?"

"Sounds good."

Megan set one on a table decorated with a spool of thread and a dollhouse spinning wheel. Her grandmother hobbled past them and over to the bar. "Those are supposed to go in the pool."

"What?" For a moment, Megan was sure her gram had finally turned a corner and gone completely senile.

"The pool." She waved her hands toward it in a shooing motion. "Your mother looked high and low for those fancy-pants bowls. She wants them in the water."

Megan picked one up and checked it over. She suspected Gram was right. It didn't make sense to add anything to the tables, and floating candles were certainly over-the-top enough to fit her mother's theme. The question was how to do this gracefully. Then again, screw being graceful.

After kicking off her shoes, Megan sat on the side of the pool, submerging her feet in the water. Josh followed and set the tray on the concrete. "Hand me the candles we set out on the tables," Megan prompted. "I'll light them and put the bowls in the water."

"Okay…" He sounded unsure, but he obeyed readily enough.

Satisfied, Gram continued on her way to the bar. "I'm thirsty. Fix me a drink, Kevin. Do you still make a mean Sex on the Beach?"

Kevin laughed and headed around the back of the bar, grabbing four glasses as he went. "I haven't made one of those since I was in high school, Gram. When you hired me to bartend for those parties you and Gramps threw."

"Until your mother found out you weren't really helping us with home repairs," she chortled.

"She had a royal fit." He shook his head with an ornery grin. "It was awesome."

"I got in trouble for that too," Megan added, calling over her shoulder. "Mom was certain I knew, so she was pissed I hadn't told her."

Gram frowned, shaking her head. "Your mother and I don't always see eye to eye."

Kevin hoisted a liquor bottle in salute. "And thank God for that."

Josh helped Megan with several more floating centerpieces before he glanced up from putting a candle in one of the bowls, a perplexed look on his face. "Wait. If Gram is your mother's mother, why doesn't she have a Southern accent?"

Megan chuckled. "That is one of the reasons Mom keeps Gram under wraps, which is harder to do now that Gram lives with them. Mom tells everyone she's from Atlanta, but she only lived there for her last two years of high school when Gramps worked for Coca-Cola. She's originally from Overland

Park, Kansas."

Josh still looked confused. "So she developed a Southern accent in a very short period of time and kept it?"

"More like she fakes it," Gram snorted, taking her drink from Kevin.

"Why?" Josh asked.

Kevin walked toward them, a glass in each hand. "To make herself seem even more special than everyone else, of course. The reason for everything she does. She'd rather be seen as a genteel Southern lady with class and sophistication than a woman with Midwest roots." He handed one of the glasses to Josh, a hard look in his eyes. "I suggest you drink this. You're gonna need it." When he leaned down and handed Megan the other drink, he searched her face. "It's like you haven't told Josh a thing about our mother, Megan. I find that surprising given how much you love your Mom stories."

He'd always been able to see through her bullshit, and she could tell he suspected something was up. Too bad he'd never guess what was *really* going on. She averted her gaze as she took the glass and instantly downed half of it, then struggled not to cough as it burned down her throat. "Good God, Kevin. Is that ninety-proof alcohol?"

"Long Island iced tea. I figured you needed fortitude."

Josh gave her a concerned glance. "I'm not sure you should be drinking at all after what happened earlier."

"Isn't that sweet of you, looking out for Megan like that." Kevin's tone was off as he turned his attention to Josh. "Has she done anything like this before?"

Josh stood and met his gaze. "No, and this afternoon was inadvertent. She had no idea she couldn't drink with Dramamine."

Kevin cocked an eyebrow. "And you didn't think to stop her?" His tone was unmistakably confrontational.

"He had no idea I took it." Megan downed the rest of her

drink. She had a feeling things were about to get ugly before the guests even showed up.

"He wasn't with you?"

Josh shook his head and stood. "What exactly are you accusing me of? Trying to overdose your sister? That doesn't seem very smart, three days before our wedding."

Kevin took a step closer with a defiant glare. "Is there a right time to overdose your significant other, Josh?"

Megan jumped to standing, her feet leaving little wet splashes on the concrete, and placed her hand on Kevin's chest, pushing him back. "Back off, Kevin. Josh would never hurt me. Otherwise, why would he suggest I shouldn't drink now?"

Kevin's eyes narrowed as his gaze turned again to Josh. "I don't trust you. Something's up, and I'm going to get to the bottom of it."

"Kevin! Enough!" Megan barked in panic. If he was this pissed without knowing the whole story, what would he do if he found out? The sooner she ended this charade and broke up with Josh, the better. "Josh hasn't done anything to make you distrust him."

"I haven't liked him since you started dating, Megan. The man's an ass. Look, maybe I've kept quiet about this for too long, but I can't let you marry him without saying my piece."

"You only just met him, Kevin!"

"Exactly my point." His voice was low and menacing. "Why?"

Megan opened her mouth and hesitated. "He's been busy. Working."

"Too busy to meet your family?"

She released a heavy breath, brushing the hair off her forehead as she glanced at her grandmother, who stood to the side listening while she sipped her drink. "*I* didn't want to come home, Kevin. Surely you of all people understand that."

He was quiet for a long moment, but then he sighed and said, "She's not the only person in your family, Megan."

She put her hand on his arm to stop him from turning away. "You're right. I'm sorry. Just don't take this out on Josh."

Kevin's jaw tightened. "Sorry I accused you of trying to kill my sister." He stared into Josh's face, his eyes filled with a challenge. "I'm sure an uptight prick like you would be much tidier with how you carried it out."

"Kevin!"

Josh tensed and took a step closer. The air between the two men was heavy with testosterone. Megan knew the slightest spark would set off this powder keg.

"Kevin, I thought you were going to get me a drink."

Kevin continued to stare Josh down before picking up Megan's glass off the patio and stomping back to the bar.

Megan let out a sigh of relief, sagging her shoulder into Josh's chest. "Sorry about that."

His arm curved around the small of her back, holding her in place. "Is your brother always that intense?"

She knew she should pull away. His physical affection was for public display, yet somehow she knew he genuinely wished to comfort her. "Only where I'm concerned."

"He wouldn't hurt you, would he?"

She laughed. "No. Definitely not. But he'd hunt down whoever did." She looked up at him. "We need to make sure he never finds out who you really are."

He nodded and looked over at Kevin, who was mixing another drink. "Seriously though, I'm not sure more alcohol is a good idea after—"

The back door opened and Megan froze in terror when she saw the blond in the gray pencil skirt and white blouse. She'd forgotten all about Blair. How could she have forgotten about Blair? Her best friend searched the yard, her face contorting in horror before she made a beeline for her.

Josh lowered his voice as his gaze moved to her friend. "Who's that and why am I suddenly nervous?"

"That's one of my two best friends. And we should *both* be scared."

"I take it she knows?" he whispered.

"Everything up until I boarded the plane."

"Shit."

From the angry look on Blair's face, Megan couldn't help agreeing with him.

Chapter Seven

Josh wasn't frightened by much, but the woman who was making her way toward them looked like she wanted to rip someone's head off. Possibly his. She didn't look dressed for a cocktail party. She wore a business skirt paired with a white shirt and jacket. The glare that her icy blue eyes shot at him made him seriously fear she might take one of her black stiletto heels and jab his eyes out. Josh inched closer to Megan.

"Blair," Megan said. "What are you doing here?"

"We had plans tonight," Blair said, her voice a monotone.

"Yeah. About that... I forgot to call you."

"I'll say," she said, stopping in front of them. She eyed Josh up and down. "Apparently you have a lot to tell me." Her voice lowered, so Kevin and Megan's grandmother probably couldn't hear. "Like how you picked up a new fiancé on a four-hour flight." Blair's eyes narrowed. "Were you the one who drugged her?"

"No!" Megan protested loud enough that her brother and

grandmother looked over at them.

Had they heard anything incriminating?

Megan grabbed Blair's arm and dragged her over to the food table, farther away from the others. Though she allowed herself to be dragged backward, Blair quirked her brow at Josh. "Oh, you better get your ass over here and join us, lover boy."

Josh knew he was going to have to dig himself out of this one. Part of him considered walking away from it all, throwing in the towel, but he wasn't ready to do that. After seeing this lavish display of wealth, he was certain that Megan's father—who genuinely seemed like a nice guy—had plenty of incentive to take Josh's plans and make a fortune out of them, snagging away their investor to boot. Josh wasn't sure there was enough money in the world to keep Nicole Vandemeer happy. He had to stay longer to see what he could uncover. He suspected some of Bart Vandemeer's business associates might be at the party, and Josh hoped to sniff out information from them in the guise of polite conversation. Tonight could help him direct his investigation. He may have fallen into this role by chance, but it was showing more potential than he could have imagined at the airport earlier.

He cast a glance at the feisty brunette next to him. And then there was Megan herself... No, Josh wasn't going anywhere yet, bitchy best friend be damned.

Megan looked over her shoulder, then back at her friend. "Who told you I was drugged? And how did you find out about Josh?"

"Kevin. He wanted to know why your fiancé *Josh* let you get shit-faced on an afternoon flight."

Megan's back stiffened underneath Josh's arm. He'd unconsciously returned his arm to the small of her back. He considered dropping it, but decided it added to the illusion of a couple in love. Even so, he had to admit that wasn't the only reason he kept it there—it felt good. The angry woman in front of him didn't seem appeased by the gesture; if anything, she looked angrier when her steely gaze lowered to his arm.

"What did you tell him?" Megan asked, her jaw clenched.

"What did *I* tell him? Why don't we talk about what you haven't told *me?*" Blair hissed. Josh wasn't sure Blair's eyes could squint any tighter as she shot daggers of hate at him. "*What the hell is going on here?*" she asked, adding emphasis to each word.

Megan rolled her eyes. "It's a long story."

"It can't be that long," Blair countered. "Eight hours ago you were single. What great love story could have unfurled in that timeframe?"

"It was all a misunderstanding," Megan said.

"Oh, *really?*" Blair kept her gaze on Josh. "A misunderstanding? Are you homeless?"

"*What?*"

"Are you mentally ill? A gigolo? A terrorist?"

"Blair, stop." Megan put her hand on her friend's arm. "And I already accused him of being a terrorist."

"And you believed him when he said no?"

"Actually," she mused, casting an ornery grin at him. "I don't think he answered me."

"Tricky bastard, aren't you?"

Josh figured anything he said at this point would be used against him, so he chose to plead the fifth.

"Blair, it's not like that. You don't even know the story."

"Then why don't you tell it to me, Megan," Blair said in a snippy tone that rubbed Josh the wrong way. Megan had already put up with a mountain of crap from her mother, princess-themed or not, and she didn't need more from her supposed best friend.

"Instead of attacking her," Josh countered in a deadly calm voice, "why don't you let her actually explain."

Blair gave him a dirty look, but she pressed her lips together and waited.

Glancing between Josh and her friend with wide eyes, Megan began, "I had a couple of drinks on the plane like you suggested, but I'd taken some Dramamine before boarding."

"What were you thinking?"

"Obviously, I wasn't," Megan said, looking embarrassed. "And I passed out on the plane. The flight attendant was going to have me turned over to security, but Josh—who was sitting by me and knew about the reason for my trip—helped me off the plane. But I couldn't walk and he ended up carrying me. People thought he might be abducting me, so he told them he was my fiancé."

"Did he, now?"

Josh leaned in closer. "I knew her family was meeting her. All I wanted to do was make sure she made it to her mother okay, but her mom heard me say I was her fiancé and they presumed I was Jay."

"Oh!" Blair cooed in mock surprise. "You know his name. And you didn't think to correct them?"

Josh's brow furrowed in irritation. "I tried to explain, but I'm sure you've met Megan's mother."

Blair crossed her arms. "So you're telling me that you didn't have a single opportunity to come out and say 'Hey! There's been a colossal misunderstanding. I'm not Jay Connors.'"

Megan's eyes flew open. "Shh! Blair! Someone's going to hear you."

Blair shook her head, staring at her friend in disbelief. "This is insane, Megan. I expect something like this from Libby, not you."

Josh's hand curled tighter on Megan's hip and he pulled her closer. How much shit did she have to endure? First her mother, then this bitch who called herself Megan's best friend...at least her psycho brother was actually trying to look out for her. Megan's fiancé—who was sounding more and more like a first class bastard—had cheated on her. Josh already knew that Jay Connors didn't deserve her, but the pain and humiliation of his betrayal still had to sting. Megan deserved sympathy and comfort from Blair, who obviously knew the truth, not full-blown hostility. Nevertheless, he swallowed his words of defense, even if it left a bitter taste on his tongue. He couldn't afford to get caught up in this drama.

Hurt filled Megan's eyes. "What's that supposed to mean?"

"Libby is the impulsive one. Not you. You're usually sensible and logical."

Megan shook her head. "No, Blair. Sensible and logical is you."

"So what does that make you?"

For a moment, he didn't think Megan was going to say something, but she finally spoke. "After twenty-five years, you really have to ask me that? Maybe you don't know me so well after all."

Blair gave her an exasperated look. "Now is not the time for *Teen Glamour* personality tests."

"No," Megan said quietly. "It's not."

"So, what? You're going to *marry* this guy to avoid a confrontation with your mom?"

"No! Of course not. He's going to break up with me. He's helping me."

Blair shot him a look of disgust. "And *of course* he's doing it out of the kindness of his heart."

"You know," Josh said, no longer able to keep quiet. "I seem to be the only person around here who's actually trying to *help* her instead of tearing her down."

Megan gasped and stared up at him, her watery eyes full of gratitude. He squeezed her side to give her reassurance.

Blair looked like she wanted to strangle him.

"Megan knows my reasons for helping her. It's no one's business but our own. Not even yours."

Blair pointed her finger at his chest. "I don't trust you."

Josh lost count of how many times he'd heard that today, a sharp contradiction to everything he'd been told for the past twenty-nine years. Josh was the steady, reliable, trustworthy McMillan boy. The one everyone counted on to be the voice of reason. He was used to everyone trusting him, so it rubbed his pride a bit raw to be treated like a cad. "I can't control that one way or the other."

Blair turned back to Megan. "Do you even know his name?"

"Josh."

"I know that already. Josh what?"

Megan shot her a leery glance, then shifted her gaze to Josh. Only moments ago, she'd told him that Kevin needed to know as little about him as possible. It was obvious that Blair and Kevin were in communication. If she told Blair, she might ultimately share her information with Megan's brother. But Josh didn't want to strip her of any defense she could use with her friend. He nodded.

"Josh McMillan."

Blair stepped closer to him, until her face was mere inches from his. "Well, Josh McMillan, you've messed with the wrong person. I'm a divorce attorney, and I specialize in digging up shit on people. By tomorrow night I'll know everything there is to know about you, including what blood type you are and whether you've been circumcised." Blair turned to Megan and pointed her finger. "And *you* better not find out the answer to that question first."

Megan's mouth dropped open in horror and…was that guilt he saw in her eyes?

Message delivered, Blair turned and walked to the bar, calling over her shoulder, "Libby will be here any minute."

Megan's face brightened.

"I take it Libby is your other best friend?" Josh asked.

She nodded, still watching Blair. Josh hoped Libby was warmer to their arrangement, because he could tell Blair had instilled some second thoughts in his pseudo-fiancée. It didn't help matters that he hadn't gotten her to agree to maintaining the ruse through the evening. He worried Blair would convince her to break it off immediately.

"Megan." He took her hand and looked into her deep brown eyes. "Don't listen to Blair. I'm not here to hurt you." He smoothed his screaming conscience by telling himself that Megan had her own life in Seattle and her father's business didn't affect her. Even if he didn't quite believe it himself. Maybe the perpetrator was one of Bart's partners and he'd be doing her father a favor. If Bart Vandemeer was innocent, surely he wouldn't want to work with a partner who was a thief and a liar.

She searched his face for something—reassurance that she could trust him? But as he held her gaze, another thought intruded—the memory of kissing her upstairs as her brother approached. His intention had been innocent enough, but the feel of her in his arms...

Despite the fact that he held her soft, warm hand in his, he knew he needed to keep his hands off her as much as possible, which would be difficult since they were attending what constituted their engagement party. If he were smart, he'd start sowing the seeds of doubt among her family members—hell, her brother was already there—but it might take him a couple of days to get the information he needed. He couldn't risk being a huge ass and giving her justification in front of her family to break up with him on the spot. In fact, if he were smart, he'd charm them by playing the dutiful boyfriend, ensuring that he could stick around as long as he needed to accomplish his task. The key to making this work for Megan was for her to come out smelling like a rose when the dust settled. Which meant as long as he was the perfect boyfriend, she'd have no justification for ending it. But no doubt about it—he'd have to tread lightly.

He dropped her hand. "We probably better get the rest of the candles in the water or your mother is going to have a fit."

She started to get back down on the pool deck but he stopped her. "The guests are starting to arrive." He motioned to the deck. Several middle-aged couples had appeared during their chat with Blair. "We can't have the bride-to-be sitting at the side of the pool and possibly getting her dress wet." He offered her a soft smile. "Why don't you hand them to me and I'll light them and set them in the water?"

She gave him a strange look, then her smile turned shy, and she dipped her head to look at the candles. "Okay."

They worked silently for nearly half a minute before she said, "Thanks for helping me."

He shrugged. "What else am I going to do? Part of the job is keeping your mother happy with you, right?" He looked up at her. "This will make her happy."

"Not just this. *This*." Her eyebrows arched with her emphasis. "Everything. I'm sorry Blair was so hateful to you. Thanks for standing up to her too."

"I never could stand a bully."

She looked surprised. "Blair's not a bully. She's just worried about me."

Josh grimaced and set the next candle in the pool. "She's your friend, so I won't butt in, but I think she could have handled it differently…with some compassion."

"That's just how she is. Blair's more of a confrontational, nip-things-in-the-bud type of person. She's never been sweet and nurturing."

"Like you?" He studied her face, which turned a soft pink as she watched him.

"How would you know that?"

He grinned, setting the last candle in the pool before

standing in front of her. "Call it a hunch."

"Megan!" A woman shouted in a happy voice.

They both turned to see a dark-haired woman running across the deck, her face lit up with excitement. She wore a gauzy orange and pink skirt and white tank topped with a gauzy button-down shirt, which hung open.

"Libby!" Megan thrust the empty tray at Josh and ran to her friend, pulling her into a tight hug.

"I can't believe you're here!" Libby shouted, waving and attracting the attention of Kevin and Megan's grandmother. Blair didn't even turn around to acknowledge her other supposed best friend, further cementing the title Josh had already assigned to her: bitch.

Libby pulled out of Megan's hold and eyed Josh up and down with an appreciative look on her face. Josh already got a better vibe from her, and not just because she'd checked him out and found him worthy. It seemed reasonable to expect she'd be more open to and supportive of his arrangement with Megan.

But Megan stiffened at Libby's announcement, an alarmed look on her face, as if it hadn't occurred to her that Libby would need to be let in on the charade. "Of course I'm *here*, Libby," she said loudly. "I'm getting married in three days."

Confusion flickered across Libby's face.

Megan glanced back at Josh, as if issuing an SOS, and he strolled over to the two women. "Hi, Libby. I'm Josh," he said, loud enough for her family to hear. "Nice to finally meet you."

Libby glanced between the two of them with a slightly open mouth. She lowered her voice when she spoke next. "I thought you broke up with Jay back in April."

Megan leaned closer, whispering. "I did."

She cocked an eyebrow. "And you're marrying him instead?"

"It's a long story. But this is Josh and my parents think he's

Jay."

Libby blinked. "Why do they think he's Jay if you're calling him Josh?"

"Megan!" Her mother waved at her, motioning for her to join the small group of people she was talking to on the deck.

Megan placed a hand on her friend's upper arm. "It's a long story, Libby. I'll tell you later, but right now I have to greet my mother's snooty friends. Please, please, please just play along."

She moved toward the couples trickling out the back door, leaving Josh with her still-confused friend. The number of guests had increased to about twenty. Bart was talking to three other men, and Josh considered joining them, but he needed to figure out a way to encourage Megan to keep him around longer. If not, he might find himself kicked out before he'd even started investigating. He had a hunch Libby would make a perfect ally.

"Why don't we get you a drink?" he asked, motioning to the bar, where Megan's brother had taken up residence. Apparently all his experience from their grandparents' parties was being put to use for the evening.

Half-empty glass in hand, Josh led the way.

Kevin gave him a measured glare before flashing a smile at Libby. "What can I get for my favorite hippie?"

Libby rolled her eyes, but her grin neutralized the action. "I'll take a glass of white wine. And how many times do I have to tell you I'm not a hippie? That generalization would apply more to your sister than to me."

Kevin grabbed a bottle of wine and poured a glass. "She works for an environmental nonprofit and that's the extent of it. You dye your own clothes, grow your own food, and make art out of recycled glass. Hippie."

Libby laughed, a happy sound that helped ease some of Josh's tension over being left alone with Megan's hostile family and friends. At least not all of them were hostile.

"Please. I dyed some clothes in high school for an art project, and I have tomato plants in pots on the balcony of my apartment. That hardly qualifies me for a commune."

Kevin handed Libby her glass. "But you *do* make art out of recycled glass. Megan told me about your exhibit. Belated congrats."

"Thanks."

Though she'd been standing to the side of the bar, listening in on their conversation, Blair finally spoke up, her gaze locked on Josh. "Maybe Megan's turned vegan or something," she said with a tight smile. "Has she, Josh?"

Kevin turned to look at him.

He froze. Damn her. "No. She definitely hasn't." He turned his attention to Kevin. "Have you got any beers back there?"

"Preference?"

"Anything alcoholic."

Kevin opened a cooler and pulled out a bottle, popping off the top before handing it to Josh.

"Spending time with your fiancée's family got you drinking?" Blair asked in a snotty tone.

"No, it's not her *family*." He took a big swig.

Libby burst out laughing. "Don't mind Blair. I don't think she's ever approved of any of our boyfriends." And swooping in to his rescue, she hooked her arm through his and dragged him away from the bar, leading to the other side of the pool which was blessedly absent of guests.

Josh scanned the deck, which was now dotted with more than three dozen people. He spotted Megan in the center of a small group. He hadn't known her long, but he could tell the smile on her face was forced.

Libby looked to see what had his attention, then shot him a grin. "How long have you known Megan?"

"About eight hours."

Libby choked on her wine and began to cough. "I'm sorry.

Did you say eight hours?"

Which was his cue to launch into an abbreviated version of the turn of events.

"So you're helping her out of the kindness of your heart?" she asked with a sly grin.

"Of course. I have a few spare days, so I figured why not?"

She shook her head. "You're lying."

He'd been accused of as much by Blair and Megan, but the way Libby said it came across differently. His breath caught. What did she know? He took a drink of his beer, seeking out Megan in the crowd. She was caught between two women who were talking nonstop. She held her hand to her face and he couldn't keep from smiling when he realized she was trying to hide a yawn. *Focus, McMillan.* Megan's best friend had just accused him of lying and he was acting like a middle-school boy with a crush. "Why do you say that?"

"The way you're looking at her right now. Like you've been fed salad for six months and Megan's a medium-rare steak."

He turned to her, surprised by the anger that smoldered in his gut. "What are you accusing me of? Do you think I'm out to hurt her?"

"No," she said, taking another sip of her wine and looking over at Megan. "Quite the opposite. I think you really like her."

"So I'm pretending to be her fiancé to get her into bed?" he asked, sounding indignant, though the thought of her in bed with him… Well, now that it was in his head, it would be hard to get it out. *Down, boy.* Wondering what Megan Vandemeer looked like sans clothes wouldn't help his case.

"No, I think you're helping her out of a difficult situation because there's a spark between you two and you want the chance to get to know her better."

"By pretending to be her fiancé?"

She shrugged, still grinning at him. "Hey, stranger things have happened."

"So you approve?"

"Wholeheartedly. The guy she was supposed to marry is a cut-throat bastard. Only Megan wore blinders the entire time and refused to see it until she saw more than she ever wanted to when she found him screwing his secretary on his desk."

Josh cringed at the mental image, but it bothered him even more to think about what it must have done to Megan. "And how do you know I'm not a cut-throat bastard too?"

She grabbed the beer out of his hand and set it on a nearby table along with her wine. Then she picked up his right hand and spread out his palm. Her index finger traced the lines. "Your love line. It runs deep and long." She looked up into his face. "Your love is very strong and loyal. You will probably only truly love one woman and you will fall head-over-heels within a day of meeting her."

He chuckled. "That doesn't sound like me at all."

A mischievous glint filled her hazel eyes. "That's what makes it all the better. You're *not* that kind of man." She traced more lines, smoothing out the pad of his hand with her thumb. "No, you're usually methodical. You think everything through and have a detailed plan. You're not prone to that sort of impulsiveness."

Josh told himself that she was guessing. But how had she managed to describe him so perfectly? Besides, she'd formed her opinion before she even looked at his hand.

"There's a branch in your life line that suggests you will veer off your usual path. That you take a risk and find love. It totally changes the course of your life." She looked up at him with a quizzical expression. "Are you on a journey right now, Josh McMillan?"

He tried not to visibly react. "That sounds like a philosophical question. Aren't we all on a journey?"

"Am I interrupting something?"

The surprise made Josh jump, and he swiveled to find

Megan standing next to him. He knew it looked bad. Libby was caressing his hand while they looked into each other's eyes. Libby was a beautiful woman. Her almost black hair, olive complexion, and dancing hazel eyes gave her an exotic look. But while Josh noticed her beauty, he wasn't drawn to it.

Libby dropped her hold on him. "I was just reading Josh's palm," she said in a careless tone.

Based on Libby's reaction, he was sure she hadn't heard the undertone of jealousy in Megan's voice. But he had…and as weird as this whole thing was, he liked that she was jealous. The smile that spread across his face as he turned to look at her was an unstoppable force.

"You still do that?" Megan asked, dragging her eyes from Josh's face.

"Of course. It's fantastically accurate," Libby murmured in a smug tone. "Just don't let Knickers know I was doing it. She threatened to hold an exorcism if she found out I was reading palms at her house again."

Josh glanced at her in surprise. "Knickers?"

"Our nickname for Megan's mom." Libby shrugged. "It's a play on her name—Nicole—because she always has her knickers in a wad."

His smile turned wry. "I can see how she earned it."

Megan grinned. "Your secret is safe with me. As long as you tell me what you read in Josh's palm."

Josh shook his head. "Nope. You first. What does Megan's say?"

"That she'll find the love of her life when she least expects it." Libby winked at Megan. "And that she'll be married by the time she turns thirty."

"How do you know that?" he asked. "You didn't even look."

"I've read it before," Libby said with a shrug.

"So how long do you have before you turn thirty?" Josh

asked.

"Don't you know it's impolite to ask a lady her age?" Megan lifted her eyebrows playfully. A rush of relief hit Josh square in the solar plexus; he was glad she wasn't holding a grudge over some imagined connection between him and her friend.

"Two months," Libby volunteered.

Megan laughed. "My palm doesn't say I'll be married by the time I'm thirty. That fortune teller did."

Blair joined their group, looking disgusted. "Not the fortune teller again."

Libby sighed, making it apparent that this was a worn-out argument. "You can't deny it happened."

"You're correct, I don't deny that we went to Santa-Cali-Gon Days and waited in line for an hour in the oppressive summer heat."

"Now who's over-exaggerating?" Megan asked. "It was Labor Day weekend, we waited ten minutes tops, and it wasn't that hot."

"We still waited in line for nothing."

"Not true." Libby turned up her chin. "She told our fortune, just not as we expected."

Josh couldn't stop himself from asking, "She told Megan she'd be married by the time she was thirty?"

Megan shook her head. "She said all three of us would be married by the time we were thirty."

Blair put a hand on her hip. "Only after she heard the three of us talking in line. Remember? We were talking about that stupid pact we made as kids. You know, how we said we'd all get married before we turned thirty and became spinsters."

"That's not all," Libby added, her face serious. "She said our weddings would be disasters, and we would all marry someone other than we'd intended. And a pact is not to be taken lightly."

Blair groaned. "You don't really believe that nonsense, do you?"

"Of course she doesn't," Megan said.

"I don't know," Libby murmured, picking up her wine glass. "So far she's right. You and Blair are engaged."

"I'm not getting married on Saturday, Libby," Megan whispered, a panicked expression crossing her face as soon as she'd uttered the words.

Libby hugged her arm. "It's okay. Josh told me what's going on." She winked at Megan. "You never know what might happen between now and then."

Blair looked disgusted again. "My wedding is in two months and everything is going perfectly. Sorry to disappoint your delusion, Libby."

Libby gave her a smug grin. "We'll see." Then she took another sip of her wine, as if closing a door on the discussion.

Megan looked between her friends for a moment before giving herself an involuntary shake. "So you two are the only ones who know about Josh. I need you to keep this to yourselves until Josh breaks up with me later tonight."

Josh jerked to attention. This was exactly what he was afraid of. And having Blair standing next to them would make talking her out of it even more difficult.

"What?" Libby asked in dismay. "Already?"

Megan's face hardened with determination. "It has to be done, Libby. And the sooner, the better. Josh has a life to get back to."

"Megan!" Just then, her mother called from the deck, waving her arm.

Megan heaved out a loud breath. "Duty calls. Again. Come on, Josh. It's time to introduce you to my parents' friends. I apologize in advance." She reached for his hand, but Libby grabbed him first.

"I need one more minute with Josh." She pulled him aside

as Megan shrugged and hurried toward her mother. Libby stared Blair down. "This doesn't concern you. Feel free to go back to flirting with Kevin."

Blair's mouth dropped open in outrage. "I do not flirt. And especially not with Kevin."

Libby gave her a shrug of indifference. "It's no secret you harbored a crush on him all through high school."

"That was ten years ago. We're friends now." She glanced back and forth between the Libby and Josh, then narrowed her gaze on Libby and pointed an accusatory finger at her. "Do not encourage this situation, Libby!"

Libby made a shooing motion. "Bye, Blair."

They watched her stomp off after Megan, intercepting her before she could reach her mother. Based on her departing glare, Josh was sure Blair hated him even more now. He hoped she didn't convince Megan to do anything rash.

Libby waited until Blair was out earshot, then grabbed his bicep and leaned toward him. "Do you want to break up with Megan tonight?" She gave him a worried gaze.

Libby thought he wanted to be here for other reasons…reasons she approved of. He'd be a fool not to take advantage of that, especially since Blair was so determined to get rid of him and Megan was set on breaking up tonight. "No."

"Then don't. Keep gazing at her like she's the last woman alive and don't do it. I'll help you out as much as I can."

Josh felt bad using Libby to help him, but he needed all the advantages he could get.

And he ignored the part of him that told him Libby was actually right about him…about how he liked Megan more than he wanted to admit.

Chapter Eight

Josh was walking back over to her, looking more relieved than he had before going off with Libby. What had her friend said?

Megan's mother was getting visibly irritated that Megan still hadn't joined her, but Blair had a death grip on her wrist. "I'm looking out for your best interest," Blair said, continuing with her mission to try and talk reason into her. "What's so wrong with that?"

Megan's back stiffened. "I love you like a sister, Blair, but this is *my* decision. If you can't accept it, feel free to leave."

"It's a stupid decision, Megan."

Megan winced but held her ground. "But it's *mine*, nevertheless. It's not like I'm marrying the guy. He's going to break up with me."

Josh cleared his throat as he stopped next to Megan, close enough to have heard her last words. "What do you want, Blair? What outcome at this moment would make you happy? Do you want me to tell Megan's parents that we've been lying to them? How will that make Megan look? She'd be worse off than she was before they mistook me for Jay."

Blair pursed her lips. "*You're* the reason she's in this situation."

"I've never denied it. I'm just trying to get her out of it the best way I know how."

"If you hurt her…"

"Yeah, I know," Josh said dryly. "You'll find out about my wicked past to throw it in my face. But good luck with that. I'm a pretty boring guy, so you'll have a tough time finding anything shiny enough to catch your interest."

Watching him now, Megan had a hard time believing he was boring, though she was fairly certain he didn't harbor a past as a hardened criminal or a member of a motorcycle gang. Blair would probably have to do a lot of digging to discover anything scandalous about Josh McMillan. But then, Megan had never harbored a hidden fantasy about dating a bad boy, and Josh's chivalry, good looks, and charming personality—everything about him—screamed the opposite of bad boy. Megan was more attracted to him than was safe to acknowledge. But she couldn't ignore the fact that their relationship had almost reached its expiration date. She couldn't get attached to him.

And that filled her with more disappointment than she had a right to feel.

Blair pointed a finger at him. "If I find *anything*, I'll whip so many lawsuits around you that you'll regret the day you boarded that plane."

Josh shrugged, looking unimpressed. "Suit yourself."

Libby, who had trailed her way to them too, laughed from behind him. "He made a pun *and* he's standing up to you, Blair. Now I *really* like him."

Josh gave her a conspiratorial grin before turning back to Megan. "Your mother doesn't look happy. Maybe we should go play the engaged couple."

"Yeah."

He put an arm around her back and smiled down at her, looking very much like the attentive boyfriend. "Then let's go make your mother happy."

"That's an oxymoron," Blair said.

Josh grabbed Megan's hand and led her away from Blair, leaning into her ear as they made their way over to her mother and her friends on the deck. "Has Blair always been so…"

"Grumpy?"

"I had another word."

Megan laughed. "She hasn't always been this way. She used to be happier and more carefree, but she's gotten much more serious and…"

"Dictatorial?"

Megan released a heavy sigh as they climbed the steps. "Honestly, she means well. She changed after what happened with her father. She found out in college that he'd been cheating on her mother for years, and took it personally. Becoming a lawyer had been her dream since grade school, but she'd planned on going into corporate law until her father filed for divorce and left her mother with hardly anything…then died five years later. Now she's a divorce attorney who specializes in representing women who've been screwed over in their marriages. She makes sure they don't get screwed over in their divorces too."

He considered her words for a moment before conceding, "It's an admirable position."

"She started out with the best of intentions, but it's made her jaded. She's changed. And not for the better."

Seeing their approach, Megan's mother waved them over to an older couple. "Megan! I want to introduce you and Josh to some dear old friends of ours from the country club."

Megan decided her mother had to be referring to the

couple's age, since her parents had only joined the country club about five years ago. "Showtime," she mumbled to Josh.

He gave her hand a light squeeze of reassurance as they joined the group.

Megan had been worried that they could never pull it off, but she and Josh sailed through the evening. He was a great conversationalist and her parents' friends loved him. Megan had heard that the art to creating good conversation was to lavish attention on the other person, taking care not to talk too much about yourself. It turned out that Josh was a master at it, diverting almost all but the most mundane questions about himself. He showed particular interest in her father's friends, and at first she worried he really *was* using her to sell his snake oil, but he didn't make so much as a peep about a timeshare or a pyramid scheme. Instead he asked how long they'd known her father, what Bart's hobbies were, and whether they would recommend Bart's financial planner. Josh smiled as he said he had to plan a future for his soon-to-be wife and their soon-enough children.

Josh smiled at her when he mentioned a future family, as though they shared an intimate secret. Her stomach fluttered, not at the prospect of having children—although she did want them someday—but at the way his gaze lingered on her face. As if he couldn't wait to get her alone so they could practice making those future babies.

Then she reminded herself that they *did* share a secret. They were breaking up before the end of the night.

Her mother may not have gotten the professional waitstaff she wanted, but the handful of teens were doing a good job of carrying around trays of food that fit the princess theme. Sugar cookies shaped like pumpkins, genie lamps, mermaids, and...*dwarves?*—were carried around on silver trays, along with other finger foods. The underage staff couldn't take drink orders, but the crowd quickly learned the bar was at the opposite end of the pool.

After Josh and Megan had made the rounds twice and her mother seemed satisfied, Blair and Libby joined them at a bistro table. While Blair was quiet and distrustful, Libby more than made up for her bad mood, asking Josh questions about his family.

"My father died when I was sixteen. My brother was still in college, but he and my mother managed to hold my father's firm together until he graduated and took over. Our business manager was a huge help."

Megan reached over and covered Josh's hand with her own. She couldn't imagine what her teen years would have been like if she'd lost her father back then. He'd been her lifeline in high school, standing up for her whenever she failed to meet her mother's expectations of femininity. Her father had always told her she was the most beautiful girl in the world and that her mother's views had warped over time and shouldn't be taken personally.

"There are things you don't know about your mother, pumpkin," he used to say. "She loves you. This is her way of showing it."

Megan had always wished she'd find another way.

"Josh," Libby leaned back in her chair and eyed her other best friend before returning her attention to Josh. "You and Blair have something in common. Her father died when she was in law school."

Blair shot him a glare. "And did your father cheat on your mother and leave her nearly destitute in a divorce before dying?"

"No," Josh said calmly. "He loved my mother very much. I hope to have a marriage like theirs one day."

"Based on lies and deception?"

He was quiet for a moment, and his answer was subdued. "No."

Libby gave her a frown. "Blair, not everyone is as cynical about love as you are."

"I'm a realist, Libby. Love is a conscious decision."

"You really think your relationship with Neil is love?" Libby questioned, turning around to interrogate her friend.

Libby was only putting a voice to what Megan had been silently thinking for months.

"Neil and I have a very compatible relationship based on trust and similar hobbies."

"And it's so romantic," Libby sing-songed.

"Romance doesn't last. It's all spiking hormones and lust." Blair glared at her friend. "Perhaps one of your relationships would last longer than three weeks if you were looking for something other than romance."

"I'd rather have a few weeks of passion and hot sex than a cold and emotionless relationship," Libby shot back, but Megan saw a hint of hurt in her eyes.

Blair turned her attention to Josh. "And how are we supposed to believe anything you say? You could very well be making it all up—your mother, brother, your father too."

"*Blair*," Megan warned.

An awkward silence settled on the group; then Josh stood. "I know you girls would like to talk without me, so I'll go make a call and leave you with some time to yourselves."

"Who are you going to call?" Blair demanded.

Josh pulled his phone out of his pocket and brought up the contact before he locked his eyes onto hers. "My brother Noah. I haven't talked to him since landing in Kansas City, so he must be worried."

Blair snatched his phone. "Let's see if you really have a brother."

"Blair!" Megan shouted, reaching for it. "What the hell are you doing?"

"Protecting you." Blair leaned out of her grasp as Josh

stared at her, his eyes wide with shock. She pressed send and held the phone up to her ear. "Hello? Noah? What is your relation to Josh McMillan?" Horror washed over her face. "No! He's fine! He hasn't been in accident! I'm sorry! He just…"

"Blair!" Megan wrestled the phone from her friend and handed it to Josh. "God! I'm so sorry."

Josh grimaced as he lifted the phone to his ear. "Noah? No. I'm fine," he said, giving Megan an apologetic look. "It was someone's idea of a bad joke."

"Go!" she motioned to him. He walked to the opposite side of the pool, moving toward the back of the yard, where there were fewer people.

"What the hell, Blair?" Megan demanded after Josh left. "You probably scared his brother half to death."

Blair shrugged. "He didn't try to stop me once I had his phone."

"Yeah, because he was stymied by the fact that a grown, supposedly professional woman would *steal* his phone," Libby said.

To her credit, Blair looked embarrassed. "Maybe I was a little overzealous…"

"You *think?*" Megan asked.

"I think he's cute." Libby kept her eyes on Josh, an appreciative gleam in her eyes. "He's got a nice ass."

"Funny," Megan deadpanned. "My gram said the same thing."

"I've always liked Gram," Libby said. "I think you should go for it."

"There's nothing to *go for.*"

"I thought you were breaking up tonight," Blair reminded her.

"Yeah…" She'd been trying to put it off as long as possible, wanting to spend more time with him. But the reality of the situation was staring her in the face, and the thought of never seeing Josh McMillan again filled her with panic.

Libby lifted her drink to her lips and gave Megan a knowing look. "I say break up with him tomorrow. You can do other things tonight."

Megan grimaced. "While sleeping around might be your style, Libby, it's not mine."

Libby shot her a haughty look. "For the record, you might as well both know I'm not sleeping around at the moment. I've been with Mitch for four months now."

Blair and Megan stared at her in surprise.

"*What?* I'm not getting any younger. We're all about to hit thirty this year, and now I'll have a date to both of your weddings. You know, when you think about it, Megan's wedding disaster isn't that much of a surprise."

"What does that mean?" Megan demanded.

Blair groaned, leaning back in her chair. "Not that fortune teller crap again. If I had known how seriously you'd take it, I never would have gone."

Libby narrowed her eyes. "It happened, Blair. Whether you choose to believe her prediction or not." She turned to Megan, who was now listening intently. "And we made a pact to get married. I told you—pacts are not to be taken lightly."

"We made that pact at a city fair because we were bored after your brother barfed on a carnival ride," Blair said. "If you remember, we also picked out our grooms. After rock-paper-scissors, you got Travis Ming. Which seems like an *excellent* way to pick your future husband, Libby. Especially in light of how Megan has picked her substitute groom." She cocked her head. "What's Travis up to these days, Libs? Your birthday is in five months. You better hurry up and track him down."

"Be a hater all you want, Blair" Libby retorted. "Megan's wedding is proof."

"You don't seriously believe any of this, do you?" Blair

asked. "You're not even engaged, Libby."

"Not yet, but I have five months," Libby mused. "Besides, look at Megan's wedding. While it's a disaster, another—significantly more charming—man is already claiming to be her fiancé."

"Hey!" Megan protested. "My wedding isn't a disaster…and as far as Josh goes…it's just not going to happen. I just met him. And under duress, I might add."

Blair scowled. "Well, my wedding is going to go off without a hitch. My wedding planner has everything under control and Neil wouldn't think of cheating on me." She cast a glance at Megan. "Sorry, Megs."

Megan shrugged, trying to make her friends believe she was over Jay's infidelity. She wasn't sure how convincing it was. While part of her was glad to be rid of him, the embarrassment still clung to her like a cheap perfume.

Reaching over, Libby patted Megan's hand. "Who knows? Maybe she'll marry Josh on Saturday."

Blair looked furious. "Megan is *not* getting married to *anyone* on Saturday, so let it go, Libby."

"Jeez, Blair," Libby said nonchalantly, sipping her drink. "You might want to consider some anger management classes." She waggled her eyebrows at Megan. "Besides, who knows what will happen tonight with Mr. Hot-and-Sexy-in-a-Pair-of-Jeans once he's out of them. Maybe he'll be so good, you'll want to marry him."

To her horror, Megan blushed.

"She's not sleeping with him tonight," Blair lectured Libby. "I'm sure Knickers gave him his own room. No one is allowed to have sex in the house of perfection."

Libby giggled. "But Knickers got pregnant twice…" Her voice trailed off in innuendo.

Blair's mouth twisted into a smirk. "I'm sure that happened in a five-star hotel so someone else's sheets got soiled. *Both* times."

The thought of her perfect mother having sex, especially with her father, was nauseating. "Actually…" Megan said. "She told Josh—thinking he was Jay—that she knew we were having sex in Seattle, so she put his bag in my room."

Blair's mouth gaped. "Knickers actually said the word sex?"

"No," Megan cringed. "She called it hanky-panky. But now he's sleeping in my room."

"Yes!" Libby squealed, drawing the attention of the guests at a nearby table. "Megan's gettin' some tonight!"

"Libby!" Megan hissed, her face getting hotter. "I can't."

"Finally," Blair groaned. "The first reasonable thing you've said today."

Libby ignored her. "Why on earth not?"

"He's not sticking around."

"So? What's the problem? You *like* him. Admit it."

Megan squeezed her eyes shut. "Maybe."

"You'd be crazy if you didn't. He's nice. He's sexy as hell. He's charming. He's attentive. And he's sexy as hell."

"You already said that."

Libby glanced over at Josh, who had pocketed his phone and was headed their way. "With a man as sexy as that, it can't be said often enough."

Megan blushed. When Libby was right, she was right, and now Megan couldn't help thinking about what he could accomplish with all that sexiness.

Chapter Nine

As Josh walked away from Megan and her friends, Noah shouted in his ear. "What the hell is going on? You scared the shit out of me."

"Sorry about that."

"Is this some new way to pick up women? Because I strongly recommend that you find a new technique."

"Not exactly," he said as he began to pace at the edge of the yard. "I left this trip up to fate, and you'll never believe what has happened."

"You got laid."

"No. I sat next to Bart Vandemeer's daughter on the plane."

That got his attention. "*What?* Did you know she'd be on that flight?"

"No. I didn't even know it was her until Bart Vandemeer shook my hand in the Kansas City airport."

"Did he know who you were?"

"No…he mistook me for someone else."

"Who?"

Josh rehashed the story and Noah released a slow whistle. "This sounds more like me than you, little brother. Are you sure you can pull it off?"

"Amazingly, I have so far. We've even made it halfway through our engagement party."

"An engagement party? Three days before the wedding?"

"Her mother's a nut job. A gold-digging, social wannabe nut job. She spent enough money on this party to sustain a family of four for a year. God only knows what she's planned for the wedding. Bart Vandemeer certainly has the motive. I think I'm on to something." He paused. "No lecture? No admonishment?"

"Hell, no. You were right and I was wrong. Your plan is pure genius. I wholeheartedly approve."

Noah's approval set off blaring alarms. Josh stopped in his tracks. "You're kidding."

"No. Is Megan Vandemeer a looker? Are you going to hook up with her while you're her fake fiancé?"

"What? No!"

"So she's a dog?"

"No. She's gorgeous, but I can't start something with her. I have to break up with her as soon as I find some solid evidence."

"Joshy, have I taught you nothing? Why not get some action while you're out there? It's perfect. You don't have to worry about a long-term commitment because you're only hanging around a few days and she knows you're bailing. Why wouldn't you go for that?"

"How's she going to feel when she finds out the only reason I'm here is to find evidence proving her father is a thief?"

"It doesn't matter, Josh," Noah said, frustrated. "You'll be gone. What's the problem?"

Maybe Josh didn't want to start something with her and be gone. He almost laughed at the irony. There had been three meaningful relationships in his life—two in college, and one he'd ended two years before. For some reason, none had ever felt quite right. By all appearances, they should have worked out. There were no compatibility issues, and Josh's mother had approved of each of his exes, but he'd always felt like something was missing.

A spark.

He'd blamed himself. Since his father's death, he'd been so driven to make his father's legacy—his business—a success, he'd given the firm priority over everything and everyone in his life. He'd told himself there would be plenty of time to find the right person and start a family when the time came. Over the last few months, when it finally seemed as though the business had found solid ground, he'd allowed himself to examine his past relationships, determined to make the next one work.

His conclusion was sobering. He realized he could have lavished all the attention in the world on each one of his exes, and it still wouldn't have worked. Though some might argue the connection he sought was the stuff of fairytales and folklore—two things Josh McMillan didn't much believe in—there had been so much spark in his parents' marriage, they'd glowed with it.

That was why Josh found acknowledging his attraction to Megan so difficult. He realized he was not only attracted to her, but he'd finally found that elusive spark…except with her, it was more like a blaze. It was crazy. He hardly knew her, but there was no denying it. And while he was tempted to take Noah's advice and indulge in his desire for her before he left, he couldn't do it. From what he could see, Megan Vandemeer's life was full of people dead set on hurting her. He didn't want to add his name to that list.

And that strangled him more than he'd expected.

"How far are you going to take this?" Noah asked.

Josh sucked in a breath and pushed it out, while simultaneously trying to force the thoughts of the sexy brunette out of his head. "I don't know yet. Bart's friends and associates have painted a pretty flattering picture of his character, but that doesn't mean anything. Desperate men go to drastic measures. He seems like an ordinary guy and he doesn't have expensive hobbies—an occasional game of golf, camping, fishing…"

"A boat?"

"It's twenty years old, with a small outboard motor."

"So the wedding is his big expense?"

"I'm pretty sure money slips through his wife's fingers like water. When I asked about Bart's financial planner, one of his friends hinted that Bart doesn't have much money to invest. A woman pulled me aside because she thought *I* might know what was going on. Joke's on her, but she had something interesting to say. Rumor has it Bart refinanced the Vandemeers' house to get the money to pay for the wedding of the year. And it *still* wasn't enough."

"So Bart could be the culprit?"

"Maybe. I was hoping Andrew Peterman, the second principal, would show, but so far he hasn't made an appearance, and it's getting late enough that I suspect he won't."

"Wow. I'm impressed. I didn't think you had subterfuge in you, Joshy."

Noah meant it as a compliment, but Josh suddenly felt dirty. "Nicole mentioned that Bart has a home office on the second floor with the bedrooms. I hope to search their house tonight after everyone goes to bed, but I suspect any real evidence is at his business office. Getting there could be challenging. Her mother is like Mother-of-the-Bridezilla. She's made itineraries for each of us and my time is booked solid up until the wedding. I have no idea how I'm going to get away to go to Vandemeer's office."

"Doesn't her family think it's weird you don't have any family or friends there?"

"Megan said the shithead she was going to marry hardly had any friends, and neither his parents nor brother were planning on coming."

"The guy sounds like a tool if his own parents weren't going to the wedding. Is Vandemeer's daughter a bitch?"

"No. Not from what I've seen. Quite the opposite, in fact. I can't figure out why she was planning to marry the douche bag."

"It doesn't matter. I think you're on to something. And the fact is, if you're busy with all the wedding plans, then you need help."

"What does that mean?"

"Your *mother* may not be coming to the wedding, but your *brother* can change his mind and show up tomorrow."

"What? No!" Josh protested in panic.

"It's perfect, Josh. I'll have more free time than you. Besides, you and I both know this is more my type of caper than it is yours." Noah laughed. "You're out of your league, Joshy. Admit it."

Josh paced, rubbing the back of his neck. Noah showing up could be a potential disaster. Noah tended to be a loose cannon. But Josh had to admit he needed help, and Noah had been the one to corner them into this situation in the first place. Time was ticking down, and he'd known going into this that he was going to have to resort to rolling in the mud. "Fine, but you have to behave yourself, Noah."

"Hey! When have I not behaved myself?"

"Consider why we're in this situation to begin with…"

"Jeez, one time—"

"*One time?*" Josh shook his head. "*Dammit.*" This plan was even more insane than the course he was currently on. "I'm not telling them that you're coming. I can't think of a single reason to justify you showing up tomorrow. Megan wants to break up at the party tonight, and I don't want to scare her into going through with it."

"You can't let her break up with you!"

"I know. And for the most part, I'm safe. Megan is trying to save face with her mother, and I've been the perfect boyfriend."

"Like that's a stretch," Noah snorted. Leave it to Noah to make an attentive boyfriend sound like a bad thing.

"The point is that she needs me to act like a first class jerk before she can break up with me, although it would come across even better for her if *I* break up with *her*. And I have no intention of doing either tonight."

"So you're safe."

In theory, but he could also end up infuriating Megan. While he'd accept that in a pinch, the better option was if he could get her to agree to the delay. And if he were being honest with himself, he didn't want her to be angry with him.

"I've told Megan we should break up tomorrow. She hasn't agreed, but one of her best friends likes me and is trying to get her to put it off. I think I can get her to hold off until at least tomorrow night. But that's not near enough time if you show up in the afternoon. I might have to try pushing the breakup off to Friday, but that's cutting it pretty close to the wedding." He paused. "Maybe I'll find what we need tomorrow."

"Not likely."

Could Josh afford to turn down his brother's help? He had four days before the axe dropped on their big deal. He was going to have to bend some of his ethics to get the proof he needed and that thought didn't sit well with him. "I don't even know what I'm looking for, Noah. How do I pin this on them?"

"See if you can get access to Bart's emails from around the time my bag was stolen. Try to find a copy of the plans with our name on it."

"You really think someone's going to keep a copy of an incriminating document?"

"Yes. I do."

Josh rubbed the back of his neck. "So where do I look?"

"The Vandemeer house is a good start. I doubt he'd want to keep the plans in the office. How would he explain it to his colleagues? But if his wife found it, no big deal…I bet none of his family would give it a second thought."

Josh had to admit that Noah was right. "This is a great start if Bart's our guy, but I still haven't figured out how I'm going to explain your sudden appearance."

"I can play the role of the surprise, drop-in brother. Send me an address."

"But why would you show up? How did you find out where I was?"

"You let me worry about all of that. You just act completely surprised to see me. Now what's the address?"

Josh had a sinking suspicion he was going to regret this. "I'll text it to you."

"See you tomorrow, Joshy."

He wasn't exactly looking forward to this family reunion.

He rejoined Megan and her friends. Libby was watching him like he was an all-you-can-eat buffet, though one she didn't care to dine at, while Megan looked embarrassed, and Blair was doing her damnedest to pretend he didn't exist.

"I need to use the restroom," Josh said, needing to escape for a few minutes. Hopefully it would also give him the opportunity to do a quick search, as he'd planned.

"You can use the powder room on the first floor," Megan told him.

Feeling someone's gaze on him as he made his way across the deck to the back door, Josh looked back to see Kevin watching him. Shaking his head, he let himself into the house and used the restroom, then opened the door, planning to head upstairs to look for Bart's office. But as he moved toward the stairs, he heard a voice from behind the partially open bedroom door at the end of the hall. He paused, looking to see if anyone would notice him eavesdropping. When he didn't see anyone, he moved closer, realizing it was Bart Vandemeer's voice.

"No…you know it's too late." There was silence for several moments before he said, "That's not what I said. You know I want to help…I'm just…tied up."

Bart was obviously on the phone, but who was he talking to and what was the call about?

"We always knew there would be casualties," Bart said, sounding unhappy. "Talk to the attorney and see what he says."

Was he talking about Josh potentially fighting the patent?

"Hear anything good?" Blair whispered behind him.

He jumped and spun around, trying to keep a poker face. "Hey, Blair. I was looking for the restroom."

"Hmm…" She crossed her arms. "You seem to have passed it." She pointed her thumb to the partially open door behind him.

"Huh." He tried to sound nonchalant. "The door was closed when I went by. I heard Bart in the other room, so I decided to ask him where I could find another bathroom."

Blair pinned him with her steely gaze.

The bedroom door opened and Bart came out. "Oh!" he said in surprise, looking nervous. "I haven't had a chance to say hi to you, Blair. How are you doing?"

"Good."

"I see you met Josh. Or had you met him before?"

Josh held his breath, waiting for Blair to expose him.

"Nope. This was my first opportunity to meet *Josh*."

If Bart heard the inflection, he didn't let on. "Are you ready for Megan's wedding excitement?"

Blair's mouth crooked into a devious smile. "You have *no* idea."

"Well..." He squeezed past the two of them. "I better get back out to Nicole. I'm sure she's fit to be tied over something." He continued toward the kitchen, but Blair didn't budge, blocking Josh's path.

Her eyes narrowed. "What are you up to?"

"I told you. I was looking for the restroom."

She shook her head slowly, keeping her gaze on him. "No. You're up to something. I can feel it. The question is what?"

Josh held his hands out at his side. "I'm just trying to help Megan."

"No. I don't—"

"You are unbelievable!" Megan said in a loud voice, walking up behind Blair. "I told you to leave him alone!"

Blair turned to face her friend and Josh slid past her, moving next to Megan. "I told you that I don't trust him, and sure enough, I found him eavesdropping outside your parents' room."

"Eavesdropping on *what?* My mother's outside and I just passed my father."

"Megan. Listen to me. Josh was listening to your father's phone call."

Josh plastered a look of what he hoped was innocence on his face. "I was looking for the restroom. I heard your dad's voice, so I was going to ask him where it was. Then Blair showed up and accused me of...I'm not sure what." Josh hated lying, but here he was, lying through his teeth. The guilt was overwhelming.

"You can't trust this guy, Megan!"

"Blair! Keep your voice down," Megan whisper-hissed. "Why in the world would Josh eavesdrop on my father? What could he hope to hear? Do you know how paranoid and crazy that sounds?"

"It might sound paranoid, but it's true."

Megan shook her head. "You'll do *anything* to prove me wrong, won't you?"

Blair looked genuinely confused. "What are you talking about?"

"You'll resort to making up lies to get me to end our arrangement."

Blair's mouth dropped open. "Have you lost your *mind?*"

Tears filled Megan's eyes. "You've already decided that I have, so why do you keep asking?"

"Megan." Blair's voice softened.

Megan shook her head. "Stop. Just stop." Then she took a deep breath and turned to Josh. "My mother wants my father to formally introduce us to their friends." He started to say something, but she held up her hand. "Yes, I know. We've already talked to every single one of them, but nevertheless…" Her voice trailed off.

Blair's anger returned. "If you think I'm going to stay here and watch this—"

"Go!" Megan said, her eyes blazing. "If you can't watch this, then go. No one is making you stay."

"Megan," Josh interrupted, his guilt crushing him. He couldn't let her ruin a decades-long friendship over him.

"You're choosing him over me?" Blair demanded. When Megan didn't answer, she pushed on. "You're picking a man whom you've known for approximately ten hours over your friend of twenty-five years."

"No, Blair. You chose for me." Megan grabbed Josh's wrist and pulled him down the hall, leaving a stunned Blair in her wake.

"Megan, really—" Josh stammered.

"It's fine," she said, forcing a smile. "I'm fine. Let's go get introduced."

By the time they reached the kitchen, her hand trembled in his clasp. She was upset whether she wanted to admit it or not.

"Megan." He pulled her to a halt. "Hold on for a second."

She stopped in front of him, looking up at him with questioning eyes. She was so agonizingly close and she looked so vulnerable. All he wanted to do was take her in his arms and kiss her, assuring her that everything would be okay…but he couldn't. He wasn't sure everything would be okay once the dust finally settled.

"Give me a minute, okay?" he asked, certain she would afford him the time she thought he needed to collect himself. He felt less guilt over this small duplicity. It was for her benefit, so he could live with it.

They were still holding hands, he suddenly noticed. He thought about dropping his hold, but couldn't seem to let go. "She'll get over it," he finally said.

She let out a deep breath, then forced a smile. "I'm not so sure."

"Libby will smooth things over."

Her smile turned genuine. "Yeah, she can't stand it when we fight."

"I like Libby." He reached his free hand around Megan's back and pulled her to his chest before he realized what he was doing. Touching her was as natural as breathing, and while that was dangerous, he didn't much care at the moment.

She relaxed into him, resting her cheek on his chest.

They stood still for nearly a minute, and with every ticking second, Josh felt more and more certain this woman was different than every other woman he had ever met. The question was what did he do with that information? He didn't see any way to achieve a positive outcome.

Nicole Vandemeer poked her head through the back door. "There you are! Aren't you too precious, stealing a moment for yourselves. You can hug later. Your father wants you out here for an official introduction."

Josh wasn't fooled. The introduction had to be Nicole's idea, but at the moment he was Nicole Vandemeer's golden boy and he wasn't about to say a word.

Chapter Ten

Josh dropped his arm but held Megan's hand again, lacing their fingers together. She liked it more than she should, just like she'd felt when he was holding her. Somehow he'd known she couldn't handle facing her mother's friends immediately after her run-in with Blair. The confrontation had upset her more than she was willing to admit to either of them. Josh had used the excuse of needing a moment for himself, but she wasn't fooled. He'd done it for her. In the entire time she'd known Jay Connors, he'd never once been intuitive about her feelings, and this man she'd known for less than a day could see right through her.

She looked up at him, suddenly feeling shy, although she wasn't sure why.

He gave her a warm smile that reached his eyes, filling her with reassurance. "We want to keep Knickers happy, don't we?"

She laughed. "You picked up on that quick."

He didn't answer as they headed out onto the deck. All the guests were still in the process of being ushered down to the patio around the pool. Her mother led Megan and Josh to the railing that overlooked the yard. Her father stood to the side, looking embarrassed and totally out of his element.

Megan's mother cleared her throat, a delicate sound that garnered everyone's attention anyway. "We'd like to thank you all—our dearest friends—for coming to celebrate the engagement of our only daughter, Megan Nicole Vandemeer." She paused and gave Megan her best fake smile, a look convincing enough to fool ninety-nine percent of the people she met, but not her own daughter. Then she turned back to the crowd. "Bart would like to say a few words."

Megan looked down at the sixty or seventy faces of her mother's dearest friends, who stood around the pool and spilled into the edges of the yard. She'd only seen three of those faces before tonight. Libby, a hopeless romantic who was currently glowing with excitement. Her grandmother, who looked like she was privy to some private joke. And Kevin, still manning his position at the bar while he shot daggers of contempt at the man standing next to her.

If she could ignore the fact that her mother had set this up—and, of course, all the blatant Disney references—the view in front of her was breathtaking. The sky had darkened and the floating candles on the water and the candle chandelier hanging from the tent emitted a magical golden glow. If she were a woman prone to falling for romance, this display would have swept her away. No wonder Libby looked so orgasmic.

She heard her father talking, so she tuned into his words. "Our daughter and our soon-to-be son-in-law..."

Suddenly the beauty of the scene hit her in a different way. Her mother had created this mostly for herself, but it had been intended as a celebration of *her* upcoming nuptials. The whole thing was a farce. Everything about it was a lie. She felt incredibly alone and panicked and messed up and...Josh squeezed her hand. She looked up at him and smiled, surprised by what she saw in his face. He was either an incredibly good actor or the lust in his eyes was real.

"...Megan and Josh."

Her mother clapped next to her, then announced, "And now we'll perform the handfasting ceremony."

That caught her attention. Megan whipped her head around. "*What?*"

Her mother was already moving behind them, a long strip of wide pink ribbon in her hand.

"Mom," Megan whispered loudly. "What are you *doing?*"

"I won't be outdone by that snotty Barbara Decker," her mother whispered as she reached for Josh's right hand. "They did this at her daughter's wedding and everyone loved it." She picked up Megan's hand and placed it palm down on Josh's forearm.

"Newsflash, Mom," Megan hissed. "That was at her *wedding*."

Her mother gave her an exasperated huff. "Reverend Snyder refuses to allow it as part of the ceremony. We'll just do it here." She looped the ribbon around Josh's wrist.

"Mother!"

Josh grinned and gave her a shrug.

There was no way she could get out of it now.

Her mother wound the ribbon around their arms and hands, weaving it in and out and making knots in various places as she spoke to the crowd about the commitment of marriage and how it would bind them together forever, trailing off when she got to a difficult part of the binding.

"Can you hold this?" she finally asked Josh, handing him one end of the ribbon.

He looked like he was about to break into a fit of laughter, but he pressed his lips together as Megan's mother fumbled with the other end. After two minutes, Megan and Josh's arms were hopelessly tied and knotted together. Her mother beamed, holding her arms out as if she'd pulled off some great accomplishment, like curing cancer or creating the world in seven days. Instead she had manufactured a mess that Megan was certain nothing less than divine intervention or a pair of sharp scissors could undo.

The partygoers graced the bizarre performance with a weak round of applause, but if Nicole was disappointed, she didn't let on. Megan's mother started to pick at the knots—a hopeless task—but stopped when a woman approached her.

"Nicole, we have to go, but thank you so much for inviting us to such a beautiful party." She glanced at Megan and Josh, her gaze dropping to their arms, which were trussed up like an unwanted Christmas present, before returning to their faces. "Congratulations to you both."

"Let me walk you out," her mother called after the woman.

"Mom!" When her mother didn't so much as glance at them, Megan released a heavy sigh and gave Josh a sidelong glance.

An ornery grin spread across his face. "It may be a little late for this question, but how *do* you feel about bondage?"

Megan was grateful that the darkness hid the blush that rushed to her cheeks. "We need to find a pair of scissors."

"We need to find someone else to use them," he added. "We're both right-handed." He gave a tiny shake of their joined hands.

She wondered how he knew that for sure, then realized he must have noticed. What else had he noticed about her? "I'm sorry about this."

"I think that may have honestly been one of the top five odd experiences in my life." Jay might have said the same thing, but it would have been dripping with derision. She could tell that Josh was genuinely amused.

Despite her suggestion to find scissors, Megan tried to pick at one of the knots with her left hand. "Stick around a couple of days," she said dryly. "I'm sure we'll be able to trump your entire top ten list."

"This is a good look for you, Megan." Libby joined them, giggling. "You're usually so straight-laced. Oh, wait. You *are* laced."

Megan shot her a glare.

"But usually when a couple does the bondage thing, the woman's mother isn't the one tying them up."

Josh burst out laughing.

"Shut up, Libby." Megan chuckled in spite of her mortification. "Find some scissors."

"I'm tempted to—"

"*Scissors. Now.*"

Libby took off for the kitchen, still laughing.

Megan looked around for her father, but she realized he'd taken off while her mother was busy hog-tying her to Josh. Gram was nowhere to be seen, but Kevin was making his way toward them with two glasses.

Still grinning, Josh took several steps backward to move them to the lower, currently unoccupied deck, then swept his left hand toward an outdoor loveseat and a coffee table tucked into a dark corner. "Would you care to sit down? I suspect this might take a few minutes."

"Sure."

He sat on the coffee table, holding her elbow to steady her as she sat on the seat in front of him.

"I'm so sorry," she said again. "I had no idea she would do something like that."

Kevin finally reached them and handed them each a glass. "This is for fortification. Good show, by the way. Do you do a matinee?"

"Oh, God. I'm so glad I don't know any of those people."

Megan took a big gulp from her drink. Josh watched her, then sipped from his own.

"Not to worry," Kevin said as he sat on the loveseat next to her, keeping his gaze on Josh. "You'll get to see them all again on Saturday."

"Saturday?" Megan asked before going in for another swallow of the fruity drink he'd brought her.

"Your *wedding?*"

Oh, shit. She choked on the drink and spit it out all over the front of Josh's shirt.

His eyes widened in surprise, but then he started to laugh.

"I'm so sorry!" Megan gushed, starting to reach for his shirt before remembering she still had her drink in hand. She finished it off and handed the empty glass to Kevin. "I'm going to need another."

Josh downed his and handed his glass to Kevin as well. "Make that two."

"I'm gonna expect a huge tip." He got up and headed down the steps to the patio.

Megan used her left hand to pat at Josh's chest. "I am so sor—"

He cut her off, reaching behind her head and pulling her mouth to his. His kiss was soft and tentative, as though he expected her to pull away. She leaned into him instead, sliding the hand pressed to his chest up to the side of his face. His tongue ran along her lower lip and she gasped.

"Megan!" her mother called.

Josh lifted his head. The candlelight shone in his eyes, and she was grateful for the blatant desire she saw there. This wasn't for show. This was real.

"Your mother's calling," he murmured.

Megan closed her eyes for a second and groaned. "I just want this party to be over." She lifted their still-joined arms. "And for us to be untied."

He chuckled, then leaned in to kiss her again. "Being tied to you has been an interesting experience."

"Megan! Come say goodbye to our guests!" her mother shouted from the other side of the pool.

Megan took comfort in the fact that her mother's gaze was swinging around the yard in an attempt to locate them. She didn't seem to notice them tucked into the corner.

"She expects us to interact with people while we're tied up like this?" Josh asked, incredulous.

"I suspect she's already forgotten that we are."

"So what are the chances of hiding out here?"

"Not so great, since Kevin's about to give us away."

Sure enough, her brother, who was on his way back to them with two more drinks, had stopped beside their mother and was motioning to them. He gave Megan a huge grin.

"That sadistic bastard," she mumbled.

He continued toward them, still grinning.

"Thanks for selling me out," Megan grumbled, snatching a glass out of his hand. "What was that about?'

He put Josh's drink on the table and leaned back, observing them for a moment, his smile having slipped away again. "I'm going to be brutally honest."

Josh picked up the drink, then said wryly, "I'm glad you decided to give *that* a go."

Megan had hardly eaten and the drink she'd guzzled down had already gone to her head. She giggled and Kevin shot her a dirty look.

"I don't like you, Connors." Kevin jabbed his finger into Josh's chest. "You've treated my sister like shit for too long, and I've decided that I'm going to stop this wedding."

Megan shook her head to clear it. "What are you talking about?"

"He's a cold-blooded prick who doesn't give a shit about you. I should have said something months ago, but I'm saying it now."

"Kevin!" she said, standing up and pulling Josh with her. "You don't know what you're talking about."

"I know all too well what I'm talking about." He stood. "I told you—Gram and I have been talking. We know what he's like." He waved his hand haphazardly toward Josh. "I know he ignores you most of the time in Seattle. I don't know what this little display of affection is all about, but your audience here in the corner is practically nonexistent. Save the show for when it counts."

He turned on his heels and stomped off.

"I'm so sorry," she said for the umpteenth time. "He had no right to do that."

He was silent for a moment, then turned to her. "Yes, he did."

"Why would you—"

"Megan," he said quietly. "From what little I've gathered, Jay *did* treat you like shit."

"How could you possibly know that?"

"More reasons than you can guess." He moved closer to her, lowering his voice. "I'm glad your brother is looking out for you. Too little too late, as far as I'm concerned, still..." His voice trailed off.

"But he thinks you're Jay."

He shrugged. "Part of the gig."

Which made her question once again the real reason he was doing this. Karma and fate felt like bullshit answers. Still, it wasn't fair for Josh to pay for Jay's crimes. "Maybe we should break it off now."

"What? *Why?*"

"Before you get hurt."

He snaked his left arm around her back and pulled her close, his face inches above hers. "I'm not going to get hurt. I'm a big boy."

"But Kevin…"

His breath was warm on her face and her skin flushed. "Kevin's not going to hurt me." He kissed her gently, then sucked her lower lip between his teeth.

Every part of her combusted and a bolt of desire shot straight to her groin.

"Don't break up with me, Megan," he whispered against her mouth. "Not tonight."

He kissed her, his tongue licking her lip again before it slipped into her mouth, coaxing her tongue. When she responded, he lifted his mouth inches from hers. "Promise me no more talk about breaking up tonight."

"Okay," she said breathlessly.

His mouth claimed hers again, demanding and insistent. She tried to press closer to him, but their bound hands got in the way.

"Where's Libby?" she groaned.

He murmured his amusement against her lips.

"Megan!" her mother shouted again.

Megan pulled away. "I'm going to tell her that we're exhausted from the time change and we need to go to bed."

He shook his head in confusion. "But it's two hours *earlier* in Seattle."

"Trust me. She always gets the times mixed up when we try to plan phone calls." She tugged him across the deck until they were standing in front of her mother.

"Oh!" she exclaimed. "You're still wearing your bindings. That's so sweet."

"Mother," she said through gritted teeth. "We can't get them off."

"I think that's a good sign." She turned to the woman next to her. "Don't you?"

Megan took a deep breath, then offered her mother and her guest a tight smile. "Josh and I are exhausted from the time change. We're going to head to bed. I'll help clean this up tomorrow."

"But—"

"Good night, Mom!" Megan called over her shoulder as she pulled Josh through the back door.

They found Libby in the kitchen, sitting on a barstool as she sipped a glass of water and snacked on a plate of fresh carrots and celery. "You're still into bondage, I see. I hope you two have discussed a safe word. Personally, my current favorite is Ferris wheel."

Why was Megan so surprised by the roles her friends had fallen into—Libby as matchmaker and Blair as prison guard? This was typical of their dynamic. "Where are the scissors, Libby?"

"*Scissors?*" she asked and winked at Josh. Then she lifted a tea towel on the counter and slid a pair across the granite counter. "I thought you might want a little more quality time."

"Well, I'm sure Josh was happy with the quality time we just had with Kevin. For some reason he's decided to go all concerned big brother. He announced that he's going to stop the wedding."

"Huh." Libby looked amused. Then she waved her hand, dismissing the subject. "I'll take care of it."

Megan shook her head. "Look, we'll sort this out tomorrow, but right now I need you to cut us loose."

Libby gave them a mock pout. "I didn't think the binding ties made in a Knickers ceremony should be so easily cut asunder."

"*Libby.*"

Libby pursed her lips, mischief in her eyes. "This has to be consensual." She turned to Josh with mock seriousness. "Josh, do you agree to cut these ties that bind?" Both of them started to laugh.

"Yes, cut us loose," Josh managed to say.

It took Libby several minutes to cut them free. Megan rubbed the deep indentations on her arm.

Wearing a grin, Libby nodded toward Megan's arm. "Looks like Knickers needs some lessons on bondage. I know a dominatrix who would be happy to teach her. Imagine how thrilled your dad would be."

Megan cringed. "Ewww. Stop."

Josh's eyes widened. "You know a dominatrix?"

"Yeah," Libby shrugged. "I can set you up with a private session if you'd like."

Jealousy rushed through Megan in a hot wave, taking her by surprise. And it wasn't the first time she'd felt this way tonight. She wasn't typically a jealous person, so what was that about? She grabbed Josh's wrist. "He'll be tied up."

"He already was tied up."

Josh chuckled.

Megan groaned and headed for the stairs, pulling Josh with her. "Bye, Libby."

"Josh, if you change your mind, let me know," Libby called after them, the merest hint of a laugh in her voice.

Megan didn't stop until she got him into her room and shut the door. He stood with his back to it, waiting for her to make a move. His smile was gone; his eyes serious.

He was probably the most handsome man she'd ever known, but this was crazy. She hadn't even known him twenty-four hours. Yet…she wanted this.

"I hardly know you," she finally said.

The corners of his mouth tipped up slightly. "I know."

"You don't know me either."

"True."

She'd had two drinks in quick succession and while she wasn't drunk, it had certainly shaved the edge off her nerves. "I like you."

His grin faded and his voice turned husky. "I like you too."

She took a step toward him. "Did you fake that kiss a few minutes ago? Was it a performance, like Kevin suggested?"

He released a breath of disbelief and gave a small shake of his head. "God, no."

She took a deep breath. "Do you want to schedule a session with Libby's dominatrix?"

Josh's eyes lit up and he released a chuckle. "*No.*"

She took another step toward him, leaving two feet between them.

He closed the distance, slowly reaching for her face with both hands and cupping her cheeks as he looked deep into her eyes. Still he hesitated.

"What are we doing?" she whispered, resting her hands on his chest.

"I'm not sure."

"This is crazy."

A hint of a smile returned. "I know." A silent war waged in his eyes before he kissed her. It was gentle at first, as if he were as shocked as she was that they were doing this.

This was so out of character for Megan. She wasn't a prude, and while she had no hard and fast rule about how many dates needed to precede sex, it didn't usually happen until after the third. She wasn't sure if she could count the engagement party tonight as their first date, but she had no doubt that she *wanted* this. She'd never believed in chemistry before, but one touch, one kiss from this man had made her a convert.

She grabbed the back of his head and opened her mouth to him, teasing the tip of his tongue with hers.

It was as if she'd released a flood gate. He moved a hand behind her back, pressing her chest tighter to his, and his mouth became more demanding. Her body answered. A surge of desire washed through her, and the urge to be closer to him, to feel his bare skin under her fingertips, was impossible to resist.

She loosened the knot in his tie, then set to work on the buttons on his shirt. He reached behind her for the zipper of her dress and pulled it down.

They broke apart, both of them breathless as Josh pushed her sleeves down her arms, his fingertips trailing softly in the fabric's wake. Her dress puddled at her feet and she stepped over it, sliding off her sandals in the process.

She stood in front of him wearing only a white lace bra and panties, thankful she'd had the foresight to not only pack matching undergarments but ones that were worthy of being seen.

Josh gasped slightly at the sight of her and then reached for her again, crushing her mouth with his.

She placed her hands on his bare chest and slid them around to his back, her hands gripping his shoulder blades. She pulled him backward to the edge of the bed, then reached for his belt, quickly unfastening it before working on the button and zipper of his jeans. A groan released from her as she felt the bulge of his erection against her hand.

She stared up at him, flushing at the desire in his eyes as he admired her body. And she expected him to kiss her again, but he took a step backward instead, conflict in his eyes.

He took a deep breath and heaved it out. "I don't think we should do this."

Horror rushed through her. "*What?*"

He closed his eyes and swallowed. "I can sleep on the sofa…"

"No. You can't." She shook her head, trying to regain her senses. "My mom…"

His mouth opened as though he wanted to say something, then closed abruptly.

She turned her back to him, mortified at his rejection. "It's a queen-size bed. We can both sleep here."

"Megan, it's not you…"

"No," she said, tears stinging her eyes. "You're right. This was a bad idea. We'll break up first thing tomorrow, and then you can get back to saving your business." She spun around to face him. "That's ultimately why you're here, right? I'm just a good karma detour."

"Uh," he looked toward the wall and rubbed the back of his neck. "Yeah." He shifted his gaze toward the bathroom door. "I'm going to take a shower. Do you need to use...?"

She shook her head. "No. Go."

He grabbed his bag and disappeared into the bathroom, closing the door behind him. She picked her dress up off the floor and opened her suitcase, pulling out a nightgown, thanking the stars above it was utilitarian and not sexy—a complete about-face from a few moments ago.

The shower turned on and she stripped off her bra and pulled the gown over her head, then dropped her discarded dress into the bag.

How in the world could she sleep with him now?

But a wave of exhaustion overcame her, so she pulled back the covers and climbed under them. The lamp on her bedside table filled the room with a warm glow, transporting her back over ten years, to when she had lived in this room. She'd failed her mother's expectations as a teen and young girl. Was that why she'd stuck with Jay, even when she knew he was so wrong? Her mother held marriage and motherhood on such a high pedestal; maybe marrying Jay had been one last-ditch effort to mend burned bridges. But it turned out that Megan was a failure at getting married too.

But the final nail in the femininity coffin was Josh's rejection. Did he wish he'd gone home with Libby instead? Was he in the bathroom thinking about her now?

Libby was like a siren. She drew men like honey did flies, and half the time she didn't even realize the power of her allure. How many times had Libby taken the attention of the boys Megan crushed on in high school? But there was never any malice in Libby's behavior. She was like a candle that burned so brightly men had no choice but to notice her. Megan didn't doubt that if Libby had gotten ahold of Josh first, he would be in her bed right now. Maybe that's what he was thinking about in the shower.

But the thought sent another blaze of jealousy through her and she had to laugh at her idiocy. Josh McMillan had never been hers. This was an *arrangement* and the sooner she not only accepted it, but ended it, the better.

Chapter Eleven

Josh stayed in the shower until the water turned cold, and then stayed in even longer. If Megan kept looking at him with that longing in her eyes, he couldn't guarantee he'd keep his hands to himself. And although every part of him demanded he go into the other room and satisfy them both, the sliver of decency still burning inside him—despite all the duplicity—demanded that he respect her enough to keep his hands to himself. So he took his time drying off and dressing in a pair of athletic shorts and a T-shirt. When he opened the door, he was prepared for an inner battle of epic proportions.

He took a few steps into the room. Megan was huddled under the covers, her eyes closed. Her long dark hair pooled on the pillow and her worry lines had ebbed away, leaving a peacefulness he hadn't yet seen in her.

She was asleep.

He let out a breath of relief. An asleep Megan made things immeasurably easier. Especially since he was still planning to escape the room and search the house for evidence of her father's deceit.

He cracked open the door and listened for a moment. Voices drifted up the stairs and he recognized one of them as belonging to Megan's mother. So the party had moved inside. He could at least search the rooms upstairs, but as he started out the door, he heard Kevin's voice on the stairs.

"Are you worn out, Gram?"

"Heavens, no. This was nothing compared to the parties your grandfather and I used to host."

Kevin laughed. "Mom's parties tend to be pretty dull."

"She's more interested in the show than she is about fun."

He laughed again. "Maybe that's why the party's over by ten p.m. Yours always went well into the morning."

"Which is part of the reason why your mother had a conniption when she realized what we had you doing."

"I learned some valuable life skills, Gram," he teased.

"Don't say I never did anything for you. Especially when you see your inheritance from me."

Kevin released a long rumbling laugh. "I've missed you, Gram."

"You and your sister need to come home more often. In spite of what you both think, your mother does love you. She just has a hard time showing it."

"I know, but it's hard to escape the Death Star once you're in its gravitational pull. It's safer to keep a healthy distance." He was silent for a moment. "I still say there's something off about Megan's fiancé."

"Josh? You promised me you'd give him a chance tonight."

"Yeah," he growled. "I did, but now I trust him even less. A guy doesn't just go from being a cold fish to being so affectionate."

"We don't know that he was cold to her. Only suspected."

"We both know her, Gram. Did she ever seem happy with

him?"

"No, but people change," Megan's grandmother said. "Maybe he came to his senses and changed. If anything, I trust him more after meeting him. He's good to her, Kevin. I know you had to notice the way he was looking at her tonight."

"Yeah, but what's behind the change? Something's up, and I'm going to get to the bottom of it."

Josh sucked in a breath. So Libby wasn't the only one who'd noticed his attentiveness? That was a good thing, right?

"You need to stay out of your sister's business."

"I've stayed out of it for too long. If he's marrying her, he'd better love her."

Josh hoped he was a couple of thousand miles away when Kevin discovered the truth.

"You're a good big brother," the older woman said. "Just make sure your motives are pure."

"What's that mean?"

"Guilt has a funny way of bending people." They were silent for a moment. "I'm getting off to bed. I need my rest. Your mother thinks she's putting on the royal wedding."

"Night, Gram."

Josh stood with his ear pressed to the door, wondering how good of a brother Kevin actually was. He'd suspected his sister was unhappy for at least two years without ever calling her on it. Where had he been while Megan was dating the bastard who'd cheated on her? Maybe Josh would let him know what Jay had done after everything had played out. He liked the idea of someone seeking retribution on her behalf.

His ears strained to hear further conversation, or at least the closing and opening of doors, but instead he was greeted with silence.

Dammit. He'd been so busy thinking about Megan he hadn't paid attention to which rooms they'd gone into. It wasn't like he could check out the office now anyway. Both Grams and

Kevin were up here and awake, and could catch him at any moment. He needed to wait until everyone was asleep.

A sudden wave of exhaustion overtook him, catching him by surprise. Although he was still partially resistant to his brother's impending arrival, he had to admit that part of him was relieved Noah would be jumping on board. The clumsy way his brother had lost the plans notwithstanding, Noah was an expert at subterfuge. Although Josh was loath to admit it, he needed him. He only hoped he came up with a plausible explanation for showing up. Maybe he should come up with a backup plan. Just in case.

But he still had tonight, even if he couldn't do anything for at least a half an hour, which left him unsure of how to pass the time. Since he was so tired, he decided to lie down on the bed and rest, maybe check his emails on his phone.

But Megan was in the bed.

He knew he should sleep on the floor—he could grab a pillow and use the blanket he'd seen in the bathroom closet. But he sank down onto the edge of the bed instead, then laid down on his side, facing her. Her hands lay on her pillow, in front of her face, and she wore a serene look that tugged at something deep in his heart.

She shifted, releasing a soft murmur in her sleep, and he resisted the urge to reach out and take her hand in his. Josh closed his eyes and breathed in her soft floral scent. It reminded him of summer and happier times before his father's death. Back before his life became so serious and his brother became a self-centered dick. While their father's death had made Josh more determined than ever to join the family business, Noah had resisted the responsibility. And although he'd done a respectable job of holding it together until Josh graduated and joined full time, Noah had been irresponsible in every other conceivable way since. If Noah were an employee, Josh would have fired him years ago.

He figured he'd lie on the bed for half an hour, then sneak out to investigate, but drowsiness overtook him. Too many sleepless nights spent worrying about his employees' futures had caught up with him. When he closed his eyes, he promised himself it would just be for a minute, yet when he woke up, Megan had rolled the opposite direction and the room was somewhat bright.

Oh, shit. It was morning.

He groped around the bed for his cell phone, eventually finding it down by his knees. When he saw the time, relief washed over him. 6:45. Time to get up and start working on the real purpose for his presence here.

Megan rolled over and faced him, her eyes still closed, her hands buried under her pillow. He watched her for several seconds, resisting the urge to brush the stray strands of hair from her cheek. She'd kicked the covers partially off as she turned and her bare legs were bent, her nightgown riding up to the curve of her ass, showing him the lacy underwear he'd gotten an eyeful of the night before. Memories of touching her and kissing her washed through him, making him hard. If he woke her up by kissing her, how would she respond?

No.

It took every ounce of restraint he possessed to keep from touching her.

He carefully slid off the bed and grabbed his bag, taking it into the bathroom so he could change. After closing the bathroom door as quietly as possible, he pulled on a pair of jeans and a cotton button-down shirt. He slipped out of the bathroom and then out of Megan's room into the hall, standing still as he listened for any noise. The question was, which room was the one he wanted?

It was still early enough that everyone was likely sleeping, so he stood in the second floor hallway and took stock. There were four doors: two on Megan's side of the hall and two on the opposite wall. Megan's bathroom shared a bathroom with another bedroom, which had to be the other door on her side. That meant the two doors on the opposite side were either both bedrooms, or one was a bathroom. One thing was sure: one of the rooms housed Bart's home office. He only hoped it wasn't currently being used as a guest room.

He moved to the door opposite Megan's and pressed his ear to the door. The light snoring he heard told him everything he needed to know. Now his odds were fifty-fifty.

When pressed his ear to the door of the room next to the occupied room, he didn't hear anything. Ditto for the room at the end of the hall. Someone was sleeping in one of the rooms, but which one? Since he hadn't heard anyone using the bathroom attached to Megan's room last night, he decided the most likely room for Gram was the one attached to Kevin's. Which left the door at the end of the hall.

Taking a deep breath, he grabbed the doorknob and turned it slowly, pushing the door gently when he felt it unlatch. He swung the door open and instantly panicked.

Megan's grandmother was stark naked next to the bed, with her hands and feet on the floor and her saggy butt up in the air, giving him a view he would—unfortunately—never forget.

Josh's brain told him "Retreat! Retreat!" but his feet refused to move.

"Josh!" Gram's face appeared between her ankles. "Good morning!"

"Sorry!" he sputtered out. "I was looking for a bathroom."

"This isn't it, but come do yoga with me."

He squeezed his eyes shut. "Uh... I'm not really a yoga fan." He started to back up and ran into the doorjamb.

"That's probably because you haven't tried it *au naturel*."

He cringed. "Yeah, I'm pretty sure that's not it."

"Come on. Don't be a prude."

He opened his eyes and turned his gaze to the opposite side

of the room. "I…can't… I told Megan…I'd get her some coffee."

Gram laughed. "That girl's like her mother. She doesn't believe in gettin' up before eight a.m. I have a hard time believing she's up."

Josh was pretty sure Megan wouldn't care to be compared to her mother. "Well, we both went to bed early…"

"What kind of positions are you kids trying these days? Back when Nicole was younger, her father and I were quite fond of the Kama Sutra. It helped us keep flexible."

Josh nodded, still not looking at her. His face felt like it was on fire. "Yes, ma'am. I'm sure it would."

"Well?"

"What?" Oh, Lord. Did she really expect him to answer?

"What positions are you kids using?"

Was she referring to the younger generation in general or to his and Megan's presumed sex life in particular? Either way, he had no desire to discuss sex of any sort with Megan's naked grandmother.

"Are you sexually repressed, Joshua?"

"*What?* No!"

"Then why don't you strip off your clothes and join me?"

"Megan's coffee…" he stammered.

"Sexual repression is a very bad thing. My daughter is the most repressed person I know and look how she turned out. I told Bart she'd be an easier person for all of us to live with if he'd just put his foot down once in a while."

Gram struggled to get upright and Josh hovered on indecision. He knew he should offer the octogenarian his help…but she was naked. And the image had already burned holes in his retinas. He had no desire to add to the damage.

Thankfully, she grabbed ahold of the bed and pulled herself to an upright position on her own.

"Well, I better get going…"

She stood in front of him in all her Lady Godiva glory. "How do you keep that firm patootie, young man? Do you do squats? Or do you lift weights at the gym?"

He started to cough. "Excuse me?" Oh, God. Was she coming on to him?

"I've enrolled in an art class—sketching nudes. I'd like to sketch your backside."

"Uh…I…" He stepped backward. "I'll need to check with Megan on that."

"And if she says yes?"

"I'll let you know." He managed to stumble into the hall and shut the door behind him. He rushed for Megan's room, heading straight for the bathroom and turning on the water. He splashed his face over and over in a desperate attempt to wash away the sight of Megan's grandmother's full womanhood staring him in the face. He groaned and washed faster.

"Josh?" Megan asked, standing in the doorway, her voice husky with sleep.

He continued to douse his face. "I just saw the most horrifying thing I can even imagine."

She stiffened. "What?"

"Your grandmother. In a downward dog yoga position. In the nude."

Megan chuckled. "Oh, dear. Mom had mentioned that Gram was going through a nudist phase, but I didn't know she'd combined it with yoga."

He stood upright, water dripping everywhere, and she handed him a towel. He covered his face with it, then pulled it down to look at Megan. He was thankful she was acting normal, as if he hadn't so abruptly curtailed their night together. He wasn't sure he could handle her dejection. His hold on his self-control with her was tenuous at best. He would probably do something he'd later regret.

She looked up at him, expecting some kind of response.

He dabbed at his neck with the towel. "She wanted me to do yoga with her in her room."

Her eyes widened in surprise. "Did you?"

"No!"

"It could have been interesting," she teased. "Have you ever tried yoga in the nude?"

He shook his head, trying to suppress the image of her grandmother that popped back into his head. "I've seen and heard things that have most likely scarred me for life."

She leaned her shoulder into the doorjamb, giggling. "Poor baby. What were you doing in Gram's room before seven in the morning, anyway?" She grinned, looking like she was up to trouble. "Did you go sleep with Gram last night?"

Horror rushed through his head. He wouldn't put it past the woman to attempt to demonstrate some of her Kama Sutra positions. But the biggest problem at the moment was explaining to Megan why he opened her grandmother's door.

"I was looking for a bathroom."

Her head jutted back in surprise. "Why? You could have just used this one."

"You were still asleep, and I didn't want to wake you."

"All the bathrooms upstairs are attached to bedrooms."

"Yeah," he said dryly. "I found that out the hard way. I thought there might be another one."

"Did you get changed in Gram's room?" she asked with a smirk, taking in his wet dress shirt and jeans.

"I got dressed in here, but I didn't want to shave or shower and disturb you."

She moved toward him and lifted a hand to his chin, running her thumb over the stubble. "Your scruff gives you a rugged look. It will give my mother a fit." She looked up at him with a mischievous glint in her eyes. "I think you should keep it."

His breath stuck in his chest at her touch, as he registered how close she stood to him, how warm her finger was against his face. He kept his hands at his sides even though everything in him was screaming to pull her closer and kiss her until she begged him to do more. "And what about you?" he forced out.

She stilled, her fingertips still splayed on his face. "What about me?" she whispered.

"What do you think of it?"

"I like it."

She was like a magnet. Not touching her would be like fighting the laws of physics. Impossible. One hand landed on her waist as the other slid across her cheek, digging into her dark, thick hair.

"There you are," Gram said, her voice coming from behind Megan. "Did you manage to get Megan's coffee?"

Josh took one look at her and cringed. Oh, God. She was still naked.

Megan broke free of his hold and spun around, gasping. "Gram! Put some clothes on!"

"Why does everyone keep telling me that? I came into this world without a stitch of clothes on and I plan to leave it the same way."

Megan chased after her. "Well, you're not going anywhere today, so get dressed."

"If I'm not leaving the house, all the more reason to go nude!" Gram insisted. "I tried to go into the Price Chopper grocery store this way, and based on the screaming and panic, you would have thought terrorists were attacking."

"I wasn't talking about running errands. What I meant is that you're not, God forbid, going to be meeting your maker any time soon."

"Don't you worry, Megan. Your mother made me promise not to keel over before your wedding. She wouldn't want anything to ruin her carefully laid plans."

Josh regained his senses and cautiously followed Megan out of the bathroom. The older woman was now wearing a skimpy robe and Megan was tying the sash around her waist.

"I'm thinking about relocating to somewhere that appreciates the human form."

"Is that so?" Megan asked, working on the knot.

"I'm considering Panama or Belize."

"I'd definitely check out Belize," Josh said, "The tax laws are more favorable to Americans there."

Gram looked interested in his suggestion. "Do they have any nudist communes?"

He crossed his arms. "You know, I've never checked. How about I look it up today and get back to you?"

Her grandmother beamed. "Maybe you kids would like to go with me."

Megan glanced over her shoulder at him, giving him a look of mock terror.

"I think we'd just cramp your style, Gram," Josh said. "I wouldn't want to be the one to hold you back. You want to do naked yoga with people who will appreciate the beauty of it. As you've already noticed, I'm too much of a prude to count myself among them."

She nodded, deep in thought. "You're probably right." She turned to Megan. "Never let this one get away, Megan Nicole Vandemeer. He's a catch."

Megan's smile fell. "I'll try my best, Gram."

"But loosen him up a bit first." She winked and gave them a mischievous grin, then left the room.

Megan shut the door behind her. "You know we'll probably find her naked in the kitchen later, but she'll have a devil of a time working that knot loose." Her words were funny, but her tone was flat and humorless.

Josh wanted to answer, but he couldn't form a response.

She moved over to her suitcase. "I'm going to take a

shower. Do you need to do anything in the bathroom first?"

He studied her back as she grabbed clothes out of the case and stood. "No," he finally managed to say. She started to walk past him. "Megan, wait."

She stopped and looked up at him, waiting. But he had no idea what to say. He only knew he couldn't stand to see her like this. He preferred the fun-loving, playful Megan and he wasn't sure how to get her back. Oh, he knew he'd totally screwed things up last night, but how much worse would it have been if he'd slept with her only for her to later find out his true purpose for being here? He knew what his brother would have done…and heck, maybe he *should* have given in to his libido. There was no denying he wanted Megan more than he'd ever wanted any other woman, but his conscience told him he had no right to want anything from her. He was using her. He could wrap it up with pretty explanations of karma and fate, but the truth remained that he was using this woman's misfortunes for his own gain. He didn't deserve her. "I'm sorry," was all he said.

She offered him a grim smile. "You have nothing to apologize for. If not for you, I'd probably be back in Seattle right now, a disowned outcast. You're offering me an out when I don't deserve one. I think I'm getting the better end of the deal here."

Little did she know. He forced an ornery grin. "Your grandmother wants to draw me in the nude. I told her I had to check with you first. We can call it even if you tell her you're too jealous to let her do it."

A smile spread across her face, returning some of her playfulness. "Deal."

"I need some coffee. I saw a coffee maker in the kitchen. Will your mother have a fit if I make a pot?"

"Probably not, and I'm willing to take the full blame if you bring me a cup."

"Deal."

He wandered down to the kitchen, partially worried Megan was right and he'd find Gram making pancakes in her birthday suit. Instead, the only person he saw downstairs was Bart, already dressed for work, pouring a cup of coffee.

"Good morning," Josh forced out. Bart had been nothing but nice to him, and despite Josh's suspicions, he couldn't hold a grudge against the man—not yet. He'd decided to withhold judgment until he had more than circumstantial evidence. So the billowing animosity he suddenly felt caught him by surprise. If Megan's father had protected her from her mother's expectations and demands, maybe she wouldn't be in this situation now. Maybe she would have felt safe telling them the truth.

"How'd you sleep?" Bart asked.

"Great," Josh said, forcing a friendliness he didn't feel. "Are you about to head out to work?"

"Sure enough. Nicole has an itinerary of things that need to be done today, but my part doesn't come until this afternoon, when I'm supposed to pick up the food for the big family dinner."

Josh decided to make his move. "I was fascinated by what I heard about your business last night. Any chance I can go into your office with you today?"

Bart glanced up in surprise. "I'm sure you'd be bored. Investment banking is bound to move at a much quicker pace than the work that's done at an engineering office."

"No, I assure you I won't be bored. I love to learn and I'd really like to know what Megan's father does for a living." He hesitated, guilt prickling his conscience before he added, "I'm marrying your daughter, sir, so I'd welcome the opportunity to get to know you better."

Bart watched him for a second, then set his cup down on the granite counter, clearing his throat. "You have no idea how happy I am to hear that. I'm giving away my baby girl on Saturday and it'll be a lot easier if I approve of the man she's chosen to spend the rest of her life with. I was under the impression you didn't want to have anything to do with us."

"There have been a lot of misunderstandings." The words were hard to get out. He hated himself for betraying this family, but if he was going save his business, he would have to continue following this course. This was what he'd impulsively signed up for. "But I'd love to spend some time with you today, and maybe you can show me around your office and tell me a bit about what an engineer does."

"Great! Can you be ready to leave in about fifteen minutes?"

"Sure thing. Let me take Megan a cup of coffee first."

Bart gave him a look Josh couldn't name. "She's got you waiting on her, huh?"

If Megan's father was hinting that she was in any way like her mother, he planned to set the record straight. Megan didn't deserve that. "If you're suggesting she's calling the shots in our relationship, I think we both know that Megan's not that kind of woman. I do things for her and she does things for me." Like he got her coffee and she was going to tell her grandmother she couldn't draw him in the nude, but her father didn't need to know about that. "She's a wonderful woman and I'm damned lucky to have her." And he knew it was true—any man who had his wits about him would be lucky to have Megan.

Bart looked him in the eye. "Yes, I can see that. I'm sorry if I implied something different."

Josh nodded and poured two cups of coffee and added creamer to both before going back upstairs. The shower was still running, and he had no idea how long Megan would be, so he cautiously opened the bathroom door, grateful there was a curtain to hide her. He wasn't sure how much control he'd have if she were naked and as willing and eager as last night.

He set the cup on the counter. "Megan?" he called softly.

She shrieked in surprise. "What are you doing in here?"

"I'm going to work with your dad and I wanted to tell you in case you're still in the shower when we leave."

Her head appeared at the edge of the curtain while she held onto it to keep herself hidden. "You're doing *what?*"

"I'm going to work with your dad."

"Why would you do that?"

"So he can get to know his son-in-law better."

A cautious look covered her face. "But we're breaking up today."

He couldn't make too big a deal of this or she'd get suspicious. "Yeah, but don't you think we should do it in front of crowd? Doesn't your mom have a family dinner planned for tonight? That would be the perfect time."

She sucked in her bottom lip, looking lost in thought. "I don't know. Wouldn't it be better if you stayed here and broke up with me this morning? Then Mom will have more time to call it all off."

"Do you honestly think your mother will *let* me break up with you? She'd be more likely to either drug me to get me to comply, and after last night's performance, maybe handcuff me for good measure. And if your grandmother is around as a witness, she'll strip me naked and draw me in my drugged state. And I don't even want to go into what she'll do with the handcuffs." He shuddered. "We need witnesses and lots of them."

She released a huff. "Damn it. You're right."

He grinned. "I brought your coffee, but I forgot to ask how you took it. You know, your father pretty much called me pussy-whipped for getting it for you. I gave him a mini-lecture about how you weren't that kind of woman, so it didn't seem like the appropriate time to mention this was our first morning together."

She fought a grin. He wondered if she had any idea how beautiful she was when she beamed like that. It was obvious that her asshat ex had been clueless. "I take creamer."

His grin spread. "Then it's your lucky day. I added creamer. Now I better get going. I want to make a good impression on your dad."

"No!" she exclaimed. "You have to make a bad one! Otherwise it'll look like our breakup came out of nowhere."

"Okay. I'll try my best to be the biggest asshole possible."

"Good."

He continued to watch her, not wanting to leave her yet.

Her grin spread. "Shouldn't you be going?"

"Yeah."

She laughed. "Have a good day, dear."

"Have fun with Knickers."

She grimaced. "You definitely got the better deal." Then her face disappeared behind the curtain.

Josh headed downstairs to meet Bart Vandemeer, feeling like he was a prisoner on his way to the gallows. This was exactly what he wanted, so why did it feel so wrong?

Chapter Twelve

Megan's mother was sitting at the kitchen table when Megan went downstairs, sipping her coffee and eating a piece of dry toast while looking over several papers. That had been Nicole Westminster Vandemeer's breakfast for as long as Megan could remember, which was one of many reasons why she still wore a size two dress. Megan, on the other hand, was a size eight, a huge disappointment to her mother.

She gave Megan a slight glance before returning her attention to the papers. "Megan, we have a very busy day ahead of us. Perhaps you could run upstairs and get ready?"

Megan, who'd been refilling her coffee cup, stopped mid-pour. "I *am* ready."

The bridge of her mother's nose wrinkled as she gave Megan a scrutinizing glance. "Really?"

Megan set the cup down on the counter. "What's wrong with how I look?"

Her mother's eyebrows rose and she released an

exasperated sigh. "We need to make a hair appointment for you at the salon. Honestly, I thought you would take care of it in Seattle before you came." She picked up her phone. "I only hope they can fit you in."

"I had a haircut three weeks ago."

Her mother released an exasperated huff as she searched through her contacts without even looking up at Megan. "How about we start with the color? It lacks depth. We'll want highlights to show off your waves when we put it up for the wedding. And it wouldn't hurt to ask them to do a dry run for your up-do."

"I want to wear my hair down," Megan said. She wondered why she was wasting her time arguing the point when there wasn't going to *be* a wedding. Maybe she was just tired of letting her mother railroad everything.

Her mother pursed her lips and tensed her shoulders in irritation. "Megan, we discussed this."

"No, Mom. *You* discussed this, or to be more accurate, you dictated it to me and I just went along with it to keep the peace."

Her mother gasped. "Megan Nicole, what on earth has gotten into you? Why can't you just be compliant?"

"Maybe I'm tired of being compliant."

Her mother waved a manicured hand covered in glittering rings. "Don't be silly, darling. Now run upstairs, change your clothes and put on some makeup."

"I *am* wearing makeup!"

"Obviously not enough. Maybe they like the natural look in that rainy, brooding, mold-encrusted place you live in, but you're home now and you're getting married in three days. What will people think, Megan? *Honestly.* Now stop acting like a petulant child and do as I say. I'll have your amended itinerary ready for you when you get back downstairs. As it is, I'm reshuffling everything since your father dragged Josh off to his office."

"Yeah, I saw the itinerary. Don't you think it's a bit much?'

"You obviously need it. Now go. And check on your grandmother while you're up there. She's coming with us. Yesterday we were almost late picking you up from the airport because she refused to get dressed."

Megan didn't even try to hold back the laughter as she walked up the stairs.

"Gram, are you dressed?" she asked, knocking on her grandmother's door.

"Not because I want to be," the woman muttered as she opened the door. "I can't untie this knot with my arthritis." She motioned to Megan's robe.

Megan flashed an apologetic grin. "Sorry about that. You freaked Josh out. I had to make sure you wouldn't accidently flash him again."

"He's already seen it all."

"So he said."

"You need to loosen that boy up."

"So *you* said, but look at it this way, Gram—he's about to commit himself to me for the rest of his life, and you're showing him everything he's giving up." She gave a half-shrug. "It's a bitter reminder of the fact that he's stuck with me." The statement was for her grandmother's benefit, but she'd spent plenty of time brooding about whether Josh had rejected her for that very reason. This morning he seemed reluctant to leave her side, which made her re-evaluate her reasoning. Had Josh McMillan left her sexually frustrated because he was a *gentleman?* She'd been too embarrassed to even entertain the idea the previous night, but now it rang true.

The older woman patted Megan's cheek. "He's lucky to have you. And I'm only giving him a glimpse of what he'll get in about fifty years."

Megan smiled as she reached for the belt and began to

work on the knot. "Mom says you have to get dressed so you can come with us."

"I'd rather have a colonoscopy."

"Do it for me, Gram. She's extended her claws today."

"When doesn't she have her claws extended?" But the older woman's frown softened as she studied Megan's face. "Fine, I'll go, but only for you. And it's my constitutional right to wear whatever I want."

"The key part of that is *wear*. You have to wear *something*."

Megan's grandmother looked up at her, her face beaming as if a particularly exciting idea had occurred to her. "Not to worry. I'll wear something."

"I've seen that look before—" Megan finished untying the belt and flashed the older woman a grin, "—and I approve."

"Ha! I'll meet you downstairs in about fifteen minutes."

Megan had no desire to wait downstairs with her mother, who would only continue to bully her about her outfit, so she went into her bedroom and grabbed the two itineraries on the dresser. She sat down on the freshly made bed and opened each cover, flipping to Thursday and then Friday. Josh had been right. He was scheduled for a mani-pedi tomorrow. Ironically enough, Jay would have appreciated how organized the itinerary was…not to mention the spa time. Josh, on the other hand, was obviously as horrified as she was. Not that there was any point in comparing the two. Jay was gone—good riddance—and Josh was going to break up with her tonight. She would probably never see him again.

The thought was like a knife driving straight into her gut.

Her cell phone rang and she jumped, digging it out of her purse and then cursing under her breath. The power was at twenty-six percent. She'd forgotten to charge it. Then she saw who was calling and cursed again.

"Hello, Blair."

She was silent for a half-second. "I called to apologize. I

came on too strong last night."

Megan couldn't stifle her gasp.

"Yeah, I know," Blair grumbled. "It's as rare as finding a leprechaun under a double rainbow."

"Actually, rarer."

"Nevertheless, I'm sorry. I just love you too much to see someone else hurt you. I feel partially responsible for not cold-cocking your ex when I visited you in Seattle last February."

Megan laughed. "I found out he was cheating on me after your visit. What grounds would you have had to justify that in February?"

"For breathing and taking oxygen away from worthier creatures. Like slugs. Or lice."

Megan's chest burned with gratitude and love. "Thanks, Blair. I love you too."

"And in that spirit, I need you to grab that imposter's wallet and make sure he was telling me the truth about his name. Get his driver's license and read off his address."

Megan knew she should get mad at Blair for continuing on in the same vein as last night, but her friend's declaration of love softened her. She rolled her eyes instead.

"Don't you roll your eyes at me, Megan Vandemeer. We may be on the phone, but I can still see it."

Megan laughed. "Do you want me to read off his height and weight while I'm at it?"

"Yeah, that will help me figure out if it's a fake ID."

"Blair, you're not really going to check him out, are you?"

"You bet your ass I am. I thought I made that clear last night. I don't trust this guy."

"And what exactly do you think he's up to?"

"I intend to find out."

"Blair, let it go."

"No. Now start reading."

"I can't. He went to work with my dad."

"He *what?*"

"Calm down. What harm could he possibly do there?"

"Is your father working on anything big? Competing for any big jobs?"

"Oh, for heaven's sakes, Blair. How should I know? I never talk to my father about business. Besides, it's an engineering firm. You and I spent plenty of time there when we worked for him the summer between our freshman and sophomore years of high school. You know how boring that place is. If anything, Josh deserves a medal for going to work with him." Then she considered it and glanced at his Thursday schedule. "On second thought, he's smarter than I've given him credit for. He's gotten out of talking to the photographer and the orchestra director—wait. What? *Orchestra?*" Megan started flipping through the pages, trying to figure out just how large the orchestra actually was and when it would be playing. There was no way this wedding only cost twenty-five grand. Panic flared up from her gut.

"Oh, my God. You actually like this guy," Blair said. "I didn't want to believe it last night, but I can see right through you."

Megan sucked in her breath, then let it out slowly. "What? Of course I don't. We were putting on an act."

"That's a lie! Your voice rose." She paused, then softened her tone. "Look, Megs, no one helps a stranger with something this big for nothing. He's got an agenda. Maybe he wants to get into your pants. You haven't found out if he's circumcised yet, have you?"

"No! You know I'm not like that." Although she would have found out if it had been up to her—something Blair didn't need to know. Megan flung herself backward onto the bed in frustration, reminding herself that her friend was trying to look out for her. Wouldn't she be cautious if the roles were reversed? "Look, I've been skeptical about his motives too…but there's just something about him, Blair. Besides, if he wanted to get in my pants, he's had a couple of opportunities. He slept in my bed with me last night and never once made a move."

"Maybe so, but I still don't trust him."

"Which you've made abundantly clear."

"I'm going to dig up everything I can, address or no address."

Megan's back stiffened. "Let it go, Blair. I'm warning you, if you present me with a dossier on him as a wedding gift, I'm never going to speak to you again."

"*Wedding gift?* I thought you were breaking up with him!"

"It was a joke. I forgot you lost your sense of humor when you became a divorce attorney." She took a second to regroup. "Look, we're breaking up at my mother's family dinner this evening." She rolled onto her side and pulled the itinerary out from under her back, then examined the schedule for Thursday night. "Although it looks like it's for Dad's side of the family." Megan read the document again. "It so weird that she would plan a party for them. Knickers can't stand them."

"Who knows with her. And don't try to change the subject. Let me do this, Megan. This is what I do. I'm *very* good at it."

"Drop it. It won't matter tomorrow anyway. Very soon I'll be on a plane back to Seattle—disowned and disgraced. I'm sure it won't make the slightest difference to my mother who's at fault in the breakup."

"Then why go through this farce?"

"Just like hell has multiple levels, so does disgrace."

"Well, if Josh McMillan is screwing you over, he's going to find himself on the lowest one."

Megan couldn't hold back a smile. "I love you too, Blair."

Blair's voice softened. "I'm just looking out for you, Megs."

"And I love you for it. Now go use your animosity and derision against the lying, cheating bastards who are your bread and butter." Megan hung up, staring at the phone's blank screen for a moment. She missed the Blair she remembered from childhood. Blair was still the strongest, fiercest person Megan knew, but she'd acquired a hard edge that could wound even those closest to her.

Megan laid back down and held up her itinerary. Florist 9:00 a.m. Photographer 10:00, Orchestra director 11:00, Lunch at noon, Pick up wedding and bridesmaids' dresses at 1:30. She was exhausted from just looking at the list. But the fact that her mother was dragging her along made it ten times worse. Did Libby and Blair know about the one-thirty appointment? Hopefully they'd agree to come. Gram definitely wasn't enough moral support. Megan needed more people on her team.

She picked up her phone again and called Libby. "Hey, Libs. Did my mom tell you about picking up the bridesmaids' dresses today?"

"Um…yeah. She mentioned it last week."

"I don't suppose you planned on showing up?"

"Seeing how you weren't engaged when she called, no."

"Do you think you can…" If either of her friends could take off work, it was usually Libby. As a professional photographer, her schedule was usually more flexible.

Libby groaned. "Lucky for you, I don't have any appointments today. What time?"

"One-thirty. At Sherri's Bridal."

"Yeah," she muttered. "I remember. I'll be there."

"You're the best!"

"I know," she laughed. "And you owe me."

Megan stared up at the ceiling. "How come you aren't asking me why I'm picking up my wedding dress when I'm not even getting married?"

"Maybe you should be asking yourself that question. See you at one-thirty, Megs."

What was Libby suggesting? She'd only just met Josh; her friend couldn't think she'd actually *marry* him. The dress was paid for, wedding or not. Hopefully, Megan would get married for real someday and she could use it. She loved the dress. Truth be told, wearing it was what she'd been looking forward to most about the wedding. The knowledge struck her again, sticking to her skin like crazy glue—the whole wedding was already bought and paid for…no take backs. Her parents were out a ton of money. The guilt of lying hung over her, sucking her energy away. Or was it the thought of spending the day with her mother?

As if on cue, her mother called up the stairs, "Megan!"

Megan rolled onto her stomach, releasing a long, low groan into her comforter. Only an act of God would get her through this day without strangling her mother.

Chapter Thirteen

Megan was tired, cranky and starving. Which was more than pathetic since she'd just left a restaurant after having lunch. Megan's mother had ordered for her while she was in the restroom. And even though Megan had asked her to order a cheeseburger, she wasn't all that surprised when the waitress served her a garden salad with fat-free dressing on the side.

Megan's mouth dropped open and she sought her mother's attention, which wasn't hard since Nicole was watching her like a hawk. "What happened to my cheeseburger?"

"You're not a teenager anymore, Megan," her mother said, picking up her fork. "You've gotten…hippy."

Gram had been quiet for most of the morning, but her interest perked up. "Megan's a hippie?" She looked into Megan's eyes. "Do you smoke the weed?"

Megan couldn't stop her chuckle. "No Gram, I don't smoke *the* weed. And contrary to what Mom thinks, I don't hug trees even if I do try to save them in the Amazon." She lifted her eyebrows and dared her mother to press the issue.

Surprisingly, her mother ignored the taunt and picked at her own salad. When the waitress came to take away their empty plates, Megan ordered a slice of cheesecake, but her mother insisted they were running behind schedule and there wouldn't be time for her to eat it. In a burst of defiance, Megan ordered it to go and told the waitress to put it on a separate bill so her mother couldn't use the cost against her later.

Now here Megan sat, in the back seat of her mother's Lincoln, eating her cheesecake with a plastic fork, offering bites to her grandmother who was in the front passenger seat.

"Don't get any crumbs on that seat, Megan Nicole," her mother said in a tight voice. "I just had the car detailed two days ago."

"I'm not five years old, Mom," Megan said as she took a bite, a tiny piece falling off her fork and onto the seat. Megan glanced up at the rearview mirror to see if her mother had noticed, while brushing away the crumb. Rather than helping, her maneuver smeared the creamy filling across the leather.

Oh, crap.

She dug a tissue out of her purse, trying not to giggle.

She was in brighter spirits when her mother pulled up to the bridal shop. Libby was standing on the sidewalk waiting for them.

Megan gave her a tight hug. "I love you, Libs!"

"You owe me drinks later for putting up with Knickers twice within less than twenty-four hours," she whispered in Megan's ear.

"Deal."

They went into shop, Gram's outfit drawing looks from other shoppers at the strip mall as she shuffled to the door She wore a red sequined vest over a black t-shirt with the words "Momma's Home Boys" printed in a sparkly red. Her black capris and red flats completed the outfit. When one middle-aged man's jaw dropped, Gram winked and said, "Give me your number and I'll set up a naked yoga session with you."

Megan's mother hustled her into the bridal shop and immediately took charge, going up to the counter and announcing they had arrived for their one-thirty fitting. The clerk took them to a viewing area and told them to have a seat.

After Megan's mother got Gram situated in an overstuffed chair, she glanced at Megan and Libby, then at the door. "Where's Blair?"

Megan suppressed a sigh. "She couldn't get off work." She'd known better than to ask.

"What?" her mother screeched.

"She has a very important job, Mother. She's a big-deal attorney."

Her mother scowled. "This takes precedence."

"I'm sure the woman whose cheating husband tried to steal her house out from under her thinks differently."

Libby sat up straighter. "I'm going to see Blair tonight, so I told her I'd pick up her dress, Mrs. Vandemeer."

"What if it needs additional alterations?"

Libby waved her hand as though it were a non-issue. "She'll be fine."

To Megan, it was obvious Libby's bright smile was forced, but her mother didn't seem to notice. "Well, let's hope so. I'd hate to see Megan's wedding ruined over an ill-fitting bridesmaid dress."

Libby started to giggle, but Megan stomped on her foot to shut her up. Of course, she knew what Libby was thinking. The dress was the least of Knickers' concerns at this point.

The employee emerged from the back, her face beaming. "Your dresses are in the dressing rooms. If you'll follow me…"

Libby went into a room by herself while the employee followed Megan into the larger dressing room.

"Did you bring the proper undergarments?"

Megan opened her purse and pulled out the bag with the strapless bra. Her mother had given it to her before they got to the store, presuming she'd forget one. It annoyed Megan that Knickers was right, even though there was a reason for it—Megan had packed thinking she wouldn't need one.

Once she had her bra on, the employee handed her a crinoline slip and Megan hooked the side, staring in the mirror in confusion. "I didn't think my slip was this full."

"This was the one purchased."

Megan let it go. She had bought the dress eight months ago, maybe she'd forgotten.

The woman unzipped a bag and told Megan to lift her arms so she could put the dress over her head. "But face the wall first. I want you to turn and look in the mirror, so you can get the full effect."

Megan did as she was told, surprised that the dress felt much heavier than she remembered. When she turned to face the mirror, she realized why.

"This isn't my dress."

The employee's eyes widened in fear. "I'm sorry, Ms. Vandemeer. I'm afraid it is."

What did that mean? "No. It most certainly is not." Megan's voice was firm as she took in the ballgown-style dress covered in silk fabric roses and a half a million crystals. It looked like fairies had puked all over it.

"Let me try to get this zipped up and I'll check on it." The woman sounded panicked as she fought the zipper. "If you could take a deep breath."

Megan took a deep breath as the woman continued to struggle behind her. "I look just like Cinderella gone wrong." Then it hit her. Surely, her mother didn't… "What size is this dress?"

"A six."

Megan picked up the skirt in her hands, ready for war. "Open the door."

The woman held it open, looking like she wanted to crawl under a chair as Megan stormed out into the viewing area.

"Oh!" her mother squealed when Megan emerged. "The dress is gorgeous!"

Gram, who'd leaned her head back in the chair, let out a soft snore.

Libby stood on the small stage, her eyes alight with horror, although Megan wasn't sure which dress had induced that reaction. Her friend was wearing a pale pink ballgown with a full crinoline skirt.

"What are these?" Megan asked, dropping the skirt with one hand and waving between Libby and herself.

Her mother looked surprised by her question. "Your dresses."

"But these aren't the dresses we ordered!"

Gram jerked awake. "What did I miss?"

Her mother shook her head in confusion. "I *told* you I decided to have a princess theme."

"You said that was for the decorations!"

"I presumed you realized it meant your dress as well." She narrowed her eyes. "Turn around. Why isn't your dress zipped all the way?"

"Maybe because you ordered a size smaller than I actually wear!"

Her mother looked exasperated. "Most brides diet before their weddings, Megan!"

"Well, I'm not getting married!" Megan shouted.

As if on a puppeteer's orders, their mouths dropped open in shock.

"What?" her mother asked.

Libby rushed toward Megan and hugged her arm. "She meant she's not getting married in this dress."

But Megan was done. The dress was the last straw. "No, Mom. That's not it at all."

Libby tugged on Megan's arm and pulled her toward the dressing rooms.

Megan resisted. "No, it's time to tell her the truth."

A cell phone rang and Megan's mother rolled her eyes and reached into her purse. "I don't have time for hysterics. Libby, try to talk some sense into her while I take this call from the caterer." She stood and walked out the front door.

"Megan, I really need to talk to you," Libby said in a low, insistent voice.

Gram, who had been taking in the whole scene like it was prime-time reality-TV drama, watched them intently, but didn't say a word.

Libby tugged again and Megan let her drag her into a large fitting room at the back of the store, where there were a couple of chairs and a full-length, three-paned mirror.

"What are you doing?" Libby whisper-shouted.

"I'm doing what I should have done in the first place. It's time to tell her the truth."

Libby stood in front of her, blocking her path. "Stop, Megan. Think this through."

"That's exactly what I should have done yesterday afternoon when I woke up with a fake fiancé." Megan leaned into Libby's face. "I can't believe I'm in the middle of this!"

"I know. I know," Libby said, rubbing her arm in a soothing gesture.

Megan sank into a chair, her massive skirt flopping up in her face. "She canceled my dress, Libby. My beautiful dress."

Libby sat in the chair next to her, shoving Megan's massive crinoline pile out of the way. "I know. I'm sorry."

"That's the only thing I wanted out of this wedding. This thing's about to swallow me whole and suffocate me."

"Megan, I shouldn't have to say this, but that's a pretty sad statement—your dress being the only thing you wanted, I mean, not the fact that this new dress is suffocating you. Although that's pretty bad in and of itself." Libby shook her head, her rich, dark waves rustling against her taffeta bodice. "You shouldn't have agreed to marry what's-his-name if you weren't excited about it."

She closed her eyes. "I know."

"What were you thinking, anyway? He was a total jerkwad."

"I don't know about that."

"That's a lie and we both know it."

Megan leaned her head back against the top of the seat. "It doesn't matter anyway. What do I do now?"

"What do you want to do?"

"I suppose I should tell Mom what's really going on." She sat up again. "She might actually kill me. If so, you can have my granddad's old cameras."

Her eyes lit up with excitement. "Including the old Brownie?"

"Yep. That one too."

Libby seemed to think about her answer before responding—perhaps trying to decide whether letting Knickers kill Megan was worth the vintage camera—but when she finally answered, she sounded more cheerful. "Honestly, Megs, at this point what does it matter if you tell her now or if you wait for Josh to break up with you tonight?"

Megan looked at her friend, her face blurry through her tears. "Because it's dishonest."

Libby took Megan's hands in hers. "And Knickers was dishonest when she changed our dresses. Can you imagine if you were actually getting married and we had to wear these things?"

Megan shook her head and laughed wryly. "No. I can't."

"So we just accept what she did with the dresses, and I'll tell Knickers you're coming with me. We'll get a drink to help you prepare for tonight. It's your big Vandemeer family reunion, right?"

"Yeah," Megan said in surprise. "How did you know?"

"Knickers Fed-Exed the itineraries to Blair and me."

"*Of course* she did." Megan smiled in spite of herself.

"Follow the path of least resistance. Let Josh break up with you later. You'll be the victim instead of the party pooper."

"Party pooper?" Megan cocked her head. "*Really?*"

"This wedding is a twenty-five-thousand-dollar party, isn't it?"

Megan groaned. "Don't remind me. In fact, she's added so many embellishments since last fall, it's probably double that by now."

When she and Libby reemerged in the viewing room, Megan's mother had returned, and was grumbling something about chicken.

"Is it free-range chicken?" Gram asked.

Megan's mother scrunched her nose in confusion. "I don't know."

"I saw a special report on one of those news shows the other day, and now I'll only eat free-range chicken. They pump those other birds full of hormones. I've been eating a lot of chicken lately and I woke up with a hot flash the other night."

"That explains something about Gram's libido," Libby said under her breath.

"Mom—" Megan's mother clenched her jaw, "—for the tenth time, it wasn't a hot flash. Someone accidently turned the air conditioner off."

"Well, I'm still only eating free-range birds. Are they free range?"

Megan's mother waved her hand. "Yes, it's free-range chicken. They're arriving from Wyoming tomorrow, then checking into their hotel rooms later."

Megan about fell over. Her mother made a joke!

Gram smiled. After spending all day with the older woman, Megan knew her game. Gram wasn't senile—not even a bit. She was egging Knickers on.

They got back to the task at hand. Libby's dress fit, so she disappeared to remove it while Megan's mother tried to convince the alterations person to finish altering the dress before the next morning. At first the store employee claimed it wouldn't be possible, but Nicole got her way the same way she usually did—by bullying everyone around her. Finally, the girl promised that the dress would be ready by noon the next day.

Guilt flooded through Megan as she watched the exchange. She didn't feel too bad about inconveniencing her mother, but the employee was obviously going to have to put in some overtime to accommodate her mother's demands. She started to say something, but Libby put her hand on Megan's arm, stopping her. With lips pursed together, she slowly shook her head.

Remarkably, Knickers didn't protest when Megan announced she was leaving with Libby. "I had hoped to get your hair done today, but they can't fit you in until tomorrow. So go have some fun."

Megan gaped at her for a moment, then took off before her mother changed her mind. Gram gave the two younger women a longing look as they headed to Libby's car.

"Just remember to be home by five, Megan," her mother called after her.

Megan felt amazingly free and lighthearted as Libby drove away in her Volkswagen convertible. But instead of going out for a drink, Megan suggested they go shopping. She hadn't planned to attend any wedding festivities, so she'd brought the bare minimum in terms of dress clothes.

A few hours later Libby pulled into the driveway and stared at the house. "Do you think Josh is back?"

Megan gave her a look of surprise. "I guess not. Dad's car

isn't in the driveway." She'd been thinking about him all day, though she wasn't about to admit she was disappointed he wasn't back yet. If he was breaking up with her tonight, they only had a few more hours together. She couldn't bear to think about it.

"Do you think Knickers would have a fit if I come in and hang out for awhile?"

"I think she'll get over it," Megan said cautiously. "Why?"

"Do I have to have a reason? I miss you. I haven't seen you since last fall…and before that it had been two years."

"Sorry. Of course you can come in. Blair's just made me paranoid, I guess."

"Unlike Blair, I approve of Mr. Sexy in a Pair of Jeans."

Megan saw the curtain in the living room window shift. "I don't think we can get away with sitting in your car until Josh shows up, which means we better go in." Megan reached for the door handle. "I'm sure Mom's got something for me to do."

They walked through the front door and stopped in their tracks. Sitting on the sofa was a very good-looking stranger. He smiled as they came inside and gave Libby a once-over. *Typical.* Gram sat next to him, giving him a goofy grin.

Oh, Lord. Gram was smitten.

But then, Megan could see why. He had thick dark brown hair and dark eyes that sparkled with the promise of trouble. Who was this guy?

"Megan." Her mother was settled in the armchair next to the sofa. "I've been trying to call you for an hour."

Megan glanced down at her purse, then back at her mother. "Oh. I think my phone died." She gave the man a second look and scrunched her nose as she tried to place him. There was something vaguely familiar about him. Maybe his eyes? He couldn't be a cousin, could he?

"Why didn't you tell me Josh's brother was coming after

all?" her mother asked, her voice thick with irritation. She hated surprises.

But Megan was more surprised than any of them.

"What?" Megan took a step back and bumped into Libby's chest.

The man stood and took a step toward her, offering his hand. "I'm Josh's brother, Noah. It's great to finally meet you, Megan. He's told me so much about you."

She took his hand, still in shock. But as she studied his face, she saw the resemblance. This man was related to Josh, all right. But how had he gotten here? And why?

He dropped Megan's hand and Libby offered hers. "Hi, I'm Libby. Megan's friend."

His mouth spread into an appreciative grin and he held her hand longer than necessary. "My brother most certainly hasn't told me about Megan's friend Libby."

Megan's head cleared enough for her to try and figure out what was going on. She cast a glance at her clueless mother. "Josh didn't mention you had changed your mind about coming." Her eyes bored into his, but he simply smiled, completely unintimidated. Damn, he was good.

"It was a spur-of-the-moment decision."

"And it's a good thing," Megan's mother said. "Josh's side of the church is going to be abysmally bare."

Noah shot Libby an ornery grin. "My job is to fill up one whole side of the church and have a little fun."

Libby graced him with one of her sexiest smiles.

Someone was going to have to take a hose to the two of them, but she needed to deal with the bigger emergency first.

"We'll have to figure out a way to include Noah in the wedding, of course." Megan's mother glared at her. "Really, Megan. A little advance notice would have been nice."

Megan held her hands out at her sides. "I didn't know he was coming. I didn't even know he knew where Josh was!"

Her mother looked taken back. "What do you mean he didn't know where Josh was? Why wouldn't he?"

Noah sidled up next to her and slung an arm around her shoulders. "That's cute, sis."

Her eyes flew open. "Sis?"

"Once you and Joshy are married…" His words trailed off, then he turned to her mother. "What Megster meant was that I didn't know he'd be with Bart at the office. Isn't that right, Megster?"

She gritted her teeth. "Yeah. That's right."

Knickers tsked. "I hope we can get you a tux with this short notice. I better call the rental store." She stood and moved to the kitchen. "If you'll excuse me."

Megan's eyes narrowed and she was about to let loose a string of questions, peppered liberally with expletives, when she remembered her grandmother still on the sofa, hanging on to their every word.

"You look shocked," Noah teased. "I hope you don't mind me coming to my brother's wedding." He glanced over his shoulder at Gram and winked.

"I like this one," Gram said, nodding her head. "Since you get Josh, I want to keep him."

"He's not staying, Gram," Megan said with a sigh.

Megan's mother emerged from the kitchen with the phone in her hand. "Of course Noah is staying at the house. Where would you have him go, Megan?"

That wasn't what Megan meant, but now that her mother brought it up, the idea horrified her. He couldn't stay in their house. In fact, she couldn't think of one good reason for him to be here at all. "Is Josh expecting you?" Megan forced out, trying to hide her panic.

Noah gave a nonchalant shrug and a cocky grin. "Nah, I thought I'd surprise him. I suspect he'll be beside himself." He turned to Megan's mother. "With happiness, of course. I told him I couldn't come, but hey—he's my little brother. I can't let him get married without me standing there beside him."

So he was one of those guys—the kind who thought he could show his mega-watt grin and every human with double X chromosomes would fall at his feet. Megan had met plenty of guys like Noah and she wasn't impressed. But that wasn't the real issue… What was his end game? Was he here to embarrass Josh?

Libby, on the other hand, appeared to fall for his schlocky charm. "And what a lovely surprise it is." She shot Megan a side glance that told her Libby planned to use her own methods of persuasion to get answers, which filled Megan with relief.

"I like surprises," Gram chimed in.

Since Libby was playing the role of her bowled-over-by-a-sexy-smile friend, it was the three of them against Megan. Was she the only sane one left? Then she remembered that she was the only one in the room who was pretending to be engaged to a stranger.

They were all doomed.

"Do we know when Dad will be home with Josh?" Megan asked.

"He said he would be home by five. There's some big to-do at the office about some silly patent," her mother waved her hand, "or some such nonsense. But I made him promise to be home in time to set up for the dinner."

"That's exciting." Noah's smile widened—as if that were even possible. "A patent, you say?"

"I told Bart there wasn't time for him to fool around and get excited over a tiny piece of metal. His daughter's getting married."

Noah nodded. "Priorities. Family takes precedence over everything and everyone, don't you think?"

Nicole's eyes softened. "Yes, I know exactly what you

mean, even if…" She forced a smile. "I'm so glad you came, Noah."

"I am too, Mrs. Vandemeer," he said, matching her serious tone. "I wouldn't miss this for the world."

"What's the theme tonight, Mrs. Vandemeer?" Libby asked, trying to keep a straight face.

A scowl almost wrinkled Nicole's Botoxed forehead. "It's Hillbilly. Red-and-white checkered tablecloths. Banjos. You know."

Noah's eyebrows shot up in surprise and amusement.

Megan groaned. "*Mom*, Dad's family is from *Springfield*, Missouri. That hardly makes them *hillbillies*."

Her mother looked unswayed.

"Does that mean I should have brought my overalls?" Noah asked, grinning. "I've never been to a hoedown before."

Megan could barely tolerate her mother disrespecting her father's family; she definitely wasn't going to take it from the strange man who had just barged into her parents' house without an invitation. "Do you actually have a pair?" Megan countered, pinning him with a scrutinizing gaze. "You don't exactly look like the type of guy who would willingly get dirty enough to need a pair of overalls."

"Megan!" her mother reprimanded. "What has gotten into you?"

Megan bit back a retort. "Nothing." She squinted at Noah. "I just *really* need to talk to Josh."

And he was going to get quite an earful indeed.

Chapter Fourteen

Josh knew he was in deep shit. In more ways than he could count.

For one thing, he'd spent the entire day pretending not to know anything about engineering at Bart Vandemeer's firm—a feat given that it was the field to which he'd devoted his entire adult life—and he was walking away with bupkis. Sure, everyone in the firm was excited over the recently granted patent—*his* patent—but whenever he asked questions about it, they treated him like a kindergartener who couldn't possibly understand anything beyond 1+1=2. Josh would have found it insulting even if he *were* an investment banker. Noah might have been able to sneak around or seduce the info out of the cute twenty-something receptionist or some other 007 scheme, but Josh was out of his league. He'd wasted the day.

And to top it off, Noah had texted Josh to tell him that Megan was pissed about finding him on her mother's sofa. Noah knew how pivotal it was for Josh to remain in Bart

Vandemeer's good graces. It was their best and only chance to get the information they needed to save their relationship with their investor. Thankfully, Noah had stuck to the plan, telling her that Josh had no idea he was coming, but apparently he hadn't gotten the chance to pull her aside and tell her why he was there. When Josh got no response to the three texts he sent asking Noah what he'd *planned* to tell her, he knew he was on his own. But she had to wonder why Noah would show up unannounced on her doorstep. What possible explanation could there be that wasn't incredibly sketchy?

He had a lot of smoothing over to do.

The patent celebration had caused them to leave the office late and Bart still needed to pick up the food for the family dinner. Using his brother's arrival as an excuse, Josh talked Bart into dropping him off at the house before making his restaurant run.

Josh watched Bart drive off, wondering if he should have stuck to the plan and arrived later. Then he wouldn't need to face Megan yet. But avoiding conflict had never been Josh's style. He met it head on. That's why this whole situation was so atypical for him. But then again, he'd never had so much to lose. The thought momentarily floored him. Losing his business or losing Megan—which bothered him the most?

Before he could reason it out, the front door swung open and Knickers greeted him in the doorway. "Josh! I'm so thrilled your brother could join us."

At least someone was happy about it. "Yes! I was shocked when he texted to say he was not only here in Kansas City, but at your house. I hope he hasn't been an imposition."

"Of course not. He's your brother. You should have family here."

He walked through Megan's parents' front door, preparing himself to face Megan's wrath, but she wasn't in the living room and he didn't see her in the kitchen either. Noah, on the other hand, was sitting at the island drinking what looked like lemonade while talking to Megan's grandmother, who—thank God—was fully clothed.

Gram glanced up at Josh and shot him a grin. "You're off the hook, Josh. Noah has agreed to pose as my nude model."

Megan's mother walked through the back door, rolling her eyes. "No one's posing nude."

Noah winked at Gram and gave her a knowing nod.

"How was your day, Josh?" Nicole asked, giving him a sweet smile. Josh was sure that wasn't an adjective normally associated with Mrs. Vandemeer, but he planned to use her temporary approval to his advantage.

"It was great, but I'm eager to see Megan."

"She's upstairs with Libby, getting ready for the dinner."

"I'll run up and check on her."

Noah shot him a glance that conveyed *good luck*.

Josh bounded up the stairs, but his steps slowed as he neared the top. He'd spent most of the day frustrated by his lack of progress, and the only thing getting him through his utter failure was the knowledge he'd see Megan at the end of the day. Granted, they were supposed to break up tonight, but maybe he could talk her out of it. The fact that she seemed to like him improved his chances. Of course, the wedding was in less than forty-eight hours, so any kind of breakup would have to happen soon, but he'd felt pretty confident he could convince her to wait until tomorrow. But now he was nervous. Any points he'd gained, he'd lost now that his brother had made an uninvited entrance.

Damn it. Why hadn't he thought this through?

The thought of her kicking him out the door made him more upset than he cared to admit. He was in a very awkward situation, with no discernable plan, but he knew one thing: Every time he thought about seeing Megan, he felt happiness blooming in his chest—a sense of peace and fulfillment he hadn't experienced since his father's death.

What in the hell was he going to do?

First thing first—he had to deal with this crisis. He knocked on the door and called out softly, "Megan?"

The door cracked and Libby's face filled the opening. She grimaced at the sight of him.

"That bad?" he whispered.

"Worse." She swung the door open wider and stepped out of the way. "She's in the bathroom, but she's decent."

"Okay." He started toward it, but Libby grabbed his arm.

"She likes you, Josh. Fight for her."

Libby's trust in him added to his guilt, but he needed her as an ally. Which meant pretending his only motive was to make a relationship work with Megan. "Thanks, Libby."

"I'm going downstairs to talk to your brother."

"He's busy flirting with Megan's grandmother."

She laughed as she slipped into the hallway. "Then maybe we can share him."

"Libby." He followed her into the hall, closing the door behind him. "Regarding my brother…" He didn't want to ring any alarm bells, but he genuinely liked Libby and didn't want to see her get hurt. Noah always left behind a string of broken hearts; it was his MO. "Let's just say he's here for the wedding, then he'll be gone."

She stopped and turned around to face him, her face softening. "You're something else, Josh, you know that?"

He froze, unsure of what she meant.

Her face lit up with amusement. "You're really sweet to be worried about me, but I'm a big girl, and I've fooled around with my share of guys like your brother. If I decide I'm interested, I know what I'm getting into." Then her eyes turned serious. "But Megan's different than Blair and me. She wears her heart on her sleeve and a lot of people take advantage of it." She stepped closer, an unfamiliar look filling her eyes. "I'd rather not go there, but let's just say if Blair's right and you're really here to hurt her, you'll find out that Blair isn't the only one with claws."

He resisted the urge to swallow, which he was sure would make him look guilty. Instead, he spread his hands wide and gave her a gentle smile, lifting his eyebrows to assert his sincerity. "Libby, I will do everything in my power to help her." Not a lie, but not the complete truth either.

She studied him for a second, then that strange glint in her eyes disappeared and her soft smile returned. "Yeah, I think you will."

He reached for the doorknob and let himself back into the bedroom. After closing the door behind him, he studied the bathroom door, struggling with what to say.

The bathroom door opened and Megan stood in the opening, wearing a white sleeveless dress dotted with tiny pink and blue flowers, her dark hair tumbling over her shoulders. Even if he'd had a perfectly planned-out speech, it wouldn't have helped him. He was struck dumb by the sight of her natural beauty. She wasn't made up with lots of makeup and fancy clothes, although he had no doubt that she'd be beautiful that way too. She was the kind of woman who was beautiful no matter what she was wearing. And in that moment, he knew he was struck with a strange certainty: he might actually want to marry this woman someday.

Where the hell had that come from?

But more importantly, what the hell did he do with that, with the knowledge that he had less than forty-eight hours with her? Because fake fiancé aside, once she knew the details of his little business problem, they would be done. And for him to give up his quest was impossible. What he was doing went beyond him personally. His employees were counting on him.

He would have to make the most of the time he had with her. If they survived this part, anyway.

Irritation was written across her face and he braced himself. He needed to stop drooling over her and put out this fire.

She pointed to the door, anger darkening her eyes. "I don't know who is down there in my mother's kitchen, but you have some explaining to do."

He lifted his hands in surrender. "Just give me a chance."

She crossed her arms and glared at him. "Is he even your brother?"

"Yes, that's Noah, my brother who Blair talked to last night."

"What is he doing here?"

Josh sighed and motioned to the bed. "Can we sit down while I explain it?"

She glanced at the bed, seemingly unsure, wrapping her arms tighter around her torso.

He sat tentatively on the edge. "I didn't ask him to come."

"Then why is he here?"

"He knew I was coming to Kansas City…" *Dammit.* He got to his feet and began pacing. Why had he been stupid enough to believe that Noah, who'd gotten him into this situation in the first place, could help? "He's worried about me."

She pointed her finger at him. "That's a bullshit answer!"

"Megan, I'm sorry! I didn't ask him to come." When she didn't interrupt him, he continued. "He knew I was coming to Kansas City and when we spoke last night he asked me where I was staying."

"And you *told* him?"

He ran a hand through his hair. Shit. This whole trip had been one ill-thought-out decision after another, which was the exact opposite of the precedent Josh liked to set for himself. No wonder he was floundering. "He didn't want me to come to Kansas City this weekend. Like I said, he was worried about me."

"Let's go back to the part where you told him you were

here!"

Josh sat back down and leaned his elbows on his knees. He looked up at her, pleading. "I told him that I was helping you. He wanted to know *how* exactly I was helping you—"

"I bet he did," she said sarcastically.

"—so I told him you were in a desperate situation."

"You *told* him that you were posing as my fiancé?"

He nodded, unable to look her in the eye. "Yeah. I'm sorry."

"Didn't he want to know why you were helping me?"

"Yeah."

"*And?*"

He took a deep breath, then looked up at her. He needed to tell her the truth. Or at least the part of it that directly impacted her. "Look, I wasn't lying when I said I never meant for this to happen. Your mother heard me say I was your fiancé. I wasn't myself…you saw me on the plane when I boarded. So when your mother assumed I was Jay, she swept me along in her cloud of…Knickers-ness… Well, the next thing I knew, I was still carrying you and we had wandered to baggage claim. How could I correct her at that point? I was in dire straits with my business, and like I told you, I'd decided to hand it all to fate, so I figured if I did a good deed, the cosmos would do one for me in return. Stupid, I know."

She turned to the side and he could feel that he was losing her. "Megan, this isn't coming out right." He groaned in frustration, then stood and moved in front of her. "When I decided to go through with this, I admit I did it for selfish reasons, but then I got to know you." He slowly lifted his hands and placed them gently on her upper arms. "As stupid as this sounds, I like you. Like *really* like you. I've never fallen for someone this quickly, and while it kind of freaks me out, I'm not ready to end this yet. At least not like this."

She looked up at him, still defensive. "You're doing all of

this because you *like* me?" She took a step back, her arms dropping to her sides. "That's not a reason."

He stopped in front of her, lifting a hand to the side of her face. "It's the oldest reason under the sun."

Her body relaxed and she pressed her cheek into his palm.

Encouraged, he lowered his head, his lips hovering over hers. His tongue ran along her lower lip, and her breath was hot on his face. "Boy meets girl. Boy likes girl. Boy does anything he can to impress girl."

She lifted her face and pressed her lips to his.

He wrapped an arm around her back and pulled her against his chest. Before he even registered what he was doing, his tongue parted her lips and plunged into her mouth as she opened to him, so lush and soft and… Her hands lifted to his head and she held him firmly against her mouth, bringing their kiss deeper. Wanting to be even closer, he tangled one hand in her soft thick hair.

It took him a couple of seconds to realize someone was knocking on the door. He dragged his mouth from hers, lifting his head as he tried to gather his senses.

"Megan," her mother called out as she knocked again. "We need you downstairs."

She groaned and closed her eyes. "I'll be right there."

"Don't dawdle like you usually do."

His hand was still in her hair, holding her inches from his face. She opened her eyes and looked up at him, her gaze dreamy. "What is this, Josh?"

He gave her a lopsided grin. "What? You've never made out before?"

"You know that's not what I meant."

"I thought I was demonstrating the lengths to which I'd go to impress you."

"Or distract me."

"Megan." His hold loosened, but he still held her close,

unwilling to let go of her just yet. "My brother is here to check up on me—and probably you, just like how Blair threatened to determine if I'm circumcised or not." He shot her another grin. When she didn't stop him, he pushed on. "He's my big brother. He's worried."

"He looks like the type of guy who's only worried about himself."

Ordinarily, he'd applaud her accurate character assessment, but not tonight. "He might appear that way, but deep down, Noah cares about me." Or at least, Josh liked to believe he did.

"We need to break up tonight," she whispered.

"But I don't want to break up with you tonight." His mouth lowered to hers again. "I want to do the exact opposite of breaking up with you tonight."

She leaned back, but stopped short of pulling out of his arms. "We are the bride and groom in a very real wedding that is taking place in two days, Josh. We *have* to break up…and very publicly, at that."

She was right. He knew it. As much as he hated to admit it. But not tonight. "Let's just play it by ear."

"We have to do this tonight, Josh. It's going to be a nightmare to cancel everything now. If we wait until tomorrow…"

"You're right." He dropped his arms. "But it has to be natural. And let me take the lead. I'll act like a jerk, so when we break up, no one will ever question why the wedding got called off. You have to come off smelling like a rose." He almost felt guilty deceiving her, but he took solace in the fact that even if his spying job was done, he still wouldn't want to break up with her. "No matter what, do not yell at me. Be the reasonable one."

She studied his shirt for several seconds before nodding. Then she looked up into his face. "And then what?"

What did she want to hear? That they could go back to

Seattle together and date? Was that really possible given that her family knew him as Jay instead of Josh McMillan? They weren't likely to approve of the pairing if they found out that he'd strung them along, particularly given how much money they were throwing down for this whole wedding. That wasn't even factoring in the whole patent mess.

"Then we'll take it one minute at a time."

Chapter Fifteen

Several hours later, Megan was furious with him, and not without cause. For one thing, Noah had been glued to Libby all night, which frankly had both of them concerned. Noah never hooked up with a girl without a purpose other than sex, but he wasn't flirting like mad with her either. What could possibly be his goal this time? He wasn't going to get any information about the patent from Libby. The most he could hope for was to get intel on Megan. And what would he want with information about *her?*

But the main reason for her mood was because he was being a *very* attentive boyfriend—getting her food and drinks, joining in conversations, making sure she was comfortable. Megan's family loved him. Most women wouldn't find fault in that—in fact, they'd revel in it—but Josh was supposed to be paving the way to their breakup. And after Josh's behavior over the last couple of hours, the only person at the family dinner expecting that outcome was Megan.

Josh had spent most of the day dreading tonight's dinner, but it was exactly the opposite of what he'd expected. Josh genuinely enjoyed hanging out with Bart Vandemeer's huge family. They were down to earth and fun, the complete opposite of Nicole Vandemeer and her friends. It made Josh wonder why Bart had chosen to marry her.

The first hour was so fun he'd completely forgotten he was supposed to be laying the groundwork for the breakup he planned to initiate. But even after realizing his mistake, he was in too good of a mood to play the part, even just enough to appease Megan, which had been his original plan.

He was having a conversation with her Uncle Jeremy about the best fishing places at Table Rock Lake when Megan wrapped her hand around his lower forearm, her nails digging into his flesh.

"Can I talk to you?" She tried to keep her tone sweet, but he heard the annoyed hitch in her voice.

"Uncle Jeremy was inviting me to come fishing with him this fall," he said with a smile, ignoring the pain in his arm.

"Yeah, I heard, but I need help with the…thing."

"What thing?" her uncle asked.

Her eyes widened in panic; she obviously hadn't expected her ploy to be questioned.

A slow smile spread across Josh's face. "I've been summoned." He gave her uncle a wink. "Never tell a beautiful woman no when she wants to get you alone. Am I right?"

Her uncle chuckled. "Smart man you've got there, Megan."

"I'm beginning to wonder," she grumbled as he stood and took her hand in his.

He leaned close to her ear and whispered loud enough for her uncle to hear, "Just where did you have in mind?"

She jerked on his hand. He stumbled slightly but contained his amusement. God, was she cute when she was pissed. But he kept his thoughts to himself and followed her through the kitchen and down the stairs to the basement.

Why hadn't he thought to check the basement rather than his botched attempt to find her father's home office? After all, what better place to stow things best left forgotten?

But he didn't have time to look around once they reached the bottom of the stairs. "Your bedroom probably has a better atmosphere for a romantic rendezvous than your parents' musty basement."

"I did not bring you down here to make out!"

"From the look on your face, you brought me down here to murder me. But I caution you to think it through. It would be difficult to hide my body, and I think Libby's too busy with Noah to help."

"Why is your brother flirting with my best friend?"

"She's a beautiful woman, Megan." He put his hands on her hips and pulled her closer. "But not nearly as beautiful as you."

"Cut the bullshit, Josh."

"I really do think you're beautiful—" his voice lost its teasing tone, "—and I don't know why Noah is so taken with Libby, but she seems like a smart girl. She can handle herself."

She jerked up her head to look him in the eye. "What's that supposed to mean?"

"It means my brother is not a one-woman kind of guy, but when Libby made it obvious she was interested in him, I mentioned that fact to her. She told me not to worry. She knew what he was."

Her eyes narrowed to slits. "When did you talk to Libby about your brother?"

"After I came home this evening and went upstairs to find you. Libby was in your room. You were in the bathroom."

"Hmm."

He was still holding her close, resisting the urge to kiss her. Although he suspected it would distract her from the next topic she was sure to bring up, he didn't want to play her that way.

"What are you doing, Josh?"

"I'm standing in your basement, waiting to see if you're going to murder me or not." He made a show of spinning his head to take it in. "I'm surprised it's unfinished. And that your mother didn't ask your father to set up his man cave down here rather than upstairs."

"You can't change the subject. Why aren't you trying to break up with me like we discussed?"

"You haven't given me much opportunity."

She pulled out of his grasp. "We've been out there for two hours!""

"Really?" he asked in what he hoped was believable surprise. "I guess I was too busy having a good time. I like your dad's family."

She shook her head, as though trying to clear her confusion. "I like my dad's family too, but you have to stick to the plan."

"What do you want me to do?" he asked, spreading his hands. "I've never purposely acted like an asshole before." She snorted and he gave her a look of surprise. "Are you suggesting I'm a natural asshole?"

"No… I don't know." She scowled. "But we have to do something, Josh. We have to end this tonight. This is getting bad."

"I know. You're right. How about I start drinking a lot and then I can act like a sloppy drunk, giving you a good reason to break up with me."

She pursed her lips, deep in thought, before nodding and looking up at him. "Yeah. That's good. If you just start acting like a jerk now, my family will wonder why you're like Dr. Jekyll and Mr. Hyde."

"Okay, so I'll start getting drunk. Let's get to it." He took her hand, surprised when she didn't protest, and led her up the stairs. When they were in the kitchen, he stopped and dropped his hold on her. "But first I need to visit the restroom before I go back outside." He patted his stomach. "That pulled pork isn't quite agreeing with me."

The look she gave him said she didn't quite trust him, but the request was too reasonable for her to deny.

"You don't have to wait for me. In fact, it might be safer for me to go upstairs." He grimaced.

She released a nervous laugh. "Don't let Dad hear you say that. He loves Gate's barbeque. He'd call that blasphemy."

"From all the dogs barking outside your fence, I'd say they like it too." The sound seemed almost appropriate given the laid-back vibe of the evening, but he knew it had to be driving Nicole crazy.

A sly grin spread across her face. "Those are the Murphys' dogs. Mom is furious they got loose. In fact, she called animal control, but apparently they haven't shown up yet."

"You really do take a perverse pleasure at your mother's aggravation."

She laughed. "I guess that makes me wicked."

He liked the thought of her doing wicked things, but not the kind she currently had in mind.

"You go on back outside," Josh said, heading for the stairs. "I'll be out as soon as I'm fit to be seen in public." He bounded up the stairs two at a time in his attempt to get away from her. He wasn't so sure how convincing his gastrointestinal issue was, but he had to talk to Noah. And maybe he could find Bart's home office while he was upstairs.

He opened the first room on his right, finding what appeared to be Kevin's room. Eliminating Megan's and her grandmother's rooms, that left one possibility. He pushed open the door, relieved to find a desk with a desktop computer and a credenza and printer. Pulling out his phone, he texted his brother. *I found Vandemeer's home office.*

Seconds later Noah responded. *I found it first. I'm sleeping there, Sherlock.* Josh could practically hear his sarcasm.

Sure enough, there was a bag on the loveseat on the wall opposite the desk. *Have you checked it yet?*

Not thoroughly, but I have all night. As long as you don't screw this up now.

Josh released a heavy breath. *She wants me to break up with her tonight.*

Obviously you can't. Figure something out.

Figure something out. Sure, no problem.

He went back downstairs and grabbed a bottle of beer from the cooler by the back door, taking a long drag from it before he searched for Megan. She was standing with a group of her cousins and aunts. She looked nervous, and he hated the knowledge that he was to blame, but he couldn't give her what he she wanted. Not yet. Now that Noah was here, they could get what they needed to save the business and he'd break up with her tomorrow night at the rehearsal dinner. He could pretend to get drunk tomorrow night, then put the moves on Blair. He almost choked on his beer at the very thought of it, but it was a good plan. Blair would raise holy hell and no one would condone Megan marrying him then.

But he couldn't tell Megan his new plan. He'd drink a lot tonight to pave the way to the big finale tomorrow and figure out a way to appease her in the meantime.

His other problem—how to appease his own hurting heart once she found out what he was about—was entirely his own cross to bear.

He took another draw off the bottle, trying to chase the feeling away. How could he already be so attached to Megan? He hardly knew her, but he knew enough not to want to let her go. He finished off the beer and grabbed another. Fuel for the performance.

Megan turned and saw him, her face momentarily lighting

up…then fading. He lifted his bottle in salute to show her he was on task.

He walked toward her and a black cat shot out from a bush, darting across his path. He stumbled to keep from tripping on it and he was sure it made him look drunk, although anyone who had been paying attention would realize it was far from true. He couldn't face Megan at the moment, so he made his way over to Noah, who was sitting at a small table with Libby. They were deep in conversation and laughing when he sat down across from them.

"What's got you so low?" Noah asked, leaning back in his seat. "You looked like you were having a great night until your fiancée dragged you away. You should be wearing a shit-eating grin right about now."

Josh glared at his brother and took another long drag of his beer.

"Have you thought of a way to keep from breaking up with her?" Noah asked.

Lowering the bottle, Josh cast a glance toward Libby.

She gave him a sympathetic smile. "He knows I'm helping you."

He couldn't contain his look of surprise. What had Noah confessed to?

Noah gave him a conspiratorial grin. "I'm all in, bro. I'll get you to the altar."

"*What?*" Josh asked.

Noah shrugged. "What can I say? I'm a sucker for true love."

Libby snorted. "Liar. You wouldn't know true love if it bit you in the ass."

Josh was relieved that Noah still hadn't fooled her. Many a woman had claimed to go into a relationship with Noah with eyes wide open only to find herself with a broken heart.

Noah shrugged and held out his hands. "Okay, you caught

me. I don't believe in love. I think what people call love is all about hormones and loneliness." He leaned his elbow on the table and waved to his brother as he gave his attention to Libby. "Take Joshua here. He's been so focused on his job that he's barely dated in the last two years."

Josh groaned. "I've dated. I just don't share all the details." He took a drink, then shot his brother a piercing glare. "Unlike someone I know."

Noah chuckled and turned his attention to the pretty brunette sitting next to him. "Like I said. Josh is lonely and he comes to Kansas City in his self-imposed exile, during which he stumbles upon a pretty girl on a plane. Said pretty girl is desperate for rescue and he instantly falls for her."

"Shh!" Josh's eyes flew open in alarm. "Keep it down."

Noah's grin widened as he looked around. "Cool your jets. No one heard."

Josh's chest tightened with anger. He was in this situation because of Noah. And now he was treating Megan's life like it was some sort of game. He was going to fuck her over for his own purposes without thinking twice about it.

No. *Josh* was fucking her over, and he could only imagine how hurt she was going to be when she found out. He had hoped that he could get out of this without her ever finding out. But it seemed pretty unlikely, especially now that Noah was involved. Noah was good for one thing—destroying everything good in Josh's life.

Why had he let him come?

Maybe he should break up with Megan tonight after all, put this farce to rest. Give up on the company. Give up on a real chance with her.

Josh finished off the beer and set the bottle on the table. He started to get up. "I need another."

Noah slapped Josh's shoulder and pushed him back down. "Cheer up there, young lad," he said in a fake British accent.

"I'll get you another pint of ale and all will be well." He stood and the barking dogs against the fence amped up their racket. The black cat Josh had seen earlier was now calmly stalking across the top of the fence.

"Knickers looks like she's about to come unglued," Libby laughed.

Sure enough, Nicole looked furious. She stomped over to her husband, nearly tripping over a cup on the deck, which only infuriated her more. "Bart!" she shouted. "Do something!"

Bart, who had been sitting with his brother on the deck, got to his feet. "What do you want me to do?"

"Make them stop!"

As he passed Bart, Noah pointed to the cat, which was still on the fence, hissing with its back arched. Then Noah grabbed three beers out of the cooler.

Libby watched Noah with more interest than Josh liked. All the more reason to seriously consider changing his tactic. "Megan has insisted I break up with her tonight."

Libby swung her gaze to him, her eyebrows arched. "You're not considering it, are you?"

He sighed. "I don't know, maybe."

She leaned toward him, desperation in her eyes. "You can't."

He rested his palm on the table, the two beers he'd drank within the past five minutes making him feel melancholy rather than buzzed. "She's right, Libby. I'm putting her in an awkward situation. The longer I wait to do this, the harder it will be to cancel everything."

Libby leaned in closer, her face inches from his. "The only person who's going to be negatively affected by canceling the wedding is Knickers. The money's gone whether there's a wedding or not. Don't let that stop you from going after Megan."

"But it's all a lie, Libby."

Her jaw set and determination filled her eyes. "Do you like her?"

"What?"

"It's a simple question. Do you like her?"

"You know I do."

"Then whatever you do, don't break up with her tonight. Wait."

"How long do I wait? Until we're at the altar and the minister says, 'Do you, Jay—what's the fucker's last name again?" The fuzziness in his head held the bastard's name out of reach.

"Connors."

"Jay Connors." The name rolled off Josh's tongue with a sneer. "So the minister says, 'Do you, Jay Connors, take Megan Vandemeer to be your lawfully wedded wife?' and I say… 'Well, about that…did I mention that I'm just her substitute fiancé?'"

She sat back, glancing over at her friend. "It doesn't have to go that far. Just make her realize how much she likes you. Make her admit that she wants this to work."

"She likes me, but what if I can't get her to admit that she does? That I'm worth fighting for?" He took a deep breath and blew it out. "I'm seriously considering giving up *everything* to try to make this work. What if she doesn't feel the same? She's in this situation to keep her mother from blowing her gasket. There's no way we can tell Knickers the truth and come out unscathed."

She didn't respond.

In the end, it didn't matter how Megan felt, not really. His original goal was honorable—saving his employees—but it wasn't worth toying with Megan's life. Maybe he could cash in his barely existent IRA and use it to make a comp package for the employees who'd have the most trouble finding new jobs.

It wasn't the solution he wanted, but he could live with it. If he had to give it all up, though, he wanted to at least enjoy one more day with Megan—twenty-four hours—before he came clean. "Tomorrow night." Saying it out loud helped cement the rightness of his decision. "I'm doing this tomorrow night."

Noah returned and set a bottle of beer in front of him. "What are you doing tomorrow night?"

"Breaking up with Megan."

Noah looked slightly panicked. "Whoa, slow down there, lover boy. What if we haven't accomplished our mission?"

Libby turned a skeptical eye on him. "*What* mission?"

An *oh shit* look crossed Noah's face and Josh groaned. He should have known Noah would screw it up.

Noah rolled his eyes. "Making Megan fall in love with Josh. What the hell else would I be talking about?"

But the seeds of doubt had been planted in Libby's head and she turned her discerning eye on Josh.

Josh picked up his bottle. "Trust me, no one's more surprised by this turn of events than I am."

"So we agree no breaking up tonight, right?" Libby asked.

"I may not have a choice," Josh said, glumly.

Noah was about to protest when Nicole, who was now standing by the edge of the deck, began screaming. "What have you done?"

Three big dogs burst through the back gate, racing for the food table. Everyone started shouting as the dogs jumped onto the deck, snarling over the pans of pork, brisket, baked beans, and coleslaw.

"What are they doing?" Nicole screamed. "Somebody stop them!"

But everyone either ran screaming or watched in silent horror as the dogs knocked over the table. The pans of food fell to the concrete, and the two candles rolled off, one of them setting the tablecloth on fire.

The black cat ran past the spilled food and burning tablecloth, hissing and screeching. One of the dogs looked up, a string of brisket hanging from its mouth, and took off running after the scared cat, which found its exit to the back yard blocked by the bar Kevin had set up the night before. The cat skidded around the corner, the dog gaining on it, while the two other dogs dragged the pans of food away from the now-raging fire.

"Fire!" Nicole shouted. "Bart! Do something!"

Bart ran toward the fire, grabbed a plastic cup off the table, then knelt by the pool and started scooping up some water and tossing it toward the fire.

The cat continued its race around the pool with the dog closing the distance. The fifty-pound lab crashed into one of Megan's younger cousins, a girl who looked like she was around six years old. The girl fell sideways into the pool, creating a huge splash that drenched the people nearby.

One of the drenched women began screaming, while Megan—who was with them—watched the melee in horror. The little girl surfaced but began flailing in the deep end of the pool.

"I don't think that little girl can swim," Josh said to Libby, his voice panicked.

"Oh, God," Libby shouted. "I think you're right." The black cat continued to circle the pool, the dog in hot pursuit. In its haste, the dog knocked over a small table, sending the cups and candle that had been on top skittering across the concrete.

The fire from the tablecloth spread to the nearby table.

"You've ruined everything!" Nicole yelled at Bart, who continued to douse the flames with scoops of water.

The back door flung open, bouncing off the house with a loud bang. Gram stood in the doorway, her feet spread apart, holding a fire extinguisher and wearing nothing but her birthday suit. "Did someone say fire?"

The girl was still in the pool, but now she was underwater.

Josh kicked off his shoes and dove in, finding the girl close to the bottom of the ten-foot-deep pool. He grabbed her waist with one arm and swam for the top. When they broke through the surface, the girl gasped for air and started crying. She flailed and kicked as Josh swam to the edge of the pool, dragging her with him.

Noah was kneeling at the edge, reaching toward them. "I'll take her."

Josh swam over to him and Noah grabbed her arms, lifting her out. As he set her on her feet, the little girl leaned over Noah's arm. Crying out in surprise, he dropped his hold on her. "She bit me!"

Josh clung to the side of the pool, heart racing.

The other two dogs, having devoured the food, joined in the cat chase.

"Take care of those *animals!*" Nicole shouted over the confusion.

"What do you want me to do?" Bart shouted, still throwing water onto the now raging fire.

Gram stopped in front of the burning food table and fumbled with the fire extinguisher. One of Bart's brothers moved toward her, trying to keep his gaze averted as he blindly reached for the extinguisher. "Maude, hand it to me and let me do it."

"I've got it," she said, exasperated.

Megan's uncle moved closer, still not looking while he held his open hand out—a tactic that accidentally led to him grabbing Gram's butt. The man shouted in horror, but a wide grin spread across Gram's face. "I think I just got goosed."

"For God's sakes, Mother!" Megan's mother shouted. "Put some clothes on!"

But Gram pulled a pin and tossed it on the ground, then

shot foam onto the fire. Once the fire was out, she kept spraying, covering two of the dogs running past. They skidded to a halt, then turned the other way, barreling into Nicole and shoving her into the pool in the shallower end. She went under and came back up, mascara streaming down her face, looking more unkempt than Josh had ever seen her.

"*Somebody get those dogs!*"

A man in a khaki uniform stood in the open gate, his mouth hanging open as he took in the destruction of the back yard. "Did someone call animal control?"

Nicole climbed up the steps at the entrance to the pool, though part of her hair stayed floating in the water behind her.

"Josh." Megan knelt next to him. "Are you okay?"

He looked up at her. "I think your mother just lost something."

She grinned, her eyes twinkling with mischief. "I've suspected for years that she wore a head piece. This disaster was worth the proof."

He couldn't help but laugh.

"The ladder's over there. We better get out of here while we can."

"What are you talking about?" he asked, swimming to the ladder on the other side. She picked up his shoes and walked around the edge of the pool, meeting him as he climbed out.

"I mean, Knickers is about to go ballistic and we need to be as far away from Ground Zero as possible. *Trust me.* I know this from first-hand experience."

"I thought she was already there."

"You're cute." She grabbed his hand, her fingers curling around his. "Let's run upstairs and get you changed first."

"What about Noah?" he asked, looking for his brother.

"I think Libby has him covered."

She swung wide of her mother, who was giving the animal control officer an earful. They snuck in the back door and headed for the stairs, leaving a trail of water from Josh's dripping clothes. "We have to hurry and leave before she notices we're gone or we'll be stuck."

"Okay." She pushed him into the room and shut the door, standing back as he rummaged in his bag and pulled out a clean pair of jeans and a T-shirt. He went into the bathroom to change.

"We don't have a car," he said through the door, unbuttoning his top button and tugging his wet shirt over his head. "How are we going to leave?"

"My dad kept my old Explorer. I'm going to sneak down to the kitchen. Come downstairs to meet me when you're done. But whatever you do, don't let Knickers see you."

"Okay." His jeans stuck to his skin and he struggled to get them off. His cell phone was in his pocket and he tried to turn it on, not surprised to find it dead. He considered leaving his soaking-wet wallet, but worried someone would find it and discover his real identity. He kept it in his hand as he crept down the stairs, making sure Megan's mother was nowhere to be seen.

Megan stood in the open doorway to the garage, motioning him to follow her. She skirted around the two cars and out a side door, Josh close on her heels. A dark blue Ford Explorer was parked on the gravel next to the house. "This was your car? Why didn't I notice it before?"

"It was a hand-me-down from my dad. When you're sixteen you'll take whatever you can get." She pointed to a tarp next to the house, shooting him a grin. "Mom won't let it in the garage and Dad can't stand the thought of leaving it to the elements. He keeps it covered." She opened the driver's door. "Get in."

He climbed into the passenger seat, setting his damp wallet on the console. "How are you going to get out? There are cars parked in the driveway."

She grinned, the Cheshire cat grin that told him she was up to no good. "Desperate times, Josh. Desperate times." Shoving the car into reverse, she put her hand on the back of his seat and looked over her shoulder. "Knickers is going to have a fit over her lawn." She backed up, driving through the grass, then angling the Explorer over the bottom half of the driveway and into the street.

Josh shook his head. "Good job." He laughed as he looked back at the yard. "And you're right. Your mother is going to have a fit over those tire ruts as soon as she finishes having a fit about the backyard."

"All the more reason to never come back." She rolled her window down and turned up the radio, driving through town and out into the farmland surrounding Blue Springs. Her hair blew around her face and she looked almost as peaceful as she did when sleeping.

"Do you have a destination in mind?"

She leaned her head toward him, grinning. "Yes, and you'll love it."

He leaned back in his seat, watching her. "I trust you."

Her face turned serious. "Thank you."

She made several turns and then she was on a back road, driving by a small lake. He almost asked her where they were going, but he'd told her he trusted her. He could ask her about it after they got there.

She drove for several more minutes, then turned down a gravel road and parked. "This is it."

He opened the door and realized they were at an empty campsite. The crickets and cicadas filled the night with their loud calls and while it wasn't too hot, the temperature felt several degrees cooler here.

She got out and went to the back of the car, lifting the hatch. "My dad used to take Kevin and me camping here when we were kids. Knickers didn't go, of course."

"Are we camping?" he asked, in surprise.

"I don't know yet," she answered, handing him a small cooler, then grabbing a stack of blankets. "Let's decide that as we go."

For once, Josh was happy to not have a plan.

Chapter Sixteen

Megan had driven here out of instinct. This was where she used to come when things got to be too much with her mother back in high school, which had happened a lot. While she hadn't been here in years, it still felt familiar and safe. It felt even more right that Josh was here with her, which was surprising. She'd never taken anyone to her special spot before.

"Let's go down this path." She turned on the mini-flashlight attached to the car key.

"That's handy," Josh said.

"My dad. He was a bit overprotective when I was in high school."

"Smart dad. He's not going to come hunt us down like a couple of kids gone parking, is he?"

She laughed quietly. "No. He has no idea I used to come here on my own. We're safe. Besides, I think he has his hands full." She followed the dirt path, turning left onto another less used path, which ended in a small clearing. "This is it."

He gasped from behind her and set the cooler down on the grass. "This is amazing."

"Thanks." She beamed with pride. They stood on top of a small bluff, overlooking the lake. A wooded shoreline was on the opposite side of the small lake, with no visible electric lights. But the real showstopper was the view of the sky. With few lights around the lake, the stars shone brighter than she usually saw them.

She handed him a blanket and two pillows. "Hold this for a minute," she said as she spread out a sleeping bag and then a sheet.

"You came prepared," he murmured, his husky voice sending a shiver down her spine.

"I used to like to lie out here and look at the stars." She grabbed the pillows from him and tossed them onto the makeshift bed.

She knew how it looked, like she had purposely brought him out here to seduce him. And maybe that was partially true. What would he think of that? For once she didn't care.

"I like stars."

She sat in the middle of the bedding, and patted the spot next to her. "Bring the cooler with you."

He picked it up and watched her with a wary face before sitting next to her and setting the cooler at the edge of the sleeping bag. "What's in here?"

"Open it and see."

Josh opened the lid and laughed. "I've already had three of these before the disaster from hell. I'm not sure if I should have another."

"Suit yourself." She leaned forward, resting her stomach across his thigh as she pulled a bottle out. She sat up and re-crossed her legs. The skirt of her dress had hitched up her thighs, and Josh's gaze followed the hem. She almost rearranged the fabric, then decided the hell with it. She was tired of playing it safe. She wanted to live a little.

Holding the bottle toward him, she asked, "Will you open this for me?"

He stared at the bottle as though undecided, then took it from her and twisted off the cap. "You like beer?" he asked, sounding uncomfortable.

"Love it. Blair and Libby are more wine drinkers, but give me an IPA from Black Raven Brewery in Seattle any day of the week."

He grinned. "You're kidding."

"That I like beer?" she asked in surprise as she took the bottle from him.

"No. That you like Black Raven Brewery. It's one of my favorite places."

She took a sip and leaned back on her elbows, her head above the pillow. "Who knows? We may have been there at the same time and never realized it."

His gaze had returned to her legs before reaching into the cooler for a bottle, twisting off the cap and taking a long drink.

"You grew up in Seattle?" she asked.

"Yeah."

"Never thought about moving away?"

"No. My father's business is there."

She took another drink, scrutinizing him as she asked her next question. "Your father's entrepreneurial business?"

His shoulders tightened and he took another drink. For a man who'd declined a beer, he was downing it pretty fast.

"Are you and Noah close?"

His gaze rose to her face and he seemed to hesitate before saying, "Not particularly."

"But he came out here to find you anyway."

He seemed to think over his response. "He was worried."

"About you or something else?"

He looked startled and she laughed before taking another

drink. She closed her eyes and let the cool liquid run down her throat. She hadn't had a drink all evening, not wanting to lose more control over the situation than she already had. And with her stomach a ball of nerves, she'd hardly eaten either, so the beer was quickly going to her head. While part of her was screaming for her to remain on guard, the rest of her said screw it. She knew that Josh had some ulterior motive for helping her. But she knew he liked her too, and in this moment, it was all that mattered.

"Relax," she said, her eyes still closed. "I don't care."

"Why wouldn't you care?"

She turned her face toward him, her eyes searching his. "Because I trust you…after a fashion."

"How do you know I'm worthy of your trust?"

She sat up and set the bottle in the grass next to the sleeping bag. Then she leaned toward him, her face hovering inches from his. "Because I can see your heart, Josh McMillan. You wouldn't intentionally hurt me."

He shook his head, pain in his eyes, confirming her suspicions. "How can you be so sure?"

Her fingertips rested on his cheek as she searched his eyes. "Will you intentionally hurt me?"

"Not if I can help it," he whispered. "That's the last thing I want."

"I know." Her lips brushed his softly and he remained still, not even breathing.

"Megan," he finally whispered, sounding like he was in discomfort.

She leaned back and stared into his eyes. "I've coasted through most of my life, Josh, letting other people direct my path, but I'm tired of coasting. I want to take charge. I want to do what makes me happy." She smiled at him. "I want you."

His eyes clouded.

"Do you want me, Josh?"

"It's not that easy, Megan."

She laughed softly. "It's a simple yes or no question, no reasoning or rationale allowed, at least not tonight." Her hand cupped his neck and her thumb brushed his cheek. "Do you want me?"

His answer was to press his lips on hers and entwine one hand in her hair as he used the other to press her to his chest. They were a tangle of tongues and limbs as pulled her onto his lap, her legs straddling his waist.

She clung to him as he took control, the hand around her back sliding down to cup her ass and press her against his erection. Heat engulfed her body and she groaned and gyrated against him, her hands sliding under his shirt. Her fingertips skimmed up his hard chest muscles.

He leaned back and pulled his shirt over his head, tossing it behind him. When he tried to kiss her again, she placed her hands on his shoulders and pushed him back. "I want to look at you."

He was more perfect in the moonlight than she remembered him from the night before. She slid her hands down to his perfectly sculpted abdomen, dipping lower to the waistband of his jeans. Using the palm of her hand, she rubbed his bulge though his jeans, feeling empowered when he squirmed.

He groaned, searching her eyes. "I thought that was my line."

Then she dropped her hands to her sides. "Go ahead."

He sat up and reached behind her back, his lips brushing the nape of her neck, his tongue dancing in tantalizing circles along her sensitive skin, sending waves of pleasure through her body. He unzipped her dress, exposing her skin to the cooler night air. She shivered and he chuckled as his teeth lightly nipped along her collarbone. His face lifted and he searched her eyes as his hands slid slowly up her back, his thumbs hooking on the neckline of her dress, then sliding the fabric down her arms.

She sat still as he pulled her arms free, the cotton dress puddled at her waist. His gaze lowered to her pale blue lace bra, but his hands dropped to her sides instead of cupping her breasts like she wanted. She sucked in a breath. The old insecurities came rushing back. Had he changed his mind? Did he find her lacking?

But his gaze lifted to hers, and the lust she saw there displaced her concerns. He pulled off her bra as his mouth found hers again, warm and desperate.

Her hands wound into his hair, holding him close as his hand moved to her breast, his thumb brushing over her nipple.

She sucked in a breath as a jolt of need shot straight to her core.

He continued to kiss her, his tongue exploring her mouth as his other hand slipped between her legs, his fingers rubbing against her damp panties. She pressed herself into his hand, moaning softly, and as if following her unspoken instructions, his fingers moved up, sliding down under her lingerie and between her folds.

She closed her eyes, her breath coming in rapid pants as his finger slipped inside her, the palm of his hand pressing against her mound as he rubbed her in slow circles. She couldn't believe how turned on she was already. She wanted more than his hand. She rose to her knees, reaching under her skirt to pull her panties off.

He wrapped an arm around her back, pressing kisses to her abdomen, then lowered her to his lap again and found her nipple with his mouth.

She arched her back as his free hand returned between her legs. "Josh," she said, hoping the sound of his name would convey to him everything she felt and needed. She needed *him*.

He pushed her back up to her knees as he fumbled with his

pants, tugging them off, then lowering her to straddle his upper thighs.

His hand cupped her cheek and he searched her face before kissing her again.

Not willing to wait any longer, she reached for him, wrapping her hand around the length of him and stroking. He released a low moan and pressed into her hand. His moan and his need turned her on even more. He wanted her. Her thumb traced his tip and he tensed, sucking in his breath. His fingers slid between her legs again, bringing her close to release.

Her sense of urgency increased as he pushed her backward, her head hitting the pillow as he moved between her legs, kneeling over her.

"*Dammit.*" He froze and squeezed his eyes shut with frustration. "I don't have a condom."

"I do." She reached inside the pillowcase under her head and pulled out a foil square.

He snagged it from her hand and ripped it open faster than she would have thought possible, then rolled the condom over his stiff erection.

She gazed up at him, reaching for him. Needing him now.

He lowered himself to one elbow and lifted her hip with his free hand, teasing her with his hardness before finally entering her, filling her perfectly.

Crying out, she lifted her hips higher, helping him slide deeper. His mouth covered hers as their movements became more urgent. As their passion built, his mouth broke free, his breath hot on her neck as he held her tighter, thrusting deeper. Faster.

She wrapped her legs around his back as she climbed higher, pressing herself against him with every thrust, until she finally climaxed, crying out in a gasp as her orgasm washed over her.

He held her tighter and gave two final deep thrusts before

coming. She grabbed his hips, holding him close for a moment until he rolled to his side, gathering her in his arms so they were chest to chest, him still inside her.

She looked up into his face and he smiled at her in wonderment and happiness. "Where have you been all my life, Megan Vandemeer?"

"Apparently, right around the corner."

Chapter Seventeen

He lay on his back with Megan on top of him, his arms wrapped around her back. Her head was nestled in the crook of his arm and her hand on his chest, her fingertips circling lightly over his sternum. They were naked on a bluff overlooking a lake. Although it was nighttime, someone could still stumble upon them, but he couldn't bring himself to let her go. Now that they'd actually done this, now that he knew with certainty how perfect they really were for each other, he wished they could just leave this whole mess behind and run away somewhere together, somewhere no one knew them or their problems.

She released a contented sigh. "I want to forget about the wedding that's supposed to take place in less than two days and just be in this moment."

His arm tightened around her.

"The only thing in my life that makes sense right now is you," she continued.

"How do *I* make sense?"

"That's just it, I don't know. I only know this feels more right than anything else. Ever." She lifted her head and grinned. "Who falls this hard for a guy within twenty-four hours of meeting him?"

"Lots of people fall in love at first sight. My parents did."

She blinked in surprise. "Your parents fell in love at first sight?"

He grabbed a strand of her hair that brushed over his bare chest. "So they claim. And they were happily married for twenty-one years."

"Well, this isn't love at first sight," she grinned against his lips. "More like lust." She kissed him with a passion that showed him how much she still wanted him.

Was she right? Was what he was feeling no more than lust? Did he have to put a label on it? He only knew the rapidly approaching wedding spelled a likely end for their new relationship…and the extracurricular sleuthing he and Noah were doing amped that "likely" up to a "certainly." He was more determined than ever to come clean in the hopes she would forgive him, not that he deserved it. But even Libby had told him Megan wore her heart on her sleeve. Maybe she would understand his desperation. Well, he wasn't sure how to fix the mess he'd created but he didn't need a solution right this minute. While the likelihood of losing her was higher than not, he had a choice to make: He could start mourning his impending loss of her now, or he could spend every minute with her while he could.

He chose the latter.

He rolled her onto her back and she giggled as he lowered his face to her neck. "So what are your plans, Ms. Vandemeer? Are we going back to your parents' house?"

"Oh, God, no."

"So we're camping under the stars?"

"Unless you have a better idea."

"I can't think of a single one." He pushed up on his elbow. "But we either need to get dressed or cover up with your blanket. Unless you're a nudist like your gram."

She laughed. "I'm not, but getting dressed is a waste of time, don't you think?" The sparkle in her eyes made it impossible not to kiss her.

"See?" she said. "You just proved my point. Besides, this spot can only be accessed from the campsite and no one's going to try camping here now that my car's parked there."

He grabbed the blanket and spread it across them, glancing back at the trail they'd used to get to the clearing.

"I think we're safe, Josh," she teased. "You're awfully uptight. Maybe Gram's right. Maybe you *are* a prude."

"You realize that sounds like a challenge…?"

She laughed. "Take it as you will. Still, we're safe from prying eyes. Unless we count the monstrous raccoons." She cocked an eyebrow. "You don't happen to have any food in your pockets, do you?"

"Nope."

"Then we're good."

She rolled on her side to face him. "So tell me more about your family. Is it anything like mine?"

"No offense, Megan, but I don't think there's any family like yours."

She laughed. "Fair enough."

"Why do you let her get to you so much?" Her smile faded and he was instantly sorry he asked, but he was curious to know. "On the plane you took on that flight attendant without a second thought. Your job is to fight corporations bent on deforestation. Hell, you'll take on a wild raccoon—" his voice softened, "—but you won't stand up to your mother." He tucked a strand of hair behind her ear. "That's such a contradiction to the woman I've gotten to know…the woman the rest of the world sees. I just don't get it."

She worried her bottom lip with her upper teeth, then looked into his eyes. "It's not that easy to answer, Josh."

"Then try."

She took a deep breath and pushed it out, looking sadder by the millisecond.

"I'm sorry," he murmured, running his hand down her arm. "It's none of my business."

A wry smile twisted her mouth. "That's not exactly true, is it? My inability to stand up to my mother has gotten you into this strange situation."

He grinned, leaning in to kiss her. "I kind of like where I am right now."

She pushed him onto his back and leaned her breasts against his bare chest. He felt himself stirring again—the sight of her bare curves driving him crazy.

"I kind of like where I am right now too." She brushed her lips against his. "The funny thing is, she was different when I was a kid. She laughed and had fun. She was a regular mom for the most part. But then when I was in middle school, she changed. Like a light switch from off to on. She became obsessed with everything being perfect." She forced a tight smile. "But nothing's perfect, you know?"

Watching her now, he considered arguing with her statement. She looked as near to perfect as he could imagine. "Perfection is difficult to reach and impossible to maintain."

"Exactly. Which is why she constantly found me lacking. I didn't suit her new view of perfection. At first I was too stunned to argue, so I said nothing. All of us did, really. Kevin and I were stunned that our mother was gone and this Stepford wife had taken her place. Kevin got involved in sports. My dad took up camping and fishing, and for a while I was the one to deal with her on a regular basis. But I didn't. I retreated. Then after a while I guess I learned that it's always been easier not to fight her. No one ever goes against her and wins. Ever. She's beaten us down enough times that we've just stopped trying. I moved to Seattle to get away from her. I've never seen my dad more crushed than the day I told him I was moving away. I think he instinctively knew I wouldn't be back much."

"But what about Libby and Blair?"

"Collateral damage."

Josh's mother had always been supportive and loving. How would he handle it if she flipped a switch like Nicole Vandemeer had done? What had happened to turn her against her family?

"No more talk about my mother." Her hand slipped into his hair and her face hovered over his, her eyes bright and large. "You were a hero tonight."

"What?"

"You probably think no one noticed in all the madness, but I did. You saved my cousin. She was drowning and you jumped in and saved her."

He shook his head, cringing. "It wasn't anything. Anyone could have done it."

"But *you* did."

"I suspect Noah wishes I'd left her at the bottom of the pool after the way she bit him."

Megan tilted her head back and laughed, and Josh decided the sound of her laugh was the happiest sound that had ever existed. "Nevertheless, you saved her. You saved me too. I'm surprised you don't have a superhero costume on under your clothes."

"I did," he teased. "But spandex shrinks in water, so I had to hang it over the shower rod in your bathroom. I hope no one comes in and learns my secret."

She laughed again, straddling his waist and leaning over him, her hair tumbling over her shoulders. "If we ever go back, will you try it on for me?"

"*If* we go back?"

Her smile softened. "We could run away together—just you and me—and never look back."

Her thoughts so echoed his own that he couldn't help but smile. "Do we end up in Seattle when we reach the end of our trip, or do we stay on some tropical island somewhere?"

"It depends. Does this island include Gram's nudist colony?"

"God, no."

"Hmm... Just how good are you at making coconut drinks?" Her eyebrows lifted playfully as she asked the question. When he started to answer, she kissed him to stop his answer. "It's a trick question, so think carefully first." Then she laughed again, sitting up.

He sat up too, grabbing her hips and settling her on his thighs. The nearness of her drove him crazy and made his thoughts stray from their conversation. "I'm going to guess that you hate coconut, so I should probably answer that I make killer margaritas."

She laughed again. "I knew you were smart."

"The question of my intelligence is yet to be decided, but I think agreeing to be your substitute fiancé was the best idea I've ever had."

"I don't remember asking," she teased.

"I have lots of things to offer that you might not have even considered."

Her eyes flew open in mock surprise. "You're full of talk, aren't you?"

He laughed. "I'll be happy to demonstrate."

The amusement on her face faded. She grabbed his face in her hands and gave him a deep, lazy kiss that reached down to his soul, stirring a longing of which he'd never believed himself capable.

He wrapped an arm around her, his hand splaying on her back as he held her close. "I think I could spend the rest of my life with you and never get my fill."

She kissed him again, this time with more urgency. In only a few minutes he was inside her again, keeping her on his lap this time. The blanket was down by his feet, leaving her clothed in nothing but moonlight and sweat. Her hands dug into his shoulders and her eyes closed in pleasure as she arched her back, trying to push him deeper with each movement. Several strands of hair clung to her shoulders, but the rest hung behind her. He held her hips as she rode him with increasing urgency, and in that perfect moment he was sure of two things. One, she was the most beautiful woman he had ever known, and two, there was no way he could walk away from her. And since he saw no way to be honest with her, to work out the tangled web he'd spent the past day weaving, he was in deep, deep trouble. His only hope was for a miracle.

But no matter what, she was his for tonight and he wasn't going to waste a single minute.

Chapter Eighteen

Megan awoke in Josh's arms. She expected to be more startled by that fact, but lying next to him felt like the most natural thing in the world. He was on his back, an arm stretched over his eyes to block out the sun.

She watched his chest rise and fall. He had a very nice chest—hard muscles covered with just a little hair but not too much. The edge of the blanket rested above his waist and she saw a hint of his abdomen. She knew what lay under the blanket and memories of the night before rushed back, making her burn, but not with embarrassment. Not for one minute did she regret sleeping with him. What happened next was a whole lot trickier. She liked him. A lot. She lusted for him. A lot. She wanted him like she'd never wanted anyone. He made her laugh and made her feel lighthearted, and part of her cringed when she let herself look toward tomorrow.

Would they have a tomorrow? After Josh broke up with her and her family sent him back to Seattle. Back to her adopted home town. She was smart enough to realize that Josh was a forever kind of guy. But they'd gone along with this deception for so long, how could she step back and say, "Sorry everyone, this was all one big mistake"?

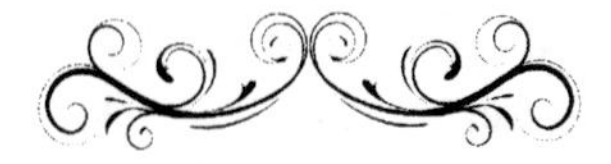

"Hey," Josh murmured sleepily, cracking his eyes open. "I know you're probably into those *Twilight* books and movies, but it's actually kind of creepy for someone to watch another person sleep all night."

"You think I spent the night watching you sleep?" She buried her face in the crook of his neck, her mouth finding his earlobe.

"Did we even have much of a chance to sleep?" he asked, rolling onto his side to face her.

"Not much."

He laughed. "Good thing you're on the pill, or we would've had to make a midnight run for more condoms." His eyes blinked open sleepily and a smile spread across his face. "Good morning."

She smiled back. "Yes it is."

"You're not one of those happy morning people, are you?" he murmured. "Because if you are, I may have to end this fake engagement right now."

"Let me guess, you don't function until after a cup of coffee?"

"Actually it's two cups. And yes. Coffee is the elixir of the gods."

Her brown eyes danced in amusement. "Are you calling yourself a god now?"

"You were a participant in last night's activities, so you tell me."

She laughed and settled her face into his chest. An ache filled his heart as he held her close, stroking her hair. He had to figure a way out of this. Could they just come clean and tell her family the truth, making it into a funny story? One thing was for sure: Her mother would never forgive them. Megan's mother's opinion was important to her, no matter what she claimed. And that wasn't even taking into account the problem of Bart Vandemeer's business.

What a screwed-up mess.

"How about I take you out for breakfast?" he asked, trying to keep his tone light.

"Are you asking me out on a date?" she asked, her voice muffled.

He leaned back, tipping her chin up to look at him. "Megan Vandemeer, would you do me the honor of letting me escort you to the International House of Pancakes?"

Her laughter lit her eyes. "How can I refuse such a gallant request? But I'm warning you that I'm a big breakfast eater—much to my mother's dismay—so don't expect me to order an egg-white omelet and black coffee."

He tried to keep his face serious. "I wouldn't dream of letting you order anything smaller than the Breakfast Sampler Plate."

"The fact you can name an item on the menu has me a little frightened. I'll agree to go out to breakfast with you, but I get to pick the place."

"Deal." He sat up, pulling the blanket down and leaving them both exposed from the waist up. "Although I might want something else first."

"Later. I need food."

She got on her hands and knees to search for her clothes and he couldn't drag his gaze away from her bare ass.

She looked over her shoulder at him. "You didn't get your fill last night?"

"I didn't get to see much of your backside—although I'm not complaining about the views I was blessed to see—so you can't fault me for admiring it now. You have a very gorgeous ass."

She smirked her amusement. "Yeah? Well, you might get to see plenty of it if I don't find my underwear."

"I thought you tossed it toward the bottom of the blanket."

"Yeah, well, we got a little creative last night. Who knows where everything ended up."

"So we just get up and look."

"Great in theory," she said, motioning her head toward the water. "I'm sure those fishermen are going to appreciate the view."

"What?" Josh's head turned to see a fishing boat coasting into view. He tackled Megan flat onto the pallet and covered her with the blanket.

She laughed, pulling him down on top of her. "I think it's too late to save my virtue."

"Maybe so, but you gave your virtue to me and I don't plan on sharing it."

"Oooh…" She grinned, pulling his mouth to hers. "I like it when you get all possessive."

"Then you should love the rest of your day, because I plan to spend it being that obsessive boyfriend every girl either loves or hates."

"And which one will I be?" she asked. "The one who loves it or hates it?"

His hand cradled her face. "I'll let you tell me at the end of the day."

She swatted him and he pulled her to him for a slow, hypnotic kiss that held the false promise of being the first of a thousand more. Her hands dug into his hair, keeping him firmly in place.

He lifted his face and gave her a genuine smile. "I promised you breakfast and the opportunity to not be gawked at by old men fishing on the lake. I'm neglecting my duties."

"You haven't heard any complaints from me."

He looked out onto the lake. They were low enough to the ground that they'd probably gone unnoticed by the fishermen. He glanced around the pallet and surrounding grass. "So any good leads on our clothes?"

"Just what you see before you."

He saw her dress, his jeans and nothing else. "Where are my T-shirt and underwear?"

"Forget your T-shirt," she grumbled good-naturedly. "That bra and panties set cost me eighty-seven dollars."

"How can you remember how much they cost so exactly?"

She cringed and turned her backside to him again. "I just bought them yesterday."

"You did?" he asked, more hopeful than he'd intended.

She turned her face away from him. "Yes, and since I bought them hoping you might see them, you're partially responsible for their return."

"Well, when you put it that way…"

"You just want to see me in them again."

"I could deny it, but that would be a lie." He pulled his jeans on and zipped them up, taking extra care since he was going commando. "And you'd never believe it anyway." He moved to the edge of the trees and spotted her bra several feet away. He held it up. "How'd this get over here?"

"Those damned raccoons," she grumbled.

"You're kidding."

"No, I told you they were the ones you had to worry about."

He dropped it by her on the sleeping bag and spotted his T-shirt on the other side of the clearing. After shaking it off, he pulled it over his head and decided not to put any effort into finding his underwear. He definitely didn't want to wear them again if monster raccoons had been chewing on them through the night.

Megan had fastened her bra and raised her arms to pull her dress over her head when Josh froze.

"Uh, Megan…how frightened are you of bugs?"

"You mean like ants and mosquitos?"

"No…more like ticks."

"What?" she screeched, jumping to her feet and dancing in place. "Get it off! Get it off!"

He ran over to her and pulled her into his arms to settle her down. "So you're afraid of your mother and blood-sucking parasites. I can see a common thread."

"It's not funny, Josh!" she shouted, trying to pull free. "Get it off!"

"Calm down. It's just a seed tick. I'll pull it out."

She took a deep breath, trying to calm down. "Where is it?"

"Close to your armpit."

She released a shriek of panic, her feet running in place, and he had to laugh despite her obvious terror.

"Stop laughing at me!"

He pulled her dress down to her waist. "I'm not laughing *at* you. I'm laughing *with* you."

She swung her face around to glare at him. "*I'm not laughing, Josh!*"

"I know. I'm sorry. You're just so cute."

"There's nothing cute about ticks!"

"Okay, hold still so I can get it off." He lifted her arm over her head and examined her skin, surprised it was gone. "I don't see it."

"*What do you mean you don't see it?*"

"It's gone."

She looked up at him, her gaze fierce. "Ticks just don't *leave,* Josh. They wait until they're engorged and drop off. Did it look engorged?"

God help him, he couldn't laugh or she would kill him. "I admit to seeing more than my fair share of engorged objects in the last ten hours or so, but that tick wasn't one of them."

"Then where is it?" she shrieked, panicked again.

"Relax, Megan. It's just a tiny tick."

"*Just* a tiny tick? It's a creature that embeds its head deep inside—" She glared up at him again when he began to snicker. "If you're going to continue to act like a twelve-year-old boy, I'm going to leave you out here with the raccoons."

Though he managed not to release the peals of laughter bubbling up inside him, he couldn't hold back a chuckle. "I'm sorry. I'm trying."

Without responding, she pulled her dress down to the ground and tried to look over her shoulder. "I can't see back there."

He grabbed her shoulders and bent at the knees so his face was level with hers. "I'll look and make sure you don't have any ticks, okay? I promise."

She dragged in a breath and let it out. "Okay."

He gave her a soft kiss and released her shoulders, then moved behind her to examine her back. Since she was now naked except for her bra and the fishermen were gone, he took his time, enjoying the view more than he'd admit to Megan right now. After looking over the backs of her legs, he moved to her sides and front, then declared her tick-free. "Nothing. You're good."

"Then where did it go?"

"I don't know." He picked up her dress off the ground. "I suspect it wasn't attached yet and fell off when you were putting your dress on." He moved several feet away from her and shook it out before handing it back to her.

She started to step into it and had it up to her hips, when she began to scream, jerking the dress off. The skirt got tangled around her legs and he lunged for her as she started to trip, keeping her from falling to the ground.

"It's crawling inside my dress!" She kicked the skirt away from her, sucking in deep breaths.

"Okay, I'll get it out." He looked into her eyes. "It's okay."

She nodded, fighting to gain control. Josh moved toward the offending dress, now several feet away on the ground, when he realized the fishermen had returned and both men were standing in the small boat, staring up at them with open mouths. They looked so ancient that Josh worried they were about to lose their balance and fall out.

Josh moved in front of Megan, blocking her from their view. He held up his hands as he addressed the men. "Everything is fine here. It's just a tick."

"That must have been some tick," one of the men muttered, his voice carrying over the water.

Megan lunged around Josh, but he held her in place—blocking her body with his and out of the fishermen's view—as she shouted, "Ticks are no laughing matter!" She pointed her finger at the men to emphasize her point. "They can *kill* you!"

Josh turned around, grabbing her arms while making sure he was still blocking as much of their view as possible. "Okay, calm down, Tick Lady of Doom. Cut those guys a break. You just gave them the biggest thrill they've probably had in the last twenty years."

She shrieked again when she realized she was naked except for her bra and dropped to the ground to grope for the blanket.

He picked up her dress again, shook it out, and checked it twice before handing it to her.

"I'm not wearing that!"

"So you're Lady Godiva now? Maybe you want to follow in Gram's footsteps." He gave an involuntary shudder. "I'm not sure they'll serve you pancakes at IHOP if you're not wearing clothes."

"We're not going to IHOP!"

"Then we'll go somewhere else, because I promised you breakfast, Megan, and damn it *I'm taking you to breakfast!*"

He heard a gasp behind him. When he turned to look, he saw two more boats in the cove, everyone onboard mesmerized by the Megan and Josh show.

He squatted next to her. "Come on, Megs. We have an audience and Knickers isn't even here to appreciate it." When she didn't answer, he pressed on, "I made sure there weren't any ticks. I checked twice. I promise."

She took another deep breath and released it, her eyes narrowing at him as she jabbed her finger into his chest. "If I even find the hint of a *tick turd* on this dress, I'm going to make you suffer."

"I accept the sentencing...er, I mean the consequences."

Her mouth pursed in disapproval, but she let him slip the dress over her head. When she stood, he zipped her up and she marched over to the edge of the bluff, looming twenty feet over the water. "You can all go home now, *you freaking perverts!*"

She was close enough to the edge to make him nervous. He moved behind her, snaking an arm around her waist to pull her back. "You told them, so why don't we go now?"

She marched over to the blanket and picked up her shoes and the cooler, then headed down the path without comment. Scooping up the bedding, Josh found Megan's panties under the pallet. He picked them up and shoved them into his pants pocket before readjusting the load in his arms and hurrying after Megan.

Her stance proclaimed she was a woman on a mission, and it looked like a major part of the plan involved leaving him behind. But he caught up to her as she opened the back hatch of the car and set the cooler inside. Josh shoved the wadded bedding into the back and quickly closed the lid so he could corner Megan against the car before she opened the driver's door.

"I know you're pissed right now, but stop a moment to take a deep breath before we leave."

She glared up at him.

"I'm sorry I laughed at you when you were clearly terrified."

"I was not terrified!"

"Says the woman who would rather face an audience of old men in the nude than put on a dress that might contain a seed tick."

A grin tugged at the corners of her lips.

"I hereby promise to do my utmost never to let another tick touch your gorgeous body for the rest of the time I know you."

Her eyes danced with mischief. "That shouldn't be too difficult, since we have to break up tonight."

How could she say it so casually? The mere thought ripped his heart out. But he was determined to make this the best day of his life, Knickers' schedule be damned. "Unless the rehearsal dinner is outside." He lifted his eyebrows to emphasize the danger.

She laughed. "You can put away your tick-vanquishing sword. It's in a restaurant."

He rested his hands on either side of her head and leaned in to kiss her. Her hands lifted to his cheeks as her lips met his. There were tears in her eyes when he pulled away, but she blinked them back and smiled.

"You owe me breakfast. Are you coming?"

He opened the car door and held it open for her. "I'll follow you anywhere." When she gave him a questioning glance, he hastily added, "Hey, I love breakfast."

The casual comment came easily enough, but if it fooled her, it didn't fool him.

Chapter Nineteen

Megan studied Josh out of the corner of her eye, trying to determine if their inevitable breakup tonight bothered him as much as it did her. He'd dropped his guard often enough for her to know he didn't want to do this either, but there really was no other way out. She couldn't tell her mother the truth, and if they didn't pick option one or two, that only left three—they went through with the wedding.

She turned over the engine and picked up her phone from the console where she'd left it, not surprised to see all the missed calls and texts. She and Josh had taken off without telling anyone where they were going. Everyone was freaked out. Nicole Vandemeer was inevitably more upset than the rest, but not for the same reason as everyone else.

She scrolled the list—calls from her mom, her dad, multiple calls and texts from Libby, one from Blair this morning, and one that came in at two a.m., which would have been midnight Pacific time.

Jay.

Her chest tightened. She hadn't talked to him since telling him the wedding was off and walking out of his apartment six weeks ago. Why was he trying to get in touch with her now?

She glanced up at Josh, whose questioning gaze told her he'd noticed her reaction. "Is everything okay?"

Shaking her head, she forced a smile. "Yeah. I'm just overwhelmed by the number of calls and texts I missed. Did Noah try to reach you?"

He grimaced. "My phone went in the pool with me last night. It's on your bathroom counter awaiting its funeral."

"So we need to get you a new phone today."

"Yeah." He was still watching her. "Did your mother send you a threatening text?" he asked, sounding worried.

"Text?" she snorted, scrolling through them. "Knickers does *not* text."

"Then what's got you so anxious?"

"I should have told someone where we were going. Libby and Blair are freaked out."

"Take five minutes to call them and let them know you're fine. Breakfast can wait."

But she wasn't in the mood to answer Libby's excited questions and Blair's accusations. Instead, she sent them a group text.

I'm fine. Josh and I needed to get away and I left my phone in the car. We're headed to breakfast now.

Breakfast??? Blair demanded. *You're eating breakfast with a kidnapper?*

Megan sighed. *If anything, *I* kidnapped HIM.*

I'm sure he wasn't complaining, Blair sent back at lightning speed. *>insert sarcasm<*

I'm not doing this now, Blair. I'm going to eat breakfast. I'll see you at the rehearsal at six.

ARE YOU FREAKING SERIOUS????

A text from Libby popped up. *I want details!!! <3*

Do NOT encourage her! Blair responded.

Is Noah okay? Megan asked.

Who is NOAH?

Josh's brother.

Megan's cell phone rang three seconds later. Sure enough, it was Blair. She silenced the phone and tossed it onto the console.

"Problems?"

"Nothing I can't handle." She put the car in reverse and backed out of their parking spot.

"Shouldn't you call your mother?"

"Yes." She kept driving and didn't pick up her phone.

"I abandoned Noah at your parents' house." He laughed in response to her cringe. "Don't worry. If anyone can handle your mother, it's my brother. But I should call him and do some recon, see how bad it is."

"Oh, it's bad." She forced a grin. "But that might be a good idea. Besides, you better check on him."

Josh picked up her phone and entered Noah's number before holding the phone to his ear. "Hey, Noah. I thought I'd let you know I haven't disappeared over state lines." He grimaced. "She's sitting here next to me, so watch it."

He didn't look happy, making Megan wonder what his brother had said.

"How are things at the Vandemeer residence?" He was silent for a long pause before he muttered, "Uh-huh." Several more moments of silence followed, broken by, "Okay" and "Wow." Finally he said, "Oh, shit. I hadn't thought about that." He ran a hand through his hair. "Okay, we'll meet you there at eleven." He ended the call and put the phone down, looking out the windshield.

"Well…?"

He jolted, turning to face her. "According to my brother,

who is prone to embellishment, your mother nearly had a stroke. Your father gave her a couple of Xanax pills and put her to bed. She got up this morning and acted like the incident never happened."

"You're kidding."

"Nope."

"Check my missed calls and see when she called."

He picked up her phone and she remembered the missed call from Jay. What if he'd left a message? It was too late to stop him now. Truth be told, she didn't owe him an explanation, but she felt unnerved all the same.

Josh studied the list. "She called five times last night and once this morning, and there are three voice messages. Do you want me to listen to them?"

It seemed like the chicken-shit way out, but she found herself nodding. "Yes."

He listened to the first one, his shoulders lifted to his ears with tension. "Okay," he said as he pressed delete. "That was mostly unintelligible, but the gist was for you to call her back immediately. It was about half an hour after we left."

"Okay…"

He listened to the second message, fighting a grin that faded before he lowered the phone. This one he didn't delete. "I think she'd taken the Xanax before making this call, so she sounded like she was drunk."

Megan snorted. "My mother has never been drunk a day in her life."

"Well, she certainly sounds like it, but she wasn't nearly as entertaining as you were on the plane."

She stuck her tongue out at him.

He chuckled. "She demanded that you call her back and chastised you for abandoning her in her time of need." He used air quotes to emphasize the last three words. "But then she asked you to call her no matter what time it was because she was worried about you."

She sobered at his words. "She must have been really out of it to say that."

"She's your mother, Meggie. She loves you even if she doesn't know how to say it."

She shot him a glare. "*Meggie?*"

He shrugged. "It's cute. And you're beyond cute when you're lecturing octogenarians about the dangers of ticks while wearing nothing but your bra." A grin spread across his face. "It fits."

She almost told him that no one was allowed to call her Meggie—that it had been a rule since a boy in first grade called her Steggie Meggie (short for Stegosaurus) and she'd punched his front tooth out—but she stopped. What did it matter? He only had one day to use the offensive name. Besides, when he said it, it sounded right.

"There's one more message?" she asked.

He hesitated and shifted in his seat. "Yeah, one more from your mother. She called about forty-five minutes ago."

"Listen to it."

He obeyed and lowered the phone after about thirty seconds, showing no reaction.

"Well?"

He sucked in a breath, disbelief spreading across his face. "She wanted to remind you that you have a full itinerary today. She said I have to pick up my tux and I'm supposed to meet my brother at the store at eleven, which Noah had already told me about. After that, she wants you to go to Powell Gardens with her, but then I have to meet you at the courthouse later to pick up our marriage license."

"Oh, crap," she groaned.

"Yeah. I know." He didn't sound any happier about it than she did. "She listed a bunch of other things like getting your hair colored." He turned to her. "Why are you getting your hair colored?"

She tilted her head slightly while pursing her lips. "My mother was horrified that I hadn't gone to a salon in Seattle before I came. When I told her my last haircut was only three weeks ago, she said it needed to be highlighted to show my waves in my up-do."

He stared at her in shock. "You've got to be kidding me." He reached for a lock of her hair and held it up. "Your hair is absolutely perfect, Megan. Don't change it."

Something warm filled her heart, mixing with the sorrow there to form a beautiful ache. How could she feel such extremes at once? "Thanks," she said softly.

"I would say skip the tuxes, but your mother said your brother's going to be there too. And Noah and I are supposed to pick up your father's tux and take it to him."

"Crap."

"Yeah."

"I'm sorry," she said.

"Hey," his hand covered hers, and he grinned at her. "For better or for worse, I'm committed to this engagement until tonight. Which means everything it encompasses."

"But Jay paid for his own tux. And I'm sure the tightwad already canceled his order."

"I can pay for the tux."

She cleared her throat. "No you won't. This is my mess. I'll pay for it."

He squeezed her hand. "Let's go to breakfast and declare it a wedding-discussion-free zone."

"Deal."

The easy conversation they shared over breakfast only proved how perfect they were for each other. He was witty and fun. They talked without pause about growing up and graduating from college, discovering what they wanted to do with their lives. Josh admitted that his plan to join his father's business had only been further cemented after his death, but sometimes he felt like he'd made the decision when he was a kid without ever having a choice in the matter. He never volunteered the specifics of what he did, and since he seemed to want to keep it to himself, she didn't ask.

"If you hadn't joined your father's business, what would you have done?" she asked, studying his face.

"I don't know," he said with a self-conscious half-shrug.

She rested her forearms on the table and leaned toward him. "I don't believe that for a second. Everyone has dreams, no matter how preposterous or stupid someone else might think they are."

"And what's your secret dream?" he teased, taking her hand in his. "If you're so eager to hear mine, tell me yours."

She gave him a wicked smile.

"You want to win *American Idol*."

She laughed. "I have no such delusions. I can hardly carry a tune."

"You want to climb Mount Everest."

She shivered. "No way. That sounds like a nightmare. I hate the cold. One of the benefits of living in Seattle. Despite all the rain, it hardly ever snows."

"I give up. Tell me."

Her smile softened. "It's stupid."

"If it's your dream, it can't be stupid." His fingers squeezed around hers in encouragement.

She swallowed, looking nervous. "I want my mom to accept me for *me* instead of trying to change me into what she wants me to be."

"How can that be stupid, Megan?"

"Because I shouldn't have to want it in the first place."

He looked into her eyes for several seconds. "I told you that my business is in trouble, big trouble, and now I find myself facing a very difficult decision. I have two choices, neither of them good. If I make one decision, ten employees lose their jobs—two of whom will have a very difficult time finding new ones—but if I choose the other, someone very important to me will probably get hurt in the process." He sighed, not looking happy.

"You're in a real Catch-22, huh?" Someone important to him. Noah? Could this be why his brother had shown up?

"Yeah."

"So is that why you're hiding out with me? Avoiding the decision?"

He watched her for a moment. "No. There's really nothing to be done at this point except for me to decide. Unless I get a miracle."

"And you have to make your choice this weekend?" When he nodded she asked, "Have you made a decision yet?"

"No." His voice was gruff and she covered his hand with her own, her thumb rubbing back and forth over his knuckles. "Like I told you, I'm leaving this trip up to fate. You're the answer I was given. I can't help thinking that has to mean something."

Horror washed through her. "Me?"

"There's absolutely nowhere else I'd rather be than with you. You were my gift from fate." When she started to protest, he stopped her. "Let's make a deal. We'll avoid talking about your mother and my business so we can make today as happy as possible."

She made a face. "Avoiding any talk about your business is a whole hell of a lot easier."

He gave her a wicked grin. "Ha! You definitely have the home court disadvantage."

"Just for that, I'm not going to take you to get a new phone," she said smugly.

His voice softened. "Who am I going to call? The only person I want to be with is here with me."

"Let's get out of here, Romeo," she said with a small smile.

"But we have to pick up the tuxes at eleven."

Her smile stretched into a grin. "I know."

Josh paid the bill and they walked out of the restaurant, his arm around her waist, holding her hip to his. He leaned down to her ear and whispered, "Do you know how distracting it was sitting across from you knowing you weren't wearing underwear under your dress?"

She laughed, but a wave of lust washed through her. "We need to shower and change clothes."

"Your mother mentioned she was going to pick up the flowers and check on the cake this morning before stopping by to make sure everyone's tux looks okay."

"So…we have an hour and a half in an empty house to go back, shower, and change?"

He stopped next to her car, pulling her to his chest. "And other things." He kissed her with more intensity than she'd expected, but she wasn't about to complain.

"*Definitely* other things," she murmured against his lips.

He broke free and opened her car door. "Tell me we're close to your parents' house."

"Define *close*." He released a long groan and she laughed. "Ten minutes. Tops."

"Paybacks are hell, Megan Vandemeer."

And they were, but deliciously so. He took advantage of the fact that she was stuck behind the wheel and pantyless by skimming a hand along her thigh, lifting the hem of her skirt, and shifting higher.

"God, you're so wet," he groaned.

She let out a soft gasp as his fingers began to coax her close to a climax but never quite there. By the time she parked in the driveway, she was hot with desire and could think of nothing but getting him inside the house and stripping off his clothes.

She took his hand and pulled him upstairs and into her

bedroom. Pushing him against the wall, she reached for his jeans. A devilish grin lit up his face as he watched her. "You're so determined."

"You drove me crazy all the way here. It's my turn now." As she lowered his jeans, she dropped to her knees and helped him step out of the pant legs.

He looked down at her, his eyes hooded with lust and desire as she licked the length of his erection, then looked up at him. His gaze met hers and he released a low groan when she licked him again while cupping his balls. He leaned the back of his head against the wall and reached for her hair, grabbing loose handfuls as she took him into her mouth. She set the pace, but he soon became impatient.

He pulled her into his arms, kissing her deeply as he unzipped her dress and pushed it off her shoulders and down to the floor. "I'm so torn," he said, dragging his mouth from hers and moving to her ear. "Part of me wants to have you in the shower and the other part of me wants you on the bed."

She pulled his mouth back to hers. "Bed."

He grabbed her thighs and lifted her as if she were weightless. She straddled his waist and wrapped her arms around his neck and back, kissing him as he walked the short distance to her bed. Laying her down sideways on the mattress, he hovered over her, his hand cupping her breast as their mouths still connected. He started to roll to his side, but she didn't want to wait. She wanted him now.

"No," she murmured. And she reached down and guided him inside her.

He accepted the invitation, lifting her hips and plunging deep into her with one thrust. She arched her back and rose up to take him in, wanting him deeper, needing more. Her legs tightened around his waist, but he pulled them loose, lifting one to hook the back of her knee over his shoulder. She gasped as his urgency increased and her body responded, wanting more.

He had her close within a minute, but she held on, fighting her release, wanting it to last, wanting to come with him. His hand covered her breast, his thumb and finger pinching her nipple, and it was enough to push her over the edge. She cried out, her fingers digging into his back as his movements grew more frantic, and he came too, pushing hard against her as he groaned.

He collapsed on top of her, unhooking her leg and rolling to his side, bringing her with him. He kissed her, his tongue seeking hers out, his hand tangling in her hair.

"This is some honeymoon we're having," she grinned against his lips.

"You, Megan Vandemeer, are absolutely perfect."

"You're not so bad yourself," she said with a laugh.

"This is exactly what I mean," he said, pulling back to look into her eyes. "We just did…*this*—and now we're laughing."

"You can't say sex, Josh?" she teased. "You really *are* a prude."

"*This* was not mere sex, Megan, and you know it. This doesn't even come close to anything I've ever experienced before." Some indeterminable emotion flickered in his eyes before fading. "But maybe it's not like that for you."

She shook her head in amazement. "My reaction five minutes ago didn't make it clear enough? This is not the norm for me—not that I sleep around."

"Neither do I."

"I've never…" Her words trailed off as she rested her hand lightly on his cheek, her thumb tracing the outline of his bottom lip. This thing between them was special. It was worth saving. "Maybe we should just tell my mom everything and let the chips fall where they may."

Indecision flickered in his eyes. "You would really do that?"

"Stand up to my mother?"

"And tell her the truth. Can you do that and live with the consequences?"

She pulled back slightly. "What does that mean?"

"If your mother walked in right now and you told her everything, what do you think she would do?"

"First of all, she would flip out to find us sideways like this. *Normal people have sex parallel to the edge of the bed, Megan,*" she mocked. "*Not perpendicular.*"

He placed his hand on her shoulder, rubbing along her collarbone as he offered her a tentative smile. "And after that," he prodded. "What would she say then?"

She shuddered. "It wouldn't be good."

"Yes, I guessed as much. But what exactly would she do?"

"She would disown me and ban my father and brother and Gram from ever speaking to me again."

"She would really do that?"

"She's done that exact same thing for lesser offenses. She has a sister. When I was in middle school, they had a stupid fight. Mom said it was over which toilet paper was better, of all things, but they haven't spoken since. Gram doesn't even mention her around my mother. And whenever I asked Gram about it, she would just say it wasn't her story to tell. That it was up to my mom if she wanted to tell me about it someday." She shook her head "Who could disown their own sister over something so ridiculous?"

Josh stared at her in shock.

"I know what you're thinking." She propped up on one elbow. "Why would I care what she thinks? But I don't want to lose my entire family. I love my dad and my brother. And while I know Gram would still call me, I'd never see her now that she's living with my parents. My father…he loves me but I'm not sure he loves me *enough.*" She sat up, anxiety forming a ball in the pit of her stomach. "To tell her everything would make me an orphan in every sense of the word."

He sat up next to her, taking her hand between both of his. "And what's the very *best*-case outcome from all of this?"

"Best-case? That we would get married tomorrow with them still thinking you're Jay." She shook her head and pushed out her frustration with a heavy breath. "But since I don't see you changing your last name in the near future, the far more likely best-case scenario is that you break up with me tonight and my mother spends the rest of her life shaming me. Every Thanksgiving I come home, I'll still hear that I single-handedly lost them fifty thousand dollars." She shrugged. "But at least I'll still have somewhere to go for Thanksgiving dinner."

No, Megan would have to find another solution to this problem, but as she stared into Josh's worried face, she wasn't sure there was one. And she only had herself to blame.

Chapter Twenty

Josh had to admit that the odds were stacked against them. Megan would have to throw her entire family away simply to take a chance on him. They hardly knew each other, but he knew enough to think she might be *the one.*

He thought back to something his father told him back when he was a sophomore in high school. His long-time crush had just broken his heart by refusing his invitation to the homecoming dance, so his father had brought him out for pizza. They'd talked about anything and everything else until they were halfway through their pie, and then all his father had said was, "There are lots of girls out there, Joshy. You'll probably date a bunch of them. Or maybe you'll only date a few. But one day, you'll find *the one.*" He'd given Josh an all-knowing smile and wiped his hands on a napkin. "It will probably knock you over when you least expect it. At least that's what happened with me. Your mother walked into my Biology 101 lab in college and there was something about her that made me take notice. We were lab partners and I could hardly focus on what we needed to do. I asked her out before we left the room. We were engaged a year later, but I knew right away I'd marry her someday. And every day I spent with her only made me more certain. She'd look at me in this special way…and my heart would melt. I wanted to make all her dreams come true and you know what? I've spent my life trying. I've never loved anyone as much as I love your mother and I never will." And with that, his father had picked up another slice of pizza. "Someday you'll find the one. And I can't wait to meet her once you do."

Josh had blown off his father's words, thinking his father couldn't possibly understand what he was going through. But now he knew…and it saddened him that his father would never meet Megan.

But the memory of his father's words gave him renewed determination. "So you're really going to break up with me tonight?"

She shook her head slowly. "No. *You're* going to break up with *me*." Tears filled her eyes and she stood. "I don't want to talk about it anymore. I want the rest of our time together to be happy."

He stood and pulled her into his arms. They had so many strikes against them, but he still held on to a slender thread of hope. "Okay."

She forced a smile. "So for today, let's pretend like we have forever and avoid thinking about what happens tonight. Happy memories. Agreed?"

He smiled softly at her. "Yes."

She grabbed his hand and tugged, her smile turning genuine and playful. "Now come take a shower with me."

"Okay, but I'm warning you now that I like really hot water."

Her eyes twinkled with wicked delight. "No cold showers

for you. I can live with that. But I don't think you'll need one today."

He laughed, but his heart was still aching, reminding him that there were plenty of cold showers in his foreseeable future.

At first he thought it might be impossible to recapture their earlier playfulness, but it slipped on easily when he was with her. They took turns washing each other, laughing about Josh confusing her shower gel for conditioner, then kissed until the water turned cold. Megan shrieked, still in the process of shaving her legs. He teased her, saying pioneer women had shaved in less favorable conditions, and she ordered him to get out.

"You know that you're actually doing me a favor, right?" he laughed. "I already told you how I feel about cold showers."

"Well in that case, I insist you stay."

He laughed and stepped to the back of the tub.

She looked up in surprise, her wet hair hanging in her face. "You're actually going to stay?"

"I take my fake marriage vows very seriously, Megan Vandemeer. Your wish is my command." He grinned and crossed his arms, pressing his back against the wall to keep out of the way of the stream of cool water.

She chuckled and returned her attention to shaving. The sight of her nude form bent over her long legs stirred him again. Good God, how many times could he have sex in a twenty-four-hour period?

She giggled. "I wasn't aware that marriage vows included staying in cold showers."

"My fake marriage vows contain many unconventional promises."

Her gaze returned to him, stopping mid-stroke with her razor. "And what would those be?"

He shrugged, grimacing with mock apology. "You'd have to

marry me to find out."

She finished with her leg and stood up, turning toward him with a seductive look in her eyes.

God, he wanted her.

Her eyes dropped down to his growing erection, then shot back up to his face. "Your vows include cold showers?" Her voice was deeper, thick with desire.

"Possibly."

She placed her hand on his chest and looked up into his eyes, but the teasing glint in her gaze told him it wasn't foreplay. "Then you won't mind this."

Before he realized what she was doing, she grabbed the detachable showerhead off the wall and sprayed him with cold water.

He yelled and tried to jump out of the tub, but she grabbed his arm, laughing. "I thought your vows included taking cold showers with me."

"Then after we exchange our fake marriage vows, I'll be happy to comply. I can't give up the milk before the wedding," he laughed. "Otherwise you wouldn't need to buy the cow."

She broke into giggles. "I bought a water buffalo last Christmas through Heifer International, so technically, I already own one."

He pulled the shower handle from her with one hand and pulled her to his chest with the other. "Then that would make you a bovine bigamist, Ms. Vandemeer."

She eyed the shower nozzle, which Josh had pointed toward the tile wall. "What are you going to do with that?"

He waggled his eyebrows. "If I were an eye for an eye type of guy, I'd hold you down and spray you."

"And if you weren't…?" A hopeful look crossed her face.

"I guess you'll never find out." He turned the water on her for a couple of seconds until she shrieked. Then, still holding her, he turned her sideways and reached for the faucet, turning off the water but leaving the showerhead dangling from the wall.

"You'll pay for that," she said between giggles.

He pressed her back against the tile and kissed her, playfulness turning to passion. Releasing the hold on her wrist, he pressed his palm against hers, interlacing their fingers. He pushed her arm against the wall while her free hand slid into his wet hair, holding him close. His erection pressed against her abdomen and she reached for him, stroking his shaft.

"You're a very resilient man," she grinned against his lips.

"Only with you," his voice deepened.

He reached between her legs and she gasped. "You really want to do this again?" she asked, spreading her legs wider for him.

He sucked in breath, telling himself to slow down, but Megan seemed to have other ideas. "I told you that I had a hard time deciding between having you in the shower or on the bed. This is what I call a win/win situation."

"So you like to have your cake and eat it too?"

He dropped her hand, then cupped her ass and lifted her higher on the wall. "I *definitely* love cake."

His mouth found hers as she helped guide him into her. She looped her legs around his waist and her arms around his neck, holding on as he began to move.

"Do you have any idea how much you turn me on?" he asked as he pushed inside her.

She tilted her pelvis to take him deeper. "I have a pretty good idea," she said, breathlessly.

Neither one of them lasted long. Her soft whimpers nearly pushed him over the edge, but he held on until she came too. When she cried out and tightened around him, he buried his face into her neck and dug his fingers into her ass cheeks as he plunged deep and hard inside her before coming.

He leaned against her and she started to laugh softly in his ear. "If that flight attendant knew how amazing you are, she probably would have fought harder to keep you."

He nuzzled her neck, making her squirm. "She never had me. You had my full attention on that flight."

"And now?" she asked.

He arched back to look into her face. "I'm all yours, Megan."

"Lucky me." She gave him a sweet smile and he marveled that she was such a chameleon—soft and vulnerable one minute, mischievous then next, then seductive and sexy.

Her eyes, focusing on something behind him, widened in horror, so he looked over his shoulder to see what had startled her. Gram was staring at them through the partially cracked shower curtain, holding up a small camera.

"I knew he'd have a nice patootie," the older woman said.

Her words jarred Megan from her trance. "Gram! What are you doing in here? Did you take *pictures?*"

"I heard all that banging and moaning. I thought we had a ghost. I wanted to get a picture of it. I figured we had a chance to be on that ghost show *The Dead Files.*"

"We don't have a ghost! Get out of here, Gram!"

"Can I just get one picture of Josh's ass?"

"No!"

Josh came to his senses and jerked the shower curtain shut, turning to face Megan. "How much do you think she saw?"

"I don't know, but I wouldn't be surprised to see your backside drawn in charcoal and taped to her wall."

"Oh, God…"

She laughed. "It could be worse. She could have seen the front."

"If your grandmother is home, does that mean your mother is? Doesn't she usually take her everywhere?"

Her amusement disappeared. "Oh, no…"

He dropped his hold on her and she slid down the wall.

Desperate to comfort her, he said, "I don't think she's here, Meggie. From what she said on her voice mail, she had a very full morning."

"Okay."

He cupped her cheek and tilted her face up to his. "Why don't you listen to her voice mail to verify, and I'll hurry and get dressed and go investigate. Okay?"

She nodded, looking worried.

"Babe, even if she's here, it's not the end of the world. She already expected us to have sex."

"But if Gram—who's as deaf as an eighteen-year-old dog—heard us, then my mother definitely did. I'll never be able to face her."

"Megan," he said, gently. "I'll take care of it."

She nodded again, looking relieved. "Okay. Thank you."

He got out of the shower and handed her a towel. "And I'll check the time too. I suspect we'll need to hurry if we're going to meet my brother at eleven."

"Where is he, anyway?" Megan asked. "Why isn't he here?"

The reminder of Noah's mission for the day hit Josh square between the eyes. How could he have forgotten? What the hell? Two days with this amazing, gorgeous woman and he was ready to toss in the towel and let his business close. But he knew he'd do anything to keep her in his life. Talking to her this morning made him realize that he'd made his father's legacy such a priority, he'd lost sight of everything else. Whether he could find a way to keep Megan in his life or not, he had some serious reevaluating to do with the rest of his life.

But he was going to work on one problem at a time. And Megan came first.

Chapter Twenty-One

Megan climbed out of the tub and listened to her mother's voice mail. Josh was right. It sounded like her mother would be tied up all day before leaving in the morning. But she noticed something else. Josh hadn't mentioned that she had a voice mail from Jay, yet he must have seen it.

Megan almost deleted it without listening, but curiosity got the best of her.

"Megan, I know our wedding was supposed to be in a couple of days and it's made me realize how badly I fucked things up with you. I want to take you out to dinner tomorrow night and we can talk things over. Give me a call."

She stared at her phone in disbelief. Did he really think it would be that easy?

Another question registered, giving her pause. Would she have gone back to him if Josh hadn't come into her world? No. There was no way she would have been able to trust him again. Jay Connors deserved whatever miserable life he'd created for himself. She deleted his voice mail, hoping her non-response would be message enough.

Josh came back to the bathroom as she put her phone on the bathroom counter next to Josh's dead one.

He leaned his shoulder against the doorjamb. "The good news is that your mother's nowhere to be found. Gram says she refused to run errands with her. Get this, Gram's excuse was that she thought she was coming down with something after running around naked last night."

Megan cringed. "Good…I guess."

"The bad news is that Gram wants to go to the tux rental place with us. Since I found her in her room with an easel and charcoal, I agreed. I figured it would stop her from immortalizing me in art…at least for the moment."

Megan laughed. "Looks like we have a chaperone."

Josh didn't look so excited. "I'd be lying if I said that idea thrilled me, but when your grandmother isn't streaking or trying to see me naked, she's actually kind of fun."

"I'm pretty fond of her myself."

"Say, I really need to check my emails, but my phone is dead. Any chance I can use the computer in the home office?"

She glanced up in surprise. Why hadn't she considered that? "Uh…sure. It's password-protected, though."

"Do you happen to know it?"

A grin spread across her face. "It's probably the same one Dad uses for everything. LoveBug4Me." She spelled it out for him. "He used to call me his Love Bug."

A strange look flickered in his eyes. "You're sure he won't mind me using it?'

"No, of course not."

He hesitated in the doorway. "How long do you think it will take for you to get ready? We have about forty minutes before we're expected to show up."

"Twenty to twenty-five minutes. I have to do something

with my hair." She lifted the damp strands hanging over her shoulder. "It only takes about fifteen minutes to get there."

"Perfect." He glanced at her phone. "Do you think I could borrow that? I need to check in with my business manager."

"Of course."

He gave her a quick kiss, then slid the phone off the counter and disappeared without another word.

Josh sat in Bart's office chair, staring at the startup screen to his desktop computer.

He knew the password that Bart Vandemeer used for everything. The implications of what he could do with that knowledge were mind-boggling.

Of course, Megan could be wrong, but Josh had seen the man in action the previous day. He wasn't technologically savvy, which would mean he probably didn't change passwords unless he had to. He entered the password into the startup screen, his stomach knotting as he waited to see if it worked. If the password was a dud, it got him off the hook with his big ethical decision.

But the password was accepted and the screen flipped to a starry sky background full of icons. Josh was relieved. He still wasn't sure he wanted to break Bart's privacy by checking email and document folders, but at least the decision hadn't been made for him. Josh had never made a choice passively when he could help it. He preferred to weigh his options and make a well-planned move. That's why he was more confused than ever since Megan had entered the equation. He'd never waffled this much in his life. Megan was his kryptonite.

First, he really did need to check his own email. The computer had two browsers. One was open with multiple tabs, including Bart's email, and the other browser was closed. Josh opened the second browser and uploaded his email account, not surprised to see fifty emails waiting for his attention. He'd only left Seattle two days ago, but he'd neglected things the day before while searching for information about PMV Engineering.

He wasn't surprised to see an email at the top of the list from his company's investor. It was Friday morning and his deadline was Monday. Sure enough, the investor wanted an update. Josh could snowball him and tell him the situation was close to being resolved—and for all he knew, Noah was making great headway at Bart's office—but instead he found himself answering that the situation was the same. While he had a promising lead that might change the patent ownership, he couldn't be sure it would pan out. He'd send an update as soon as he could.

The investor wouldn't be happy. He was a man of action as well, which Josh respected and could appreciate.

His breath caught when he saw an email from Angie, his business manager, which had been sent at four a.m. The title read "URGENT," and Josh felt sick to his stomach as he read it.

Josh,

I know you're out of town, although Noah won't tell me where…or why he flew off too. I also knew that you'd answer your phone if I called so late at night, and since there's nothing you can do, there's no sense in that. Still, I wanted to let you know as soon as I could.

Ted Murray's had a heart attack.

His wife called and said they took him to Harborview. He needs a quadruple bypass and will be off work for at least a month or more. Marilyn cried and said to thank you for covering the insurance premiums after the rate increase last year. If you hadn't increased the company contribution, he wouldn't have coverage. When things settle down, she plans to bake you a batch of her famous cinnamon rolls.

I know I'm old enough to be your mother, and although I've never acted like one to you, tonight I'm going to make an exception. I'm proud of you, Josh. You stepped up when your brother wouldn't. I know you've made sacrifices, even if no one else noticed. You could have easily given up, but you hung on instead. We both know how hard it would be for a fifty-seven-year-old man to start over in his career. Poor Ted would probably be jobless and destitute if you hadn't gone above and beyond to keep this place afloat. I just wanted you to know it hasn't gone unnoticed.

Angie

A lump burned in Josh's throat and he blinked back tears. He'd known Ted since he was a kid. The guy was like an uncle to Josh and Noah. Part of him wanted to say screw it all, hop on a plane, and go check on him. But the email was also a sharp reminder of the original purpose of his trip. He would do Ted more good here. His father's business wasn't something he could drop in the dust behind him just because he was considering a life with Megan Vandemeer. Hell, there was a good chance her father had played a part in the subterfuge that might well lead to Ted Murray's future joblessness.

He'd spent almost half his life sacrificing his personal life to keep the business from floundering. Now was not the time to change course. Lives hung in the balance. With newfound determination, he pulled up the document folders and began to search for any titles that could lead to evidence incriminating Bart Vandemeer. While he suspected the man wasn't devious enough to pull something like this off on his own, he could very well be part of the scheme. And moreover, he might be the weakest link. Josh couldn't ignore the phone call he'd overheard two nights ago.

Bart had more folders on his hard drive than Josh had expected, but most bore clients' names and contained reports.

After several minutes of searching, he decided his time would be better spent searching Bart's emails.

Turned out he had two email accounts open—one business, one personal. He checked the business account first. He started his search by reviewing the emails sent and received around the time his firm would have gotten ahold of the plans for the part, then moved on to the timeframe during which they would have applied for the patent. When he didn't discover anything significant, he moved to Wednesday and the days preceding. There were in-house congratulatory emails regarding the notification that the patent had been approved, and a few about Megan's upcoming wedding, but everything else was client-related.

So what was up with the phone call?

Noah had said he suspected the perpetrator still had the plans but wouldn't keep them at the office in case someone came across the incriminating evidence. What if the same principle could be applied to his emails? If he wanted to hide evidence from the firm, it would be safer to use his personal account.

The search took more time than he'd planned. Twenty minutes had passed and Megan would be ready to go any minute. Josh switched over to the personal account, and he was thankful to see Bart had fewer emails in this one. That made one stand out all the more: The sender was Herman, Moore, and Snyder, Attorneys at Law. He clicked to open it and started reading.

Mr. Vandemeer,

After examination of the paperwork you've provided, we feel you are safe from litigation—

"Josh?" Megan said softly.

His head jerked up, and though he tried to hide the fact he

was startled, the grin on her face let him know he wasn't off the hook. He sucked in a breath, overcome anew by her beauty. She wore another dress, a pale pink that contrasted with her dark hair.

Focus, Josh.

"I didn't mean to scare you," she said, entering the room.

He clicked over to his own email tab, trying to keep the action smooth so she wouldn't notice.

"You must be intent on your work. Did you get an answer to your problem?"

He swallowed as she moved next to him, her hand resting on his shoulder.

"Actually, I got a little more clarity."

Her fingertips moved to his neck, massaging the tense muscles at the base of his neck. "That's a good thing, right?" she asked sweetly.

His eyes sunk closed as he fought an inner battle. Could he continue carrying on with her this way, knowing full well that he and Noah were doing everything in their power to bring her father's firm down? Up until now, everything had been circumstantial. He had no idea what else that email might say, but he had a feeling it was their first piece of hard evidence.

"Yeah," he murmured, unable to make eye contact. "It's a good thing."

"Then why do you sound so glum?"

He looked up at her, trying to keep his voice from breaking. "Sometimes the answer we get isn't always the one we want."

Talk about the understatement of his life.

Chapter Twenty-Two

On the way to the tux rental shop, Gram talked nonstop about her drawing of Josh's backside, her research into nudist colonies in Belize, and the dress Megan's mother was making her wear—a very conservative pink suit paired with pearls. Knickers had seen the Queen Mother of England wear something similar and insisted it fit perfectly with the scheme.

"I'd rather strip down to the pearls before I walk down the aisle," Gram said. "But I'm afraid it would give your mother a heart attack and that would ruin your wedding."

Megan's eyed bugged out.

"*That's* what would ruin this wedding?" Josh murmured without his usual humor. He looked behind him to make sure Gram hadn't heard him, but she'd moved on to the cake Knickers had ordered.

Megan nodded and uh-huhed every so often, but most of her attention was fixed on Josh. Something had happened while he was reading his emails in her father's office. He was withdrawn and distant. Did he regret what they'd done? But surely that wasn't it. There was no way he could fake so much happiness and playfulness. She reminded herself that their fake engagement wasn't his only concern. In fact, it was probably a small fry compared to whatever impending decision he faced. He'd told her someone would be hurt no matter what he decided, so if he'd received information leading him toward one of the options, it was bound to bring him down. Josh McMillan was a good man. Hurting people wouldn't sit well with his soul.

She reached over and slipped her right hand under his, lacing their fingers. He didn't respond at first and she almost pulled away, but then his fingers curled over hers, squeezing tight.

He was still silent when she parked outside the store, though he helped Gram out of the back. She shook him off as soon as she was on her feet. "I can walk on my own."

"I wouldn't dream of helping you," Josh laughed, but it sounded forced to Megan's ears. "You could probably run laps around me, Gram."

"Damn straight," she muttered as she made her way to the door.

Josh started to follow her, but Megan snagged his hand and pulled him back.

She looked down at their linked hands, then up into his troubled eyes. "Josh, I know you have bigger issues than my stupid wedding. I want you to know that if you need to bail to take care of your business, you're free to go. Don't let me stop you."

He studied her for a moment before pulling her into his arms and crushing her lips with his. One arm encircled her back while the other dug into her hair, holding her firmly against his mouth.

The intensity of his kiss scared her. Was he telling her

goodbye?

But he pulled back and slid his hand down to her cheek, the corners of his lips turning up with a hint of a smile. "I have a job to do here first. Let's go get a tux."

Josh put an arm around her back and led her into the shop. Gram had already wandered in and found a chair to sink into.

As if Megan were a heat-seeking missile, she instantly spotted her mother in the back of the store. Kevin and Noah were with her, and they looked like two bucks ready to butt antlers. Apparently Kevin held the same animosity for both of the brothers McMillan. But Noah was holding his own. Megan figured Noah was the type of guy who could be dropped into a camp of cannibalistic pygmies and come out of the incident revered as a god.

Her mother gave her a disapproving frown as she approached. "Megan, I'm glad to see that you could manage enough responsibility to bring Josh to pick up his tux for your wedding tomorrow." She puckered her mouth. "Let's hope you can show up for your own wedding. I didn't spend fifty-six thousand dollars just to throw it all away."

Fifty-six thousand dollars? It had snowballed even more than Megan had realized. Her irritation grew, heat burning her cheeks. Josh had more important things to attend to than this sham wedding, and she was through with pretending. "Miss my wedding? Funny you should mention it, Mother—"

Josh's hand tightened, snugging her firm against his side. "Megan wouldn't dream of missing the wedding. Isn't that right, Meggie?"

"Meggie?" Kevin snorted. "She lets you call her that? She tried to beat the shit out of me every time I said it."

"Tried," Megan sneered, lifting an eyebrow. "You still can't admit that I beat you up almost every time!"

"I didn't fight that hard, *Meggie*," Kevin said. "You're a girl, in case you haven't noticed."

"I can still take you, *Kevio*!"

Noah watched their exchange with an amused grin. "Kevio?"

Megan's mother rolled her eyes, clearly irritated. "Kevin always attracted a lot of interest from girls in high school and had quite a few girlfriends. Megan compared him to Fabio one day, then started calling him Kevio." She shot them both a reprimanding look. "You two are too old to be bickering like children." She turned her back to them in dismissal of the subject. "Now we need to pick out a tux for Noah. He has to match because he's going to be in the wedding."

Ignoring her mother, Megan stuck her tongue out at her brother and he flipped her off. It was a shame that Gram had nodded off. She loved when Megan and Kevin pushed Knickers' buttons.

Josh's arm was still around her waist and she was surprised when his chest shook from a suppressed chuckle.

"How is Noah going to be in the wedding?" Megan asked her mother. "I thought you had the bridesmaids-to-groomsmen ratio perfectly figured out."

"I'm making your cousin Vince an usher now."

Noah shifted his weight. "I'm good with just sitting in the audience."

"I was tempted," Megan's mother said, giving her attention to a shoe display. "Especially since Josh's side is shockingly bare. But I think it's more important to have his brother standing beside him. Oh, here's the salesperson now."

A man emerged from the back room holding a black tuxedo.

Noah grimaced, clearing not impressed.

"I think this will fit you," the man said, handing the suit to Josh's brother. "I have the groom's tux out already." He eyed Josh up and down. "Are you the groom?"

Josh hesitated before nodding. "Yeah."

Megan tried to hide her surprise that Jay hadn't canceled his order. That type of slip-up was totally out of character. Still, she wasn't sure what good it did them. Josh was taller and broader than Jay, so there was no way the tux was going to fit him. She supposed it didn't really matter since he wasn't going to wear it anyway.

Unfortunately, the salesman shook his head. "They must have really screwed up your measurements in Seattle. I'm not sure the tux I pulled is going to fit you."

Megan's mother jolted. "What are you talking about?"

"I can tell the pants aren't long enough, and I don't think the jacket will fit his broad shoulders."

"*Please* tell me you have something that will fit."

The man looked worried. "It's June, Mrs. Vandemeer. We were lucky to have a tux for the groom's brother. I'll check, but I can't make any promises."

"You better take care of this or heads will roll!" her mother shouted.

Gram jerked upright in her chair. "We're having dinner rolls?" she asked, looking excited. "I'm hungry."

Kevin laughed, not a friendly sound, and his gaze landed squarely on Josh. "No one's head is going to roll…yet."

The clerk still looked nervous. "I also pulled the tux for the bride's brother." He turned to Kevin. "If you could go back and try it on to make sure it fits. Especially after this…situation." He nodded to Noah. "You can go back with him to try yours on too."

Noah looked even less thrilled than the other men did.

The clerk turned to Josh. "I'll need to re-measure you to see what we have." He grabbed the tape measure and quickly took Josh's measurements. "They were definitely off," he said quietly. "As I suspected, the tux we have won't fit."

"How could you people be so incompetent?" Knickers' voice took an icy tone. "It's such a simple thing. You just write down numbers."

The anxious clerk started to twitch and guilt ate at Megan's resolve. The poor man had Jay's measurements, not Josh's. And he was right. Josh was taller and broader than her ex-fiancé. There was no way the tux would fit. "Mom. Stop. It's not his fault the measurements are wrong."

She put her hand on her hip. "What on earth does that mean?"

Megan started to answer, but Josh's grip tightened on her side, and he cleared his throat. "Mrs. Vandemeer, what she means is that we suspect the salesperson in Seattle was dyslexic."

"What?" she asked in disbelief. "Why on earth would they put a dyslexic person in charge of taking measurements?"

"That's what I said," Josh said in exasperation. "In fact, I told Megan I didn't trust him, but she insisted I was overreacting." He looked down at Megan, his mouth pinched in disapproval.

Megan gasped in surprise. What on earth was he doing throwing her under the bus like that? Then she realized he was paving the way for their breakup. The thought made her heart beat faster, but in a way that was strangely close to panic.

Still, if Josh expected her mother to take her side, he was wrong. "Josh, I'm sure you've figured out by now that math isn't Megan's strong suit."

His arm stiffened and Megan was sure he was going to say something, but the clerk emerged from the back. "Good news, Mrs. Vandemeer! We have a tuxedo that will fit him."

She held her hand to her chest, fingering the pearls at the base of her throat. "Thank goodness."

"We'll need you try it on to make sure it fits."

Josh snuck a glance at Megan. For the first time since they'd started this charade, he looked uncertain.

Fear twisted in her stomach. Was he going to break up with

her now? She knew it had to be done, but even after what she'd said in the parking lot, she wasn't ready to let him go yet. She lifted on her tiptoes to give him a kiss. "I want to see you wearing it."

"Yes," Megan's mother said. "I need to see it on."

"Okay…" He still sounded unsure, but he followed the salesman to the back.

Megan pulled back her shoulders, waiting for her mother to attack now that they were alone with Gram, who had closed her eyes again after realizing they weren't about to eat.

"It pains me to see that you're still so irresponsible, Megan," her mother said. "I had hoped the fact you're getting married tomorrow would help you mature."

Megan considered responding, but what was the point?

Her tone softened. "Honestly, Megan. I was very worried after you and Josh disappeared last night. I understand why you left, but the least you could have done was call and let me know you were okay."

Megan met her mother's eyes and saw unexpected sincerity there. This was the first time she could remember her mother ever putting her concern for Megan's safety over the need to look good in front of other people. "You're right. I'm sorry."

Her mother's eyes widened in surprise. Megan knew why she was startled—she had never so willing volunteered an apology to her mother.

Maybe they were both growing up.

Kevin and Noah walked out of the dressing rooms, both wearing black tuxedos. Her mother's attention turned to the men, fussing over seams and hem lengths. But Josh was the one who stole her breath away when he emerged from the dressing rooms a moment later.

He wore a black tuxedo with shiny black lapels. His shirt was white and it was paired with a white bow tie. He stood in the doorway, the uncertainty on his face more pronounced than before. He was a handsome man. She'd recognized that the first moment she saw him, but it was what was in his heart that had drawn her to him. As his gaze sought out hers, she walked to him, unable to keep away. She stopped a foot in front of him and placed her hands on his lapels. "You are the most beautiful man I've ever seen," she whispered, tears filling her eyes.

His eyes searched hers for something—she wasn't sure what, but she offered him a soft reassuring smile and the twinkle in his eyes returned.

They stared at each other for several seconds before Kevin made a production of releasing a groan. "Save it for the honeymoon."

Sadness flickered in Josh's eyes, but only for a second before he wrapped an arm around her back and pulled her gently to his chest. "Give the girl a second," he said to her brother. "She's been overcome by my ruggedly handsome good looks."

Noah laughed, but Megan didn't so much as spare him a glance. Josh was her sole focus. She didn't want to lose him. What was she going to do?

The men went back to take off their tuxes and after a couple of minutes, Megan's mother's no-nonsense voice returned. "I'm glad you finally deigned to make an appearance because we have things that need to be done and we're desperately behind. I have an updated itinerary for you in the Navigator. Let's go."

Megan spun around to face her. "Go? What about Josh?"

"He's going with his brother."

She shook her head, adamant. "No. Whatever I'm doing, he's coming with me."

"It's the day before your wedding, Megan," her mother groaned in an exasperated tone. "After tomorrow, you can spend your entire life with him, but I need you today. It doesn't help that your irresponsibility has added more things to our TBD list."

"How has my disappearance last night added to the list?"

Her mother rolled her eyes. "Not last night, Megan. I'm talking about your weight and your hair." She shuddered. "We were lucky my stylist could fit you in this afternoon."

Megan stared at her in disbelief. Her weight? Was she seriously bringing that up again?

"What's wrong with Megan's weight?"

She turned to see Josh, who had reappeared from the dressing rooms, now dressed in his jeans and shirt. There was an unmistakable undertone of menace in his voice.

Gram sat up again, and Megan suspected the older woman's nap had been faked to avoid interacting with Knickers. Smart woman.

Surprisingly, her mother looked slightly embarrassed. "It's…well…most brides lose weight before their weddings, and her dress was too small because she didn't."

Josh's eyes widened and a stunned silence followed her mother's words. When he spoke, his voice was controlled and tight, showing more authority than Megan had ever heard him use. "Lose weight? Why would she lose weight? She's absolutely perfect the way she is, and without being vulgar or crass, I like her curves just as they are. And as for her hair—" he closed the distance between them, "—it's perfect too." He glanced at Megan's mother, his gaze allowing for no argument. "This woman by my side is the woman I want to marry, exactly as she is right now. I don't want her transformed into some cookie-cutter Barbie doll, so don't you dare try to do it."

Her mother gaped at him, her mouth drooping open. He had done what Megan had previously thought impossible: He'd stunned Nicole Vandemeer into silence.

Gram started to chuckle.

His hand snagged Megan's, his fingers curling around hers

and holding tight. "So now that the stylist appointment can be canceled, what else do we need to do?"

That shook her mother out of her stupor. "It's on the itinerary."

"It's a damn wedding," Josh said, trying to keep his anger in check. "Not a global summit. What do Megan and I need to do today? Absolute musts only."

Her mother's face reddened, although Megan wasn't sure if it was from anger or embarrassment. Perhaps both. "She needs to pick up her dress and make sure it fits after the alterations. You both need to pick up the marriage license."

Megan's hand grew clammy at the mere mention.

Her mother's resolve seemed to be returning, along with her haughtiness. "As I said in my message this morning, I have an appointment at Powell Gardens at two to go over everything for tomorrow with the event planner. I would prefer for Megan to come to that, but I need you both at the Platte County courthouse at three-thirty."

"Why so precise?" Megan asked.

Her mother's scowl deepened. "It's all in the itinerary, Megan. Did you even bother to read it?"

Megan figured her silence was answer enough.

Her mother rolled her eyes again. "I have a photographer scheduled to be there to take your pictures."

"*Getting our marriage license?*"

"It's an important moment to preserve."

Megan shook her head, at a loss for words.

"So Megan needs to pick up her dress, and we need to meet you at three-thirty at the courthouse," Josh said in a tone that was all business. It was obvious he'd axed the Powell Gardens stop as must-do. "Anything else?"

"You were supposed to go see Bart at his office to take him his tux and make sure it fits before the shop closes today." Her eyes hardened and she shot the clerk a glare. "And after today's fiasco, it's a good thing I already budgeted in time to make sure it worked out."

"Josh's tux issues weren't this poor man's fault, Mother."

"Nevertheless…"

"I'll take care of it," Noah said, stepping forward and clapping Josh on the shoulder. "You go spend the day with your bride-to-be. I'll take Bart his tux."

Megan's mother looked dubious.

"I'd love to do it, Mrs. Vandemeer," Noah said, using a toothpaste commercial smile that Megan was sure had gotten him more women than he could count.

"If you're sure…"

Noah's grin spread. "Well, that settles it. You two crazy kids go have fun picking up wedding dresses and getting that marriage license." He turned slightly so Megan's mother couldn't see him snicker.

"We'll see you at three-thirty." Josh tugged on Megan's hand and dragged her toward the front door.

"Run, kids!" Gram called after them. "Escape while you can!"

"Megan!" her mother called after her. "Do *not* let him see your dress."

"See you later, Mom," she said as Josh continued out the door, not stopping until after he opened the car door for her.

"You just bowled over my mother," Megan said as she climbed into the driver's seat. "Thanks."

His hand tightened around the edge of the car door and his eyes darkened. "I probably should have let you handle it, but she infuriated me." He shook his head in disbelief. "Does you seriously think you need to lose weight?"

Megan looked up into his face, floored by the protectiveness radiating off him. "It doesn't matter. Let's just get the dress, then eat lunch." She gave him a wicked grin. "I seem to have worked up an appetite."

"Sounds good to me."

The bridal shop was only ten minutes away and they made an unspoken pact not to talk about their impending troubles. Megan told Josh about all the spats she and her brother used to get into as kids and how all her friends used to crush on him, Blair included.

"No offense," Josh said in a dry tone, "but I have trouble imagining Blair developing a crush on anyone. It seems like she'd be happier if she were actually *crushing* them instead."

"I told you that she wasn't always like this. She means well." When he didn't respond, she said, "Tell me more about growing up with *your* brother."

She pulled into the bridal store parking lot and Josh held out his hands, beaming. "Looks like my Noah stories will have to wait."

"You can tell me at lunch."

Josh followed her into the bridal store, holding the door open for her. The saleswoman recognized her and smiled, probably in part because her mother was nowhere in evidence. "We have your dress ready for you. Go on back to the fitting room and I'll bring it to you."

Josh looked around, wariness in his eyes as he took in the racks of lace, satin, and organza dresses.

Megan laughed. "You don't have to be in here, Josh. You can wait in the car."

"No, I want to see you in your dress."

"My mother specifically forbade it."

He gave her a wicked grin. "Since when do you obey your mother?"

His words caught her off guard. Her entire life had been one act of secret disobedience after the other, except for her major, impossible-to-hide decisions like running off to college and moving to Seattle. It wasn't that she was purposely hiding her defiance. She was avoiding conflict. Megan had no problem standing up to anyone else. So why couldn't she stand up for herself with her mother?

"Megan?" Josh asked, his smile fading.

She threw her arms around his neck. She couldn't believe she was considering what she was considering. Was this man, whom she'd only known for two days, worth the risk? What she felt for him scared her, but the thought of losing him scared her more.

His arm tightened around her back and his hand cupped the back of her head. "Hey, are you okay?"

She leaned back and searched his face, not even sure what she was looking for—perhaps some sign that he was right there with her, that fate really had seated them together on that plane. Could there actually be something to the fortune teller's prediction?

"Do you want to just skip this?" he whispered, his eyes filled with worry. "It's not like we're really getting married."

She forced a smile. "No. I'm just being silly." She broke loose from his hold. "You have a seat and I'll show it to you."

His eyes searched hers. "Are you sure?"

"Sit," she ordered, her good mood returning. "I'll be out after I wrestle this monster on."

"Okay."

She found the saleswoman in the back waiting with the crinoline skirt. "Do you have a strapless bra?"

Megan cringed. "No."

"Not to worry. Your mother had us set one aside."

"Of course she did," Megan mumbled.

"You get undressed and put on the bra, then I'll be in to help you with the dress."

Megan didn't waste time disrobing and putting on the bra. The saleswoman returned moments later and helped her pull the fluffy skirt over her head.

"Tomorrow I'm sure your hair will be done, so you'll

probably want to step into the slip, but the dress will still have to go over your head."

"Okay," Megan said, only half listening. None of it mattered. She would never wear the dress again anyway.

The clerk removed the dress from the hanger. "Ready?" the woman asked, holding the dress toward her.

"As much as I'll ever be."

The clerk gave her a questioning look, but kept silent.

It took several minutes to get the dress over her head and laced in the back. The clerk opened the door and helped her maneuver the massive skirt through the opening. "Are you sure you want the groom to see you?" the woman asked. "Some people believe it's bad luck."

"I've had enough bad luck to last me a lifetime. I'll risk it." She picked up the skirt and rounded the corner.

Josh was sitting in a chair, his legs extended and crossed at the ankles, his arms crossed over his chest. When she entered the viewing area, he sat upright, his gaze combing her from head to toe.

She stepped onto the short stage and dropped the fluffy skirt.

Josh still eyed her, his face expressionless.

Megan cocked an eyebrow. "That bad, huh?"

He shook his head and stood. "The opposite of bad."

She looked down at the massive skirt, her nose wrinkling in disgust. "I look like Cinderella…if she stuck her finger in the light socket just before running off to the ball to seduce Prince Charming. Now all I need is a pair of glass slippers. But it fits the princess theme, so if Knickers is happy, everyone is supposed to be."

"But *you're* not happy?"

"What does it matter? It's not like there's going to be a wedding anyway."

The sales clerk, who had begun inspecting the seams on the

dress, jerked her head up in surprise, but refrained from comment.

"Why did you buy the dress if you hate it so much?"

"First of all, I don't really hate the dress. It's beautiful. It's just not what I wanted. And I *didn't* order it. My mother did." She took a deep breath to keep from tearing up, but her voice still broke as she continued, "Apparently, the dress I chose—the dress I *love*—didn't fit in with her princess theme so she ordered this one."

"You're kidding?'

"I wish I was."

"That's just not right."

She lifted one shoulder into a half shrug, trying to convince herself it didn't matter, even though it still hurt. "It is what it is."

"Which one did you pick?"

Her head jerked up in surprise. "It doesn't matter now."

"It matters to me. Which one did you pick? I want to see it."

A warmth spread through her chest, and she resisted the urge to hug him. "I don't even know if they have it anymore."

"We do," the sales woman said, standing upright.

"How do you know about it?" Megan asked, looking over her shoulder at her. "I don't remember you being here when I tried on dresses last fall."

"I wasn't. But I took the call when your mother changed the order. It was too late to cancel the first dress, but your mother pitched such a fit the manager let her order the new one, taking the loss and hoping we'd sell the original. I've never heard of a bride's mother canceling a bride's dress behind her back like that. It was the talk of the store for weeks. We would have called you if any of us knew how to reach you."

"*You still have it?*" Megan asked

The woman nodded.

"Can she try it on?" Josh asked.

"Sure…" the woman said. "But you can't trade it. This dress has already been altered to fit you. No refunds."

"That's okay," Josh said. "I still want to see it on her."

"This one looks beautiful," the woman said, fluffing the skirt, then stepping off the stage. "But I'll pull the other one if you want to see it."

"Thanks," Josh said, offering his hand to Megan.

"Why are you doing this?" she asked as she stepped down next to him.

"Don't you want to try it on again?"

Did she? "I don't see the point." She loved the dress, yes, but this whole charade had gotten out of hand. Her mother had spent the equivalent of a year's salary on the wedding and for what? Wasn't a wedding supposed to be the commitment of two people who not only loved each other but genuinely *liked* each other enough to promise a lifetime commitment? This wedding would be no less of a farce if Jay were here with her now. She had thought she loved Jay, but now she wasn't sure she'd even *liked* him. She was embarrassed to admit it to herself, but there it was. The truth. Finding Jay nailing his secretary on his desk was the best thing that had ever happened to her.

But if she were teasing the truth out of this screwed-up mess, she also knew that the dress she'd chosen meant something to her. It had been her symbol that she would get married someday and have a different marriage than her parents did. She'd almost screwed up with Jay, but she was realizing what was important. And the man in front of her ranked very high on that list, even after only knowing him a few days.

He gave her a coaxing smile. "Indulge me."

She returned to the fitting room and waited for the woman

to come back and help her change. The dress she'd chosen was lighter and rather than the crinoline skirt of the Cinderella dress, its skirt was made of swathes of silk with scattered gatherings around the skirt and a small train. The bodice was like a wrap dress, with a V-neck that showed off her chest without revealing too much cleavage. The first dress had been strapless, but this one had short, silk, off-the-shoulder sleeves.

"This dress does suit you better," the saleswoman said as she zipped up the back. "You need a different veil. I don't think the tiara your mother picked would work. Wait a moment. I have one in mind."

She was back within seconds, holding a comb with an attached veil, which she carefully arranged on top of Megan's head. "That's much better," the woman said, but there was regret in her voice. "It's such a shame your mother didn't stick with this one. I really do wish we could exchange it."

"It's okay. I'm not getting married anyway." The saleswoman started to say something, but Megan interrupted her. "It's a long story. Josh is just filling in."

The woman took it in stride, which made Megan wonder how many weird stories she heard in her line of work. "Well, let's let your *substitute* groom see you."

"Okay," Megan said, butterflies fluttering in her stomach. The sales clerk was right. This dress was so much more *her*. While she hadn't thought anything of showing the other dress to Josh, this one mattered. What if he didn't like it?

His back was turned, his eyes gazing out the shop's windows, but he must have heard the ruffle of silk because he turned slowly to look at her.

She took several steps toward him, then stopped, searching his face for a reaction.

He must have seen the worry in her eyes because he closed the distance between them, gently slipped his hand behind her head and pulled her mouth to his. It was a soft kiss, gentle and reassuring. When he lifted his head, his eyes were filled with warmth. “God, Megan. You’re beautiful.”

She flushed, slightly irritated with herself that his opinion meant so much.

“Your mother is an idiot,” he murmured, picking up her hand as he took a step back. “This dress is so much more you.”

The clerk stood behind Megan, smiling sadly. “It fits perfectly. This dress looks like it was made for you.”

Megan stepped up onto the stage and studied herself in the mirror.

A group of women entered the store, chatting excitedly, and an anxious look filled the saleswoman’s eyes. “My next appointment is here, and the other consultant called in sick.”

Megan forced a smile. “That’s okay. I’m done.” She stepped off the stage, ignoring Josh’s offer to help, confused by her feelings. She couldn’t name all of the emotions brewing in her chest, but she could name one, pushing its way to the front, demanding attention—sadness. She didn’t know if it was over the man she was possibly walking away from or the dress she’d never have, because after wearing it for Josh, she knew she could never wear it for another man.

Chapter Twenty-Three

When they got back into the car, Josh told her that he'd changed his mind. He wanted to get a phone after all.

She told herself it didn't mean anything, but somehow she sensed it did.

Nevertheless, his earlier distance was gone. She stopped at a phone store next to the shopping mall and stayed with him while he picked out his replacement. He touched her nonstop—either holding her hand or putting an arm around her. And she teased him about how he'd told her earlier in the morning that he was going to be the attentive boyfriend she would either love or hate.

"And which is it so far?" he asked with a grin.

She lifted her eyebrows playfully. "I'll let you know later, but I have no complaints so far."

He snaked an arm around her back and pulled her close, searching her eyes.

"You two are so cute," the sales girl gushed. "It's so

wonderful to see couples in love."

She expected Josh to pull away or protest, but he only pulled her closer and placed a sweet kiss on her forehead.

In love? It was too soon to make that kind of pronouncement, yet there was no denying she was heading there fast. What if they didn't go past tonight? How would she live with that? But something told her focusing on the future would be a mistake if it meant missing out on the present.

They left the store and she drove him to a crummy little strip mall, refusing to tell him where they were headed until she parked. "Don't let the exterior fool you," she said, pointing at the sign. Faded cartoon characters adorned the sign. A man on a horse carrying a Mexican flag was next to a man with a huge handlebar mustache holding a set of maracas. A third man was about to take a bite out of a huge taco. "Three Amigos has the best Mexican food I've ever eaten. And they make great margaritas too."

"You don't have to sell me on it. We're already here. And I'm starving, so let's go get a table."

Fifteen minutes later, their orders were in and Megan had already polished off one margarita and, after Josh's assurance he'd drive to the courthouse, asked for a second one. They had fallen back into their lightheartedness from earlier when Megan's phone rang. "It's probably my mother making sure I haven't run off again," she said, faking a cringe. But when she saw the name on the screen, her smile fell. Why was Jay calling her again?

"Is it your mother?"

She silenced the ringer and stuffed it back into her purse. "It doesn't matter. You were telling me a story about your brother scratching your name in the side of your mother's car with a key when you were kids."

He studied her for a moment and she wondered if he suspected something, but he resumed his story.

They had finished their lunch, Megan had polished off her second drink, and they were sharing fried ice cream when Josh pulled his phone out of his pocket and glanced at the screen. He set his spoon on the table. "It's Noah. I better take it."

"Sure. Of course," she said, but she wasn't prepared for him to leave the table and go outside.

Why couldn't he talk to his brother in front of her? But before she could think it through, her own phone rang again. She pulled it out, planning to take advantage of Josh being outside so she could tell Jay to take a flying leap. But it wasn't him at all; it was Blair.

She answered, her tone sweeter than usual, "Hello, Blair."

"Please tell me you've changed your mind."

"About what?"

"The rehearsal dinner." Megan could tell Blair was trying to be civil.

"I suggested pasta, but my mother insists on chicken, and you know Knickers, so no changing my mind about that."

"Very funny." Her sarcasm was heavier than usual. "Seriously, Megan. Just how far are you planning to take this?"

"This is going to end tonight, Blair. Calm down. It's under control."

"*Calm down?* You're sleeping with a man who's lying to your parents about his name…a man you've known for less than three days. Not to mention the fact that you're asking me to come to a rehearsal for a wedding that's not even taking place. Why should I *calm down?*"

"Who said I was sleeping with him?"

"Please. Don't insult me. I can hear it in your voice."

No wonder Blair was such a great divorce attorney. She was like a human lie detector. "My sex life is no one's business but my own."

"Maybe so, but it's my job as a friend to point out when you're being irresponsible."

Megan remained silent, worried about what she'd say if she didn't give herself a second to calm down. Several seconds of silence passed, but she still didn't trust herself. "I think I better hang up before I say something I'll regret."

"Megan." Blair's tone softened, but it wasn't enough to appease Megan.

"The rehearsal is at six at Powell Gardens. Come or don't come. I'll understand if you don't." Megan hung up before Blair could respond. She stared at the phone, wondering if she was being too hard on her friend. What would she do if their roles were reversed? Probably have Blair admitted for a psych evaluation.

Josh slid into his seat, not looking much happier than Megan.

"Everything okay with Noah?" she asked.

He scowled, but tried to force a smile. "Fine. Just a brother thing."

He was obviously hiding something from her, but what business was it of hers?

He gestured toward the phone in her hand. "Another missed call?"

She shrugged. "Blair."

"I take it that it didn't go well?"

"Once again, she's made it abundantly clear that she doesn't approve of what we're doing."

He was silent for a moment. "You can't really blame her, can you? She's trying to be a good friend."

"Whose side are you taking?" It was a complete turnaround from his previous attitude toward Blair.

"I'm not taking anyone's side. But you've been friends with her for what? Ten years?"

"Over twenty."

"Don't throw that away on an asshole like me."

She gaped at him. Where was this attitude coming from?

"What did your brother say that bothered you so much?"

"Nothing." He pulled his wallet out. "Shouldn't we get going? We need to get a marriage license."

She dug inside her purse and pulled out a credit card. "I said I'd pay for lunch, Josh."

"Megan, will you just let me pay for it. *Please.*" His tone was shorter than he'd used with her before. What did she really know about him, though? Maybe this was normal for him.

No. She may have only known him for a short period of time, but she knew something was up. And it had to do with that phone call.

"Fine. I need to go to the restroom anyway."

She went to the restroom and checked her own phone. Blair hadn't called her back, but she felt a sudden urge to talk to Libby.

"Hey, Libs," Megan said when she answered. "I just needed to hear a friendly voice."

"Is Knickers that bad today? She must have been furious after your disappearing act last night. She was fit to be tied when she couldn't find you two. Poor Noah got the third degree. And Knickers was even more furious when Noah couldn't reach Josh's phone."

"Sorry to leave you with such a mess on your hands. And thanks for taking care of Noah."

"Hey, if you ran off with Josh and had a good night, it was well worth it. And there's no taking care of Noah. He's a player, plain and simple."

"So there's nothing between you?"

"What? I'm dating Mitch."

"I know, but…"

"No, Megan. There's nothing between us. We're friends. Friends who like to flirt, but friends nonetheless."

"Is someone like Noah capable of being just friends with a woman?"

"That's pretty judgmental, Knickers Junior."

"I know you're right, but you have to admit that you've met more than your fair share of men like him. How many of them have been good at having platonic female friends?"

"You hardly know Noah."

"So I pegged him wrong?"

Libby paused a beat, then laughed. "No. You have him exactly right. But before you say anything else, I'll just say our friendship is based on an alliance."

"What alliance?"

"The goal of keeping you and Josh together."

"I'm not pinning any hopes on a future just yet."

"Why?"

"Look, today I'm just living for the moment. That's the gift I was granted. I admit that I want more with him, but there are just too many variables in play for me to count on anything. And at the risk of beating a dead horse, we can't forget how my mother's going to react to all of this. You remember the mess with my Aunt Heather."

Libby sighed. "Damn. I forgot about her. You're in deep shit."

"I know," Megan said in defeat. "But it doesn't matter. Josh has been wonderful all morning—even sticking up for me with Knickers—but he just took a call from Noah and now he's acting cold and distant. I can't help thinking Noah said something to make Josh have second thoughts about me."

"Impossible. Noah wants you two together."

"That's weird, don't you think? Noah doesn't seem like the type of guy to play matchmaker."

"It's his kid brother and he knows you make him happy. That's all it is. Quit being so suspicious or you'll start to sound like Blair."

"Very funny."

"He likes you, Megan, and you like him too. I see the way

you look at him. I've never seen you so taken with a guy, and Noah says the same is true of Josh."

"It's all just happening so fast, Libs. What am I supposed to do?"

"Just go with it for now. Fate put you together in the first place. It will keep you together. The fortune teller said so."

Libby had always been the dreamer, while Blair was invariably the voice of reason. Both qualities were constantly at war in Megan. She wasn't so certain fate would work everything out—and she definitely didn't believe some fake fortune teller—but this one time she really hoped Libby was right.

"Go have fun with him. Just enjoy the ride, Megs. Stop stressing. It'll all work out."

"Well, fate only has until tonight."

"Don't throw this away," Libby said, taking an uncharacteristic serious tone. "If you do, I have a feeling you'll regret it for the rest of your life."

That's exactly what Megan was afraid of.

Chapter Twenty-Four

Josh signed the check and left the restaurant, then started to pace the sidewalk as he waited for Megan. Noah's phone call had left him conflicted. He played it over again in his head, hoping for a better resolution.

Josh had told Noah about Bart's password and the suspicious email while they were in the dressing rooms at the tux shop. He'd no sooner picked up Noah's phone call than his brother said, "She's right. The password works on everything…everything but his personal email account. Is there any way you can quiz her to see if she knows of any alternate passwords?"

"No. That one was a fluke, and even if I could work it into a normal conversation, I suspect she wouldn't know. She said it was the password he used for everything…so we're screwed."

"Slow down there," Noah laughed. "We may have struck out there, but that doesn't mean I came up empty-handed."

It turned out that Noah had already made more progress in two hours at Bart Vandemeer's office than Josh had made in a day. "Don't ever become a detective, Joshy," Noah chuckled. "You couldn't investigate your way out of a paper bag."

"Hey, I got the password."

Noah just laughed. "Which you already admitted was a lucky fluke."

"Who did you screw to get what you needed?" Josh asked dryly.

"While I'm flattered you think I could seduce someone so quickly during a weekday, and in an office to boot, that's not how I did it."

"So how *did* you do it?"

"Flattery and asking the right questions."

"That's great. Gloat all you want. What I really want to know is what you've found."

"I think you might be right about Bart Vandemeer being a part of this."

Josh's heart sank. He had hoped to be wrong, even though the email seemed like pretty substantial evidence. "Why would you say that?"

"The bookkeeper let it slip that Bart has been siphoning money off the company. Thousands of dollars."

"That's no surprise. Nicole Vandemeer spent fifty-six grand on a wedding Megan didn't even want."

"Down boy. You nearly jumped down Nicole's throat at the tuxedo rental store."

"She deserved it."

"Well, cool your outrage. You need to stay in that woman's good graces."

"Why?" Noah didn't answer and an anxious ball formed in the pit of Josh's stomach. "Noah? Why do I need to stay in the woman's good graces?"

"You can't break up with Vandemeer's daughter tonight."

A disarming mixture of relief and dismay washed through him. "Why not?"

"Because the partner's son, Drew Peterman, is showing up for the wedding tomorrow. I saw a photo of him in the partner's office with his fiancée."

"Is that supposed to mean something? Do I really care who's on the guest list?" Josh was still trying to decide whether postponing his inevitable breakup was a good thing or not.

"Peterman's fiancée is the woman I slept with the night the plans disappeared."

"Holy shit."

"Exactly." Noah sounded smug, not that Josh could blame him. It was a monumental find. Of course, Noah was the one who'd lost the plans to Drew Peterman's fiancée in the first place.

"If Drew Peterman stole the plans, how does Bart Vandemeer come into play?"

"Bart's been taking so much money from the company that the firm needs this patent to survive just like we do."

"Shit. That's the proof we need." This should have made him happy, but all it did was make him nauseated.

"Yep. It's shitty as hell, but it's their firm or ours, and they didn't play fair, so which one do you pick, Joshy?"

"You know damn well which one I pick."

"Maybe, maybe not," Noah murmured. "But all of this is to say that we need to be around tomorrow. I'm going to corner the fiancée and get her to admit she stole the plans."

"How in God's name do you propose to do that?"

"I have my ways, now you need to use yours. Convince Vandemeer's daughter to keep the charade going."

"We're getting a marriage license this afternoon, Noah."

"I heard."

"I'm pretty damn sure you have to provide ID to apply. Megan's mother is going to be there."

"Take care of it."

"That's helpful."

"Look, Josh. I know this is totally unlike you, but it's obvious you like the girl, so keep playing house." He paused and his voice softened. "Dude, I know I've sucked as a brother, and what I'm asking you to do sucks more than any of it all combined, but we *need* this. Think about Ted—yeah, I know about Ted. Where's he going to be if we close our doors on Monday?"

Josh didn't answer. He didn't need to.

"Maybe you can get the happy ending you truly deserve, Josh, but for now we need you to keep this going."

"I don't think I can do that." Josh's voice cracked.

"You can and you will. Now I have to go. I'll see you at the rehearsal."

The conversation had sucked something out of Josh and he'd taken it out on Megan. She didn't deserve any of this. Not her mother, not her cheating ex-fiancé, and especially not Josh and the havoc he brought with him.

Now, as he waited for her to join him, he wrestled with his conscience. The way he saw it, he had three options: One, tell her everything right now. Two, break up with her at the rehearsal dinner like they'd originally planned. Or three, follow through with Noah's crazy plan. But what would happen then? Was he supposed to ditch her before the wedding?

She studied his face as she stepped out of the restaurant, probably trying to judge his temperament. Her brow was lowered with worry and cautiousness. He vowed to make this as easy on her as possible, but he had no idea what that entailed. So he followed his gut, which meant recapturing their earlier happiness.

He closed the distance between them and pulled her into his arms, kissing her with abandon, his deep fear of losing her fueling his passion.

Her hands clutched at his chest, trying to pull him closer, as his arm tightened around her back and his other hand nestled the nape of her neck. He could feel her pulse racing and the knowledge of how he affected her only turned him on more. But they were standing on a public sidewalk, and even if it wasn't prime lunch time, they'd already made enough of an exhibition of themselves. He lifted his head, pleased to see she was just as breathless as he was.

"I'm sorry," he said, his hand caressing her neck. "I was irritated with Noah and I took it out on you."

"Josh, it's okay."

"It's not, but I promise to try my best not to be an ass for the rest of the day."

"Until tonight," she said.

Rather than answering, he took the car keys from her hand. "Let's go get a marriage license."

As he drove to the courthouse, he reached over and interlaced his fingers with hers. She turned and offered him a soft smile and something in his chest felt warm and overwhelming. His hand squeezed hers tighter as he tried to decipher what he felt. He wasn't big on hand-holding. It had always felt clingy and confining, yet here he was, not only instigating it, but enjoying it.

Using the map app on her phone, she gave him directions until he pulled into the parking lot of the gray stone building slightly after three-thirty. "My mother is going to have a fit that we were late."

"Only by a few minutes."

"It's enough to release the kraken," she teased.

As they walked to the building, he held her hand again, grateful that she didn't seem to mind.

When they entered the office of the recorder of deeds, Megan's mother was sitting in an ancient vinyl chair, drumming her fingers on the arm. Josh was surprised she'd sit on something so tacky and most likely germy, but maybe she'd wiped it down with an antibacterial wipe first. A very unhappy man who appeared to be in his thirties sat next to her. A camera bag rested on the floor at his feet. He shot a glare at the both of them, then glanced at the phone in his hand.

"Hello again, Mom," Megan said with a cheerful tone.

Her mouth pressed into a tight line. "You're late."

"Only by a few minutes."

"Every minute counts. The office closes at four."

"So why didn't we do this sooner?"

"This is the only time the photographer could come."

Megan turned her attention to the man who now stood behind her mother. She extended her hand to him, most likely as a peace offering. "Hi, I'm Megan. Thanks for indulging my mother's eccentricities."

She winked and he laughed and winked back, his mood visibly lightening.

Josh offered the man his own hand. "I'm Josh. *The groom.*" He hadn't meant to add that part, but he hadn't liked the way the photographer was acting with her.

What the hell? He'd never been jealous of previous girlfriends. But he had more serious issues to deal with than self-analysis—like the fact that he was here to not only file for a very real marriage license, but he had to keep his real last name a secret from the other two people in room besides Megan.

They approached the counter and filled out the application, the photographer taking photos of them. Megan seemed irritated, but Josh was more concerned someone would announce his real last name and blow his cover.

A clerk took the application and their driver's licenses. "That will be fifty-one dollars," she said, giving them an expectant look.

"Do you take a credit or debit card?" Josh asked.

The woman's mouth pursed with disapproval. "Cash only. Exact change. It's very clearly stated on the website."

Megan looked up at him, her eyes wide. There went his hope that she was prepared. He was surprised that Nicole hadn't already slapped the bills on the counter in anticipation of their ill-preparedness. Apparently, even she had her limits. But she'd slipped out the door, presumably to the restroom, and the photographer felt no need to pony up.

Megan and Josh started digging through their wallets and together they managed to come up with the exact amount. When they found the last quarter, he breathed a sigh of relief.

"I didn't think we were going to make it," Megan said, shaking her head as she closed her wallet.

"Can you imagine the look on your mother's face?"

"I'd rather not."

The clerk handed back their driver's licenses and told them she'd be right back.

"What exactly am I supposed to get photos of?" the photographer asked.

"The two of them filling out the application," Nicole said, sounding disgruntled as she walked back into the small office waiting room.

"I got that, so can I go?" he asked, looking at the clock at the wall.

Megan's mother rolled her eyes. "Fine, leave."

The man grabbed his bag, not even taking time to put his camera away. But the clerk was on her way back with the license and Nicole stopped him.

"I want you to get a photo of them holding it."

"Maybe you should wait until tomorrow, Mom," Megan suggested, casting a nervous glance at Josh. She must have been thinking the same thing he was. If they were taking photos of the license there was a good chance Knickers would see his real name. "When we actually sign it."

Megan's mother gave her an exasperated look. "Oh, we'll get that too. You can never have too many photos."

The clerk returned to the counter with the paperwork. "Here you go, Mr. Mc—"

Josh reached for the paper, cutting her off. "Thank you."

Megan's mother gave the clerk a strange look. "What did you start to call—?"

"Mom," Megan interrupted, putting an arm around her mother's shoulders and squeezing as she pulled her away from the clerk. "How about you and I get a photo together?"

"Really?" she asked, sounding shocked.

"Of course," Megan's tone softened as she said it. Josh was surprised by how happy the older woman looked.

The photographer shook his head and grimaced. Two days ago Josh might have reacted the same way, but now he was learning to take things in stride. The photographer snapped several shots—Josh joining halfway through—before Megan dropped her hold on her mother.

"Thank you, Mr...?"

"Steve," the photographer supplied, picking up his bag off the chair.

"Thank you, Steve."

"See you tomorrow," he said, waving as he walked out the door.

Josh saw Megan's slight flinch, and he knew it was from guilt. How could he get her to agree to carry this on through tomorrow?

Before he was even out the door, Knickers looked Megan and Josh up and down, her disapproval returning. "The rehearsal's in two hours. You two better hurry home if you're going to be at the gardens by six."

She grabbed the corner of the folded license in Josh's hand and tugged, but Josh didn't let go. "I'll hold onto it until tomorrow."

"No, that's okay." He tugged back. "I've got it."

She pulled harder. "I think it's better if I take it."

Josh didn't want to get into a tug-of-war with Megan's mother, but there was no way in hell he was letting Nicole Vandemeer take the marriage license, which included his full, proper name, with her. He pulled back. "No, Nicole. *I insist.*"

The clerk stood behind the counter, her mouth hanging open. She shook herself out of her stupor. "If you rip that up, you'll have to pay for a new one."

Josh and Megan had barely scrounged together the money to pay for the first one. He gave a hard jerk and pulled it free. Knickers gasped as she stumbled backward, righting herself before she fell over.

Megan just watched the wrestling match with wide eyes.

Holding the paper to his chest, Josh said, "Megan, your mom's right, we better go if we're going to get to the rehearsal in time."

She nodded, still speechless, and rushed toward the door, snagging Josh's hand as she bolted. Nicole still hadn't moved an inch—apparently frozen in place with shock—but she came to her senses as they hurried out the door.

"Whatever you do, do *not* lose that paper."

Josh slowed down once they were halfway down the hallway, and Megan gave him a questioning glance.

"She does realize we're adults, doesn't she?" His disbelief was bleeding into irritation. "Professional, fully functional adults."

Megan laughed as she opened the door to the stairwell. "Hello. Have you *met* my mother?"

Josh followed her and let the door close behind him. "She accused me of potentially losing our marriage license, Megan. Who would lose their marriage license?"

She stopped and wrapped her arms around his neck, pressing her lips to his. "You're pretty cute when you get all indignant like that."

He laughed, pulling her to his chest. "Cute, huh?"

A playful grin spread across her face as she looked up at him and said in a mock serious tone, "Okay, you looked so sexy wrestling that paper from my fifty-eight-year-old mother."

He leaned his head back and laughed. "It wasn't easy. She has an iron grip."

"Well, I'm glad you hung in there and won. I almost died when she tried to take it. That would have been a disaster."

His smile fell, and he searched her eyes. "What if she had gotten it?"

She turned serious. "But she didn't."

"What if she found out I wasn't Jay?" He held his breath as he watched her inner battle play out on her face. He wasn't sure why he was asking, except he still held out a cockeyed optimistic hope that they'd figure out a way to make this work when it was all said and done.

She closed her eyes and leaned her forehead against his shoulder. "Josh."

His hand slid up her back, rubbing in slow circles. "It's okay. Don't answer that. I just..." His voice trailed off.

"I know."

He leaned back and offered her a smile. "Let's go get ready for our wedding rehearsal."

"You mean our breakup."

He didn't answer. He'd lied to her enough. He didn't feel like lying anymore.

Chapter Twenty-Five

Hours later, Josh was frustrated for so many reasons. He and Megan hadn't counted on how badly Friday rush hour traffic would delay their drive to her parents' home. Knickers had shown up only minutes behind them, along with everyone else, to get ready for the evening. Everyone congregated in the living room as Knickers barked out last-minute orders, as if she were in the marines with Kevin. Megan was already on edge, thinking dinner would be ground zero for their breakup, so when Knickers announced that he needed to pack his belongings because he wouldn't be spending the night at the Vandemeer home, Megan flipped her shit.

"*What?*"

"Megan," Knickers had said in her snooty, condescending tone. "It's the night before your wedding. You can't spend the night together."

Megan stood at the base of the stairs. "I'm a grown woman! I can make my own decisions!"

Her mother pursed her lips with determination. "It's already been decided. Your father and I have booked a hotel room for Josh."

"You can't just decide on something like that without asking us first!" Megan shouted.

Josh was proud of her for finally taking a stand, even if it was for a cause she had to see as pointless. She thought he was breaking up with her tonight, in which case he wouldn't have stayed at the house anyway. But he worried that she was going to spill everything. That couldn't happen yet…not when he and Noah were so close to getting the answers they needed.

Josh put a hand on Megan's arm. "Megan, it's okay."

She turned to look up at him, tears in her eyes. "No it's not, Josh."

Then it hit him. She was upset that he was leaving. Period. Relief seeped through him before the aftertaste of guilt bit in. While he was grateful for the confirmation that she wanted more with him, he hated to see her this upset.

He pulled her into his arms. "It's okay, Meggie," he whispered in her ear as he stroked the back of her head. "We'll work everything out. I promise."

She clung to him, and in that moment he wanted nothing more than to run away with her. But he couldn't, as much as it killed him. His employees were in trouble because of someone else's wrongdoing, and they needed his help. "Nicole," he said over the top of Megan's head. "It's fine. I'll pack up before we leave, and I'll have Noah take me to the hotel later."

"Noah's welcome to stay here tonight, or he can stay with you if you'd like," Knickers said.

Noah stood next to the sofa, watching the scene unfold. Josh cast a glance toward his brother, who gave him a short shake of his head. They hadn't found the original plans, so Noah probably wanted to search the basement. Finding the documents would spell game over for PMV Engineering; it would be proof enough to convince their investor to hang tight. "That's okay. I'm going to be anxious and nervous. Noah won't get any sleep if he stays with me."

Gram had been standing to the side watching. "I'll go with him."

Knickers rolled her eyes. "Mother, you can't stay with Josh at the hotel."

"He promised to help me with my research on nudist colonies in Belize. He hasn't done it yet."

Josh couldn't help but grin.

"I bet he'd feel less anxious about the wedding if I kept him company. We could have a yoga session. It does wonders for stress."

Josh was pretty sure he'd be anxious about something else.

"What do you have to feel nervous about, Josh?" Kevin asked with a sneer, leaning his shoulder against the doorjamb to the kitchen and crossing his arms over his chest. "Having second thoughts about marrying my sister?"

Josh's anger surged, but he tried to control it. This was Megan's brother, after all; he needed to play nice for as long as possible. "When you get married, Kevin, we'll talk. Then maybe you'll have an idea."

He pulled Megan upstairs to her room so she could get ready and he could pack. She'd settled down some, but he could tell she was still fluttering with nervous energy. "We need to figure out how you're going to break up with me."

Wrapping his arms around her, he tugged her to him. "Maybe we can put it off."

She pulled free. "How can we put it off? The wedding is *tomorrow*. We have to break up, Josh."

He hesitated, worried about pushing her, especially since she was already distraught. "What if we don't?"

She froze, her face a mask. "What does that mean?"

He pulled her to the bed and sat down beside her, holding

her hand. "Look, the wedding is paid for whether we get married or not, right?"

She shook her head in confusion. "Well…yeah, but…"

"Wait," he said, a little more desperately than he would have liked. "Just hear me out, okay?"

"Okay." She looked uncertain.

"What if we don't break up tonight?" His brain scrambled to come up with a plan. He knew he needed one, but he had yet to think of anything that might actually work. "What if I break up with you before the wedding?"

"You're going to ditch me at the altar?" she asked in dismay. "Do you have any idea how humiliating that would be?"

He hadn't thought about it that way. He squeezed his eyes shut for a second. "Okay, what if we *do* go through with the wedding? It's already paid for. Everyone might as well get their chicken dinners."

"But then we'll be married!"

"No," Josh said, breathless. "Only if the marriage license gets sent to the courthouse. I'll take it from the minister and make sure that doesn't happen."

"But everyone will think we're married." She shook her head again. "Scratch that. They'll think I'm married to Jay."

"Then tell them you got a divorce. Or an annulment. Or," he gushed out, trying to figure out a solution, a way to buy himself more time for both of his dilemmas. "You can tell everyone the wedding wasn't legal because we had a fight and I tore up the marriage license instead of sending it in."

"Josh." She stood and turned to face him. "This is *crazy*."

He jumped to his feet in front of her. "I know."

"I don't understand why we don't just break up tonight…"

He pulled her into his arms. "Do you really want to end this in a few hours?"

"That's beside the point."

He cradled her face with both hands and she covered his with her own. "No. It's not. It *is* the point. Do you want to break up? Yes or no?"

She released a heavy breath and looked down. "No."

He kissed her hard, then pulled back, surprised at his own building excitement. "I don't want to either. So let's not."

She shook her head again. "So you're suggesting that we go through with the wedding?"

"Meggie, I told you that I left this trip to fate. Maybe this is our fate. Maybe we're supposed to do this."

"But…" He could tell she wasn't sold yet, but he'd planted the seed and she hadn't outright dismissed the idea. In fact, she'd been more receptive than he'd expected.

"Don't decide yet. Just think about it."

"But I don't have *time* to think about it."

"You do. You have at least a couple of hours or so." He searched her eyes. "I know it doesn't sound like long, but just go with your gut, okay? You'll know whether you want to go through with it or not."

"And if I decide I want you to break up with me tonight?"

He searched her face. "Then we'll set the wheels in motion. You only have to say the word."

Despite his dislike for Blair, Josh was happy she'd arrived for the rehearsal, if only because it so clearly pleased Megan. The tension in her shoulders eased when her friend showed up, but Blair let them both know she was on guard.

"This in no way means I condone what you're doing," Blair said under her breath, just out of hearing distance of Knickers. The group was waiting in the parking lot for some last-minute stragglers, so everyone could enter the grounds together.

Megan pulled her to one side of the lot, Libby and Josh following close behind.

"So basically you're here to spy on me," Megan teased.

A wicked gleam filled Blair's eyes. "Pretty much."

"I can live with that."

"You're always so cynical, Blair," Libby said. "It's almost like you don't believe in marriage." She looked around at the people gathered for the rehearsal, which included a few of Megan's cousins and aunts and uncles. "Where is Neil, anyway?"

The bridge of Blair's nose scrunched with disapproval. "Neil is still at work. He'll meet us later. Where's your new boyfriend, Libs?" she asked, her tone barbed. "Mitch, is it?"

Libby shot her a tolerant smile. "Mitch is meeting us at the restaurant too."

The gardens had rented out the chapel for another wedding that evening, so they were directed to the small lawn by the main entrance. Knickers told everyone what time they needed to show up for the wedding and where, although Josh was confused by some of the instructions. He could see the chapel on the other side of the pond and he overheard something about the rooms underneath, but he was too focused on Megan to give it much thought. She was jittery and wide-eyed as they all took their places for the run-through, and he knew exactly what was getting to her. This felt like a farce. A fake rehearsal on top of a fake wedding, made worse by the fact they had very real feelings for each other…and no idea if their relationship was about to meet its sell-by date. Hell, it was getting to him too, but she was a wild card at the moment, her nerves apparent enough to gain her mother's attention.

"Megan?" she asked as Megan took her place beside her father. Blair and Libby were getting ready to practice their walk down the aisle. "Care to join us here at the rehearsal? You're obviously a million miles away."

Megan's mouth opened as if to say something, then she took a deep breath and dropped her father's arm. She took several steps into the center of the lawn, clasping her hands in front of her, her face paler than usual. "Actually, there's something I have to tell you." She lifted her gaze to Josh, who stood at the end of the imaginary aisle with Noah and Kevin, next to the sidewalk that led to the gardens.

Josh's eyes widened, and he shook his head slowly.

She glanced down at her hands. "I…this…"

Josh's heart seized in his chest. How could he stop her? *Should* he stop her? This wasn't some game they were playing, after all. He was screwing with her life. But truth be told, his business issues aside, he wasn't ready to lose this woman. He was certain he'd never find anyone like her again. He didn't even want to try.

Libby rushed toward Megan and wrapped an arm around her shoulders. "I think Megan's got some pre-wedding jitters. We all know how this marching down the aisle thing works. How about we just skip it and go to dinner?"

"No," Kevin said, stepping away from Josh and Noah. "I don't think that's it at all." He moved closer to her. "Megan, you don't have to marry this dipshit. Come on, let's go home."

Without replying to her brother—or even looking at him—Megan glanced up at Josh, her eyes glassy with unshed tears.

Josh held his breath, clenching his fists at his sides as he silently pleaded with her.

Relinquishing her position at the head of the group, Knickers marched to the center of the lawn, her imperiousness slightly undermined when her spiky heels sunk into the wet sod. She swung her legs in an exaggerated movement to break them loose of the earth. "Stop the wedding? Have you lost your *mind*, Kevin? I always expect *you* to be the sensible one."

"The sensible one?" Josh said, louder than he meant. "What the hell is that supposed to mean?"

Bart, who now stood several feet behind Megan, had a panicked look on his face. Things were spiraling out of control pretty quickly, and Josh could easily guess who would bear the brunt of it later.

Finally reaching Megan, Kevin grabbed her hand and pulled her to him, his face red. "Mom, we've all sat back and let you ramrod this family for long enough. Enough."

"Ramrod this family?" she shrieked.

Kevin flung his arm toward Josh. "Megan's not marrying this guy."

"Of course she's marrying him!" Nicole shouted, her face twisted with a mixture of surprise and anger. She wobbled as her heel sunk deeper, pitching her to the side.

Josh took a moment to survey the rest of the scene: Gram, who'd been seated in a folding chair at the side of the group, was watching it all, her eyes glittering with excitement. Megan's cousins stood toward the back of the lawn, looking all at once uncomfortable and enthralled. Blair seemed like she was about to rush over and drag Megan away, but Libby was blocking her path. The minister stood behind, wisely keeping his mouth shut.

Shaking Josh out of his stupor, Noah leaned into his ear and whispered, "You have to put a stop to this. *Now.*"

"I know." But did he? Part of him wanted to let it play out, to let Megan make her choice without any intervention.

"Well, Megan?" her mother demanded, hands on her hips as she tottered back and forth like a baby giraffe. "Are you going to tell your brother to go back to the groom's line so we can finish this rehearsal and go to dinner?" She shook her head, looking like she was about to implode. "If Josh will even let Kevin stand up with him." She pointed her French-tip-manicured finger at him. "Your behavior is *deplorable.*"

Megan looked from her mother to her brother, then finally rested her gaze on Josh, tears streaming down her face as her chin quivered.

His heart twisted with a pain that sucked in his breath. He couldn't do this to her. He couldn't hurt her. Not her.

"Megan." He took a step forward as he said it; his voice cracked, but he didn't care. "You are singularly the best thing that has ever come into my life."

She dropped Kevin's hand and studied Josh as a fresh trail of tears tumbled down her cheeks. Kevin's fists balled at his sides, but Josh didn't let that stop him. He continued to take slow steps toward Megan, moving around Knickers. "You fell into my life and turned it upside down. You've made me question everyone and everything, but when I sort through it all, the only thing that makes sense is you." He stopped in front of her, her eyes looking up at him in confusion and sorrow.

He cupped her cheeks, his thumbs wiping her tears. "Don't cry, Meggie. We'll do whatever you want. You just say the word. If you want to end this right now, we can. I won't fight you. But if you want to keep going…" He pushed past the lump in his throat, ignoring the fact they had an audience. "Can I tell you how I feel before you make your decision?"

She nodded, fresh tears breaking free, the sight hurting his heart even more.

"I can't imagine walking away from this mess without you. I don't know how this happened. I only know it did. You know how I said I left it all up to fate?"

She nodded, sucking in her lower lip to stop her chin from quivering.

He smiled at her and picked up her hand, cradling it between his own. "We're supposed to be together. *I know it.* I don't want to go back to Seattle without you. Don't give up on us, okay? Don't give up on me."

She watched him, indecision wavering in her eyes.

He pressed his forehead to hers, lowering his voice to a

whisper. "It's up to you, Meggie. Either I walk away, or we keep going. I just want you to be happy. What will make you happy?"

A soft smile lifted her mouth. "You make me happy, Josh. I've never been happier than I am with you."

Relief flooded through him, and he released the breath he'd been holding. "So what do you want to do about it? Do you want me to take you away from this mess?"

She looked around at her family, then at the crowd of botanical gardens visitors who now lined the sidewalk by their practice lawn. They were watching with open mouths, as if they'd happened upon a particularly trashy episode of reality television. Finally she returned her gaze to him, her orneriness returning. "And walk away from a fifty-grand party? Not on your life."

He kissed her, his joy overshadowing the fear that lurked in the shadows of his heart. He still had to come clean, but not yet. Not now. He might lose her when he did, and he wasn't ready to take that risk.

She wrapped her arms around his neck, clinging to him and kissing him back.

The crowd of onlookers—strangers and friends and family alike—broke into applause and a round of "Woots," undoubtedly led by Libby.

When he lifted his head, he noticed two people were not participating: Kevin and Blair. They stood together now, glaring at him as if he were public enemy number one. He could deal with their animosity—even hatred—as long as they didn't try to take Megan from him.

"Well," Knickers said, breaking into the celebration. "Now that this nonsense has been taken care of, can we finish the rehearsal?" She pointed a finger at Kevin. "I'll deal with you later."

Josh returned to the other end of the lawn next to Noah,

Kevin shooting darts of hate at him the whole time. Too relieved to care, Josh took a deep breath, letting himself relax. He couldn't believe how close he'd come to losing her. He couldn't believe how panicked he'd felt at the prospect.

Noah clapped his hand on Josh's shoulder and leaned in close. "Good save there, Joshy."

Anger rushed over him, and before he could think about it, he hissed, "This isn't a *game*, Noah. She's important to me."

An uncharacteristic solemnity covered Noah's face. "I know she is."

Josh blinked, words escaping him.

"I know you, Josh… You love this girl. I'm sorry for what I…" He cleared his throat. "We'll figure out a way to make it work."

In the entirety of his twenty-nine years, Josh couldn't remember Noah taking the side of love or romance. He thought it was a hyped-up emotion that quickly ran its course. But as he sorted through his shock, he registered the word Noah had used: *love*. Josh started to protest, but Kevin, who'd been standing as far from them as the situation could warrant, leaned closer. "Do you boys have something you want to tell me about my sister?"

Josh shook his head, his back tensing. "*No.*" If this wedding were real, he'd be tempted to invite Kevin to the parking lot to *discuss* this further. But he reminded himself that Megan's brother's animosity was really for Jay. He wasn't sure whether to deck him or cheer him on for finally coming to her defense.

Kevin edged closer, not stopping until he stood a foot away. "I don't trust you. Something strange is going on here, and I'm going to prove it before Megan makes the biggest mistake of her life."

"*Kevin!*" Nicole shouted while pointing to his preordained spot. "This is your last warning. Get back into place."

Knickers began the practice drill, and since Josh's job

seemed to consist mostly of standing at the front, he had time to think about his brother's words. Could Noah have read him correctly? He really liked Megan. He lusted for her like he'd never lusted for a woman before, but *love?* How could you fall in love with someone in a matter of days?

They wrapped up the rehearsal and left for the restaurant. Megan's mother had reserved a private room at a steak restaurant closer to their home. Because of the delay from all the drama, Neil and Mitch were already waiting for the group at the restaurant.

As everyone headed down the hall to the room, Josh snagged Megan's hand and pulled her out the front door, into the warm summer evening. She seemed almost relieved; her brother, of all people, had ridden to the restaurant with them, so there hadn't been an opportunity for them to speak privately. Josh led her a little ways down the sidewalk, then took both of her hands in his. "I'm worried about you. How are you doing?"

She gave him a hesitant smile. "I'm better."

"So we're doing this?"

She searched his eyes for a moment. "I guess we are."

He lowered his mouth to hers, giving her a gentle kiss. When she sighed and leaned into him, something tightened in his chest. Suddenly he knew with certainty that if it came down to her or his employees, he wasn't sure he'd pick his employees. He was seriously considering giving up a thirty-year-old business for a woman he'd known a few days. And that scared him.

She pulled back and gave him a sweet smile that melted his heart. "We better get inside before my mother has a coronary."

"You're right." But he kissed her again, not wanting to let this moment go.

"Maybe I can stay with you at the hotel tonight," she murmured against his lips.

"I don't know." He grinned. "Gram's promised to make my last night as a bachelor a memorable experience. She keeps talking about the positions she wants to show me. All I remember is something about a camel and a baby."

Megan laughed, a pure melodious sound that he tried to bottle into a memory he could pull out later and reminisce over if things went south.

The others were already seated when they entered the room, but no one seemed surprised they were coming in late. They probably figured Megan and Josh had had some spat before the rehearsal and needed to iron things out. Thankfully, Kevin and Blair hadn't conspired to split Megan and Josh up with the seating chart. There were three tables. One was for Megan's parents and aunts and uncles; the second was for her cousins, Kevin, and Gram; and they were seated at the third, with Noah, Blair and Neil, and Libby and Mitch. Josh held Megan's chair out for her and she flashed him a mischievous grin. The certainty of how much he needed her—not just wanted—hit him square between the eyes.

Josh was surprised by how civil Blair was toward him. After a couple of drinks, she let her guard down and seemed to actually be having fun, albeit not with her fiancé. Neil was a quiet, unassuming man, and Josh couldn't at all see the attraction between him and Megan's tempestuous friend. By the time the entrées had been served, it was apparent their marriage would be one of convenience. Blair brought her prestigious career to the deal, but he couldn't figure out what Neil had to offer.

Mitch and Libby seemed like a much better fit. He was funny and attentive to her and she seemed to genuinely like him. But while Josh could hardly claim to be an expert at love or matchmaking, he thought something was missing—maybe that essential spark he himself had only felt with Megan. Noah must have noticed too. He spent the entire dinner by Libby's side, deep in conversation with her. If Mitch felt threatened, he never let on. Josh worried that Kevin would come over to talk with them at some point and ruin the friendlier atmosphere, but he stayed where he was, seemingly content to continue sending evil glares across the room. Josh was suddenly glad he'd been exiled from the Vandemeer home. He wouldn't put it past Kevin to come into Megan's room in the middle of the night and hold a pillow over his face.

How had nice guy Josh McMillan acquired so many enemies in such a short time?

During dessert, Josh leaned over and gave Megan a kiss. "I need to go to the restroom. I'll be right back."

She gave him a wry smile. "Okay, but no guarantees your cheesecake will still be here when you return."

He laughed, feeling happier than he'd felt in a long time. "I guess I'll take my chances." When he reached the doorway, he looked back to see her fork hovering over his dessert plate. He laughed, shaking his head as he made the short trip to the men's room. After he finished his business and emerged from the restroom, he wasn't surprised to see Blair waiting for him in the hall.

"Blair," he said, his voice tight.

"Scumbag."

He tried to suppress a grin. He shouldn't enjoy riling her up so much when she clearly had Megan's best interest at heart.

"You find all of this so amusing, do you?"

Any hint of a grin fell. "No. Actually, I don't."

"I need to talk to you in private."

Josh considered blowing her off, but if he had any hope of a long-term relationship with Megan, Blair was part of the package. "Okay."

She led the way out the front door and sat down on a nearby concrete bench. Josh only realized she'd brought her large black leather purse with her when she pulled out a folder and set the bag on the ground next to her. She patted the concrete seat. "Sit down. Let's take a look at what I have here."

His heart leapt into his throat. What could she have in that folder?

"So you carried through with your threat," he said as he sat next to her, trying to keep his tone light.

"Oh, you bet your fine ass I did." She opened the folder.

There was a recent photo of him stapled to one side, a photo that had been in the *Seattle Times* two years ago, along with a small piece about Josh's firm.

"Joshua Thomas McMillan."

"You found my middle name. You really *are* a super sleuth."

"I could list all the boring stuff," Blair said, ignoring him, her tone breezy and casual. She actually sounded happy, which was surely a bad sign. "Like your birthdate, parents' names, where you went to grade school..."

"But then you don't seem like the type of woman who wastes time."

She turned to him with a radiant smile. "You *do* get me."

He shrugged, forcing himself to act lighthearted even though he felt like he was about to throw up. "Why don't we just get to the good stuff?"

"Yes. Let's." She sounded like a giddy schoolgirl as she flipped through a stack of papers. "Does Megan know you're an engineer?"

He could deny it, but what was the point? "No."

"Hmm…" A twinkle lit up her eyes. "Now why is that?" But she didn't give him a chance to answer, rummaging instead through several printouts of press releases and financial statements on his company letterhead.

He grabbed a page from the stack, his anger surfacing. "How did you get this stuff? It's confidential."

"I told you I'd find out everything." Her gaze dropped to

his crotch before returning to his face. "Circumcised," she sing-songed.

"You obviously think you found something important, so why don't you spit it out?"

"Oh, Josh," she pouted. "I could go for the clean, humane kill, but what fun would that be? I'd rather toy with you first." Her eyes narrowed. "I like to watch the sleazeballs squirm."

Josh jumped to his feet, trying to control his temper. "This is a *game* to you?"

She looked up at him, clearly unnerved. "Everything's a game, Joshua. You, of all people, should know that."

He shook his head, pointing to the restaurant. "Not her. Not this."

She got to her feet too, tilting her head slightly, her eyes icy cold with rage now. "Yes, this. *Especially* this. You're using my best friend to gather information to steal her father's patent."

"*Steal his patent!*" Josh shouted. "He stole *my* design!"

She shook her head, glaring at him. "No, Josh. Protest all you want. He filed the patent first."

Sick dread gave him a chill despite the warm night air.

"He came to me three years ago. He told me that he had a revolutionary design his firm wanted to patent. I couldn't help him, but I had a friend who could, so I made the introductions. I met Tim in law school, and now he works for one of the best patent firms in the country, Haverty and Simmons in Boston." She took a step toward him. "You filed your patent, but it was a week too late. So now you're here trying to steal information that will paint Bart and his firm in a bad light."

"If you know so much, then you must know my firm will be dead by Monday morning if I don't get proof my design was stolen. Ten employees will lose their jobs."

"Boohoo. They'll find new ones."

"These aren't nameless people to me, Blair." He held his hand out, pleading with her to understand. "Some of them were hired by my father when he first opened the doors thirty years ago. They have families to feed."

"People lose their jobs all the time, McMillan," she sneered. "They'll live."

He shook his head in disbelief. "How are you friends with that incredibly sweet and sensitive person in there?" He jabbed his finger toward the front door of the restaurant.

"You were counting on that, weren't you?" she said. "You studied her, found out she'd broken off her engagement. You bought the seat next to her on the plane so you could use her."

He shook his head again, his eyes wide in horror. "No. *No.*"

"*Yes.* You purposely sat by her and played her like a freaking fiddle." Her face contorted with hate. "You took advantage of her vulnerability and *used* her."

He took a step back, trying not to panic. What if she told Megan her twisted version of events? Worse, what if Megan believed her?

She shook her head in disgust. "I swear to God, if I had a gun right now, I'd be tempted to shoot you myself."

He ran his hands through his hair. "I'm surprised you're not inside right now, presenting your case to that room full of people. It seems to me you'd want to broadcast my imperfections to as many people as possible."

"*Imperfections?* This reaches far beyond imperfections." Her eyes narrowed. "And I actually care about Megan. I'm not telling anyone else but her. She's been embarrassed enough over the last couple months."

He breathed a silent prayer of relief.

She laughed, a bitter sound. "I think we can make a deal, Joshua McMillan."

Fear seized his heart. "What kind of deal?"

She began to pace the sidewalk, her hands behind her back, the folder still clutched in her grasp. "I'm sure we can reach a compromise that's satisfactory to us both."

He highly doubted it. "Go on. You obviously have the terms worked out in your head."

She released a haughty laugh. "In my head? Oh, no, Joshua, I'm an attorney. I'm the queen of paper." She pulled another document out of the folder and handed it to him.

He took it with shaky hands. "What's this?"

"Your agreement to slink away into the night and never speak to Megan again."

"No."

"Don't be so hasty in your decision." Something in her voice caught his attention.

"What am I supposed to get out of this?"

"Pride for doing the right thing?" Blair asked. "What? Not enough? I know you need money from your investor to keep your firm afloat." She paused, her eyes piercing his. "I have the connections to find you another investor. One who will support you without the patent."

He shook his head. "Bullshit." He threw the offensive paper to the ground. "And even if you could, no deal."

He turned to head back into the building, but she ran in front of him, blocking his path. "Don't be so hasty, Josh. I thought you wanted to save those employees of yours."

"No. Not like this. I love her, Blair. I can't just walk away from her. Not like this."

They both gasped at his declaration.

He loved her? But he knew it was true as soon as he said it. As impossible as it seemed, he loved Megan.

"*Love her?* Who are you trying to fool here? Is this a bargaining chip?"

"What? God, no!" he spat in disgust as he walked away from her. "You can take your fucking deal and ride your broom back to hell." One persistent thought ran through his head: He had to get to Megan before Blair did.

"Your brother agreed to it." Blair's calm voice called out

into the night air.

He froze, his eyes sinking closed.

"Oh, yeah. Noah couldn't sign that deal fast enough."

He turned around and watched as she squatted and picked up the paper. "You didn't notice his signature?"

He stomped over and snatched the document from her hands. Sure enough, Noah's unmistakable scrawl was at the bottom. Fury rushed through him.

Noah had betrayed him.

Again.

Josh ripped the paper in half, then ripped it again and threw it into the air. "Here's what I think of your deal. And my original suggestion stands—go to hell."

He marched toward the front door of the restaurant.

"If you hurt Megan, I will rip your balls off myself," Blair shouted, her voice cracking. It was the first sign of genuine emotion he'd heard from her since she'd staged this little scene.

"Get in line." Once inside, he raced to the private room and threw open the door. There he was. Noah was still in his seat beside Libby as if nothing had happened, a flirtatious grin on his face while Mitch looked at his phone.

The entire room turned to stare at Josh as he threw the door against the wall. Megan's eyes widened in surprise. "Josh?" she gasped, getting to her feet. "Are you okay?"

He turned his attention back to Noah. The amusement in his brother's face crumpled into an expression that clearly read *oh shit.* Noah stood and started around the table to intercept him.

"Josh, let's go outside," Noah said.

Josh strode toward his brother, stopping only when he heard Blair's voice from behind him. She stood in the doorway now, a smug grin on her face. "Yeah, Josh. Why don't you and Noah go outside, and I'll have that chat with Megan."

Megan glanced between Josh and Blair. "What's going on?"

So this was what it felt like to really be backed into a corner.

Kevin stood next his seat, looking ready to implement plan B to stop Megan's wedding: beat Josh to a bloody pulp, while Gram's eyes glittered with excitement. Poor Bart looked concerned over the second drama that was clearly about to erupt. Knickers remained shockingly silent, but perhaps that could be credited to the empty wine glass in front of her.

Noah took several cautious steps toward him. "Now, Josh. Let's go outside and I'll explain everything." He started to push Josh toward the door.

But Josh dug in his feet. There was no way he was going to let Blair get to Megan first.

He turned to Noah, a wave of hurt engulfing him out of nowhere. It wasn't the first time his brother had let him down, of course, but somehow it was the worst. "How could you?" Josh choked out.

Noah's eyes filled with some unnamable emotion. "When I signed…I didn't realize…I'm sorry, but maybe it's for the best."

"*Like hell it is*," Josh growled as he swung his fist into his brother's face.

Noah stumbled backward, holding his hand up to his eye as the room erupted into chaos.

Knickers finally sprang into action. "Someone tell me what's going on here. Right. This. Instant!" she shouted, standing next to her seat.

Josh turned to Megan and held out his throbbing hand toward her. "Come with me," he pleaded. "*Please*." She took one hesitant step toward him and paused for a moment before quickening her pace.

"*Go?* Go where?" Knickers screeched.

Blair blocked Megan's path, but she cast a confused glance to Josh, as though no longer certain what to make of him. Josh hoped to God she realized how wrong she was, but her indecision faded, quickly replaced by cold determination. "Don't do it, Megan. There are things you don't know."

"Megan, *please*," Josh called to her, desperate.

Megan looked between the two of them, then shoved Blair to the side. "Sorry, Blair." She hurried to him, and he nearly cried with relief as she took his hand. He led her outside and to the passenger's seat of her Explorer. Then he got into the driver's seat and took off without a word, wanting to get the two of them as far from reality as possible.

Chapter Twenty-Six

Megan was terrified as Josh drove away from the restaurant, but not for her own safety. She knew he would never harm her. In fact, she had a feeling this was an attempt to save her somehow; she just didn't know what he was protecting her from.

"Josh, what happened?"

His hands tightened on the steering wheel, and he shook his head, his jaw clenching as he swallowed.

"Okay, we don't have to talk about it yet. Where do you want to go?"

He was quiet for several moments. "Our spot."

Our spot. How could two little words fill her with such contentment and hope? "Okay, we can try it. It's a Friday night in June. It might already be taken."

"Let's try anyway."

His hands on the wheel relaxed. She tried to release some of the tension in her neck. What had Noah done to elicit such rage from his brother? What had Blair done to instigate it? Because this had Blair's handiwork all over it.

Josh reached over and grabbed her hand, squeezing with an intensity that worried her, but she kept silent. There was plenty of time to ask questions. They had all night.

Fate was on their side. The campsite was vacant. The bedding from the previous night was still in the back of the car. After Josh parked, Megan climbed out and went around to the hatch to pull it out. Josh met her and snagged it first, both of them silent as they walked to the bluff. Josh handed the pillows to Megan as he spread out the sleeping bag and sheet, then laid the blanket on the pallet. Megan tossed the pillows down and turned to Josh, waiting.

The whole night had been an overwhelming roller coaster of emotions. Something big was happening, and she was intuitive enough to realize this would be a defining moment in their relationship. Whether they moved forward or called it quits. The thought of losing him was suffocating.

She stared at him, overcome with how attractive he was. He could have his choice of just about any woman—the flirty flight attendant was proof of that—but he was here with her, dealing with her mess and all that it encompassed. Despite the huge hassle, this gorgeous, thoughtful, humorous man had chosen to be with her.

The starry sky was his backdrop, the moonlight giving him an ethereal glow. Pain and regret welled in his eyes, and she did the only thing she could to show him that she was there for him in the way he'd been there for her.

She slowly reached for his cheeks and pulled his mouth to hers.

He grabbed her hands and tried to pull away. "Megan."

"Shhh." She slipped her hand around to the back of his head and held him in place, her tongue probing his parted lips.

He groaned, opening his mouth to her as he wrapped his

arms around her back, tugging her close. Her tongue teased his and he released another groan, though she could sense he was holding back from her.

She reached for the buttons of his shirt, unfastening blindly as she continued to kiss him. He pulled back and searched her eyes. When she cupped his cheek and smiled, he opened his mouth as if to say something. Then he stopped and kissed her instead, pulling her lower lip between his own and raking his teeth lightly along the tender flesh. She released a soft whimper, grabbing handfuls of his shirt. His urgency increased as he reached for the zipper on her dress, jerking the fabric down until it pooled at her feet. She resumed her work with his buttons, smiling when he unfastened the last one, clearly impatient for her to finish. She spread his shirt open, her hands skimming his chest. His abdominal muscles tightened under her touch as her hands continued their downward pursuit.

She quickly unfastened his belt and the zipper on his dress pants, then pushed them over his hips so they fell to his feet.

Her gaze on his face, she stepped backward onto the pallet, wearing nothing but her bra and panties. He dropped his underwear and followed. Reaching a hand behind her head, he pulled her mouth to his, claiming her with more intensity than she'd expected, sending desire shooting through her lower abdomen. His hands reached around and unfastened her bra, tugged it down her arms, then stripped off her panties so they both stood naked in the moonlight.

She wanted this man, and not just his body—although she wanted that too, desperately. She wanted to go home to Seattle and start a life with him.

The whole idea scared the crap out of her. How could she be so certain so quickly? She used to make fun of girls who claimed to fall in love on a first date, but here she was, wanting a fairy-tale ending with a man she'd met three days before. *Three days.*

But it was *Josh.* Sweet, gentle Josh who made her laugh. Who made her feel cherished. She trusted him more than she'd ever trusted Jay, and no one was more surprised by any of this than she was.

She wanted this man in every sense of the word, and she intended to let her actions prove it to him. She dropped her knees and took him into her mouth, her tongue teasing his tip, dancing in circles.

"Oh, God, Megan," he moaned, grabbing handfuls of her hair as she began to suck the length of him, his grunts and rapid breath sending hot desire through her veins and straight to her pelvis. She coaxed and teased him with her mouth until he put his palms on her head and pulled her back. Then he dropped to his knees in front of her, their chests just inches apart.

He stared into her face as his hand caressed her cheek and sank into her hair, grabbing the strands loosely into his fist. His gaze penetrated hers before he gently tilted her chin. He placed a kiss at the corner of her mouth, brushing a line of them to her jaw line, then moved down to her neck, finding her sensitive spot and making her squirm.

He pushed her back and gently laid her down on the pallet, her head on the pillow. His knee nudged hers, spreading them apart so he could kneel between them. She watched him as he lowered himself over her. The lust and passion in his eyes sent a shiver down her spine, straight to her core.

His face lowered to her neck, his lips brushing the sensitive skin there. His tongue worked circles down her sternum before easing to her breast to tease her nipple. Then he took it in his teeth.

She lay panting and breathless, lifting her hips in involuntary need, but he moved to her other breast, continuing his exquisite torture. A light breeze swept over her wet skin, making the hairs on her arms stand on end. His mouth moved lower, over the swell of her breasts. His tongue and lips licked and sucked a path down her abdomen, setting her skin on fire with need. He continued his torturous descent to her pelvis, her inner thigh.

He lifted her hips, cradling her ass cheeks in his palms as his face hovered over her folds, his warm breath sending a tingling jolt into her lower abdomen. By the time his tongue started to caress her, she cried out with relief, surprised by the intensity of the pleasure shooting through her.

She arched her back, lifting into him, trying to stifle her moans. After a minute of his sweet torture, she blindly grasped his hair and pulled him up, sure she'd come if he didn't stop, and she wanted to do that when he was inside her. His head lifted and he slid his chest up her abdomen, his chest hair brushing over her sensitive nipples, making her gasp and press her groin into him.

He rested his weight on his elbow next to her head, looking down at her as she fought to catch her breath. His hand brushed several strands of hair from her cheek, then he leaned in to kiss her, soft and gentle, his tongue skimming her long bottom lip, the taste of her on his mouth.

Wild with need, she lifted her hips, the movement pressing his erection into her thigh. She took control of the kiss, frantic for him and for release. His hand moved down and brushed her nipple with his thumb.

Megan sucked in her breath as her back arched in desire. "Josh," she cried out, that one word channeling the force of her raw desire.

Moving his hand under her ass, Josh lifted her up, then teased her entrance with the tip of his erection.

She moved under him, encouraging him to take her completely. His palm covered her hand next to her head, and he laced their fingers together before pushing into her, moving with agonizing slowness.

The ache for release was overwhelming as he pulled out and repeated his slow thrust. "*Josh*."

He moved his hips more quickly, leaning down to kiss her as she gasped in pleasure and relief. Wrapping her legs around his waist, she tilted her hips up to take him deeper.

The pressure built until she shattered, crying out his name. He covered her mouth with his, muffling her sounds. He was close behind, thrusting several more times before he pushed deep inside her and groaned into her mouth. Her arms wrapped around his upper back, holding him close, her wordless way of telling him that she never wanted this moment to end.

He gently eased her hips down to the pallet, staying on top of her. As he kissed her, slow and deep, Megan realized she'd never felt so connected to anyone in her life.

"Don't leave me tomorrow," she whispered.

"I will never willingly leave you, Megan."

She studied his face. "What does that mean?"

"You might change your mind about me."

"Why would I do that?"

He gave her a soft smile, but it was full of sadness.

"Does this have to do with what happened with Blair and Noah at the restaurant?"

Surprise flickered on his face and he rolled to his side, bringing her with him. He grabbed the blanket next to him and flipped it over to cover them both to their waists. "What do you know about it?" he finally asked.

"Nothing. Only that Noah must have done something terrible to make you hit him like that, and I suspect Blair instigated the whole thing since she was hot on your heels when you came back from the restroom."

His body stiffened below her. "Noah betrayed me."

What could that mean? "Does this have to do with your business decision or me?"

His hand tangled in her hair and tightened. "Both."

Both? "And Blair was involved."

Wariness filled his eyes. "She loves you, Megan. She's going to do what she thinks she needs to do to keep you safe."

Megan pushed up on her elbow. "What did she do?"

A gentle smile lit up his eyes and his hold on her hair loosened, but he continued to play with the loose strands. "It doesn't matter. She'll tell you tomorrow, I'm sure." He searched her eyes. "I thought about talking to you about this first, but I've decided to let her. I know her version and you know most of mine. All I ask is that you think of what we have—what I'm so desperate to keep—before you make up your mind."

What was he talking about?

"But if you decide you believe me and you believe that I care about you, I still want to go through with the ceremony tomorrow. Let's give Knickers her last hurrah."

"You really want to go through with *the wedding?*"

"Yeah, but don't worry. I'll stick with the plan and tell her I lost the marriage license. You'll be off the hook, but Knickers will still get her fancy party. We'll figure out this—you and me—later."

It was still a crazy idea, but for some reason it didn't seem so crazy anymore. She would do it for him. "Okay."

He took her hand in his. "I'll take you home in the morning, and I'll be at the gardens in time to do my part tomorrow afternoon. If you decide to go through with it, I want to talk to you before the wedding, before you go down the aisle."

"But—"

"Please."

"Knickers will have a *fit* if she knows you've seen me in my dress before the wedding," she said, trying to look serious. It didn't last; her face broke out into a huge grin. "Count me in."

A smile spread across his face. "That's my girl."

She lay her head on his chest, desperately hoping she really was.

Chapter Twenty-Seven

Megan and Josh spent the night under the stars, making love until the sun rose. They went for breakfast before he drove her back to her parents' house.

He turned to face her once they were parked in the driveway. "I feel like I should walk you to the door," he teased, taking her hand in his.

She chuckled. "Trust me, you don't want to do that right now."

His smile fell. "Then maybe I *should* go with you. You shouldn't have to deal with the fallout from last night on your own."

She leaned over and kissed him, her lips lingering on his. "I love that you want to protect me from my mother. But I think it's time I started standing up for myself."

"Does that mean you don't want to go through with the wedding?"

She paused, studying his face. "No, as strange as it sounds, now that I'm used to the idea, I kind of want to do it. What about you?"

He didn't answer her for several seconds. "I want what *you* want, Megan. From here on out, you're calling all the shots. You want to have the wedding, we'll do it. If you change your mind and decide to say screw it all and hop on a plane back to Seattle, we can do that too." He hesitated and swallowed. "And if you decide you don't want to see me again, you only have to text me and tell me to go to hell."

She forced a smile. "I can't break it off. I don't have your number." How could that be? How could she have experienced so much with this man and still not have his cell phone number? Maybe because they had spent nearly every minute together.

"Give me your phone."

She dug it out of her purse and turned it on, entering her passcode before she handed it to him.

He entered his number and gave the phone back to her. "See you at our wedding."

She reached for the door handle, but he grabbed her arm and pulled her back, kissing her as though he was never going to see her again. "Josh, you're scaring me."

"Maybe that's because *I'm* scared, Meggie."

"Tell me what Blair's going to tell me."

He shook his head. "I want you to decide for yourself."

She got out and walked to the house, checking her phone before she walked through the door—there were multiple missed calls and voice mails from her mother, as well as calls, texts, and messages from Blair, Libby, and her brother. And there was one text from Jay.

Call me.

She pressed delete. She never wanted to hear from that asshole again.

The front door opened before her hand could reach the

knob.

"Where have you been?" Her mother's voice was icy. "I've been worried sick about you. I was about to call the police."

"The police? Why would you call the police?"

"Josh punched his brother in the face, then dragged you to off to God knows where. I was frightened for you, Megan..." Her mother's voice broke.

Oh, God. She really *had* been worried.

Megan pushed her shock aside and wrapped her mother in a hug. "I'm sorry, Mom. I'm fine. We both just needed to get away. I was getting cold feet, and Josh knew I needed some time alone with him to sort everything out." She shut the door behind her, then hastened her mother into the living room, where Gram sat munching from a box of fiber cereal.

They'd only just walked in when Kevin stalked in from the kitchen, a coffee cup in his hand. He set it down on the end table next to the sofa. "Did he threaten you?" he demanded of her, the veins on his neck bulging.

Megan released her hold on her mother and turned to look at Kevin. "What? No!"

"I don't see what all the fuss is about," Gram said, still crunching on her cereal. "So Megan wanted to have one last night as a single woman." She grabbed another handful. "You can't blame her for wanting wild, single sex."

Knickers' face turned beet-red. "Mother!"

"Gram," Megan laughed. "I don't think it counts if you're having wild, single sex with the man you're marrying."

Kevin looked even angrier. "I do *not* want to hear about my little sister's wild sex. Especially with that violent asshole."

She shook her head. "Josh would never hurt me. His brother did something related to their business that he saw as a betrayal."

"*Their* business?" he asked, incredulous. "I thought he was an investment banker. Does he own the freaking bank?"

Oh, crap.

Gram continued, oblivious to the change in topic. "I heard something on the news about how all you kids are into BS stuff because of that *Fifty Shades of Steele* book. I read it, you know." She lifted her eyebrows at Megan, grabbing another handful of cereal. "Are you and Josh into whips and colored rooms?"

"*Mother!*" Knickers gasped in shock.

Megan began to laugh, despite her horror. She cast a glance at Kevin, who looked close to losing his breakfast. "It's BDSM, not BS, although some people might call it that too." She tried to get serious. "You really don't expect me to discuss my sex life with Josh in front of my mother, do you?"

Gram shoved some of the cereal in her mouth. "It might loosen her up. Maybe she and your father should try it."

"*Gram!*" Kevin shouted.

She shrugged, reaching into the box again. "I'm just saying a little spice in the bedroom might loosen her up. Or she could put some of those contraptions in the basement. There's room for a dungeon down there."

Megan burst into laughter.

"Although I'm worried Bart might get carpal tunnel if he uses a whip." Gram lifted up her hand and began to flick her wrist, mimicking the motion.

"*Mother!*" Knickers shouted.

Gram gave one last wave of her hand and cereal went flying across the room, a piece of it hitting Knickers in the face.

"Oww!" she screamed, covering her face. "My eye."

"Mom," Megan groaned. "Don't be so dramatic. It was a piece of cereal."

"It was a piece of cereal that hit my *eye*." She staggered past a chair as tears streamed down her cheek. "I need to wash it out." But as she stumbled across the floor, her foot slid on a piece of loose cereal on the wood slats, and she knocked her shoulder into the kitchen doorjamb. Releasing a loud cry, she started to fall.

Kevin hurried over to her to keep her on her feet, but she cried out again.

"Mom?" Megan asked, running over to her. "Are you okay?"

But as soon as she reached her, she knew she *wasn't* okay. Her shoulder was sticking out at a weird angle. "Dad!" she shouted, then looked up at Kevin. "Where's Dad?

Kevin's eyes bugged out and his face turned pale. "I…I…"

Megan groaned. "Don't you wimp out on me and pass out, Kevin. I haven't forgotten what happened when we were kids and I needed stitches in my hand."

"If you pass out, fall that way," Gram said, waving her hand to show him where to fall. More cereal spread across the floor. "It would be better if your head hits the overstuffed chair than the coffee table."

"Put that cereal away!" Kevin shouted, probably in an attempt to take attention off himself. "It's a deadly weapon!"

"Nobody's passing out," Knickers said through gritted teeth. "And your father's at the store getting me a pair of pantyhose."

"No one wears pantyhose anymore, Mom," Megan said as she led her mother to a chair.

"*I* wear pantyhose."

"I rest my case. Kevin," she said, turning to look at him once their mother was settled. "Call Dad. We have to take her to the hospital. I'd do it, but Josh has my car."

Kevin looked livid. "You gave him your car?"

"He has to get to the church somehow. Besides, in ten hours or so, it'll be his car too."

Kevin scowled at the reminder, then glanced at his mother and turned a shade of pale gray.

Megan's mother tried to wave her hand and cried out in

pain. She glanced up at Megan with one eye. The other was bright red and squinted shut. "No one is going to the hospital."

"Mom! Your shoulder looks like a Barbie doll part popped out of it socket. You have to go to the hospital."

"I don't have time for that. There's too much to do."

Megan glared at Kevin. "Call Dad!"

He stood next to the front door, peering through the side window and looking like he was preparing to bolt. "I don't have to. His car just pulled up."

Moments later, the front door opened and Megan's father stood in the doorway, his gaze landing on the group. "What happened?"

"Mom dislocated her shoulder. She needs to go the hospital."

Her mother shook her head, gritting her teeth. "I don't have time to go to the hospital."

Bart took one look at his wife's shoulder and his face turned ashen.

"You can't pass out, Dad!"

Her mother narrowed her one good eye. Leave it to her to make a one-eyed squint look intimidating. "The women are the strong ones in the Vandemeer family."

Her father took a deep breath. "I'm okay."

Taking in his pale complexion, Megan wasn't so sure. "We have to get her to the hospital."

"I'm not—" Megan's mom started to say.

"Yes, you are!" Megan shouted. "Now shut up and come out to the car with us."

Her mother looked shocked, as did everyone else in the room. No one spoke to Nicole Vandemeer that way.

"Now is not the time to be stubborn! If you try to go to the wedding like this, you'll gross everyone out. If you go to the hospital now, you'll probably be there in time to help me get dressed."

"I...okay."

Megan blinked, sure she'd heard her mother wrong, but decided to trust her hallucination. "Okay, then. Dad and Kevin, get her to the car. Mom, what else needs to be done for the wedding?"

As her father and brother lifted the unwilling invalid out of her chair and led her to the door, Megan walked beside them.

Knickers grimaced as she hobbled along with their support. "We need to make sure the cake gets delivered and that the orchestra sets up on the west side and not the east. The staff at the gardens can handle both of those things. Just make sure everything goes according to plan."

"I can do that."

"You need to be at the church two and a half hours early. It's in the itinerary, but I know you didn't read it."

For once, Megan wished she had.

"The hairdresser will be there at one." They led her out the door and down the sidewalk. "Be sure to eat, Megan. You'll probably be too excited and nervous to eat, but otherwise you'll get lightheaded standing up there so long for the ceremony."

"Okay, Mom."

As Bart sprinted around the car to climb into the driver's seat, Kevin helped Megan's mom get settled in the passenger's seat. She gripped Megan's hand. "I'm so sorry, honey. I wanted this day to be perfect for you, but I've ruined everything."

Megan squatted next to her. "You didn't ruin anything, Mom. It *is* going to be perfect. I promise."

She nodded, tears now streaming from her good eye too.

Megan gave her a kiss on her forehead. "I'll see you in a few hours."

Kevin and Megan watched the car drive away, both in shock.

"Did what I think just happened really happen?" Kevin asked.

"Which part?"

"The whole convoluted mess."

"Yep." She grabbed his arm and pulled him toward the house. "Come on, we have work to do."

"We?"

"You don't think I can do everything by myself, do you?"

"So you're really going to marry this guy?"

She stopped on the front porch, a step up from him, putting him at eye level. "I know you're looking out for me, and you have no idea how wonderful that makes me feel, but Josh isn't the man you think he is. Take everything you knew about Jay Connors from all my insinuations and unsaid truths and toss them out the window. Josh is not that man."

His eyes narrowed. "Why not?"

"I hope to explain it to you later, but for now you'll have to trust me." She took a deep breath, then poked her finger into his chest. "I'm marrying Josh this afternoon, so let this evil plot to stop my wedding end now."

"Damn straight," Gram said from the sofa through the open front door.

Megan leaned toward him and whispered, "And you're in charge of making sure Gram wears clothes to the wedding."

"Eww!"

"And it has to be that pink suit Mom picked out. I need a shower." She headed for the staircase as he continued his protests and shut herself in her room, feeling better about herself than she had in a long time. While she was in the shower, washing her hair and reliving the shower she'd taken with Josh, a new thought occurred to her. If she was actually going to go through with this wedding, she should wear the dress she wanted…no matter how much of her heard-earned money she had to spend on it. When she finished, she toweled off and pulled up the bridal shop's number on her cell phone.

"Hi," she said when the salesperson answered. "This is Megan Vandemeer. I came in a couple of times this week to try on my dress and get alterations."

"Oh, yeah, I remember you. Your mother is the dragon lady."

Megan hesitated. She understood why the woman felt that way, but after seeing a more human side to her mother, she felt indignant on her behalf. "Yeah," she finally said. "That's her… Anyway, my mother changed my original dress order."

"Oh, I know."

"Okaaay…" Megan took a deep breath. "Do you know if it's still there? I'd like to buy it."

"But you already have a dress. I was assured you picked it up yesterday."

"I know, but I want to know if you have the other one. I realize I can't exchange it. I just want to buy it."

"I'm sorry, Ms. Vandemeer," the salesperson said, her voice thick with regret. "We sold it."

Megan let the words sink in. "Are you sure? I just tried it on yesterday."

"Oh, yes. That dress is pretty famous here. It was sold this morning."

This morning? Why hadn't she thought to buy it yesterday? But all the regret in the world wouldn't change the fact the dress was gone. "Okay. Well…thank you."

"Have a good day," the salesperson said before she hung up.

Megan sat down on the edge of her bed. *Sold.* It was such a final word, but she told herself not get upset. She was determined to make this the best fake wedding ever. It sure was expensive enough to qualify.

Blair continued to call her multiple times. She knew avoiding the calls wasn't the best idea, but she was terrified to hear what her friend had to say and wanted to put off the conversation for as long as possible.

Megan fed them all sandwiches that her mother had prepared and stored in the refrigerator, then she and Kevin loaded his car with her wedding dress, shoes, and a change of clothes for after the reception. She wondered if she'd forgotten anything and suddenly wished her mother were around to oversee it all. The thought shocked her enough that she fumbled with the door handle as she put Gram in the front passenger seat.

Megan was squished into the back seat next to the monstrous dress bag, which inevitably made her think of her mother. Her dad had called not long ago to tell them her mother hadn't even been seen by a doctor yet, and now Megan was worried her parents wouldn't make the wedding at all.

They rode in silence all the way to the gardens, even Gram staying remarkably quiet. When they pulled into the back parking lot, Kevin helped Gram out as Megan gathered her things. As soon as she had everything, she started toward the bridal changing room.

"Megs, wait up," a gruff voice called out from behind her.

Butterflies flapped in her stomach. "I don't want to fight with you anymore, Kevin."

He shook his head. "No more fighting."

"Really?"

"Well," a teasing grin lit up his face. "Not *all* fighting."

She grinned back. "Good."

"I just wanted you to know that I've thought about what you said, and I've decided to respect your decision. If you want to marry that asshat, I'll let you."

"There are so many things wrong with what you just said." She laughed. "But I'll take it." She kissed him on the cheek. "Thanks."

She took off for the dressing room, one of the rooms in the

walk-out basement under the chapel, grateful to discover she was the first to arrive. After her morning, she needed a few moments to herself.

The room was furnished with a sofa and several wingback chairs that faced a wall of windows overlooking the flowering gardens. A full-length mirror stood in one corner, and Megan knew the door across the room led to a bathroom. She sat in one of the wingback chairs and stared out a window, trying to let the peaceful setting settle her unrest.

"Megan?"

She turned around to see Gram standing in the doorway. She looked older than usual in the Pepto-Bismol suit Knickers had chosen.

"Can I come in?"

Megan hopped out of her seat and crossed the room. "Gram. Of course. I'm glad you're here." She helped the older woman into the chair next to hers and they sat together, taking in the view.

"It's a beautiful day for your wedding," Gram finally said.

"Isn't it?" Megan sighed. The sun shone bright in the sky, and the temperature was comfortable in the shade, which would be perfect for the outdoor reception later. She almost wished it were for real.

Gram released a sigh. "I'm sorry I ruined everything for you. Your mother…"

Megan hugged her grandmother's arm and leaned her head on her shoulder. "Good heavens, Gram, you didn't ruin anything. Think of the stories we'll tell."

Gram chuckled. "Your mother will never let me live it down."

"True," Megan laughed. "And it will be awesome."

"I know you two have your differences, but a girl should have her mother with her on her wedding day."

"She'll get here in time. I *know* it."

The older woman fingered her pearls, then smoothed an imaginary wrinkle from her skirt. "There's a reason your mother acts this way, you know." Megan sat up and turned to face the older woman, who patted her hand. "I kept hoping she'd tell you herself one day, but she never did. She can hardly admit it to herself." She swung her gaze to the gardens. "You wonder why you never saw your Aunt Heather again... I know your mother told you some ridiculous story about a fight over toilet paper." Her mouth lifted into a weak smile.

Megan took her grandmother's hand in her own, sensing what she had to tell her would be bigger than she ever anticipated.

"It wasn't true, of course. Heather was always interested in your father, but he only had eyes for your mother. I hoped Heather would get over her infatuation, and I honestly thought it had died down. But one day when you were eleven, your mother came home and found your father and Heather together."

"Together?" Megan asked in confusion, then horrified understanding set in. "*Oh, no.*"

Gram nodded. "They were in your mother's bed." She took a deep breath and released it. "Your mother was devastated. She saw it as the ultimate betrayal. Her sister and her husband in her own bed. You and Kevin came and stayed with your grandpa and me for a week, remember?"

"Yeah…"

"That's when it happened. Your mother didn't take it well, as you can imagine. She and your father vowed to stay together, and your father was truly sorry. He did his best to make it up to her, giving her anything and everything she wanted. He still does. But Nicole was certain he'd cheated on her because she wasn't *enough.* She'd always thought Heather was the prettier of the two of them. Since that day, she's tried her best to be perfect, and she's made herself and everyone around her miserable in the process."

Megan closed her eyes, fighting back tears. "I can't believe Daddy cheated on her."

"He's always sworn it was a one-time thing, and I believe him. Heather was a lot like your Libby."

Megan started to protest, but Gram squeezed her hand. "No, Libby would never try to steal another woman's husband, especially from someone she cares about. But Libby catches men's attention without even trying." She sighed. "Heather was like that too. Only she had no scruples. Bart wasn't the first married man she went after and I'm sure he wasn't the last. As her mother, I tried to ignore it for many years. Until Nicole." She was silent for a moment. "Heather had tried to snag your father since your mother first brought him home. I'm sure she just happened to catch him at a weak moment." Her voice turned stern. "I'm in no way condoning what your father did, but I *do* believe he regretted it."

"Yeah, because he was caught," Megan said in disgust.

"Maybe. Maybe not. But he truly loves your mother."

"Poor Mom." She could sympathize with her mother after Jay's betrayal. Now she wished she'd come clean weeks ago. Her mother would have probably understood. "And she really hasn't spoken to Aunt Heather since?"

"No, and Heather died in an accident several years ago, so they never had a chance to reconcile." She released a heavy sigh. "She loves you, Megan. She just has a hard time letting anyone close now. She's always waiting for them to betray her."

Had her mother viewed many of Megan's decisions as betrayals?

"And please don't hold this against your father. Even though this is news to you, it happened nearly twenty years ago. Water under the bridge for both of them. Trust me, he's more than paid for his crime." Gram climbed to her feet, releasing a groan. "I didn't get a chance to do my *au naturel* yoga yesterday, and today I'm all stiff."

Megan's mouth lifted in a small grin despite her emotional stew.

"Megan," Gram turned and paused. "The boy you're marrying today is better than the one you were supposed to marry."

Megan stood, sure she'd heard her grandmother wrong. "*What?*"

She gave Megan an ornery grin. "I know that man isn't Jay Connors. I talked to that idiot several months ago on the phone. The man you're marrying today isn't him."

Megan started to protest, but what was the point? "How long have you known?" she asked in shock.

"Since I met him at the airport."

"And you didn't say *anything?*"

Gram shrugged, then hobbled to the door. "I wanted to see how it played out." She paused at the doorway. "I could tell he was a good man, and I figured you'd come clean eventually."

"We're not really getting married, Gram. It's all a misunderstanding. I was afraid to tell Mom I broke up with Jay. She'd spent *so* much money—"

"You don't have to explain. But I hope you don't give that boy up after this wedding." She winked. "He does have a very nice patootie."

Megan started to assure her that she had no plans to let Josh go, then stopped herself. She needed to save the assurances for after Blair dropped her bombshell.

She only hoped her heart wasn't blown to pieces when Blair was done.

Chapter Twenty-Eight

"Oh, Megan," Libby gushed. "You're beautiful."

Megan stared at her reflection. Libby had helped with her makeup and the hairdresser had just finished her hair. It wasn't the up-do her mother had wanted. The front was pulled into a loose knot at the base of her neck, and the rest of her hair tumbled in soft curls down her back. "I'm not even wearing my dress yet."

"What if your mom doesn't get here in time?"

Megan chuckled, but her stomach twisted with nerves. "She'll be here. Dad says she's raising holy hell, insisting it shouldn't take so long to fix a dislocated shoulder and a scratched cornea."

It had been hard to talk to her dad on the phone without confronting him, but she'd forced herself to set her anger aside. She knew without a doubt he loved her mother—his voice practically broadcast it as he relayed Nicole's current status—and was mature enough to realize things weren't always black and white. She only had to look at her own mess to see that. Still, a new heaviness had settled over her heart. Her father wasn't the perfect man she'd always believed him to be.

"Do you think she'll really wear an eyepatch?" Libby asked.

"Maybe she's wishing she'd picked a pirate wedding theme instead."

Libby laughed. "If anyone can pull off pirate chic, your mother can."

"I know." Megan cast a glance at the door, feeling heavy-hearted. "I don't think Blair's coming."

Libby put her hands on Megan's upper arms. "Blair *will* show up. We all made a promise to each other."

"The pact."

"*Yes*, the wedding pact. We promised we would be married by the time we were thirty. We'd be in each others' weddings, and we'd be the first ones to see each other in our dresses on our wedding days."

"We were nine years old, Libby."

"But it still means something to us all, whether she admits it or not. She'll be here."

"It's almost time to get dressed." Megan's nerves were getting the best of her. "She hates me. I haven't answered any of her calls today and I wouldn't listen to her last night. She's not coming."

Libby gave her a side hug. "She doesn't hate you. Give her a few minutes. She'll be here."

They were silent for a few moments, and Megan started to pace. Finally, she stopped and turned to Libby. "Aren't you wondering why Josh and I are going through with this wedding?"

"No."

"*Really?*"

Libby smiled. "No, this feels right. You feel it too, or you wouldn't be here right now. You and Josh are perfect for each other."

"But Blair would say—" Megan lowered her voice to a growl, "—'then go on a date, Megan. Don't do something rash, like marrying someone you barely know.'"

The door swung open. "I don't sound anything like that," Blair said, marching through the doorway with a brisk stride, an enormous dress bag slung over her shoulder. "My voice isn't anywhere near that deep. Although the rest is reasonably accurate."

"Blair." Megan clutched her hands in front of her, feeling like she was about to puke.

"You've been ignoring my calls, texts, emails, voice mails, and carrier pigeons, Megs."

Blair not only showed up but used her nickname. Megan grinned. "I never got the carrier pigeons."

"Ah-ha!" Blair pointed at her. "You just admitted that you received and ignored the other three."

"You're playing the role of an attorney, Blair. I need you here as my friend."

"Well, you're going to have to tolerate the attorney for a little while longer, because there's something I need to talk to you about. If you feel like going through with this preposterous endeavor once I've said my piece, I will be here for you one hundred percent."

Tears stung Megan's eyes. "Thank you."

"Don't thank me yet." She hung the garment bag on the rack that held Megan's wedding dress, spread out in all its bedazzled organza glory. Blair stopped in her tracks as she took in the sight of it, her mouth gaping. She pointed to the dress, then Megan, then back at the dress. "*Really?*"

Megan shrugged, over it all ready. "Knickers."

Blair looked around. "Where is she anyway? I expected to find her here with a riding crop and a whistle to keep us malcontents in line."

Libby snickered. "I haven't heard her call us malcontents for years."

"She's not here. And after Gram asked me earlier today if Josh and I were into BDSM, I don't want to hear another mention of whips or crops for a very long time." Megan shuddered. "She's at the hospital with a dislocated shoulder and a scratched cornea. She'll be here soon."

"*You're kidding?*"

"I'm more interested in finding out how Gram knows about BDSM," Libby said.

Megan rolled her eyes. "She says she read *Fifty Shades of Grey.*"

Libby burst out laughing. "That explains so much."

"Tell me about it," Megan grumbled, her nerves pinging with anxiety. She was ready to seal her fate.

Blair lifted her eyebrows. "What happened to your mother?"

Megan sighed. "It's a long story, but I'm more interested in the story you have to tell me. I'm ready to hear it now." When Blair blinked in surprise, Megan added, "I know you have something important to say. Josh told me that much, but not the details. You investigated him, didn't you? After I expressly ordered you not to."

All the fight left Blair, who looked more vulnerable than Megan had seen her in years. "What would you have me do, Megan? I wasn't willing to stand by and watch you get hurt by one more jerk, especially when the last one still can't seem to take no for an answer. I swear, if Jay makes one more annoying call…"

"What are you talking about?"

"That man's been calling me nonstop since Friday morning. Finally, after your fiasco of a rehearsal dinner last night, I told him you were in Kansas City, which meant you couldn't go out to dinner with him so he should *stop calling* me. To his credit, he seemed genuinely surprised to hear you were here. I said the only way you would even fathom going out with him was if he hopped on a plane, found you here in KC, and groveled at your feet. Thank God, that seemed to do the trick, and my phone has been mercifully silent ever since."

"Why would you tell him that? I wouldn't go out with him if he were the last man on earth. Especially after meeting Josh."

"Yeah...well, you shouldn't put Josh on a pedestal just yet." She put a hand on her hip and cocked her head. "What did he tell you?"

"I told you. He didn't tell me anything. I figured out you had something to do with it after he punched his brother—oh, God!" she said, realization hitting her. "I have no idea where Noah is or where he stayed last night."

Libby's mouth contorted. "I know the answer to both of those questions."

Megan froze, narrowing her eyes. "How do *you* know?"

"You didn't!" Blair gasped.

Libby's back stiffened in defense. "What? He didn't have anywhere to go, and he was really upset."

"Libby!" Blair said. "What about Mitch?"

"What about him?" she asked in genuine confusion. "Oh! You think—no! I didn't cheat on Mitch." Disgust washed over her face. "Is that really what you think of me?"

"There was that one time..." Blair's voice trailed off.

"I was a kid—barely nineteen—and he told me that he and his girlfriend had broken up. *He* was cheating on his girlfriend, but I would never purposely cheat. Especially after Megan found that prick..." Her voice trailed off.

Megan grabbed Libby's hand. "It's okay, Libby. I'm over it. I'm thankful for it. Otherwise, I might be marrying said prick now." She gave a shudder.

"There's nothing between me and Noah. He just needed a friend last night."

"A friend?" Blair asked, turning her attention to Libby. "That kind of guy doesn't do *friends*."

"Yeah, I know," Libby said. "That's what was so confusing. We stayed up almost all night talking." She widened her eyes, as if sensing they were about to pounce on her. "What? It's true. And he never once made a move on me. Honestly, I think he's lonely."

Blair stared at her, speechless for several seconds before shaking her head. "Lonely? Whatever. One McMillan man at a time." She turned her gaze to Megan. "There are a few things you need to know. I can't believe he didn't tell you everything before I could get to you."

"No, Blair," Megan said, her tone brisk. "He told me to listen to what you had to say, then make up my own mind."

Blair sighed. "He's playing you, Megs."

"No, Blair. He trusts my judgment. He said if I decide I don't want to see him again, he'll respect my choice." She took a deep breath. "So tell me."

Blair cast a glance toward the still-silent Libby.

"Libby can stay," Megan said. "She's part of this too."

"I think you should sit." Megan obeyed and fought her rising nausea as Blair told her about the patent, Josh's business, and how she wasn't sure it was a coincidence that he'd sat next to her on the plane. And when she was finished, all three women sat in silence.

Megan stood and wandered over to the window, looking out at the flowering gardens. Parts of it made sense. She knew Josh's company was in trouble. He'd told her that he had two choices—either his employees would lose their jobs or he'd hurt someone he cared about.

She had thought that someone was Noah. Turns out it was her.

So why had he continued with this charade?

Because he hadn't stolen the information he needed yet.

If he left, he couldn't look for it. She felt like an idiot when she realized she'd given her father's password to him, providing him with carte blanche to all of her father's electronic files. What had she done?

She was going to throw up.

Then she thought about the man she'd gotten to know—a man who would never steal something for personal gain. He had too much integrity. It might not look that way, since he'd helped her for reasons that weren't on the up and up, but she couldn't ignore how he'd refused to have sex with her that first night. He'd wanted to—badly—but he'd stopped because he was afraid of hurting her.

But what about his feelings now? When she examined every minute they'd spent together, she kept coming up with the same answer. What he felt for her—what they felt for each other—was genuine.

"Why was he so upset with Noah?" she finally asked, turning to face Blair.

"How should I know?"

Megan stared at her, lifting her eyebrows. "Try again. I know you had a part in it."

"Why would I interfere with their relationship?"

"*Tell me.*"

Blair released a sigh. "You know how much I love you, Megan. I may not say it often, but I figure actions speak louder than words. So I acted."

"What did you do?" Her words were tightly controlled.

"I had a document prepared. After I presented my key evidence, I gave Josh an out. I found another investor to take the original one's place—one of my divorce clients who received a very large settlement—but if he wanted my help, he had to promise to leave you and never speak to you again."

Megan felt lightheaded. "You did what?"

"He refused to sign it. I know he wants that patent, but if he doesn't have the money by next week, he'll have to shut down. For all his whining about how devastating it would be to his employees if he had to shut his doors, he never even stopped to consider it."

Megan put her hand on the back of her chair to help support her shaking legs. "He gave up his business for me."

Blair scowled. "I know it looks that way, but you don't know that."

Megan shook her head. "No, Blair. I do. I know how desperately he wants to save his employees. He came on this trip for no other reason. And give me a break, there's no way he could have arranged to sit beside me on that plane unless he hacked the airline. He said he left this trip up to fate, and sitting by me was definitely fate. He cares about me. I know it." Her voice broke. "If he didn't, he would have signed that document and gone with the sure thing." She pressed her fingertips to her temple. "This morning he told me it was up to me if I wanted to move forward with the wedding…and with him. He wouldn't do that if he didn't want to be with me." She looked up at her friend. "Tell me I'm wrong."

Blair's mouth twisted as she considered her words. "I admit that it confused me when he tore up the document. While I expected a half-hearted denial, I didn't think he would act so offended."

Megan lifted her chin. "Why was he so furious with Noah?"

Guilt washed over Blair's face. "Noah had already signed the document. I caught him before the rehearsal."

Megan sat in the chair, feeling even more lightheaded. "Oh, Blair. What have you done?" She glanced at Libby, who was sitting on the other side of the room, to gauge her reaction. There was a strange look on her friend's face, and when she didn't say a word, Megan narrowed her eyes. "You already knew. That's what you talked to Noah about all night."

Libby gave a tiny shrug. "He was upset. When he signed it, he had no idea that Josh was in love with you."

Megan bolted out of her chair. "He's *what?*"

Libby's eyebrows rose. "You didn't know he's in love with you?"

"No..."

Blair snorted. "Hell, he told me himself last night when he tore up the paper. I didn't buy it when he told me, thinking it was some way to outmaneuver me. But now I'm reconsidering, and I'm more cynical than the two of you put together. Supposing there are no other mitigating circumstances, what man gives up his family legacy for a woman he *kind of likes?*"

"Oh, God. I have to talk to him." Megan bolted for the door, but Blair blocked her path.

"Wait. He stopped me when I was on my way in here."

"What? He's here?"

Blair rolled her eyes. "Of course he's here. He said if you were still open to going through with this after I talked to you, he wanted me to give you something from him."

"And you agreed?" Megan asked in shock.

Blair shrugged, looking irritated. "I have to admit, before I talked to him, I was convinced he was guilty as hell. But after I talked to him... I'd be lying if I didn't admit that I see some flaws in my theory."

"What does that mean?" Libby prodded.

Blair scowled, looking aggrieved. "I *may* have been wrong."

"What?" Libby teased. "The all-knowing Blair might have been wrong?"

Megan shook her head. "Get back to the present part."

"It's out in the hall. Like I said, he asked me to give it to you if you didn't hate him after hearing my version of events."

"And you agreed?"

She shrugged. "I'm not *entirely* cold-blooded, and like I said, there were some holes in my theory." She left the room and came back with a white box that was almost as big as she was. "If I'd known it would be this hard to carry, I would have asked for a delivery fee."

"What is it?" Megan asked, pushing makeup aside on the large table to make room for the box.

"No idea. I'm just the delivery person. Open it and find out."

Megan's hand shook as she tugged on the end of the giant white bow and pulled it loose. When she lifted off the lid, she gasped. "It's my dress," she whispered in shock.

"What dress?" Blair asked, peeking around her.

"Her original dress," Libby gasped in awe. "But how? Knickers canceled the order."

"They said it was too late to cancel it. So both were delivered to the store, but they wouldn't exchange it."

A card sat on top, which she pulled out to read.

Meggie

I know how much this dress means to you. If you decide to go through with the wedding, you should feel like the most beautiful woman in the world, although it doesn't matter to me what you wear—you are already the most beautiful woman in the world.

Josh

Libby picked up the small veil on top. "That is the most romantic thing *ever.*"

Megan grabbed the corners of the dress and lifted it out of the box. "I can't believe he bought my dress."

Blair grunted. "This still doesn't mean he's innocent."

"Yeah," Libby mumbled. "Because a guy who's trying to scam her would obviously buy her a three-thousand-dollar wedding dress."

Megan held it in front of her, studying her reflection. "I

can't believe he did this."

"Well, what are you waiting for?" Libby asked, putting the veil back in the box. "Let's get you dressed. There's less than an hour until the wedding."

Twenty minutes later, Libby and Blair were dressed in their pink puffed monstrosities, arranging Megan's veil in her hair. They stepped back and studied her.

Tears filled Libby's eyes. "I can't believe you're getting married."

"I'm not really getting married," Megan gushed out.

"It looks like you are from where I'm standing," Blair said.

"It's not real. It's all for Knickers, and she's not even here to enjoy it."

Libby squeezed her arm. "She'll be here, Megs. Wild horses couldn't keep her away."

There was a knock at the door and Blair went to answer it, poking her head through the opening. She turned around with a scowl. "He wants to talk to you." A tiny grin broke through her tough exterior. "And I suppose the fact you're wearing the wedding dress means you want to talk to him too." Blair tugged on Libby's pink organza. "By the way, it's not fair that you got to dump the fairy princess dress and we're still stuck with ours." Her eyes lit up with a devilish gleam. "But I'm getting married soon too, and paybacks are a bitch."

They filed out of the room, leaving the door open to reveal Josh. He was gorgeous. He wore the black tux he'd tried on the day before, but today he looked different. Nervous, but there was something else she couldn't put her finger on. He stood at the threshold, hesitating. "Can I come in?" he asked in a hoarse rasp.

She nodded, not trusting her voice.

He entered the room and shut the door behind him. He openly stared at her, his eyes wide in awe. "You're beautiful," he whispered.

She smiled softly, feeling shy in the spotlight of his unabashed wonderment. "You saw me wearing this yesterday."

He shook his head. "Not like this." He moved closer, stopping several feet in front of her. "You didn't tell me to go to hell. I'm going to take that as a good sign."

"I have some questions."

He pressed his lips together. "Okay. Anything. Total honesty."

She took a deep breath. "Did you know I'd be on that plane?"

He shook his head, his eyes pleading. "No. I had no idea…I didn't have much of a plan either; I just knew Bart Vandemeer's daughter was getting married. But I freely admit that I boarded the plane with the intention of finding evidence that your father's firm stole my design."

"*Your* design?"

His gaze held hers. "I came up with it, and Noah and I were working on funding and paperwork for the patent. Noah had a spare set of plans with him at a convention and he…lost them."

"Lost them?"

He grimaced. "He slept with a woman and when he woke up the next morning, the bag and the plans were gone."

She couldn't believe her father would involve himself in such a thing, but two hours ago, she would have sworn an oath that her father wasn't capable of cheating on her mother. "How do you know this isn't some big coincidence?"

"Because when Noah was at your father's firm yesterday, he saw a photo of the woman." He paused. "She's Drew Peterman's fiancé."

"Miriam?" Megan gasped. "I knew Drew was underhanded, but to have his girlfriend sleep with your brother…"

"So you believe me?"

"Of course I believe you, but I still don't understand how

you ended up as my substitute fiancé."

"Everything I told you is true. I carried you out of the plane, and your mother heard me telling people you were my fiancée. I did try to correct her, but then your father introduced himself, and…I figured I was being given the chance to help us both out. I really did leave this trip up to fate, and it seemed like this giant gift had been delivered to me, wrapped up in a bow." He took her hand in his. "I never meant to hurt or humiliate you. You have to believe me."

She nodded. "So the reason you didn't want to break up with me in the beginning was because you hadn't found what you needed?"

"Yes, at first."

"And then Noah came to help."

"It seemed like a good idea at the time."

"And then yesterday? When you used my father's computer…?"

"I was ready to let the business die. After our night together, I knew I couldn't lose you."

"But something changed."

"When I checked my email, I got a note from our business manager, Angie. She told me that an employee who's been with the firm for over thirty years had a heart attack." He swallowed and reached forward to squeeze her hand. "He's counting on me, Megan. How will he survive if my business fails? I felt like I had to make a choice between saving him and the other people in my firm and my own happiness. I've sacrificed so much for this business, but I didn't want to give you up. It ripped my heart out to even consider it—"

She closed the distance between them and kissed him. "You're not giving me up."

He squeezed his eyes shut and pulled her into a hug, kissing her softly for several seconds before releasing her.

"Do you have any hard evidence against my father's

company yet?"

Guilt flickered in his eyes. "No. Just circumstantial."

She hesitated, not knowing if she wanted the answer to her next question. But she was tired of hiding from the truth. "Is my father involved?"

He didn't answer and she pushed out a breath, trying not to cry.

"We don't know, Megan. That's circumstantial too."

But there was a good chance he *was* involved somehow, and the thought nearly killed her. "How'd he pay for this wedding, Josh? My parents don't have that kind of money."

"I don't know."

She pressed her lips together and nodded, taking in a deep breath. "So we need to get the evidence to save your business, right?"

"*You want to help me?*"

"You have people depending on you, don't you?"

"Well…yes…but…"

"Do you have a plan?"

He shook his head, as though letting the realization that Megan was there for him, that she wanted to help him, sink in. "Drew Peterman and his fiancée are supposedly coming to the wedding. Noah is going to pull her away and try to get her to confess to stealing the plans and capture it with a video recording. If we can get her confession, the rest falls into place."

"And how does Noah plan to get her to confess?"

His face reddened. "He has his…methods."

"Oh." She was sure he did.

"Libby's agreed to help him too. She's going to record it all." When her eyes widened in surprise, he added, "Noah stayed with her last night. Supposedly they're BFFs now."

"I heard. And what about you and Noah?"

He grimaced. "We're working it out. He's making an

effort."

"So if Libby and Noah are trying to get a confession, what is there for me to do? I want to help you."

His eyes were soft as he smiled at her. "Your job is easy. You just be you."

"And what's *your* job in this?"

"To stand next to you and be the luckiest man in the world."

Her face flushed. Were Libby and Blair right? Did he actually love her?

Did she love him?

She glanced down at her dress. "Thank you for this."

"If we're going through with this, I wanted today to be as wonderful for you as possible." He started pacing, then stopped in front of her and said, "I have another gift, if you'll accept it."

Why was he so nervous? "Okay."

He reached into his coat pocket and pulled out a silver ring. The band was engraved with an intricate pattern. Two smaller but still good-sized diamonds flanked a large round diamond. "I don't want to stand in front of all your mother's friends and go through this ceremony with Jay Connors' ring on your finger. Noah called our mother on the way to the rehearsal dinner last night—after he'd realized what a screw-up it was to sign that damned paper—and asked her to overnight this." He held it in front of her. "This was part of my grandmother's wedding set. I figured we could swap out his engagement ring for mine. There's a wedding band too." He searched her eyes. "And maybe when the ceremony is over, you'll keep wearing the engagement ring."

Her mouth dropped open in shock as he got down on one knee. "Megan Vandemeer, sitting by you on that plane was the best thing that ever happened to me. And when I thought about losing you, I was devastated. I don't want to live without you. I don't know how I fell in love with you so quickly, but I did. I know it's probably too soon, and this is *so* unlike me, but I love you. I know deep in my gut that I want to spend the rest of my life with you. Will you marry me?"

She laughed between her tears.

"Are those happy tears?" he asked, still on his knee. "Please tell me those are happy tears."

She nodded.

"Is that a yes? You're leaving me hanging, Meggie, and this floor is hard. But I'll grovel if I have to. I'll do anything to prove myself to you."

"Yes. Yes."

He stood and pulled her into his arms, kissing her until she forgot everything around them.

When she looked into his eyes, she smiled. "I love you too."

He laughed. "I sure as hell hope so. You just agreed to marry me for real."

Chapter Twenty-Nine

Josh was more nervous than he'd expected. This was a fake wedding, arranged for his now-fiancée and another groom, so why was he so nervous?

Fake wedding or not, it felt incredibly real, especially since there was a real wedding in their near future. He knew Megan was worried that her parents wouldn't arrive in time, and he wished his own mother were present. All he could do was hold Megan's hand and stand by her side.

Megan and Josh waited behind the glass chapel and around the corner by the flower garden, out of sight of the guests who were being seated. Libby, Blair, Noah, and Kevin were with them. Josh was happy that Kevin's animosity had softened, even if he wasn't overly friendly. Noah kept grinning like a fool, as though he had something up his sleeve, and Libby, who was probably in the know since she and Noah were besties now, seemed perkier than usual. Josh pulled his brother to the side.

"What are you up to?" Josh asked, scrutinizing him while waiting for an answer.

Noah held out his hands. "What? I can't be excited my baby brother is getting married?"

Josh leaned into his ear. "It's not like this is our real wedding, Noah." He stood upright. "But thanks for having Grandma's rings sent." He swallowed. "It means a lot, especially since she left them to you."

Noah clapped his brother's upper arm. "You and Megan deserve them and all the happiness that comes with them." He glanced over his shoulder at the bride. "It looks good on her finger."

Josh studied his brother before whispering, "She's going to keep wearing it after the ceremony. I asked her to marry me, and she said yes."

He expected more surprise from his cynical brother, but Noah's face lit up with a radiant smile. "That's the best news I've heard in a long time."

"You—a firm believer that true love doesn't exist—think me proposing to a woman I've known for four days is the best news you've heard in a long time?"

Noah shrugged, glancing at Libby, then back at him. "What can I say? I've been convinced this is true love. And I have to admit that I've never seen you happier." He turned serious. "You deserve all this happiness and so much more, Josh."

A lump clogged Josh's throat. "Thanks, Noah."

Noah shrugged again, an arrogant grin slowly spreading across his face as he straightened his tie. "I'll try not to outshine you up there."

"With that black eye?"

He winked his bruised eye, then winced, still grinning. "It only adds to my rugged charm."

Josh's gaze fell on Megan, once again stunned this woman who was so beautiful—inside and out—was his. "We're both going to be outshone."

Noah rested his hand on Josh's shoulder, following his gaze. "I think you're right about that one, little brother."

Bart and Nicole arrived with minutes to spare—Nicole hopped up on painkillers, with an arm sling on her right side and an eyepatch on her left. The instant Megan saw her parents, all the tension drained from her body, leaving her with a radiant glow. She gave the go-ahead to start the wedding procession.

"Thanks for keeping me calm, but I'm good now." Megan reached up and placed a gentle kiss on his lips. "See you at the altar, Mr. McMillan."

Her mother's unfocused eyes darted around. "Did she just call him Mr. McMillan?" But just then the usher came around the corner to lead her to her seat. Josh started to head for the chapel but stopped when he saw Nicole pull away from the usher and stumble toward her daughter. She was probably planning to give her an earful about letting Josh see her dress. This wedding might not be real, but he wasn't going to let her mother screw this up for her any more than she already had.

Sensing that Megan's mother was chemically impaired, the usher reached for her good arm to lead her away, but she shrugged him off again.

Josh was about to bolt toward them to intervene, but stopped when he heard Nicole's first words. "You're a good girl, Megan. I wanted you to have the perfect wedding. I've been a terrible mother to you, and I know it. This was my way of trying to make it up to you, but I went ahead and screwed that up too."

"No, Mom." She shook her head, tears glittering in her eyes. She looked up at Josh and he offered her a reassuring smile. All the drugs must have shook some warmth and affection from Megan's mother, and he was relieved. Granted, Knickers hadn't handled the wedding arrangements the best way, but as a gesture, it was appreciable.

"It's the most beautiful wedding ever. Thank you," Megan said, placing a hand on her mother's good shoulder.

Assured that Megan was okay, Josh took his place at the altar of the all-glass chapel, the view of which overlooked the gardens. Knickers had outdone herself with the organza draping gracing the ends of each pew. Flowers were everywhere—roses in varying shades of white and pale pink. Josh hated to admit it, but Knickers' wedding madness had paid off. The glass chapel was gorgeous on its own. The plethora of flowers made it stunning.

Kevin stood on the altar with him, and Noah stood in the best man position. He leaned over and whispered in Josh's ear. "I know Knickers was worried about your side of the church being too bare." He pointed to the right. "There's a surprise for you."

Josh turned his attention to the front row and was shocked to see his mother. Tears filled her eyes, and she gave him a warm smile. He turned back to Noah, silently demanding an explanation.

"You can't get married without Mom. She'd kill us both." When Josh didn't avert his gaze, he continued. "When I asked for the rings, she demanded to know why, so I told her everything. She overnighted the rings, but her plane barely landed in time."

Josh leaned closer to Noah's ear. "But this wedding isn't real."

Noah smirked. "You just keep telling yourself that."

The string quartet switched to the wedding march, setting Josh's heart to racing, and first Libby then Blair walked down the aisle.

Bart walked down the aisle next, Megan on his arm. She was gorgeous in her white silk dress, her dark hair hanging down her back. A short veil—the one the sales clerk had recommended—was pinned to the top of her head. She carried a bouquet of soft pink roses. All eyes in the chapel were on her, but her gaze remained fixed on him as she made her way to the front of the room. The love in her eyes sucked his breath away, and he once again thanked God above that this woman was his. His chest warmed as she approached him, and before he knew it, they were standing in front of everyone.

When the minister announced it was time for the vows, Josh interrupted him. "Uh…I wrote my own vows."

Megan's eyebrows lifted playfully as he reached into his pocket and pulled out a napkin.

"Okay," the minister said, sounding uncertain. Josh knew Knickers had told him to stick to the traditional vows, and this was throwing off the pre-scripted ceremony.

Josh opened the napkin and began to have second thoughts as he looked down at the list in his hand. His gaze lifted to hers and she smiled, giving him the silent encouragement he needed to speak.

"Megan, I promise to stay in the shower with you when the water turns cold."

She giggled.

"I promise to carry you off planes when you overdose on Dramamine, but I draw the line at letting your Gram take pictures of my bare butt." He turned to the audience and found her grandmother on the front row. "Sorry, Gram."

"That's okay," Gram called out to him. "Noah will pose for me."

The crowd snickered and laughed.

He turned back to Megan, who was obviously struggling to keep a straight face.

"I promise to walk the dog when it's cold and rainy," he continued.

"Wait," she whispered, loud enough for only them to hear. "You have a dog?"

He leaned closer and whispered, "No. Do you?"

She shook her head. "No, but I want one."

"So do I. I'll walk it." He straightened and looked at the bottom of his list. "And if you agree to keep me around, I promise I'll always bring you milk."

She started laughing.

"I promise to throw my laundry in the hamper and always keep your feet warm." He looked up at her. "I'll be there to share your joy, and I'll always be there to wipe away your tears in your sorrow. I will support you in every choice you make—unless it involves snow peas—but I'll definitely be there for everything else." He took her hand, turning serious. "No matter what, I promise to always love you. I want to thank you for turning my life completely upside down." He looked into her eyes. "You are my once in a lifetime, Megan Vandemeer. Thank you for giving me a second chance."

She squeezed his hand and bit her lower lip. "I didn't write any vows, Josh."

"That's okay."

She took a deep breath and pushed it out. "I don't know what I would have done without you over these last few days, and I had no idea what I was missing until you showed it to me, but now that I've had the milk, I wouldn't dream of giving up the cow. Thanks for crashing into my life."

He laughed.

"And thank you for giving into fate, Josh. I can't imagine spending the rest of my life without you."

He grabbed her hand and squeezed it as she stared up at him with so much love he had to fight the impulse to kiss her right then and there.

They turned back to the minister who was gaping at them, his eyes wide. He shuddered, then took a moment to gather his wits. "You can exchange the rings," he stammered out.

Josh knew from the rehearsal that the minister had been

planning to recite something, but the unorthodox vows had clearly thrown him for a loop.

After pulling the wedding ring from his pocket, Josh picked up Megan's finger and held the ring over it. "This was my grandmother's ring. My grandfather had it specially designed for her, and they were married fifty-two years." He glanced at his mother in the audience, wondering what she thought, but she just gave him a loving smile and wiped tears from her cheeks. He turned back to Megan, suddenly wishing this wedding had been planned for the two of them—that it was real. "I hope we can have a marriage as strong and long-lasting as theirs was." He slid the ring over her finger.

"I don't have a ring," she whispered. "I forgot a ring."

Kevin cleared his throat. "I have one. Mom worried that you'd forget, so she gave me Grandpa's," he grumbled, walking over and handing her a ring. "And for the record, this is the most bizarre wedding I've ever been to," he said, soft enough for only them to hear.

Josh grinned. There was nothing traditional about how they'd gotten here. Why would their wedding be any different?

Megan put the ring on his finger with little fanfare, and the minister, who was clearly eager to be done with this mess, said, "May I present Mr. and Mrs. Josh McMillan."

"Who?" Knickers asked Bart, loud enough for everyone to hear. "Why did he call them that?" Hopefully the pain medicine was still in full enough effect that she'd forget the slip.

"You may kiss the bride."

Josh pulled Megan into his arms and kissed her, then lifted his head as applause filled the chapel. "We really did it."

She beamed up at him. "We really did."

Chapter Thirty

Josh endured several rounds of photos with the drunk photographer, who hiccupped in between shouting out orders, a wedding cake that nearly fell over, and Knickers' spiraling mood swings as she came off her pain meds. Luckily Knickers seemed to have forgotten the minister's use of his real name, though, and everyone was having a wonderful time.

It was the best day of his life.

When Bart introduced him to Drew Peterson and his fiancée Miriam in the receiving line, Josh realized he'd completely forgotten the original purpose for carrying on with the charade of the wedding. His back stiffened, and he forced himself to shake the man's hand. Megan wasn't as gracious, and barely acknowledged either of them. Her father gave her a confused glance, but the next guest approached, and Drew and his date moved along to their table.

Josh looked over at Noah, a couple of places down the line. They exchanged a nod, then Noah's gaze followed Drew to his seat.

A couple of minutes later, Josh's stomach tightened when he glanced into the face of his mother. She'd seemed happy enough during the wedding, but what would she say now that it was all over?

"Mom..."

She reached up and pulled him into a tight hug. "I'd ask you if you're sure, but it's too late for that now. Besides, the happiness rolling off you tells me that you are."

He swallowed. "I'm sorry."

She broke loose and looked up into his eyes. "Why would you be sorry?"

"For not telling you sooner."

"From what Noah told me, there wasn't much *sooner* you could have told me." She grabbed his hand, tears in her eyes. "You're so much like your father. Even when it comes to love."

His face warmed and he realized Megan was watching them, both fear and worry on her face. He took her hand in his and turned to his mother. "Mom, this is Megan Vandemeer...the most amazing woman in the world." He turned to his mother. "Next to you, of course."

His mother laughed. "Now that you're married I'll relinquish the title."

Megan held out her hand. "Mrs. McMillan...I'm so happy you came."

His mother ignored her outstretched hand and hugged her. "None of that Mrs. McMillan stuff. Call me Marla."

She squeezed her one more time and Josh let out a sigh of relief. So she wasn't going to hold this impromptu wedding against either of them.

His mother gave him an ornery grin. "And why are you calling her Megan Vandemeer? She's Megan McMillan now." Worry filled her eyes and she hastily added, "Unless, of course, you plan on keeping your maiden name. I realize women do that nowadays."

Megan laughed and wrapped her arm around Josh's, leaning her temple into his shoulder and looking up into his face. "No. I like the sound of Megan McMillan."

He leaned down and kissed her. "I like the sound of that too."

His mother smiled. "I can't wait to get to know you better, Megan. Anyone who can make my son beam with so much happiness is a very welcome addition to our family." Her gaze landed on Noah, who was joking around with Libby. "Now if Noah could just settle down with a good woman."

Josh snorted with a grin. "I wouldn't hold my breath."

Knickers had outdone herself with the reception as well. The dinner was served under a huge organza-draped tent filled with flowers and candelabras. After the dinner, the guests made their way to the makeshift dance floor on the lawn, dancing to music played by a band.

Hours into the reception, the open bar had helped the atmosphere shift from formal to fun-loving, but Noah still hadn't made his move. Finally, Josh saw Miriam head up to the administrative building, where the restrooms were located. Noah followed about thirty seconds later with Libby close behind. The heavy sense of responsibility that had been plaguing him finally sloughed away.

Josh spun Megan around on the dance floor under the stars. The band Knickers had hired was surprisingly good. He knew they should be mingling with their guests, but he couldn't bring himself to lose this perfect moment with her.

A couple of dances later, Megan noticed his attention drift up the small hill, and she glanced around. "Where's Noah?"

Josh gave her a knowing look. "He's getting our proof."

"Do you think he'll get it?"

He grinned. "Yeah."

"What about my dad?" Worry lines wrinkled her forehead.

"Hey." She looked up at him. "Let's find out what Miriam tells Noah, then go from there."

"Okay." She nodded. "Did you get the marriage license from Noah yet?"

Josh had told the minister he'd take care of mailing the license, but he'd seen the minister hand the stamped envelope to Noah, who'd been evasive about it all evening. "No. But I'll get it. I promise."

"Josh! What if Noah loses it?"

He stopped dancing and kissed her, making them both forget about Noah and what he was up to. "How much longer do we have to stay at this thing?" he asked, his lips brushing hers. "I'm very eager to start our honeymoon. Although, I just now realized that I have no idea where we're staying tonight."

She giggled. "As much as I love making love to you under the stars, I need a bed tonight."

A wicked gleam filled his eyes. "All this talk about beds is only making me want to drag you away *now*."

"Patience, Mr. McMillan."

His gaze returned to the small hill. He had to at least stay and see how Noah's scheme played out.

Ten minutes later, Noah emerged from the administrative building, searching the crowd. Josh nodded, then gave Megan a lingering kiss.

"Keep that up and *I'll* want to skip the rest of my own reception."

He grinned. "Hold that thought. I need to talk to Noah."

"Okay."

"Your mother has been shooting us dirty looks for the last five minutes. Why don't you go appease her and after I finish with Noah, I'll steal you away."

"Deal."

He made his way through the crowd and met Noah at the

edge of the tent Knickers had rented for the reception.

"Did you get it?" Josh asked, keeping his gaze on Megan.

"Piece of cake. Peterman's kid put her up to it. His dad didn't want to make him a part of the firm, so he needed to give them something they couldn't refuse. We were at the same conference, and Peterman knew about the design because I ran my mouth a bit too much. His girlfriend was with him, and you know the rest of that part."

Josh scowled. "It's the next part I'm interested in."

"Drew gave the plans to his dad, passing them off as his own."

"So, no one else knew they were stolen?"

"No, I don't think so."

"But what about the email from the attorneys in Bart's personal email?"

Noah grinned. "I cracked his email."

"What? When?"

"While you and Megan were busy making goo-goo eyes at each other during dinner, I kept trying different combinations until I broke it."

"Combinations of what?"

"His nicknames for Megan."

That made sense. "And…?"

"It looks like Bart caught wind of our application being denied. He realized that Drew had acquired the plans illegally. He was checking to see what ramifications it would have on the firm, given that the others principals had no prior knowledge of the crime."

"That means Bart is innocent."

"In this? Yes."

Josh lifted his eyebrow in question.

"There's still the issue of him taking money from his company, but that's their problem, not ours."

"So we won?" Josh asked, incredulous.

Noah looked over at Megan. "You won, all right."

Libby slipped out the side door of the building and walked over to them, a sly grin on her face.

"Has it been taken care of?" Noah asked.

Libby's grin widened.

A man walked up to the party, his gaze scanning the crowd. He looked to be in his early thirties, with dark hair and a medium build. He wore jeans and a polo shirt, so he obviously didn't belong at the wedding. Something about him set Josh's nerves on edge.

But something else told him that Libby and Noah were the more immediate concern. "Has *what* been taken care of?"

"Your wedding gift," Libby said.

Libby had his full attention. "Why am I suddenly scared?"

"There's no reason to be scared," Noah said. "It's exactly what you wanted. Megan."

Josh's chest tightened. What had they done? "I already have Megan."

"This is more permanent." Looking pleased with himself, Noah slapped Josh's arm. "Libby put your marriage license in the mail. I told you this was the real deal."

Terror washed over him. What was Megan going to say? Would she think he tricked her in this too? "Get it back!"

"No can do, Joshy." Noah laughed. "It's a public mailbox. Breaking in is a federal offense."

"*Fix this.*"

"It *is* fixed. It's done."

Josh turned back to the crowd, trying to sort through his options. Surely Megan wouldn't hold it against him if he could get Noah and Libby to confess. His eye caught the man at the edge of the crowd. He studied him closer, thinking he'd seem him somewhere, then realized he looked like an actor on Dawson's Creek. The guy stood on the periphery, his body stiff, as though he were looking for a fight. How did he know him?

Josh turned to Libby, his heart racing now. "Who *is* that guy?"

The man started to push his way none too gently through the crowd, heading straight for Megan.

"Oh, God," Libby said, breathless. "It's Jay."

"Shit!" He took off running, his heartbeat pounding in his ears as he pushed people out of the way.

Megan was talking to her mother and several of her friends, oblivious to the booby trap headed toward her.

Jay reached her first. He grabbed her arm and spun her around to face him.

"What the hell is going on here?" he shouted, still holding her arm.

She cried out in surprise and tried to pull out of his grasp, but he held on tight.

Finally reaching Megan, Josh positioned himself beside her, hands balling into fists at his sides. "Get your hand off her now." His voice was calm, but it held a deadly edge.

Knickers appeared from behind him, livid at what she had to see as a wedding crasher—one who was accosting her daughter, no less. "Just who do you think you are?"

"Who am *I?*" Jay shouted, spittle flying out of his mouth. "*I* am Jay Connors. *The groom!*"

A collective gasp spread across the crowd.

"*What the hell is going on here, Megan?*" He jerked on her arm.

Josh wanted to beat the shit out of the dirtbag, but the guy had to let go of Megan first. "I'm warning you," Josh said, taking a step forward. "Let go of her *now*."

"Who the hell do you think *you* are?"

"I'm her *husband*. Now. Let. Her. *Go*."

Josh weighed his options as the other man turned to face him, his mouth gaping wide open. He could try to deck Jay, but he didn't want Megan to get caught in the middle. He heard someone come up behind him, and when he glanced back, he wasn't surprised to see that Noah literally had his back.

Megan's face was pale, and she cast a glance at her mother, then at her ex-fiancé. "Jay, let's go somewhere more private, and I'll explain."

A black look washed over his face. "Oh, you're going to explain all right." He moved through the crowd, dragging Megan with him.

As Josh followed, he waved over Libby and Blair, who'd hurried over to them. "Call the police."

Blair held up her phone. "Already done."

Jay didn't stop until he reached a concrete pad at the edge of the gardens. Josh took comfort in the fact that it was at least a somewhat private place. Not that this was a private moment. There were six people watching Jay maul Megan—Kevin had joined the group, looking like he was going to murder Jay Connors himself—but one look at Megan's face told Josh how humiliated she was.

"Start talking, Megan." Jay's fury grew, and he jerked on her arm. "Who is this clown?"

Josh's own temper raged and he started to lunge for the man out of instinct, but Noah held his arm and growled under his breath, "Not yet."

Megan took a deep breath to keep from crying. "Josh." She shot a glance at her mother. "Josh McMillan."

Anger spread across Knickers' face when she realized she'd been duped.

"*Josh,*" Jay said with a sneer. "Were you screwing him while we were together?"

"*What?*" she asked in horror, then her fear gave way to anger and she glared at him. "No, Jay. I'm not a cheating bastard like you are!"

"We broke up six weeks ago, Megan, and you're marrying

this—" he waved his hand toward Josh, "—this shithead. You're telling me you weren't *sleeping* with him all along?" He jerked on her arm again and she winced in pain.

Josh had about reached his limit. "If you care about her at all, let her go."

"You mean care about her like *you* do?" He released a bitter laugh.

"I love her." Josh held up his hands, pulling loose from Noah's hold. "I wouldn't dream of hurting her, but you're hurting her now. So let her go, and we'll talk about this like adults."

Jay shook his head, seeming to just notice the others who'd trailed after them. "This doesn't concern the rest of you of you. Everyone leave, but you." He pointed at Josh.

Knickers' face twisted with rage. "You are manhandling my daughter, you miscreant. Let go of her *now*." She was a force to behold.

Jay's gaze turned to Megan's mother, and his grip loosened as if by instinct.

Megan took the opportunity to stomp on his foot and elbow him in stomach. Releasing her arm with an angry shout, Jay reached up to hit her.

Josh didn't waste a second. He lunged for Jay, knocking him to the ground as Noah pulled Megan out of harm's way.

"You son of a bitch! Keep your hands off my wife!" He swung at Jay, connecting with his jaw. "You never deserved her!" Jay pushed Josh away from him, then got to his feet and punched Josh in the stomach.

"Jay!" Megan shouted. "Leave him alone!" She tried to lunge for them, but Noah held her back.

Josh got two more punches in before the men broke apart and leered at each other.

"What do you want, Connors?" Josh asked, breathless. "Do you want her to say she cheated on you? Why? So you won't feel like such a fool for letting her go?" He clenched his fist then flexed it. "That's why you're here in Kansas City, right? Because you realized what a complete idiot you were to cheat on her? Now she's moved on, and you can't accept responsibility for that, so it's easier to blame her." He stepped closer and jabbed his finger at Jay's chest. "But that's on you! You had two years to treat her right, but you were too stupid to see what you had."

Jay's face hardened. "She's not yours."

"We're *married*. Deal with it."

Jay swung at him again and Josh stepped backward and out of the way.

Hundreds of sprays of water suddenly shot straight up from the ground in a twenty-foot diameter. They pulsed, spraying on and off, completely drenching the two men.

So that explained the concrete pad.

Jay swung at him again and Josh took another step back, evading his fist.

"Enough!" Megan's mother shouted, the authority in her voice unmistakable.

Both of them stopped and turned to face her, still standing in the oscillating water sprays.

"Jay Connors, you have five seconds to leave my sight. Never contact my daughter again." Her eyes narrowed "And if you do, I will hunt you down all the way to the Pacific West and chop off important parts of you that you'd probably prefer to keep."

His gaze shifted to Megan, a question in his eyes.

"We're done, Jay," she said without hesitation. "*Go.*"

Nicole's voice was icy. "Your time starts now, Mr. Connors."

"You'll regret this someday, Megan," he shouted.

"You keep telling yourself that."

He stomped up the steps and toward the entrance to the

gardens.

Bart appeared at the edge of the group, panting. "What happened?"

Knickers ignored her husband and turned her attention to Josh. "Mr. McMillan."

He lifted his chin, shivering in his wet suit and trying not to feel like a grade school boy sent to the principal's office. "Yes, Ma'am."

"How long have you known my daughter?"

"Four days."

"*Four days?*"

"Yes, ma'am."

"You met on the plane?"

"Yes."

"And you just got *married?*"

"Yes."

Megan pulled free from Noah's hold. "Mom, I can explain."

"You can explain why you told me this man was Jay Connors."

She hesitated, looking over at Josh. He nodded his encouragement.

Taking a deep breath, Megan turned toward her mother. "I broke up with Jay six weeks ago, and I was afraid to tell you."

"Why?" her mother demanded. "Do you really think I would want you to marry a man who would cheat on you?"

Megan looked torn. "You kept telling me how much the wedding cost and that you couldn't get refunds."

The fury in her mother's face dissolved into sorrow and her shoulders sagged. "You really think I'm that much of a monster?"

Megan started to say something, but kept her mouth shut.

"So you chose to marry a stranger rather than tell me your fiancé cheated on you?"

"We're not married. It wasn't real."

Josh cringed. Things were about to get uglier. As if that were possible. He took several steps toward her and out of the fountain, water dripping from his hair onto his face. "Meggie, we are."

Confusion wrinkled her brow. "We are what?"

His eyes pleaded with hers. "We're married."

She blinked. "What?"

"The marriage license got mailed in. We can't get it back."

"*What?* How?"

Libby raised her hand, a sheepish look washing over her face. "Me."

"And me." Noah stepped up next to her, as if presenting himself for punishment.

Libby stepped up beside him. "Josh didn't know anything about it. We had just told him when Jay showed up."

Josh knew he had to take control. "It doesn't matter. As far as I'm concerned, this wedding couldn't be any more real. I'm glad they mailed it in, but they should have consulted us first." He searched Megan's face, hoping to get a read on how she felt, but it remained expressionless. He decided to go for broke and took several steps toward Knickers, his hand extended as he presented his case. "I love her. I've never met anyone like her before, and I know it's crazy. I *know* it. But it's right too."

Knickers watched him for several second before turning to Megan. "We can get this annulled."

"What?" Josh asked in panic. Noah and Libby voiced their own protests too, but he was too distraught to register what they said.

Megan gasped. "You would do that?"

"Of course, I would do that." Her no-nonsense countenance had returned, and she was ready to take charge once again. "You're not stuck with this. I'll take care of it."

Megan looked between Josh and her mother and took a

deep breath. "What if I want to be stuck with this?"

Josh leaned over his knees, weak from relief. "Oh, thank God," he mumbled under his breath.

Knickers eyes widened. "Why on earth would you want that, Megan?"

"Because I love him."

"How? You hardly know him."

"I don't know. I just do."

"So you're married to Josh McMillan?"

She gave him a bright smile that sucked his breath away. "Yes, I suppose I am."

Epilogue

Two months later, Megan McMillan pushed open her apartment door, terrified she was too late. "Josh!"

"In the bedroom."

She shut the door behind her and dropped her purse on the entry table before she hurried down the hall. Josh was bent over a suitcase, zipping it closed. "I got tied up at work, and I thought I missed you." Her voice broke and she felt ridiculous. He might be flying to Kansas City, but she'd see him in two days.

Josh stood upright and turned to her, the look in his eyes making her tingle from head to toe. How could he always look at her with such wonder, as though he were seeing her for the first time?

He pulled her into his arms and kissed her. When he lifted his head, he smoothed the hair back from her face, searching her eyes. "I think I should postpone my trip and leave when you can get away on Wednesday."

"No, don't be ridiculous," she said, more for her benefit than his. "You have to be there tomorrow for the big meeting with the new investor. It was your idea to merge your business with my father's. You have to be there to oversee everything."

"You're more important than some business meeting, Megan. Besides, Noah can take care of it."

She snorted. "Noah? He can barely feed and clothe himself."

"He'll be there anyway. He's flying with me."

That was news to her. "Why? He hates business meetings."

"I have a feeling it has something to do with Libby."

"What? But she's still with Mitch."

He kissed her again, taking her breath away, along with all thoughts of Noah and Libby. Her knees weakened and he wrapped an arm around her back, holding her to his chest. "I really think I should postpone this trip," he whispered huskily into her ear. "I'm not sure I can be away from you for two days. The longest we've been apart is twelve hours."

She looked up at him and forced a smile. "Some people like Blair would find that nauseating."

"Good thing we're not like that."

She looked down at his chest and smoothed several imaginary wrinkles from his shirt. "No." She forced her voice to sound firm. "You need to go, and I can't come with you today because of my meeting tomorrow. I'll fly in on Wednesday for Blair's wedding weekend like we planned."

He sighed and placed a lingering kiss on her lips. "Being responsible sucks."

She laughed. "I couldn't agree more."

"I'll stay with your parents until I pick you up from the airport, then we're staying in a hotel. Because after being away from you two nights, I can't promise to be quiet in bed."

He kissed her again, making her wish she had time to strip off both their clothes.

"Do me a favor," he murmured against her lips.

"Anything," she sighed.

"If some man sits by you on the plane and offers to stand in as my proxy, refuse."

She gave him an ornery grin. "I don't recall having any say in the matter the first time." She laughed. "But I couldn't imagine my life any other way."

"Nether can I, Meggie." He placed a soft kiss on her lips, filling her with love and contentment. "Neither can I."

About The Author

New York Times and USA Today bestselling author Denise Grover Swank was born in Kansas City, Missouri, and lived in the area until she was nineteen. Then she became a nomadic gypsy, living in five cities, four states and ten houses over the course of ten years before she moved back to her roots. She speaks English and a smattering of Spanish and Chinese which she learned through an intensive Nick Jr. immersion period. Her hobbies include witty Facebook comments (in her own mind) and dancing in her kitchen with her children. (Quite badly if you believe her offspring.) Hidden talents include the gift of justification and the ability to drink massive amounts of caffeine and still fall asleep within two minutes. Her lack of the sense of smell allows her to perform many unspeakable tasks. She has six children and hasn't lost her sanity. Or so she leads you to believe.

CPSIA information can be obtained at www.ICGtesting.com
Printed in the USA
LVOW06s1429110815

449683LV00005B/931/P